Breach of Sanity

BREACH OF SANITY

Patricia Neary

Library of Congress Control Number:		2012900942
ISBN:	Hardcover	978-1-4691-5286-8
	Softcover	978-1-4691-5285-1
	Ebook	978-1-4691-5287-5

This is a work of fiction. Names, characters, places and incidents either are the
product of the author's imagination or are used fictitiously, and any resemblance
to any actual persons, living or dead, events, or locales is entirely coincidental.

This book was printed in the United States of America.

To order additional copies of this book, contact:
Xlibris Corporation
1-888-795-4274
www.Xlibris.com
Orders@Xlibris.com
109591

To my loving husband Serge for your loyal support.
And, to my eldest son Matthew who made so many sacrifices.
I couldn't have done it without you guys.

Chapter One

It was a lovely, almost cloudless Monday morning. The Rockies surrounding Morial Hospital stood majestic with their snowcapped gleaming peaks so enticing yet dangerously aloof. Uninhabitable. The golden sun's rays cast a brilliant sheen over the hospital's ashen brick building. The doors at the front of the building were for emergencies only. The parking lot's yellow lines far outweighed the parked cars. Three ambulances waited in the wing for the next hospital crisis. The grounds were immaculately maintained by Calosoes Gardening Services. The rainbow of flowers and luscious lawns were breathtaking. Birds were singing gaily from the copious treetops, awakening the world to life.

At half past six, Dr. James Blake crossed the grounds of River Edge Mental Health Institute and cut through the parking lot and then entered the front doors of Morial Hospital. It was a walk the length of a football field. He nodded unsmiling at the receptionist and continued walking briskly down the long white corridor to the first-floor medical laboratory.

His distant demeanor didn't surprise the receptionist. In the four years since being hired by the hospital board, she could count on one hand the number of times he'd actually spoken to her. She'd been warned in advance about his not-so-charming personality. She shrugged. Some doctors were odd ducks. She rolled her eyes and went back to keying in last night's casualties on the computer.

Dr. Blake stood in front of the white door, rummaging for the proper key in his jacket's left side pocket. Unlocked, with confidence he pushed wide the door. He paused before entering, his eyes scanning for signs of life other than the bacterin: a vaccine prepared from dead pathogenic bacteria contained in the fridge. The lab reeked from the pungent odor of disinfectant that hung thick as fog, destroying any leftover germs that might have crept in undetected.

The black and white tiles were polished to a radiant shine. Four rows of lab tables on each side lined the room in perfect sequence. At each counter, a set of medical test tubes was racked neatly in order. Next to the test tubes, two sets of science and biology texts were bound by steel book holders. Old-fashioned Bunsen burners sat mutely waiting to be fired by the qualified technicians. The chrome sinks and faucets sparkled brilliantly. Positioned at the front corner sat a large oak desk littered with papers, files, spilled pens and pencils, and one empty coffee mug. Alongside the west wall stood a huge iron freezer secured with locks to protect the chemicals stored inside from falling into the wrong hands. Dr. Blake didn't have to break into the fridge; he had a poison of his own. A four-foot chalkboard hung directly in front of the room. Scribbled in white against the black surface was the solution to the schematics of yesterday's experiments.

Dr. Blake stood unmoving, pondering which chair would best serve his demonic need. Finally, he turned around and, checking the lab's doorknob, ensured it was locked. Yes, he nodded. The black stool at the very far rear of the room would best serve his purpose. It was out of view of the tiny window at the top corner of the door. Blake's boyish smile twisted into a devious grin. He was about to commit an act so unnatural and brutal that his legacy of destruction would live on forever.

He took off his white doctor's coat and spread it neatly across the marble surface of the tabletop, then sat down. Reaching into the right-hand pocket, he placed a hypodermic needle, rubber band, alcohol swab, cotton ball, and one Band-Aid in a perfect row. The minutes clicked on as he deliberately calmed his mounting feeling of power. He took in deep breaths of air through his flared nostrils and exhaled slowly the carbon dioxide from his lungs. Now he was ready. The doctor used his mouth to assist his hand in securing the rubber band tightly around his bicep to decelerate the fast-flowing circulation. He gazed down at the purple vein swelling until it was ready to burst. Swabbing the area with alcohol, with his right hand he brought the needle into close focus, staring at the murky poison within its core. He smiled, flicking the valve not once, not twice, but three times, releasing any trapped air. He stretched his arm across the countertop, feeling the cold marble against his elbow, before pushing the point of the needle way into his pulsing blood duct. Eyes gleaming with resolve, he watched the tiny cluster of nerves around his radial artery spasm. His arm stiffened with pain when the blood intermingled with the deadly mixture in the hollow core. He took a deep breath. There was no backing out now. He plunged the rest of the toxin into his bloodstream. Seconds later, he felt hot fluid feeding his every artery, forcing his heart to palpitate savagely. He eyed the last couple of drops in the syringe. Using his teeth, the doctor released the pressure and pushed down on the plunger. Its contents emptied. Swiftly, he pulled out the needle. Its deadly deed was done. His arm throbbed as though from the stings of a dozen wasps. He gently placed the syringe next to his jacket, then rubbed his finger over the slight bleeding and licked it clean.

Blake wiped the tiny beads of sweat off his lower lip, waiting for his pulse to slow. His mind wandered back to the face of the woman haunting his every waking moment. Even in his dreams she came alive. There was no escaping her. He had tried desperately to gratify her gluttonous appetite for perfection; with each attempt to please her demands, he failed. His face reddened as beads of sweat formed on his brow and trickled into his eyes. The pink fold of flesh around his mouth turned ashen. His strength began to weaken, yet his mind raged on. Vivid flashes of the brutality of his earlier existence blinded him to his surroundings. Bowing his head, he clasped his hands over his ears in a vain attempt to silence her harsh, condemning words, but her tormenting accusations struck at him like fierce bolts of lightning.

"You pathetic mistake for a boy!" She was screaming in his mind's eye. "You're a good-for-nothing little brat. I warned you about getting your clothes dirty." She seized him by the scrawny shoulders, shaking him violently. "I told you not to play in that sandbox before church, didn't I? Why are you so stupid? Filthy boy. Now we're going to be late." His bottom lip quivered as tears streaked white lines down his dusty face. "Don't you dare cry, or I'll give you something to cry about. Do you understand me, boy?" She smacked him across the face, knocking him to the floor. "Get up this instant and get yourself washed and redressed. You have five minutes, now move!" James scrambled to his feet and rushed upstairs two at a time.

"I'm sorry, Mommy," he now whispered into the lab's sterile air.

Her castle in the air for him was to become a world scientist. Someone she could brag about to her churchgoing friends: the winner of all manner of prizes and acclamations, among them the Nobel Peace Prize. Alma nagged him every day to excel in the field of science. She forced him to study biology and physics as soon as he could read. Not often enough was he allowed the luxury of being a child. No baseball or soccer after school activities, unless it had to do with science. At the age of thirteen, James had a nervous breakdown. Unable to sleep at night, he stopped functioning. He could no longer string sentences together without stuttering. Each night, he trembled beneath his covers, waiting for another malicious beating with the belt because she felt he deserved it. This was her way of bringing him back to normal.

Alma didn't measure an ounce of compassion for her son's mental crash. He was an attention seeker and worthless, a kid too stupid to get a good grade. The nurses on the ward hated seeing Alma. Any progress made that day was diminished within the first ten minutes of her visit. She was known as "the heartless bitch." Alma never once took responsibility for pushing young

James over the brink of sanity. Even when a team of medical professionals told her he was not faking his condition, she disclaimed their prognosis. He was worthless and stupid. His IQ of 167 could not change her judgment. Her ruthless criticism turned James into an emasculated genius whose mind sought refuge from insanity. Alma committed James to a mental hospital in Oak Bay. He spent almost a year in the "crazy house"—as the patients called their home away from home. After six months escape from the mental torture and pressure at home, James regained his faculties and was discharged with a new lease on life; he decided to become a doctor. He wanted to help others the way he'd been helped . . .

The doctor could feel his tension rising. Face flushing, his hands shook with the rush of memories of his wretched life raced through his mind like a fast-forward horror film.

One scene in particular stood out from the many.

It was the end of his senior year of high school. Summer kicked off with scorching temperatures in the midthirties. The heat didn't bother James; he was preoccupied with more important things, like which university he'd be accepted in to. He'd stopped at the end of their driveway and eyed a large envelope sticking out of the mailbox. It was addressed to him. He'd been praying this letter would come. He tore open the envelope, excitement surging as his eyes flew to the last sentence on the page. He gave a yelp of cheer and raced into the house. His mother was sitting at the kitchen table doing a crossword puzzle.

"Mom! Mom, look! I've been accepted into Mill View Medical University right here in British Columbia. Isn't that great?" He waved the letter of acceptance proudly in the air. This was his moment to shine. Surely now, at long last, he had earned his mother's approval! She snatched the paper from his hand and frowned as she read it.

"Am I supposed to be impressed?" She tossed the paper across the kitchen table and took a deep drag of her cigarette. James's lifelong dream for her approval immediately withered with her frosty reaction.

"Isn't this what you wanted? Jeez, you've been yelling at me for years to succeed. I finally make it to the university of my choice, and it's still not enough for you, Mother?"

Her stare cold as granite, Alma stubbed out her cigarette in the ashtray and rose to her feet. "You won't become a 'real' doctor working in an asylum," she sneered. "You'll be cleaning bedpans, wiping drool, and changing diapers. Those retards are beyond help, so why throw a potentially great career away?" Then she walked away. Never before had he wanted to kill someone. Assisting to heal the mentally sick had been a lifelong dream. Heart pounding, jaw and fist clenched, he watched her disappear. He had always feared his mother. But for the first time, that fear was replaced with pure hatred that boiled in his veins like hot lava.

Each and every cruel word was like a nail being hammered into his skull. Even now, Blake cried out against the unbearable pain. "Father would have been proud of my accomplishments. I know it. But you made sure he didn't live long enough to see my triumph. But you will, Mother. I'll see to that!" In the empty and silent room, he raised a fist and shook it.

The sound of the floor polisher in the hallway banging against the lab's door catapulted James from the past to the present. James glanced down at the discoloration on his arm where the needle had punctured the skin. He placed the adhesive bandage over the slight stain and rolled his starched ivory shirtsleeve.

Briefly, an impish grin lifted the corners of his lips at the memory of his mother coming to his bed only days after his father's murder. "At least I was good for something." He shrugged back into his doctor's coat.

A final glance around the lab assured him all was in order. All the paraphernalia was hidden in his pocket. He patted over to the biohazard disposal container and tossed in the evidence. He heaved a sigh of relief before exiting out into the glorious sunshine.

*   *   *

The serene stroll back to River Edge was shattered by screams of foul profanity. He spotted the police car parked at the front entrance. A young woman—probably in her midteens—was being ushered by two uniformed police officers through the institute's front doors.

"Another fun day at Hotel Crazy," Blake muttered.

Chapter Two

Well-known street kid, fifteen-year-old Franki Martin didn't appreciate being committed to River Edge. She was clad in two pink hospital gowns, one facing forward the other backward. Otherwise, she was butt naked. Middle-aged officer Michael Vaser held Franki's arm at the elbow. His frustration was evident by tight lips and forehead furrowed like a washboard. If permitted, he would have gagged her with one of those pretty pink gowns, just to shut her up. Ten steps away from the front doors, Franki was kicking and screaming at the top of her lungs.

"Get your hands off me, pig. Let me go, you bastard. Let me go or I'll press charges against you two assholes."

"You'll be free soon enough, my dear," Vaser grunted through gritted teeth. His younger partner, Barney Funct, was also at the end of his rope with the foul-mouthed girl who wouldn't quit fighting.

"Stop struggling before you get hurt," Officer Funct ordered.

"Then get the hell off me. I can walk on my own," Franki shouted, trying to shake them off.

Officer Funct arched an eyebrow. "Yeah, like you tried to do back at the hospital?"

"Fuck you, asshole."

"Girl, you really need a lesson in manners."

"And I suppose you're the tough pig to teach me?" she sneered.

"Almost home." Funct held open the glass door.

Franki screeched as the officers dragged her down the hallway. She was going, the officers had determined, willing or not. And Franki was demonstrating a loud not. No way was she going to be incarcerated into a nuthouse!

At eighty-one pounds, Franki Martin looked like a walking skeleton. Her once pretty face was cavernous from lack of nutrition; her big sapphire eyes, now pools of dark emptiness. But she was giving it her all as each step brought her closer to the main foyer. Her shoulder-length blond hair was matted with tangles and sweat, her chest heaving from combating a battle she couldn't win. Two hygienic bandages shrouded each wrist, protecting her fresh wounds from infection. On her feet were old, worn-out sneakers without laces. Officer Funct carried her duffle bag overflowing with everything she owned. All she had left in this world was stuffed into that bag. Dirty clothes, diary, old worn-out photographs of her family, a pack of smokes, a couple of Mars bars that by now had melted over her things. Chocolate wasn't the healthiest of snacks, but it gave her energy when starving.

The three reached a small glass-enclosed office known as the receiving station for admittance. Franki's neatly uniformed escorts waited impatiently for someone to arrive and sign the commitment forms. Then the officers' faces relaxed at the sight of two nurses striding toward them. They introduced themselves: Sandy Miller and Gertrude Calder. Officer Funct handed over Franki's duffle bag to Sandy, while Officer Vaser chanced unlocking the cuffs. Sandy placed the bag inside the office door at the receiving station. Gertrude handed the clipboard over to Officer Funct to sign the commitment form.

"Hey, shithead, give that back!" Franki yelled.

"We have to search through it first, Ms. Martin," Sandy explained. "Don't worry, it's just policy."

"Policy my ass."

"I don't think you have anything worth stealing," Officer Funct grunted.

"Who the hell asked you?" she glared at him.

"Don't you dare run, girl! It's too hot to chase you." Officer Vaser wiped his perspiring forehead with the palm of his hand.

"Lose a few pounds around the midsection and you might be able to keep up, fat boy."

Funct turned his head, snickering quietly.

"You are one heartless, girl," Vaser shook his head, knowing she was right.

"Shut up and do your job," Franki laughed.

Vaser looked at the nurses and rolled his eyes as if to say, "You two have the she-devil herself on your hands!"

Franki carefully rubbed each wrist, releasing the blood flow back into her veins. The steel cuffs had dug into her injured wrists. The nurses stepped forward quickly, each taking an arm at the elbow to prevent her from bolting out the door.

"Franki, I don't want to see you in my neighborhood again, understood?" Vaser warned.

"You don't own the damn world." Her chin jutted defiantly.

Sandy thanked the officers for delivering Ms. Martin to their facility. With Franki in tow, she and her new escorts marched down the main hallway. *I'm screwed,* Franki thought, mind racing frantically. She noticed a jock-built orderly standing on guard for any sign of trouble. *This is worse than lockup,* she thought.

*   *   *

The officers strolled out into the glorious warm sunshine, drained of energy and relieved to be rid of that belligerent brat, Franki Martin. This wasn't the first time they'd picked up Ms. Manners. Two weeks prior, she'd been busted for prostitution and sent to juvenile lockup, where she escaped. Vaser prayed silently that Franki would get the help she needed before she wound up dead in some alley downtown. If she continued her destructive lifestyle, it wouldn't be long.

"If this morning is any indication of how the rest of our day is going to go, we're in serious trouble, buddy," Funct swore.

"Hope your intuition is wrong."

"Me too!" Funct laughed.

Shaking his head, Michael Vaser opened the squad door and slid into the driver's seat.

*   *   *

The nurses were dressed in sparkling white uniforms, matching nylons, and Hush Puppy shoes with enough lace to tie a perfect bow. Gertrude was a heavyset woman with short curly white hair and black-rimmed glasses framing cold, steely-gray eyes. Heavy rouge-colored pale, stone-carved cheekbones. Hooker-red-lipstick-emblazed thin lips. Sandy Miller's meadow-green eyes graced a marred face by a purple scar slicing the length of her cheek, disfiguring her innate beauty. Five foot five and one hundred thirty pounds, she was in great physical shape, unlike Gertrude who was as frumpy as she was tall. Sandy smiled pleasantly at Franki, yet the secured hold on the young girl's elbow left no doubt as to who was in charge. Franki struggled to pull away, but Gertrude locked on to her arm with a death-grip hold. Franki's empty sapphire eyes pierced Gertrude with hate and contempt. Without warning, Franki turned her head in Sandy's direction.

"You're ugly," she yelled and spat in the nurse's face.

This unexpected act of nastiness took Sandy by surprise. Momentarily, she loosened her grip, and Franki pulled free her arm. Gertrude grabbed both of

Franki's arms and yanked them behind her back. She wasn't going anywhere. Out of the corner of her peripheral vision, Franki eyed the big scary dude heading toward the trio. Sandy raised her hand, letting the orderly know they had the situation under control. This power play was over. The nurse took a tissue from her uniform pocket and wiped the gob of spit off her cheek.

"Crude behavior of that nature is totally unacceptable, young lady," Sandy stated, matter-or-factly.

"You ain't seen nothing yet, bitch."

Franki arched her eyebrows.

"Aren't you a pleasant little one?" Sandy snapped.

Franki pulled from side to side. "Let go of my arms, or I'll—"

"What?" Gertrude tightened her grip. "Spit at me? It would be your last."

"Ready to be nice, Ms. Martin?" Sandy questioned Franki.

"Screw you."

"Whenever you're ready, we can continue on."

"We should lock her in the basement, is what we should do with her." Gertrude held her grip like a pro wrestler.

"Get this Amazon off me," Franki yelled.

"Are you ready to be nice?" Sandy asked again.

"Do I have a friggin' choice? Amazon, off me."

"Please let go of her arms, Gertrude. I trust Ms. Martin will behave herself."

Gertrude dropped her arms, glancing quizzically at Sandy. Why was she being so nice to this rotten brat? If she had it her way, she'd give her a few well-deserved smacks and lock her up in solitary, throw away the key.

*   *   *

The seemingly endless hallways were painted white high-gloss latex. No pictures softened the cement-block corridors. No warm carpets quieted the sharp staccato of the nurse's heels echoing within the confines.

This place sure isn't home sweet home, Franki thought wryly. Not that it mattered. It had been a long time since she'd seen anything resembling a home spiced with sweetness. The foster homes were rotten to the core, just fronts for child abuse. So the streets had become Franki's new world—ugly, dirty, and dangerous, but anything was better than what she previously had escaped.

The ceiling's fluorescent lights hummed off electricity. Each fixture, mounted three feet apart, filled the hallway with an icy-white glow. Finally, they stopped in front of a slate gray fire door. Gertrude pushed it open, and they climbed the next two flights. The cement stairs told of neglect and indifference. At last they'd arrived on the third floor, Franki huffing and puffing.

"Doesn't this nuthouse have elevators?" Franki barked, panting.

"We figured a little exercise was a good way to work off all that excess energy," Gertrude scoffed.

The barred windows were heavily screened, shutting out most of the natural sunlight. As all three marched along the dimly lit corridor, Franki's heartbeat quickened. Where were they taking her? To hell, it felt like.

All three finally arrived at their destination, stopping at the second door from the elevator: a steel windowless door numbered 321. Gertrude scrawled Franki's name with magic marker on a piece of paper and attached it to the door with two strips of masking tape. *What a great homecoming to this pill factory shit hole,* Franki thought.

"You got a hold of her?" Gertrude glanced at Sandy.

"Sure do. You're better now. Right, Franki? I think it was just a case of the nerves back there." Sandy gave Franki a friendly wink. Franki averted her gaze. She wasn't buying into the niceness crap.

The key slid into the lock as easy as hot steel slicing through butter. Franki tensed, every fiber of her being wanting to bolt for freedom. After her last attempted suicide, she vowed to never again allow herself to be locked up. She had to get away. She just had to . . . Sandy put her arm around her shoulders and coaxed Franki into the room. Gertrude stood guard at the door.

It was every bit as awful as Franki expected: coldly impersonal with a faint smell she'd rather not contemplate. The room was large enough to hold a metal off-white nightstand and single bed. On the surface of the nightstand sat a Gideon Bible. So was God going to wave his magic wand and get her the hell out of there? Not likely. The cot had a gray pinstriped mattress that looked old and worn. The pillow's plastic covering protected the foam stuffing from drool. A fluorescent light illuminated her depressing prison. Where the hell's the bathroom? Franki wondered. Then she spotted a stainless steel bedpan with a roll of toilet paper sitting on the middle of the mattress.

"What the hell is this? No toilet?" Franki stared in wide-eyed disbelief at the two nurses.

"The bedpan is for emergencies. All you have to do is ring the red bell on the wall beside your bed. Someone will come and take you to the washroom."

"What? I need a bodyguard to use the goddamn toilet. This is such bullshit. What about my privacy rights?"

"Franki, this is only temporary until we get you better situated," Sandy soothed.

"Meaning?"

"You need to be evaluated, and I'm afraid you're not yet trustworthy to have the freedom of second-floor residents."

"This place is worse than jail!" *And I oughta know,* she thought.

At the foot of the bed sat a folded set of starched sheets and a pillowcase. Under the white sheets was a brightly flowered yellow-and-green bedspread. Franki shuddered at its ugliness. The walls in her prison-sized cell were coated with a cream-colored paint. A portable metal table stood below the window. This lifeline to the outside world was secured with black bars. White wire mesh crisscrossed the thick pane no larger than a basement window—precautionary measures to ensure patient's safety.

"Why do I have to be here? It's not like I'm going to get all freaky from drug withdrawal. Been there done that at Morial Hospital, what a week ago."

"This room is short-term, Franki."

"Temporary or not, this sucks."

"Franki, I need your shoes." Sandy held out her hand.

"Hell no!"

"You either give them freely or we'll have to take them."

"You serious?"

"Afraid so."

"Jesus Christ. My fucking freedom is gone. Shoes. What the hell is next? Hair and blood samples?" Reluctantly, Franki took off her running shoes and threw them at the door, narrowly missing Gertrude's shoulder. "You want them, you pick them up."

Gertrude kicked them into the hallway. "You won't be needing these, little Ms. Attitude."

"Bite me. Oh, on second thought, forget I said that. You probably would."

Franki gazed down at the battleship-gray cement floor. Black scuffmarks hinted at what previous prisoners had endured. Her body stiffened, and she clenched her hands into such tight balls her knuckles turned white. She threw back her head and let out a strangled scream that sounded like the keening of a wounded animal caught in a hunter's trap. Both nurses tensed, waiting for the preteen to lose control. Instead, Franki stomped over to the nightstand and grabbed the black book off the table.

"Get this religious crap out of my room now!" she screamed, sailing the Bible at Gertrude's head. The nurse wasn't quick enough to catch it. It missed her head but caught her in the chest before plummeting to the floor. Face flushed with anger, Gertrude started toward her when Sandy put out her arm, stopping her. Sandy bent over and retrieved the Bible.

"Franki, that's enough," Sandy ordered. "You won't make any friends around here with that attitude. Getting violent isn't the answer to solving anything."

"I have enough friends," Franki fired back. "If I wanted to read that bullshit, I would have brought my own version."

"You owe Gertrude an apology."

"You take my shoes, lock me up in Crazy Ville, and I owe that fat thing an apology? Are you on glue?"

Sandy sighed. "Franki, I think—"

"This is what I think," she interrupted. "Fuck her, fuck you, and fuck everyone associated with this shit hole!"

"Keep it going. Keep it up, my dear, and I'll have you restrained by the end of the day. If I have to do it myself," Gertrude threatened.

"Oh . . . I'm scared. Get the hell out of my room, you old battleaxe and take ugly with you."

"Relax, we're leaving. You might want to make your bed." Sandy nodded in its direction.

"Whatever!" Franki flipped them the bird, her defiant smirk, a thin slash across a colorless face.

*   *   *

The mere sight of the Bible stirred up a horrific potful of memories of what had been done to her while in the care of the Wilkins. *"Doing God's work" my ass,* she thought. Anyone could quote scriptures. That didn't mean they were right in the head. The Wilkins proved that. Anyone who dared to step out from under his or her tent of religion was a sinner. They would surely perish in hell, they proclaimed. Franki's eyes took in her cold, inhospitable room. Maybe the Wilkins were right. This was getting closer to hell than she'd ever intended.

Once the nurses exited the room, in utter defeat, she dropped down on the cot. She understood why she'd been committed to River Edge Mental Health Institution, but part of her still couldn't accept the painful truth. She had arrived at her final stage of the game. Franki never allowed herself to show anyone her despair or sadness. Anger was not a problem. Weakness, on the street, was an enemy you couldn't afford if you wanted to survive. Defeat, to Franki, meant she was weak in spirit. Now she was even more pissed off not only with herself but the hero who rescued her in the alley. He should have kept walking and minded his own business. But, oh no. He had to interfere and call the ambulance. "Fucking cell phones should never have been invented," she grumbled.

She leaned over the bedpan and clutched the sheets into her arms. As if holding on to a cherished teddy bear from long ago, Franki rocked back and forth with the bundle pressed against her chest. Nervousness moved like a current through her body. Her muscles felt drawn and taut as on a torture rack.

She sat this way and that on the thin mattress. Hard as she tried, she couldn't get comfortable in her own skin. She slapped her feet on the cold floor and then paced back and forth from window to bed. She had to think of the advantages of being in a place she hated. Three meals a day, toilet privileges, maybe even a hot shower once a day. For their sake, they'd better let her take showers. For the first time in weeks, her freshly scrubbed skin, from her stay at Morial Hospital, glowed. Her five-foot-two frame was no longer ravaged with lice and creepy crawlers from sacking out in garbage-infested alleys. She wouldn't have to give a blowjob to get high. On the other hand, life on the street was tough, but at least, she didn't have to put up with rules and regulations from strangers who thought they knew what was good for her.

She grabbed the steel bedpan and flung it as hard as she could at the wall. It careened onto the wall then hit the floor with a metallic clang. "Make my bed, piss on that. Go to hell." She stretched onto the cot and had barely closed her eyes when another bout of anxiety gripped her to the core. Haunting images swirled like a tornado in her mind, and she bolted upright, wrapped herself in a tight little ball and rocked. Drugs kept the demons at bay. The only time she did sleep was when she was blotted. She was now physically exhausted, and yet her mind would not rest. She rocked faster and faster as though the action of her movement could rid her mind of its relentless flashbacks of abuse.

She was too worn out for the battle. Her body and soul needed peace, but she couldn't find it anywhere anymore, not even in the booze and drugs. That's why she finally decided suicide was her only answer out of hell.

Franki was jolted back to reality when the door sprang open. There stood Gertrude in all her manly glory, her steely-gray eyes piercing the room for anything problematic. In her hands was a tray of food. The nurse entered the room and walked to the table, placed the tray down, and rolled it next to the bed. Franki eyed the old fifty-year-old woman suspiciously. The yummy aroma of breakfast quickly filled the air; it didn't entice Franki to open the lid. Before leaving, the nurse stopped at the door and turned around to face Franki.

"You're going to be here for a long, long time."

The short statement was long in letting Franki know where she fit in the scheme of things. Resistance was useless. She had already demonstrated that character flaw downstairs. Gertrude was correct; Franki did belong to the medical system. No matter how hard she fought, she couldn't win.

Trust was something earned, not given in Franki's world. Believing in strangers with certificates hanging on the wall was a joke. These people didn't care about her; they were doing a job and getting paid. Sparkie was different. She always told it like it was. Sparkie never needed to bullshit Franki into believing what life held for them both; they were living it day in and day out on the streets of Victoria, surviving the madness as best they could. Whatever they needed to do, they did it, selling their souls for shelter, food, and drugs. They loved and trusted one another.

Gertrude waited for a response.

"That's what you think, dumbass."

"Oh, you and I are going to have problems."

"We won't if you get your fat ass out of my cell." Franki shot daggers at the nurse.

"You're a real mouthy brat who needs a good attitude adjustment."

"Look it, Ms. Professional, you know nothing about my life. So don't stand there pretending to be a badass. You're old, homely, and know-nothing."

Gertrude spun on her heels and left the room, slamming shut and locking the door behind her. Franki shook her head and laughed out loud. How many times had she been told those words before? Threats from morons with authoritative degrees were just irritating noises that didn't mean squat.

She was sick of professionals' sanctimonious bullshit. You-can-change-your-life-if-you-change-your-attitude speeches. What did she have to live for? She was fifteen, a homeless, broken-down shell struggling through life alone. Her parents died in a car crash when she was nine years old. The comfort of their smiling approvals and loving arms was now but a distant dream. She missed the warmth of her mother's hugs and the assurance of safety and the laughter of her father's zest for living. The amazing way they made her feel about herself. All snuffed out in one senseless, tragic moment. She even missed fighting with her older sister. Her shame was overwhelming at what her life had become. Without a doubt, her life would not have turned out so wrong if her parents were still alive. Who knew where her sister had been taken. And life sucked. Franki was sick of life's what-doesn't-kill-you-makes-you-stronger bullshit. Pain, fear and betrayal were hurdles she was too tired to jump over anymore.

CHAPTER THREE

Franki had no idea the time lapse when the door swung ajar. In the hallway stood a peculiar-looking man. Franki rolled her eyes: another geek with a degree. She tried not to stare at him but couldn't help it. There was something very chilling and disturbing about this one. The fine hairs on her neck bristled in warning. Why, she couldn't put her finger on it. Around him was an aura of unexplainable darkness. Maybe, she hoped, it was a shadow from the hallway. Either that or she was losing her mind altogether. This guy wore dark-blue dress pants; perfect seams ran down the middle. Black patent leather shoes with pointed tips and laces. Matching socks, one could safely assume. His receding hair was flecked with gray. His wire-framed glasses sat on a hawkish nose, enlarging his small dark eyes. His ivory pressed shirt hung on his gangly, five-nine frame like an IV pole.

He was no sun worshiper. The ivory shirt really emphasized his pasty complexion. His Allessoudro tie pressed as immaculately as his trousers. Pinned to the lab coat was a gold-plated name tag: Dr. J. Blake. He stood against the doorframe, arms folded across his chest, leering in at Franki who was sitting on the bed, pretending to ignore everything around her.

"Remove the tray of food from her room. Bring her to my office in twenty minutes," he ordered.

"Yes, Dr. Blake," Gertrude oozed sweetly.

Franki's lips silently mimicked the nurse. He pivoted on his heels, leaving as fast as he'd appeared. Gertrude stomped across the floor to the table, lifting the lid. "I see you haven't eaten your breakfast. Now it goes in the garbage. What a waste." Gertrude shook her head.

"If you're so worried about throwing it out, you eat it! Not that it looks like you've missed any meals." Franki stared pointedly at the rolls beneath the uniform.

"You are the most disrespectful girl I have ever met," Gertrude said, pinching her lips together. "I'll be back. Be ready," Gertrude commanded, her tone louder than necessary.

"I'm not deaf, and I don't need a doctor. See, stupid, my wrists are bandaged." Franki extended her arms as proof. "Get out of my room and take your stupid tin tray with you."

Gertrude leaned into Franki's personal space, almost spilling the tray. Gertrude managed to grab control again. Fearless, Franki laughed in her face. The nurse felt the hot air waft into her nostrils. Gertrude's eyes narrowed in for the kill.

"Don't you ever disrespect me like that again if you know what's good for you," she hissed.

Franki averted her gaze and shrugged. No nurse was going to intimidate her; that was for sure. Without warning, Gertrude slammed the tray back onto the table and seized Franki by the arm, squeezing with considerable force. Spittle flew from her mouth. She howled, "You may be queen on the streets of hell, but in here, you're nothing more than a little bitch with head problems. If you don't want to be strapped down to a bed, you'd better change that attitude and start doing what you're told. Freedom days are over, missy-miss. Now last warning. Get that bed made before I get back. You don't want to mess with me anymore, you little crazy freak!" She pushed Franki onto the cot, grabbed the tray, and marched out of the room, slamming the door behind her.

Franki wiped the saliva from off her cheek with the back of her hand. *And they lock me up,* she thought, shaking her head. She waited for the clicking sound the door made when the lock engaged. Nothing. She waited a couple more seconds, and still nothing. The door was unlocked.

Franki leaped off the bed like a professional sprinter. Her plan of escape in motion and time was undeniably against her. She had no idea which direction to run. The maze of corridors she'd been led through earlier would get anyone confused as to how to get outside. She had less than twenty minutes, if that, before the old battleaxe returned. Her hand trembled as she touched the knob. She was in luck! The door was really open; it wasn't her imagination playing tricks. Cautiously, she turned the knob, inching the door open ever so slowly. Franki squeezed her head out enough to glance up and down the hallway. No guards were posted at her door like she'd anticipated. Heart hammering with excitement and dread, she inched the door open a little more. She could almost smell the sweet scent of freedom. She stepped into the deserted hallway . . . then, out of nowhere, voices came toward her from around a bend in the hall.

"Shit! Shit!"

She leaped back into the room and released a trembling breath.

God, she'd almost made it . . .

*   *   *

She was unaware her every action was being monitored from a hidden camera in the corner of the room. Whatever she did or said was on tape. This was for patient protection in case of injury.

Franki looked up when an orderly stepped into her room.

"Is everything okay?" John's boyish smile topped his two-hundred-pound frame.

"Go to hell," she spat.

"Come on now, it's not that bad. I know it takes a little while to adjust. Hang in there, kid."

"What would you know about adjusting? You're free to go wherever the hell you like. I can't go for a piss without an escort. So save your happy speeches for someone else."

"Don't get upset. I'm leaving."

She turned her back on him. "Yeah, you do that."

"Try and have a good day, kid." John closed the door. "She's a pistol." The lock clicked behind him.

Not long after, Sandy and Gertrude materialized in the doorway. Franki was sitting on the bed, rocking back and forth, the sheets enveloped in her arms, instead of on the bed. She didn't care what the old battleaxe thought when she eyed the unmade bed. What could they do, put her in a cage?

Sandy announced she had to go and get Franki a pair of slippers; she'd be back shortly. Gertrude's eyes narrowed at the unmade bed. She was at the end of her rope with Franki's deliberate rebellion. She reached for the sheets. Franki held on. The nurse tugged harder, yanking Franki off the bed and staggering the young girl against her.

"Let go, Franki," the nurse growled through clenched teeth. Anger exceeding self-control, Gertrude raised her hand high above her head and struck the side of Franki's face so hard the impression of her hand rose up in a red welt. Both Franki and the sheets crumpled to the floor.

"You fucking bitch." Franki looked up at the nurse, pure hatred turning her blue eyes into black orbs. She was on the floor, but that position had its advantages. Franki stopped herself from kicking the hell out of the older woman. If she attacked Gertrude, she'd be strapped down for sure, and that's exactly what Gertrude wanted.

"This isn't over yet." She sprang to her feet.

"Have you had enough yet?"

"Watch your back, bitch. Remember, I'm the crazy one." Gingerly, her hand touched the side of her face.

"You don't scare me," Gertrude panted.

Maybe you'd just better be scared, thought Franki.

CHAPTER FOUR

Dr. Blake rushed down the hall to an appointment he dared not to miss. He glanced down at his Cardinal. Exactly eighteen minutes to do what must be done and get back to the office in time for his first appointment with Franki Martin. His visit would be memorable. The doctor checked his pocket, ensuring it held the correct syringes. Yes. This was another experiment he was eager to try out. This one was a little too loud for his liking. He rushed along one dark hallway after the next. Hiding her in another part of the facility was genius. No one would ever find his secret. She wasn't even in the same wing. A year and a half ago, River Edge added another wing on to the south side of the building and closed down the north side. Eventually, it would be back up and running when the facility found the funding, but right now, it was vacant. The last four corridors, the doctor began to sprint. He rounded the last corner, huffing and puffing like a heavy smoker. The doctor stopped to catch his breath. Taking his breathing apparatus out of his opposite pocket, he pumped two shots of mist into his lungs. Before going on, he removed a copper key from his other pocket. With each step, particles of dust flew up into the air, strangling his asthmatic airway. Coughing and wheezing, he inserted the key into the lock, turning it counterclockwise. The security device clicked. He pulled down on the steel handle and entered. Dust almost thick as ash mantled the room and the doctor's mystery patient.

The abandoned room hadn't been used in over a year. The windows were streaked with heavy black soot. Each corner had its own collection of dirt, dust, and thick cobwebs. No warm memorabilia graced the walls. In the middle of the room stood an antique hospital bed built with a long iron shaft anchored at the foot. To move the bed up and down required manual labor. In the corner of the room were the skeletal remains of a bathroom: a dirty sink secured to the wall with rusty one-inch bolts and a lidless toilet bowl layered thick with dried black mold. A corroded stain ringed the water bowl's level. A shower stall was big enough to accommodate one person. The musty, humid air was pungent with the stench of excrement. Dr. Blake inhaled deeply at the doorway before running across the room to the window. He grabbed the handle and jerked upward. The lilac-scented summer breeze hesitated as though not wanting to enter such an awful place and then gusted through the open window. Dr. Blake took several clean breaths into his already restricted windpipe. He turned and stared across the room at the woman sleeping soundly in the bed.

The woman, once a tyrannical ruler in her son's life, had been reduced to this helpless state. Alma Blake could no longer fend for herself; she was too feeble and old. Life and death fascinated James Blake. It amazed him how the passage of years could steal away vitality. No one could escape the inevitable: death. When James was a young boy, he believed there wasn't a more beautiful woman on the planet next to his mother. Denial was a hell of a lot softer on the soul than reality. At the age of five, James wanted to marry his mother. Later, he learned one must be careful about what one wishes. He didn't have to marry his mother to have that special relationship. Whether it was out of fear or loyalty, not even James could comprehend the real gravity of his depraved situation. And there were times he did pleasure her, without guilt.

Before waking his Sleeping Beauty, he moved the wheelchair out of the way and then reached down, shaking her on a shoulder that was more bone than muscle. Slowly, her eyes opened.

"James? James, is that you?" She called out to him in a deep rasp. She blinked, trying to focus her blurred vision.

"Yes, Mother, it's me."

"I'm so hungry, James," Alma Blake pleaded.

"I know, Mother."

The doctor smiled. *So nice to be needed,* he thought. The one thing that hadn't slowed with age was her enormous appetite. Her son crossed over to the dust-covered dresser positioned along the north wall. Pulling out one of the six drawers, he retrieved clean bedding, a hospital gown, and one Depend Diaper. Standing at the sink, he filled the washbasin with warm soapy water. No time for a shower this morning. A quick sponge bath would have to do. He reached up into the medicine cabinet, grabbing skin cream, antibiotic ointment, and baby powder. The older a person became, the more dehydrated the skin, especially confined to a bed. Bedsores were a common result. Gagging, he changed her soiled diaper. This was one loyal duty he hated. He suspected she was soiling herself on purpose, one way of avenging her helplessness upon him. He scrubbed her down before placing her in a fresh diaper and clean gown. Then he lifted her weak frame out of bed, placing her in the wheelchair so he could change the soiled sheets. He had the power in his pocket to stop all his misery had he wanted. Throwing the soiled sheets into the laundry bag, he strolled to the foot of the bed, cranking the handle manually. The mattress rose to a more comfortable angle.

"Feel better? That diaper of yours weighed ten pounds."

"I'm starving, James." Her voice rose to an irritating whine. "Where's my food?"

"I know, Mother." He rolled his eyes. "I'm sorry, I didn't have a chance to go to the kitchen this morning. I have to see a new patient in just a few minutes. I promise I'll make it up to you at lunch."

"A 'patient' is that what you call them? I say they're head cases looking for sympathy for their miserable lives. I'm the one you should be helping." Her lips curled derisively. "Now, where is my breakfast?"

James twisted the lid off a jar of baby food, not saying aloud what he was thinking. Alma had no right to judge anyone. Look at what her life had succumbed to: seventy-three, living in an abandoned dirty room, hiding from the world in fear of being found out for the crime of murder she had committed a lifetime ago. Reduced to a paranoid, bitter old woman clinging stubbornly to life. A life she didn't deserve. Not being able to control her bodily functions was a sign that death was near.

"Look, Mom, it's your favorite, peaches." Smiling, he extended the jar of fruit toward her. In a fit of fury, she swung her arm, knocking the jar from his hand. It landed on the floor, glass, peaches, and sticky juice splattered everywhere.

"I want decent food, stupid!" She shook a fist at him.

"Mother! Jesus, I said I was sorry. I told you, I didn't have time to get to the kitchen." He grabbed a roll of paper towels from beneath the sink and knelt, cleaning. "Give me a break please. I'm doing the best I can."

"You're always saying sorry. I'm starving, damn it. I want real food not some mush in a jar. Go to the kitchen this instant!"

"No! I have an appointment, remember me telling you?"

His face flushed red from frustration. "You could afford to miss one lousy meal," he mumbled under his breath. James rushed to the foot of the bed, quickly cranking the lever counterclockwise.

"What . . . what are you doing?" She struggled to sit up.

"I'll come back at lunchtime with something yummy . . . maybe some more dessert. Would that please you?"

His last-ditch effort to satisfy her was pointless. Now she was thrashing around the bed and yowling like a wounded animal. He shoved his hand into his jacket pocket and removed his weapon: a tranquillizing needle. He tore the plastic tip from the sharp end and spat it on to the floor. The doctor held her right arm down to the bed with his knee and stabbed the sharp point of the needle into her brachial blue vein, emptying 5 cc of curare directly into her bloodstream. James needed this to work fast. He was just sorry he couldn't stay to find out how long it would take before the drug took effect. She moaned as the curare surged through her body.

"That drug should knock you on your ass," he laughed. "I hope."

When he locked the door, before heading down the steps, he could hear her screaming at the top of her lungs, "Don't you leave me in here, you little bastard? I hate you! Come back here this minute."

"Tell me something I don't know, Mother. Love you," he wheezed, grabbing his inhaler from his lab jacket. "I wish you could love me as I have loved you," he whispered.

He flew down the rest of the steps two at a time until he gained enough distance, he could no longer hear the screeching obscenities she was hurling at him. Straightening his tie and jacket, he rounded the corner to his office.

CHAPTER FIVE

Sandy returned with a pair of pink cotton slippers to find Gertrude forcefully shoving Franki toward the doorway, arms bent behind her back, like a prisoner. Sandy gasped at the large four-finger welt below Franki's eye. This incident needed to be reported. Before she asked Gertrude what transpired, something inside of her already knew the answer. Since Franki's arrival, she'd kept pushing for a fight. From the look on the girl's face, she got what she asked for. Franki found out quickly she'd picked the wrong person to test. Gertrude had a short fuse. On a couple of past occasions, the nurse had been disciplined for using excessive force against a couple of River Edge patients. She'd been warned to just walk away. And if it happened again, further disciplinary action would be necessary, and that meant a suspension. The rules applied to all staff.

Sandy blocked the doorway. "What happed to Franki's face?"

"It's been dealt with. She knows now who the boss is." Gertrude shrugged like it was no big deal.

"Franki, what happened?"

"Are you blind or just stupid? This bitch hit me for no reason, not that you'll believe me. You'll take her side anyway. What do you care?"

"Watch your mouth." Gertrude tugged her arms up higher on her back.

"Or what? You'll beat me up again?"

"Please let go of Franki. I want to speak to you privately." Sandy motioned Gertrude out into the hallway.

"Can't you see I'm busy?" Gertrude snapped.

"I suggest you make time to discuss this matter with me," Sandy stated firmly.

"Right now, Dr. Blake is expecting this patient, and we all know how he is about punctuality."

"By the end of this morning then." She flashed Gertrude a no-nonsense glare. "Franki, I'm very sorry. Let me assure you, it's not our policy to go around beating up patients. I promise it will never happen again."

"Could have fooled me." She pointed to her swollen cheek.

The two waited in the corridor while Gertrude locked the door.

"I'm reporting that bitch," Franki barked.

"Don't worry, this incident will be handled."

"Something better be done or I'm filing assault charges against that animal."

"Consider it done." Sandy nodded. "How old are you, Franki?" Sandy smiled.

Franki gave her a quizzical glance, deep wrinkles forming between her brows. Then a half smirk unfurled around her mouth. The deep creases of tension disappeared as though by magic.

"Hey, sorry for being mean earlier and calling you names, it's just—"

"Thank you, apology accepted. It's just that you trust no one." Sandy winked knowingly.

"I should have spat at that bitch instead of you!" She glared at Gertrude.

Gertrude started to say something; Sandy shut her down with a warning scowl.

"So, how old are you?" Sandy asked, trying to defuse an already explosive situation between nurse and patient as they all walked along the hallway.

"Fifteen going on eighty."

"You are a beautiful, young, spunky adolescent. Tell me, do you have any dreams or hope for your future?"

"Do you know where I come from, Nurse Optimistic?"

"Yeah, I do. You have had a lifetime of troubled experiences that few only read about. I can't imagine street life being pretty . . . was it?"

"Nope. You'd be surprised what you do to survive. Even a naive chick like you could do it. You learn the ropes fast or get beat up."

"Your life can change for the better if you want it to." She ignored Gertrude's disdainful grunt. "Make the choice to stop surviving and learn to live. Life has a way of surprising us, Franki." Sandy's warm, green eyes smiled at her.

"I doubt it."

"Consider River Edge a time out to rest and get healthy again."

"Yeah, okay." Franki rolled her eyes. Silently, she hoped this nurse was different from the rest of the phonies that had crossed her path. *A little over the top with her happy bullshit, but maybe, she could become cool with my help,* she thought. It wasn't that Franki didn't want to reach out and trust someone, but right then, she couldn't risk knocking down her concrete wall, especially in this psycho ward. She had been betrayed and discarded so many times by adults in authority; she didn't see how she could ever truly allow herself to be vulnerable. If Sandy wanted Franki's trust, she'd have to earn it.

*   *   *

On a finely carved birch door was a brass-plate sign that read Dr. J. Blake MD. Gertrude's stubby knuckles rapped against the grain.

The door opened, and the anomalous-looking man appeared. He stood with his hands tucked in his jacket pockets, smiling as if he had the world by the balls. His dark eyes though held no warmth or humor. His low voice was barely audible as he invited Franki into his office.

"Come in."

Franki hesitated, warning feelers clawing their way up her spine. With the help of Gertrude's little shove, Franki crossed over the threshold.

"Thanks for the help, troll," Franki gave her an evil glare. Sandy groaned silently. It was obvious these two were going to do battle, and it wouldn't be pretty.

"Thank you, nurses. I'll send for someone when I've examined Ms. Martin."

"Doctor," Sandy nodded.

When the door closed and they were several paces up the hall, Sandy stopped and faced Gertrude.

"Give me your side of the story, or do I have to rewind the tape?"

"A simple request turned into a power struggle. She's been itching for a fight since her arrival. She's no longer queen of the jungle in here."

"A power struggle over what?"

"She wouldn't give me the sheets. I warned her to let go. She played her little defiance game, and that's when I slapped her."

"You do understand she has the right to file an assault charge against you?"

"She's too stupid to do such a thing."

"Don't bet on it. As your supervisor, you may finish out the rest of the day and consider this your final warning toward permanent dismissal. You are suspended for the next two days without pay. Pay heed to my words: this will not happen again."

"I promise it won't happen again," Gertrude concurred verbally but thought, *That you'll know about . . .*

*   *   *

Franki always made it a habit to carefully scrutinize her surroundings, something she'd learned from living on the street. Trusting her instincts kept her out of some pretty harming situations most of the time. Now, everything inside of her was screaming, "Run!" She shivered. There seemed an unexplained chill in the air—the rest of the institution was warm enough—and far from the doctor's office being cozy and inviting, it radiated danger. Yet everything appeared normal. His cherry—wood desk and matching leather chair conveyed expensive taste. The desk surface held neatly arranged voluminous medical texts, a glass container of pens and pencils, and a computer humming to the same electric beat as the fluorescent fixture on the ceiling, which was odd, thought Franki, because it had been turned off. Directly in the middle of his desk sat a blue folder, which she assumed to be hers. In front of his desk were two beige cloth chairs.

The room was fairly dim, with the blinds almost closed, shutting out any trace of natural sunlight. A black banker's lamp sat at the corner of the desk. Her first thought was, why did he only have the lamp on and not the ceiling's fluorescent light? The medical textbooks on the bookshelf were sorted from largest to smallest. *This guy,* Franki thought, *is a bit anal-retentive.*

He requested she have a seat in one of the chairs at the front of his desk. Out of the corner of her left eye, she noticed another door in the doctor's office. *What secrets,* she wondered uneasily, *lie beyond that entrance?* Nervous energy formed on her palms; she wiped the salted sweat on the hospital gown, trying to hide her mounting fear. Sparkie had groomed Franki on how to be cool in all situations. "Even if you're scared shitless," she'd said, "never show it." *Oh, Sparkie,* she cried out silently, *I sure need you here.* The doctor opened her file and soundlessly thumbed through the pages. His beady eyes scanned line by line the pages that revealed her life, his eyes dissecting her privacy with the cold impartiality of a biologist cutting into the innards of a frog.

His elbows on his desk, he leaned his chin on his hands. "What happened to your face?"

"The old battleaxe gave me a sucker slap."

"Gertrude," he smirked. "One piece of advice, my dear: you will want to stay on her good side. I've heard she has a hot temper."

"Nice tip. I'll keep that in mind."

"You have quite the extensive file I see for someone so young."

"Shit happens."

"It states that you're currently homeless. Someone found you in the alley with both interosseous arteries slit wide open. Consider yourself fortunate you didn't severe the radial artery."

"I beg to differ."

"Thought you would." He chuckled.

"What's so fucking funny?" Franki questioned, sounding tough.

"Oh, you are a harsh one, aren't you?"

"Good observation, Sherlock, you catch on quick Dr. Whoever You Are. Why am I here?"

"My name is Dr. Blake. I'm assigned to your physical needs. I think you already know why you're here. As for how long you'll be staying, that will depend on you. You know, Franki, you and I could become intimate friends. A girl of your caliber, I think, would like my offer." A cold chill crept up her spine. Suggesting to Franki that this guy was a real creep.

He rose from his chair, his slender form slithering around the desk like a serpent. He leaned forward, his face inches away from hers. *Here we go,* Franki thought. She had encountered his kind before: men with money, believing that power could compensate for the small dick in their pants. Her every muscle strained against the idea of kicking him in the nuts and bolting for the door. Trepidation made her stay put. She didn't know exactly how much dominance this guy wielded over her life.

"So, tell me, how did a pretty little thing like you survive on the big bad city streets?"

"What do you mean?" She knew from his voice, he wanted to hear the dirty things she did as a prostitute.

"Dirty little girl like you shouldn't be embarrassed about disclosing a few intimate details. After all, it's medically useful to know a little something about you."

"You read the file. Shall I say no more?"

"Sweet thing like you. I know what you like." His eyes glittered like a boa about to devour a trapped mouse.

"Excuse me? What's this trash you think you're talking?" Franki leaned away.

Dr. Blake slid his cold, bony fingers along the edge of her chin. Franki tried to slap his hand away, but he caught it in a surprisingly strong grip for such a slight man. "Franki, you're not the one in charge here. This is not the streets, little girl." *No, this is worse. At least out there, you know the predators that prey on vulnerable girls,* she thought, *not inside a looney bin!*

"Hey, dude, whatever you think is gonna happen, ain't happenin'. Why don't you do us a favor and sign my release form, and I'll be on my way?"

"Not so fast." He chortled. "The party is just getting started."

"Stop jerking my chain! There are about a thousand other nutcases you can molest. So forget me and let's not waste each other's time."

"Relax, Franki. I'm afraid I couldn't release you even if I wanted. One, you tried to commit suicide. Two, you haven't been assessed, and three, you're a detoxing junkie."

"Then I guess your idea of a little fun is out of the question."

A cold silence filled the room.

"How does the idea of being restrained in a straightjacket and placed in a rubber room appeal to you?" Blake leaned against the doorframe and grinned, enjoying his little game of cat traps mouse.

"A straightjacket and rubber room? No, I don't find that fucking appealing, fuck you very much."

"I more than suggest you do what you're told. And Franki, no one will hear you scream in here."

"You can't do this to me!" Her heart began hammering against her ribs like a jackhammer.

"I'm not the one committed to the crazy house. I can do whatever I like."

Powerlessness rose in her like an empty jug filling with toxic waste. All her life she had tried to win against authority. There was no way to beat them. They were too strong, too smart, and too manipulative. She shuddered at the thought of being alone in the dark, helplessly confined within a straightjacket while this twisted maniac did horrible things to her. Franki knew what it felt like to be locked away in the dark, all alone, waiting for her foster mother to have enough mercy to let her out. Hours and days would slowly drag by before that act of kindness would happen. The mere thought of that flashback sent hot prickles up and down her spine.

Reluctantly, Franki rose out of her chair and followed the doctor. She was expecting a torture chamber with whips, chains, and gag balls and was almost relieved to find it an ordinary examining room, equipped with the usual examining table, stool, blood pressure apparatus, and so forth.

"You had me worried." She blew tense air from her lungs. "I was expecting a death chamber or somethin'."

"Want it to be?" His eyebrows rose.

His arms reached out as if he were going to hug her. She flinched and pulled back. Instead, he set a long, bony finger under her chin, lifting her head so their eyes locked. She read his perverted thoughts.

"Hell no!" She jerked away.

"Franki, this is not a game. I'm going to have you, whether you like it or not." His tongue slowly moved across his thin upper lip. "Take off your clothes."

She could smell mints trying to mask the morning breath.

"No!" She shook her head. "I was examined at the hospital a week ago."

From the set of his chin and determined look in his eyes, Franki knew instantly there was no getting out of this situation. She didn't believe in a God, but that didn't stop her from praying for help to whatever entities might be listening. Alarm bells rang in her head like a school fire drill. Her mind swirled with denial. This can't be happening. He's a doctor for Christ's sake. He's supposed to take care of me. Out there on the streets, perverts and pimps were expected to pull this inhumane crap but not honorable doctors. This authority figure had a respectable position in society and was believed to be helping civilization, and right now, she was supposed to be a part of that humanity.

Fear crept up her body like an eerie Nova Scotia fog. She froze, unable to speak or move. He turned and keyed the door's lock from the inside. She heard him unzip his trousers.

"Remove your clothing. It's not your mangled wrists I'm interested in seeing."

CHAPTER SIX

Sandy helped Franki into the wheelchair ordered by Dr. Blake.

"You've had the biscuit, haven't you?" she quipped.

All of a sudden, Franki grasped onto Sandy's arm with the ferocity of someone drowning clinging to a life preserver. Their eyes locked. Sandy saw the fear. Something strange and unnatural took place between Blake and the kid, but what? This wasn't the same girl they'd dropped off an hour ago. Before the doctor retreated behind the closed door of his office, Sandy noticed his small dark eyes were peculiarly gleaming and his face unusually flushed. Sandy expressed her concern to Gertrude, who merely shrugged. Gertrude didn't seem the least bit concerned about Franki's lethargic condition. But Sandy was troubled. The girl could not walk without assistance; she was heavily narcotized. She'd been fully alert and mobile when she walked into the doctor's office. The hair on the back of Sandy's neck bristled, giving her a shiver. Sandy somehow sensed that Franki was in danger of some sort but had no idea why she felt this way. This had never happened before, and she had taken and retrieved many patients to and from the doctor's office. Although heavily sedated, in the deep wells of Franki's eyes, Sandy recognized, fear, pain, and shock. But if there were something to tell, Franki didn't utter a word. Her feistiness had vanished as though by a sorcerer's wand, and Dr. Blake had the power. What had he done to reduce the girl to this?

The trio descended down the corridor, heading for the elevator, when a redhead named Gloria Shelby sashayed toward them. She had been a resident at River Edge for several years.

"Hi, Gloria. How are you today?" Sandy asked with a smile.

Gloria's eyes fixed on Franki as she approached, and her answering smile fell flat.

"Fine," she murmured and hurried toward the doctor's office door.

Even in her drug-induced haze, young Franki tried to scream out a warning for the redhead to get the hell away from the pervert's door. The words remained trapped in her mind, her lips frozen. There came the sound of Gloria's knuckles rapping at the door and then silence.

The two nurses wheeled Franki into the elevator and rode to the third floor. Once in her room, they helped Franki into bed where she could rest. Sandy was pulling up the starched sheet when she noticed black bruising on the inside of Franki's thighs. *That looks painful and fresh,* she thought. Sandy pulled the sheet up onto Franki's shoulder, promising to check on her in a couple of hours. As soon as the door closed, Franki fell into a bottomless sleep. Her brutal ordeal was over. Every noise, thought, and ache vanished.

*   *   *

Later on that day, Sandy returned as promised. Franki was sitting upright, resting against her pillows. Sandy gave the patient her usual gleaming white smile.

"So, minus the injury to your wrists, did Dr. Blake give you a clean bill of health?"

Franki didn't know how to respond. If she told the truth about what the doctor did to her, she'd be running the risk of his threat becoming her reality. She thought about his glinting eyes, his cruel mouth, and his strong hands and shivered. He was even crazier than some of the johns she'd bedded. This guy—he held the real power over her. She did not doubt his warning.

"You might say that," she answered after a long pause; she had to be careful.

"You look tired, dear."

"I've had a hell of a few crazy days."

"You'll get better while you're here with us."

"Can't get much worse." She meant it.

"Hungry?"

"Not really."

"It's almost lunchtime and you didn't touch your breakfast. You must be starving by now?"

"No."

"I made the bed for you while you were visiting with Dr. Blake."

"You fishing for a thank-you?"

"No, but I would appreciate you being a little nicer to me. I am not your nemesis, little girl."

"I'm not a nice person, but thanks." She turned her head and stared at the wall.

"Franki, do you need to use the bathroom?"

"Yeah, you could say that."

"Are you strong enough to take a walk down the hall or should I get a wheelchair?"

"I can walk." Franki swung her legs over the side of the bed and tried to get to her feet. Instantly, pain racked through her body as though a fist had pummeled her.

"Ooooo!" she gasped.

"I'll get the wheelchair." Sandy moved toward the door.

"Don't! I'll make it on my own." With supreme effort, she forced herself erect and made it to the washroom and back. She'd long ago learned from her own stubborn streak that not always asking for help could sometimes make a person stronger. It had been a long haul down the corridor, but she managed.

"Okay, sweetheart," Sandy said on Franki's return, "I'm going to get your lunch and no arguments about eating. I'll be back in a few minutes."

"Hey, what's your name?"

"Sandy."

"'Sandy' sounds pretty girly. Oh, can you bring me something to read 'cause I sure as hell ain't gonna read that Bible-thumping crap."

"Sure. *MACLEAN'S* magazines, okay?"

"Yeah, anything."

"Not a problem. See you in a bit."

Alone again, Franki moved slowly across the room to the table in the corner. She pushed it back to the side of the bed and waited for the nurse to return. Warm comforting memories floated in her mind like fluffy white clouds in the sky on a summer's day. It was the picture-perfect moment of having a picnic in the park with her family when she was seven. She and Beth throwing a Frisbee back and forth while her parents set up the wooden picnic table with delicious food. She'd saw off her own limbs to have them alive for another ten minutes. As the memories faded, despair took their place. Every minute felt like hours, the hours like days, and there was nothing to do but wait. She counted ten steps from the bed to the window. She gazed between the bars, barely able to make out the people below. She wanted to shout down to them, "Help! Help! A crazy deranged doctor is holding me prisoner in here. Get me out of here. Please . . ." The pain of what had occurred in the doctor's office only hours ago would not slip silently into her Pandora's box. Controlling the horrific memory was like trying to hold back the ocean with a straw broom.

*　　*　　*

She saw the excitement gleaming in his eyes as she started removing her hospital gowns. At first, she contemplated making a run for the door, but fear of what he would do to her was a stronger deterrent.

Dr. Blake's threat of a straightjacket and rubber room and much worse could become an actuality. Her chance of ever leaving this place would become a distant dream. No one would believe her side of the story; after all, she was the one that tried to commit suicide. Being taken to juvie for prostitution didn't help her already tarnished reputation. She'd only prostituted when there were no other options. Hunger and withdrawal pains weren't a pleasant feeling. Franki did what had to be done in order to stay alive, and she would apologize to no one for it. Glancing down at her hands, she watched them tremble as her mind replayed every ugly detail . . .

Under her gown, she was almost naked, except for a Morial's Hospital special. She deliberately fumbled with the ties on the back of her hospital gown.

"Hurry up. Finish the rest of your undergarments," he hissed.

"I beg you, don't do this to me."

"Take everything off, Franki."

Jesus Christ, she thought. *Who the hell would believe that this psycho-piece-of-shit is about to rape me?* Then she turned to face the monster, staring into the dark pools of lust. Her heart hammered against her ribs as the truth of what was about to take place hit her like swimming against a cold river's current.

"Why in hell are you doing this to me?" Her bottom lip quivered with fear and betrayal, but she held back her tears. She would not let him see her cry.

"Franki, we've already discussed it. I thought this is what you wanted?"

"Ye-yes, N-no! I'm a patient, you're the doctor," she stuttered, mind racing like a gerbil on a treadmill. The door was locked, and she was sure the room was soundproof. If she went along with him, chances were he'd not go off the deep end. If she resisted, she was certain he'd inflict the greatest amount of pain possible. From past experiences, she knew what psychopaths were capable of doing.

"Remember, if you cooperate with me, you'll be released a lot sooner."

It was that damned smile of his that creped her out, eyes that were cold and calculating pools of evil.

"Nope. I've changed my mind. Keep me in here for as long as you want." She started dressing.

"No, bitch!" he screamed. "You'll do what I tell you to do."

He paced back and forth in front of the examining table, a certifiable nutcase about to blow a gasket. "Why do you bitches keep changing your minds? You're worse than Mother. She used to change her mind a lot too. Get me all excited and then brush me away like I'm nothing." James's hands flailed in the air. "James, try and do it this way. Now you're going to slow. Try again, James. You know how to please Mother . . ."

"We made a deal, Franki. Now you think you can change you mind? You have no regard for my feelings. Pretty sluts like you just snap their manicured red nails, thinking well-established men like me will come crawling with our pants down around our ankles ready to service you despicable filthy whores." Franki backed slowly away from this lunatic. His eyes bulged, high blood pressure spreading like a spider web up his neck and face. Then he stormed out of the examining room and into the outer office.

*   *   *

Circling the gray carpet behind his desk, his mind fueled with rage, guilt, and an overpowering desire for her warm flesh, his inner chastened, "Don't hurt her, James. You don't want to do this. You are not your mother. Control your hunger. If you don't, you'll lose everything. The experiment. What about the experiment? Stop being a loser, James, and get a grip! Stop hungering for her nice warm flesh."

Franki had a couple of moments to suffer the shock of this supposedly sane doctor and all she could think was *And they committed me? Holy shit, this asshole is a certified demented freak! He belongs inside one of those padded rooms, but I'm not gonna tell him, that's for sure.*

Her body trembled with terror, knowing he meant business. She could hear him rambling on the other side of the door. If she didn't do what he told her to do, she would get hurt. How badly, she didn't know. But she wasn't ready to take the risk. Her heart pounded so loudly, she thought her eardrums were going to burst. Braced by her elbows, Franki leaned over the papered examining table, rubbing her temples in a desperate attempt to regain control of her shocked nervous system. Her legs were quivering so much she thought her knees were going to buckle. Queasiness swirled in her stomach, threatening to unload bile. The agony seemed endless. Franki felt like that abused ten-year-old that no one believed. She was powerless, vulnerable, and very much alone. After all, she was locked up in a mental institution, certified as crazy girl for wanting to take her own life. If only whoever was in charge knew about this medical misfit, maybe he'd be fired . . . unless his boss was just as nuts.

*   *   *

Dr. Blake returned; he reached out and grabbed a fistful of hair and threw her up onto the examining table. She scrambled for shelter against the wall. He ordered her to lie on her back and place her feet into the steel stirrups. When she hesitated, he slammed his fist into her stomach, demonstrating his supremacy. Franki gasped for breath. Taking a long needle from the mobile sterile stainless table, "You'll feel a sharp prick," he said, his voice flat. Franki winced as the Horocaine emptied into her mammalian circulatory system. She watched the second hand on the wall clock circle twice around before her body went numb. As hard as she tried, she could not pull her feet out of the stirrups. Whatever local he'd shot into her worked.

Her body weighted down by medical poison didn't stop her mind from lifting into hallucinations. She saw ghastly visions of Blake cutting her up into little pieces with a razor-sharp scalpel, without any local. With each slice, she felt the razor's sharp burn inching into the tendons, muscle, and bone until body parts filled a plastic bucket.

The doctor hovered over her like a vulture waiting for its prey to die. His beady eyes were as black as the devil's heart. Icy black ice.

He began touching her. "Oh yes, your tits feel nice, so white and firm and excited to see me." He gave her left nipple a playful flick, as would a lover. His touch repulsed her. She closed her eyes and waited for the assault to be over. Leisurely, his hands traveled downward, touching each of her twelve ribs. Without warning, he pressed his bony fingers into her visceral cavity and then her liver. The pressure of his so-called doctor's exam became more and more fierce. This animal, Franki realized, was deliberately trying to break her down.

Franki opened her eyes and shut them as quickly. She knew what he was doing with his gloveless fingers. Then, she heard his zipper come down. She felt thankful that whatever drug he injected into her body had made her numb.

"If you hadn't given me such a hard time earlier, we'd both be enjoying the pleasure of my loins. I control you now."

Franki kept her eyes shut tight.

"This is better than a straightjacket and rubber room, don't you think?"

The doctor laughed as if he'd just told a witty joke. With each hard thrust, her tiny frame slid back and forth on the table. She hated the hot tears that slid down her temples, disappearing into her hairline. Never did she want this animal to know that he'd gotten through to her and hurt her. She suffered the pains of abuse, betrayal in silence as she had always done.

Chapter Seven

Day by day, after being brutally raped in Dr. Blake's office, Franki grew progressively more agitated. The prescribed medication only masked the ugly face of her tormented soul. Unpredictable eruptions of rage at staff members would burst out of her as though fueled by demons from hell. One minute she'd be sitting quietly on her bed, and the next she'd be screaming at the top of her lungs for no apparent reason. If she couldn't get her way, she'd resort to physical violence or pound her fists against the walls until her knuckles bled. Her favorite was ripping the mattress off her bed and hurling it at the barred window, shouting profanities. But throughout all of this, she remained mute about the truth. Who would believe her? She had no proof that Blake—this fine upstanding pillar of the medical community—was a cruel and dangerous pervert. Her accusations not only would be fruitless, it would backfire. Blake would avenge himself on her. Somewhere, somehow, sometime, he'd get her good.

She was taking high doses of anti-anxiety medication: Benzodiazepine, to try and stabilize her mood, but it was not working. Franki begged the staff to give her something more powerful to numb her inner pain. Dr. Blake ordered Seroquel, a mood stabilizer, along with Amitriptyline. Rarely her mind would be numbed to her predicament. At the end of each week, someone, and it wasn't always Sandy, reviewed the tapes documenting how Franki would be sound asleep and then, without warning, would bolt from her bed and blindly throw herself around the room, kicking and screaming and lashing out at demons that weren't there. On several occasions, Sandy would be called into Franki's room to try and calm the young girl. It would take some time getting her settled back to sleep; perhaps an hour later, she'd be wrestling the same demons. On the worst nights, usually an injection of haloperidol would finally relax her tormented mind enough to sleep through the rest of the night.

Franki was barely eating enough to keep herself alive. The psychiatrist, Dr. Viewer, who was filling in while Dr. Smith was away on holidays, diagnosed Franki's condition as the first stages of borderline depressive. But he also suspected she was seeking attention too. During a weekly meeting among the third-floor staff, they all recommended Franki remain where she was until the violent outbursts subsided. She could not be trusted to go to the second floor. They all believed Franki would run and complete her suicide mission—the main reason she'd been committed to River Edge.

Four times a day, she gobbled down mood stabilizers and antidepressant medications from a little paper cup, always hoping for that trip to numb land. Although it dulled a bit of the edge, she remained trapped inside her private world of isolation and horror. She felt utterly helpless, hopeless, and defenseless. She vomited copiously as if this would expunge Dr. Blake's touch, his smell, his taste, and his brutal invasion of her body. She had become Dr. Blake's sex slave. There wasn't anything she could do to stop him, no one she trusted to tell. In order for her to survive, Franki forced herself to accept his sexual assaults. As least, she justified, she didn't have to live on the street. She had traded one nightmare for another. Blake was dangerous but so had been the strangers she'd given her body over to.

Franki devoured every magazine Sandy gave to her, welcoming nourishment for a mind starving for diversion and escape. From the pages of pretty pictures, Franki could fantasize their lives belonged to her. She too could have beautiful clothes, living in a mansion far away from this sterile confining cage like prison.

Throughout the long, tiresome hours confined to her room, Franki saw strange flashes of light out of the corner of her eye and heard terrifying screams telling her to do unthinkable things. She was like an explosion, eyes ping-ponging around the room in search of the disembodied voices and glowing spirits. The stench of rotting flesh was unbearable. She'd pace the floor, babbling, sniffing like an animal at food. The putridness of herself cloyed inside her nostrils and flavored her meals with the taste of fetid food. She'd flung her tray at the wall on numerous occasions, refusing to eat the poison. Under Sandy's orders the nurses were not to confine Franki to the bed but to lead her down the corridor to the shower room. Sometimes it worked, but most time, the cure was fleeting.

On this one particular morning, Franki awoke literally gagging on the nasty odor. She could not breath. Frantically, she began buzzing the call button. Minutes ticked by like hours. Franki began cussing obscenities at imaginary people in her room. Finally, when she thought she could take no more, the door opened, and in stepped Bobby and her burly male partner, Art.

"About time! Jesus, how long does it take to walk a few steps down a bloody hallway? See this buzzer? When I push the button, you're supposed to come and help me. Not take your diddlly sweet time!"

"You want my help, be nice Franki," Bobby ordered.

Franki launched her familiar tirade of how excessively bad the smell was this time, sticking her arm under Bobby's nose so she could smell and bear witness to the reek odor.

"There is no bad smell," she assured Franki. "If anything, there's only the fresh scent of sweat." *It's going to be one of those days,* Bobby thought.

Immediately, Franki freaked out. Shaking her head from side to side, yelling, "I'm not crazy! You animals are trying to poison me. That's what this bastard smell is. Admit it, just admit it!" Yet, in the deep recesses of her mind, Franki was starting to believe that it was her mental faculties that were on malfunction. Could it possibly be . . .

*　　*　　*

Leaving Art on guard, Bobby returned to the nurse's station and paged Sandy to the third floor. When Sandy arrived, the two nurses quickly compared notes. A pattern had crystallized. A day or two after every appointment with Dr. Blake, these strange behaviors would manifest: flashes of light, voices, and smells. There seemed to be a correlation, but they needed proof. Together they laid out a documented map of Franki's daily events, searching for a destructive pattern—if there was one. Sandy wanted to get to the root before more visible damage was done.

Art returned to the station. Sandy could see on the monitor that Franki had fallen back to sleep. Seeing no point in waking her, she resumed her usual duties.

That afternoon, around one o'clock, Sandy made an unscheduled visit to Franki's room. She was huddled in the corner on the floor, clawing frantically at her arms and legs enough that blood was seeping from her wounds. Her long nails were doing the job of sharpened scissors. Franki cried in terror, scraping and digging away at the decomposing flesh only she could smell. Sandy was livid; hadn't anyone even bothered to check the monitor, she thought. Not even a minute later, Bobby opened the door.

"Page Dr. Viewer," Sandy barked as Bobby stood in the doorway watching the grizzly scene unfold.

"Tell him Franki needs an IM injection of haloperidol."

In minutes the psychiatrist was administering the 5 cc's of haloperidol. This drug was a temporary solution. He did not linger once the injection was completed. He left almost as quickly as he came. Sandy and the other nurses found it odd that Viewer never took the time to investigate further into the reason why Franki was having these hallucinations. His sessions with Franki included no such prodding in his reports.

Once Franki nodded off to a chemical-induced dream state, Sandy left the room briefly and returned with gauze, tape, antibiotic ointment, and a pair of nail clippers. The nurse bandaged Franki's cuts and clipped her nails. If kept short, she'd be unable to do as much damage to herself or others. She treated Franki's arms and legs with bactericidal ointment and thickly wrapped gauze to protect the skin from infection. Her emaciated arms were like chicken's that had gone through the meat grinder. Pink and white folds of flesh resembled rip tides in an ocean from previous suicide attempts. Fresh scars rose in ugly crimson mounds from more recent attempts with sharp object. Open wounds seeped from self-inflicted cuts only minutes ago. As precautionary measures, Sandy covered Franki's hands with oven mitts—a trick she learned from a very wise nurse who retired two years ago from River Edge. Franki wouldn't be able to wipe herself after using the toilet, blow her nose, or even read a magazine. She'd need assistance—and she'd be hopping mad. But her life was at stake. It had to take priority over such inconveniences.

Sandy settled into the chair beside Franki's bed and glanced at the folder Viewer had left behind. It was Franki's medical records. In one swift motion, Sandy snatched it off the table and opened it, her meadow-warm green eyes scanning the psychiatrist's scribble; her blood rose to a quick boil. These episodes, he wrote, and allegations of smelling rotten flesh were Franki's way of gaining attention and a strategy to get booted out of the institution and back on to the street. Her violent outbursts and unnatural behaviors were only attempts to manipulate by using any possible means she thought might work. It was in his opinion that the third-floor staff should not participate in these charades.

Sandy marched out the door to find the five-foot-nine, medium-build, blond-hair, blue-eyed doctor waiting at the elevator. She waved Franki's file under his nose.

"Dr. Viewer, I don't believe we should ignore Franki Martin's so-called attempts at attention. Have you even bothered to read her entire file and ask questions?"

"No need. I know what I know, and I know what I see. I suggest you do your job of bedpans and keeping company with lonely heart patients like Ms. Martin. Leave the expertise to the ones who've devoted a lifetime to studying minds and what makes them tick."

Sandy was shocked but only momentarily.

"Look, you arrogant bastard"—she placed a hand on her hip and took her stand—"I am not going to let you sedate her anymore without you knowing what's in her file. Why don't you get down to the root of what is really going on with Franki Martin. Have you even bothered to inquire why she can smell her own flesh decaying? Or is that not in your realm of expertise, Doctor."

He didn't comment. "And let me tell you one more thing: when Dr. Smith returns from her holiday, I am going to inform her immediately regarding your unprofessional conduct toward this young girl, that you state clearly"—she poked her finger at the folder she held fast in her right hand—"she's an attention seeker."

He shrugged. "Do what you will. Just remember, nurse." Viewer took a lingering glance at her nameplate. "Nurse Miller, you don't have the degrees that I have to form such a psychiatric prognosis."

"I don't need a goddamn degree to be a human being."

"I suggest you do another humane act and go change a diaper or bedpan."

"You are truly despicable."

Dr. Viewer turned on his heels and marched into the open elevator, leaving Sandy staring after him in disbelief. "That arrogant, snot-nosed creep," she fumed to herself. "I hope he lands in here one day. I'll show him the same treatment he gives to his temporary patients." Nostrils flaring, she stormed to the nurse's station. Whispering followed in her wake as she passed other staff members who'd overheard her lose her temper. Sandy couldn't remember the last time she'd been so angry. Dr. Viewer was fresh out of university, a conceited ass who needed a good kick. Having his own practice downtown, he believed to be above the rest of the professionals that worked in substandard conditions, such as mental hospitals. He preferred moneymaking clients. Sandy's grandmother taught her to never get angry to make a point. The best points made in an argument were the ones that came from calm rational, not irrational people.

Sandy understood the pains of growing up all too well. It seemed like a lifetime ago, but the images were still crystal clear in her mind. Franki was so lost and alone. She wasn't an angel, but Sandy knew she sure deserved better treatment than what Viewer was giving. Franki was inwardly suffering and needed treatment, but most importantly, she needed TLC. Her spirit was dying.

*   *   *

Over the next few days, Sandy came to visit Franki as often as she could. This kid was special. The nurse was determined not to let Franki fall through the cracks of the system under which she worked. Sandy had seen a lot of patients come and go over the last twenty years. She knew which ones were seeking attention from those in serious trouble. Patients didn't mutilate their bodies for simple attention. It was pain manifesting itself like an SOS on the beach of a shipwrecked passenger. Why these ignorant doctors couldn't see this was way beyond her comprehension.

The sun was shining, the birds were singing, and it had been four days since Franki's last episode. A cheerful Sandy opened the door to Franki's room, expecting to find her propped against her pillows, reading one of the many magazines she'd left behind.

Instead, Franki was hunkered on the floor in the corner, hysterically clawing and biting at her arms, literally tearing away pieces of flesh away with her teeth. Bloody gauze straggled along the floor. Her body beaded with sweat as her chest heaved for breath. Her eyes were saucer wide, and pupils dilated as she swung out at the imaginary evil only she could see. This time, it appeared she'd gone over the edge with no return ticket.

Franki stopped, looked up at the noise of the door closing, eyes dark as coal, blood speckling her chin and cheek. She growled, a warning to stay away.

"Franki, it's me, Sandy."

"Cut them off," Franki screamed.

"Cut what off, Franki?"

"My arms. My arms. The smell, help me get rid of the smell." She panted.

"Honey, what smell?"

"My skin. It's dying."

"No, Franki it's not. Honey, it smells like soap and sweat. Here, let me show you."

Sandy knelt down beside her. She took Franki's injured arms and held them directly under her nose, so Franki could realize that there was no putrid smell.

"You're lying to me, Sandy," Franki screamed, tearing away at her arms. Then she began digging deeper with a nail file. How she got such a weapon, Sandy had no idea.

"I wouldn't lie to you, I promise. Please, let me have the nail file, sweetheart." It took a few more minutes of coaxing before Franki let it drop to the floor. Sandy threw it farther away from Franki's reach. Sandy pulled the slouched girl in close, rocking her back and forth until her sobbing became quieted intakes of air, and waited. The door swung open, and Sandy glanced up: Dr. Know It All, Dr. Viewer, and two husky male orderlies stepped into the room. It was time to sedate Franki once again. Sandy tried to get them to back off, but she was overruled. Like a scared puppy, Franki scrambled, hiding behind Sandy's back for protection. Sandy reluctantly moved aside, letting John, the first orderly, lift Franki up off the floor while the second orderly restrained her blood-covered arms. Dr. Viewer swiftly injected Thorazine into Franki's arm. The potent sedative took affect within seconds, allowing the orderlies to calmly carry Franki to her bed. As soon as they left, Sandy ordered Bobby to bring her the medical supplies needed to bandage Franki's wounds. She wasn't certain if Franki needed stitches, but she'd find out soon enough. It hurt

Sandy's heart to look at her little face; tearstained and blotchy from another battle she didn't win.

*   *   *

That very same evening, Sandy came back to stay with Franki. She didn't want her waking up alone and shackled to her bed. Sandy stood staring down at beautiful little Franki Martin, who was in so much distress. The world had not been kind to this little one. Obviously, she was getting worse instead of better. Why? This was a puzzle that needed solving, and fast. How much more could Franki Martin withstand? Something was terribly wrong. It had to be more than being confined to her room. Although it was isolating, it was doable.

Sandy managed to get a hold of Franki's entire chart and began reading it, word for word. When she'd finished, she tossed it onto the table, disgusted. Throughout the years, Franki Martin had been diagnosed with every mental illness from borderline depressive to psychotic menace. In her opinion, the lack of evidential facts regarding Franki's diagnosis from Shiffer to Mayberry and now Viewer was a pile of horseshit. Could none of them see that young Franki was depressed due to how her life had horribly unfolded after losing her parents? She'd worked in the mental facility long enough to correlate theory and practical study with human observation. There was something offbeat with their findings. She would make it her mission to find out the truth. She settled into the single fold-up chair and watched Franki sleeping. Everyone in the world deserved love, respect, and above all, validation. Franki needed a friend, and she was the right person for the job.

*   *   *

Around midnight, Sandy called it a night. She gave Kathy, the nurse in charge, her cell number, telling her if Franki woke up in a bad state, she was to phone her immediately. But hopefully, Franki would stay asleep until morning.

"Sandy, I hope I'm not out of line here, but what is it with you and this girl?"

"Meaning?"

"I mean . . . I have never seen you so concerned about one patient. I don't mean that in a bad way. It's just . . . well . . . you're very nice and all, but . . ."

"I understand what you're saying. I usually don't spend my time off sitting next to patients while they sleep, but . . . there is something real special about this girl. A connection of the soul or something."

"How? She's always so angry?"

"Justifiably so. Wouldn't you be pissed at the world if your parents died and you'd been bounced around in foster homes and then forced to live on the streets?"

Kathy flushed. "Oh, I didn't . . . know. That explains why she's so hard. My mistake." She paused, then, "Is there anything I can do to help?"

"I doubt she'll talk to you about anything personal. Try asking her questions about what clothes she likes in the magazines. She loves fashion, stories. Those are all openings to initiate conversation."

"I'll try anything if you think it might help."

"Thanks, Kathy. Remember, call if I'm needed."

Sandy strolled over to the elevator and pushed the button. The door slid open, and she stepped inside the large metal box that would take her down to the underground parking garage. She gave Kathy a wave as the doors slid closed. Driving home, Sandy thought about what Kathy had asked. Why was this kid so special to her? She didn't have a solid answer.

CHAPTER EIGHT

The following morning, Franki awoke, fear coursing through her veins like the current of a lightning rod in an electrical storm. Her mind raced as she tried to sit up and couldn't. She was strapped to the bed with leather straps at her wrist and ankles. She thrashed frantically, straining against the bondage. Not being able to move was one of Franki's worst fears. Primal screams of terror escalated from her throat. She hadn't noticed Sandy standing at the window. "It's okay, baby, I'm here." Sandy rushed to her side. "It's okay, you're not alone." Sandy stroked her hair.

"Why am I tied up? Untie me! Untie me!"

"It's okay, I'll untie you."

Sandy didn't want her ripping out her stitches.

"Who the hell did this to me?"

"It was Dr. Viewer's orders. I had no choice."

"Why? How could you do this to me?"

"You freaked out again. Franki, you were clawing and biting and digging into your arms with a nail file. You had to be restrained. If your cuts were a millimeter deeper, you'd have more stitches."

"So what? It's my skin."

"Franki, you were screaming that your skin was rotting. You were ripping off chunks of skin with your teeth!"

"So what if I did? No one in this hellhole believes me anyway. It's obvious you don't care?"

Franki had no idea how long Sandy had sat next to her while she'd slept, consumed with worry.

"So you're not denying it?"

"I don't want to talk about it."

"You will have to tell someone sooner or later."

"Yeah, yeah. Get these belts off my legs." Sandy quickly freed Franki. Franki noticed the bandages taped around her wrists and then did a double take at the yellow-flowered oven mitts.

"Oven mitts again?" She held up both hands.

"Yep."

"What the hell is wrong with you people?" she spat.

"Honey."

"Doctor's idea of a sick joke?" She tried to swipe at the tears.

"You can't keep hurting yourself. You have slashes across both wrists that Freddie Cougar would be proud of. Where did you get that nail file?"

"My business."

"Fine. Okay, this smelling rotten flesh . . . care to enlighten me please?" Sandy smiled gently. "Franki, I think it's more than your skin that's tormenting you. Is there something going on that I should know about? Did Gertrude threaten you in any way? Tell me something so I can help you."

"No. Yes. I can smell the rank odor of my skin but not always. The lights go real bright and then I hear screams. Everyone thinks I'm making this up. Do you think I like being poked with needles and strapped down like some wild animal? I can't get away from the smell once it's here. Why won't anyone believe me?" Franki looked pleadingly into Sandy's eyes.

"I believe you. I want to know what's causing this?"

"You think if I knew the answer you would have to belt me down to these goddamn rails? You have to help me."

"Then tell me what's going on? The truth."

"I'm losing my fucking mind, genius. And that prick that keeps jabbing a needle into my arm thinks I'm doing this for attention. He can go straight to hell. He's not inside my head when this strange shit happens to me. I don't even want to be in my body. So how would he know what I smell and don't smell?"

"Is there a scary memory that flashes before this happens?"

"My entire fucking life is a bad memory, Sandy. You want me to figure out which one, like a trigger you mean? They come like they're all mushed together, for Christ's sakes."

Throwing her arms into the air.

"Can you share one with me?" Sandy took one of Franki's mitted hands into her own.

"No. I don't like to talk about that stuff!" Franki pulled away her hand.

"I think if you talk about your fears or regrets, they won't seem so unmanageable in your mind," Sandy said softly.

"Sure, that's what the last shrink told me before throwing me into another shitty halfway house for unruly street kids."

"Want to tell me what happened?"

Franki felt the mattress sink down beside her.

"You're not going to stop bugging me until I give you something to chew on."

"Works for me. Sit up and tell me."

Franki leaned back against the pillows. "What do you want to know?"

"Talk to me about one of the halfway houses."

Franki sighed and rolled her eyes. "It's a placement house. You go there first before a bleeding-heart family takes you in, if you're lucky. It's a sweet lie. There are no nice bleeding hearts that want to take strays into their protected precious lives. The house is called Playroad. Nice house as far as homes go, full of juvenile delinquents that society has thrown away. After a couple of days of being there, I was brought into the office with one of those social workers, being interrogated of course, when a huge fight broke out in the kitchen between this fat white chick and a black working girl named Honey. This chick is tough as nails. They were trying to kill each other with knives, pretty serious stuff. Anyway long story short, staff bolts to the kitchen to break up the fight, and I quietly grabbed my gear and exit out the front door. Guess they didn't care much because no one came looking for me."

"You just walked out without anyone noticing? How old were you?"

"Eleven, not sure. Years are blurred together. My nickname on the street is Houdini." Laughter, dry as autumn leaves crunched underfoot, rasped from her throat.

"I guess River Edge is different?"

"Prison, you mean? And yeah the streets are different. The drugs you guys keep shoveling down my throat every four hours that's supposed to help me, ain't. And you guys frown on applejacks and smurfs. Why is beyond me." She rolled her eyes.

"Are you an addict?"

"That's what they labeled me. But I don't think so. The high gets me comfortable is all."

"The antidepressant you're taking is to level out the chemicals in your brain because of your comfortable-drug use, as you like to call it, and the mood stabilizer drug is for your panic attacks and hallucinations."

"A little too late, don't you think?" She held up both arms.

"I know you don't believe us, but you are getting proper medical treatment."

"Treatment? You call this treatment? I'm in lockdown like a prisoner."

"Not true."

"You can't keep me here against my will! It's cruel punishment and you know it." She flopped back against the propped pillows.

"This institute will keep you here, Franki, until we feel you're safe. If that means protecting you from yourself, then that's what this institution is prepared to do. I don't want anything bad to happen to you. I kind of like you, kid, in spite of that tough facade."

"Are you hitting on me?" Franki smirked.

"Get real. This may come as a surprise, but I have a lot of respect for you."

"Now I know I need my dad's old hip weighters for the landslide of shit that's coming my way."

Sandy laughed. "And I love that sarcastic wit too. You are awesome, Franki Martin, and I hope one day, you'll see that."

"You sure you're not making a pass? Cause . . . if you are, it's going to cost you like everyone else. No freebies." Franki winked.

"Honey, you must be starving?"

"No. I don't know what the hell I am."

"Come on. I'll take you for your morning shower."

"Don't you have anything better to do?" Franki stared at the nurse, distrust measuring Sandy's intentions.

"Nope." She gave Franki a warm smile. "I am here to help you, my dear, and that's exactly what I am going to do. Is that okay with you?"

"I guess. Where's the uniform?"

"I'm off today."

"What? And you decide to spend it with a crazy person? Are you sure you don't need any mental help?" Franki raised a brow.

Sandy laughed, messing Franki's hair that was in dire need of a good wash. "I assure you, my little friend, I'm fine. Besides, what is wrong with wanting to spend time with you?"

"It doesn't happen very often, let's put it that way." She grimaced as her wrists throbbed inside the mitts.

"Franki, I want you to understand that I'm not just a nurse. I am a friend you can trust. I know under that layer of rage, there is someone really sweet awaiting the chance to come to life."

"You're a weird wonder." Franki snickered and shook her head.

Sandy stood. "I have to go and get plastic wrap for your arms to keep the bandages from getting wet."

"What about these ridiculous things on my hands? How do you expect me to hold the soap?" Franki demonstrated as she tried to pick up a magazine. "Or do you intend to wash me?" She cocked her head.

"Have no fear, the oven mitts are coming off. Try and behave."

It was Sandy's turn to pucker a brow.

"A shower in plastic wrap sounds like fun to me." Franki laughed.

"An experience, no doubt. I'll be back in a minute."

It didn't take long for a newer and cleaner version of Franki to emerge. Sandy handed over a fresh pair of pajamas.

"Hey, new ones!" She quickly dressed.

On the way back to the room, Franki tugged at Sandy's shirt like a child seeking attention from a loving mother.

"When I came here, I had a duffle bag. Where is it?"

"The duffle bag?"

"The only bag I own."

"It's in lockup. Why?"

"I want it!"

"Sorry, but it's not allowed on the third floor."

"Jesus, rules," Franki said glumly.

"Is there something special you need in the bag?"

"Yeah. I have photos of my family. It makes me scared sometimes because I can't always remember what they look like. I need my pictures close to me."

"Franki, I will get the pictures for you, promise."

"When?"

Sandy viewed the vulnerability momentarily cascading over the angry pain in her eyes.

"The minute I go."

"And you'll come right back with the pictures?"

"Have I lied yet?"

"No, not unless you were hitting on me earlier," she teased.

"I love that rawness about you."

Sandy understood when she started bringing Franki magazines that there was a chance she could get into trouble. She decided it was worth the risk. It would be more therapeutic for Franki to occupy her mind than whether or not she got in a little bit of trouble. She had been a nurse at River Edge for twenty years and had spent long hours working her way up to supervisor. Most of the time, she held the respect of her peers. She had always followed the rules—at least up until now.

The two sat on the bed most of the day, viewing the photographs. They were wrinkled and yellowed from time. Franki's mother was a beautiful woman with shoulder-length blond hair and a petite frame. Her father was tall and handsome with a carefree smile. Franki and her sister looked like twins, except Beth was taller. Happy moments captured in time. Precious. For a long moment, Franki stared at the four of them, out at Rockie Point Road longing to relive that treasured moment one more time. Sandy made sure there was a balance of conversation like girl stuff, boys, clothes, dreams, and goals. They went through the designer magazines picking outfits they both liked and what they enjoyed about the models that were parading the designer's masterpieces.

Finally, it was time for Sandy to leave young Franki. Her shoulders were starting to slump, and clearly, she was in need of some serious rest. Sandy left with a spring in her step. At last, she'd established the beginnings of a relationship. For the first time, Franki had shared about her family, along with life on the street and how she survived day to day. Sandy couldn't imagine herself trying to endure Franki's horrific ordeals. It had been more than a tough life. It had been hell!

Sandy gave Franki a hug, leaving the photographs and magazines behind. She'd stop by the nurse's station and tell them those things were not to be removed.

"I'll see you in a day or two, depending on my schedule. Try and be good."

Franki smiled. "Sandy, thanks." She held up her photographs.

"My pleasure. Friends?"

"Maybe in time." Franki smirked.

As the nurse waited for the elevator, she got a sudden brainwave. On her way to her house, she'd make a detour and stop by Ellen's place. The two had become dear friends over the course of her career. She wanted an expert opinion on Dr. Viewer and the medication Franki was taking.

She stepped out of the gloomy world of mental illness into the glorious sunshine. Hearing the birds singing in the trees brought joy to her soul. She crossed the parking lot to her shiny black BMW and slid in behind the wheel. She popped in Keith Urban's CD, *Road to Be Here*, cranked it up as loudly as her eardrums could stand, drowning out the wild life.

CHAPTER NINE

A couple of days later, after the visit with Sandy, Franki was sitting up with her legs dangling over the side of the bed, reminiscing. She didn't want to accept that she'd had a good time with the nurse, but she had to admit that Sandy was different. They weren't best buddies or anything, but at least, she now had someone decent to talk to. She glanced around at the jail-sized space where she spent a majority of her time, except for showers, bathroom trips, and short walks up and down the hallway when she felt up to the challenge, accompanied by her bodyguards—orderlies. She debated which of the two evils was worse: life on the street or being locked up. The streets offered freedom to come and go as she pleased but didn't provide an inside bed, toilet, and regular meals. The institute provided physical comforts and should have been a safe haven; instead it was a concrete jungle where two-legged danger lurked. Dr. Blake was a beast far worse than any she'd encountered on the outside. And now, she was locked in the same cage with him. Trapped with nowhere to run. No way to escape. Tears coursed down her cheeks as she stared at the metal door blocking her from freedom. It would take a battering ram to knock it down.

Franki had become habituated with the routine: eat breakfast, then shower, brush her teeth, comb her hair, and change into a clean nightgown. Franki hated being supervised while she shaved her legs and armpits. In moments of rebellion, she refused all human luxuries, including hygiene. Who in the hell did she have to impress? It's not like she wanted to pretty herself up for Blake the Rape Hound. Breakfast arrived. Today's fare was two fried eggs, toast with jam, orange juice, and fruit of the day: sliced apples sprinkled with lemon juice to prevent browning.

Following the morning ritual, she stood gazing out her room's wire-meshed window. She closed her eyes, her face trying to absorb summer's warmth. After some moments, her eyelids fluttered open to view the broad stretch of manicured lawns, bordered by brilliant arrays of floral color. The sun hugged the residents, privileged to have yard passes; they strolled the cobblestone pathways and sat on benches scattered throughout the greenery. The Rockies never looked more majestic. Franki imagined herself outside, basking in the summer sun's warmth. She couldn't get a clear picture because the window mesh obscured the beautiful view.

She struck a clenched fist against the screened window that was obstructing the marvelous view.

"I deserve to be outside. Instead, they've locked me in this fucking broom closet. I should have killed myself when I had the chance. I'd rather die than live like this!" She threw back her head and screamed at the top of her lungs, "Get me the fuck out of here!"

She flopped onto the bed, punching the pillow in frenzy until her fury became a quiet despair. Her spirit was broken.

It all began the night her parents were killed in an automobile accident. The system stole her older sister, Beth, and placed them into separate foster homes. Hers was more abusive and vile than she had ever imagined possible. She begged foster care to reunite her with her sister, but they flat-out refused. Franki set out determined to find Beth. She'd run away on several occasions, searching for her, only to be found hours later and brought back. She vowed that one day she'd find Beth and they would never again be apart. At the age of eleven, the streets had become Franki's permanent home. Now fifteen, the end had come. What the streets hadn't gobbled up, this place surely would. A dangerous predator was lurking inside the facility, hiding behind a mask of professional power and prestige.

Lost in her own thoughts, Franki hadn't heard Sandy enter her room.

"Good morning, Franki."

Startled, she leapt to her feet. "Go away! I'm in no mood."

"Why are you so grouchy this morning? Didn't sleep well last night?"

"All I do is sleep goddamn it. Piss off."

"Sorry, honey, you know I can't do that. What's making you so upset?"

"How would you feel if you were locked away like some rat in a cage? How do you think I feel? Leave me alone!"

Sandy frowned. This was not the contented Franki she'd left a couple of days ago.

"You are allowed to be in a bad mood, but you're not allowed to take your anger out on me, little buddy."

"Piss off. I'm not your buddy."

"No can do, besides, you don't want to loaf around in a smelly old gown, do you?"

"Not like I'm going anywhere important." She sank back on to the bed and burrowed her face in the pillow.

"Okay you're upset." Sandy sighed.

"What does it matter if I take a shower or not?" Franki grumbled.

"It matters. This goes on your progress report. Good hygiene, remember?"

"Who gives a holy hell what those assholes write about me? It's their word against mine. I could be a model prisoner it won't matter. Crazy people don't stand a chance in here. Leave me alone, Nurse Wonderful? Go find another nutcase to harass." She glared a killing look.

"You'll feel better after a shower. Come on, Franki, let's go." She clapped her hands to get her moving.

"Fine! Fine! Fine! Let's get it over with so you'll leave me the hell alone, I hope?"

"That's the spirit. Thank you."

Franki marched down the corridor, each hard-hit step punctuating her anger. Had something in particular set her off? Sandy wondered. If so, she wanted to know what it was.

This time, Franki heard loud moaning behind the doors as she stomped past. Had she heard these cries before and not noticed? Or was she losing her mind?

*   *   *

Dr. Blake was enjoying poisoning his mother in the name of research, injecting her daily with small doses of curare. Exalting in his power over life and death, he became increasingly more sadistic.

It was the middle of June, midmorning. As Alma Blake lay in a state of unconsciousness, he delighted in yelling in her face and pinching her thin frail arms and legs as hard as he could to bring her back around. Her fragile arms and legs were blanketed in blackish bruising. He was being what she always wanted him to be: a bona fide scientist. Of course, scientists needed guinea pigs. Unbeknownst to Alma, she'd become her son's. *Quite fitting*, he thought. She would awaken with no recollection of the night before. This was a great feat for James. Gradually, he had become less and less attached to pleasing her. The emotional wounds of childhood had materialized. He fought against the ardent current like a drowning man caught in a whirlpool, but it was no use. His long suppressed fury was unleashed.

He brought her meals only when it suited him. And when he felt generous, they were hot and on time. The nights when he was in a good mood, he only injected sleeping aid into her system. It was fenced between hate and love.

Those were the nights he made a point of staying late to keep her company so she wouldn't be lonely. In his mind, he was being the loving son she always wanted him to be. Weekends were different. He couldn't just stupor her and abandon her without food and water; that would be cruel. What if she woke up? What if the drug wore off and she got out of the room? His high-powered standing amongst his colleagues would be ruined. He didn't fear being seen after hours though. He carried his pager with him wherever he went. The institution's staff would never catch on to his secret. He was much too clever for those "lame brains," as he referred to them. No one knew where he hid out each weekend. His colleagues assumed he was held up in his office or home studying something to do with medicine. Dr. Blake snickered to himself; he was beyond research. He was the epitome of greatness. If Alma were nice for a whole week, he'd reward her with chocolate. She had been, so now he sat in the wheelchair next to the bed, reading *A Midsummer Night's Dream*. Her eyes sparkled with enjoyment while listening to her son narrating the story. Sometimes she closed her tired eyes, allowing her imagination to flow with Shakespeare's characters. It tickled Blake's soul to hear her laugh.

With old age, she'd become less high-strung. Life had taken most of the mania out of her, but she still wasn't fully placid. From time to time, she complained of not having a television, but James stood his ground. The chance of someone hearing it blaring wasn't a risk he wanted to take. This game of hiding his mother was enough for him to handle. On rare occasions, she'd get him to lie next to her. He'd stroke her frizzy white hair, telling her what she wanted to hear and how sorry he was for being such a disappointment. She loved to hear him grovel. A couple of times, James got brave enough to sneak her outside so she could soak up some fresh air. Of course, he would take her to a different part of the city where he was certain no one would recognize him. He wasn't prepared to answer questions from people who knew nothing about his private life. She in the wheelchair and he pushing would enjoy nature's winding trails on the outskirts of the city.

He had concocted a not only reasonable but also believable story. If he did run into someone from work—he was taking his neighbor's mother out for an airing. If in the unlikely event Alma started babbling of her son's experiments, he would merely look confused, shake his head, and tap his temples: she's mad as a hatter, plain and simple. People would commiserate and continue on their way.

* * *

It was now the end of June, the sun warm and glowing in a clear blue sky. Its rays gleamed through the trees, so bright he had to squint. Elk Lake forest lined each side of the trail. Blake hadn't realized there were so many brilliant shades of green. Fallen trees lay on the forest floor, their stumps making homes for the creepy crawlers needing shelter.

It had been exactly four weeks since his first experiment in the lab, and Blake was bursting to share his accomplishments. He had to remain cautious. Even to himself, it seemed way off the chart of sanity. A hint would give him a bit of relief. Before returning his mother to River Edge, he stopped and knelt before her wheelchair. Nervously, he adjusted his glasses, took two hits of his lung mist, and smiled tremulously.

"Why are we stopping, James? Keep going."

Blake held her skeletal age-spotted hand into his and clearing his throat. "Mother, I have something important to tell you."

"Can't you push and talk at the same time?" she snapped.

"It's important that you hear this from me."

"What stupid thing have you gone and done now?"

"I am aware of your disappointment in me."

"Oh, here we go. What did you do? Get fired?" She pulled away her hand.

"No, nothing like that, Mother." He gritted his teeth.

"Get on with it before you spoil the entire outing."

"I know you wanted me to become a scientist, right?"

"Yes, why?"

"And I went to med school and became a doctor, right?"

"Yes, yes, go on." She flapped a hand.

"Since I entered med school, I have never lost interest in science."

"A lot of good it will do you working with crazy people," she scoffed.

He took a deep breath. "Well, I did an experiment on myself."

"What are you going to do, become good-looking or something?" she heckled.

"No, better. When word gets out eventually, the whole world will know who James Blake is."

"How?" Her eyebrows raised a notch.

"I can't give you the details until I'm sure. But if it works, it will make me superior to mankind. More famous than Einstein even. And you, Mother, will be the first to know. I can't wait to see that proud look on your face."

"When will you know for sure?"

"That part I'm not exactly sure."

"Are you telling me that we stopped our stroll so you could tell me that you've gone and done something that might make you famous but you're not sure when?"

"Yes. I . . . guess." James bowed his head.

"And you can't tell me the exact science of what you've done?"

"I'm optimistic that this won't fail."

"Tell me what you've done. You owe me that much."

"I think . . . I mean, I know you will be proud of me. All I can say is that I have dabbled with creating a deadly mixture so extreme that no one has thought about the idea or its ramifications. Mother, if it works, I will be unstoppable. The scientist you will be proud of. I did it all for you, Mother."

"Sounds like a load of crap to me." She frowned. "James, I don't have much time left. Make me proud before I die."

James tried to give his mother a kiss on the cheek; she deliberately moved her face.

Her rejection of his gesture of love didn't surprise James. Any intimacy between them had ended a long time ago.

CHAPTER TEN

Since Franki Martin's admittance to River Edge, the chip on her shoulder about following rules had not been whittled into shape. As she stood at the screened window watching the "outsiders," as she called the privileged residents, taking their strolls or sitting in the sun, an especially painful keepsake was triggered that still tore out her heart.

Her foster mother, Susan Wilkins, demanded perfection, a mark of excellence so high it was impossible to obtain. Human beings are flawed creatures. It was the end of October, Halloween night. It had been a hard transition for Franki, being shunted from home to home without her sister, Beth. She was a deeply wounded little girl of ten by the time she arrived at her final foster home. In the beginning, Franki felt wanted with her new foster family. This was her first real feeling of excitement since being betrayed and abandoned by the system sworn to protect her. And collecting candy and goodies on Halloween was a wonderful experience she looked forward to. Susan had made her a fairy-tale princess costume to wear. Franki beamed. The dress was white and pink and glittering with silver sequins. It looked just like the one worn by Cinderella when she went to the ball to meet her Prince Charming. Being a fairy princess was the best costume in the world, for fond memories of her daddy calling her "his little princess" still warmed her heart.

That morning, Ms. Leacher gave the class a spelling quiz. Franki felt confident she'd do well, having spent hours studying in her room the night before. By noon, the test papers were marked and handed back to the students. Ms. Leacher knew of and sympathized with Franki's struggles, but the girl constantly amazed the teacher with her determination to excel. She was a bright student with a zest for learning. And this was another test proving how smart this little girl truly was. Her mark was a large A on the top of her paper. The quiz had to be signed by the parents and returned to the teacher. At lunchtime, Franki skipped happily the whole way home, glowing with pride. She kicked off her shoes and dropped her coat at the door, then ran excitedly through the house, searching for Susan, to show her the spelling quiz results. She found her in the sewing room, putting on the finishing touches of her beautiful princess gown. Franki jumped up and down, waving the paper in the air, bursting with excitement.

"Let me see," Susan said, smiling.

Franki handed it over beaming with joy.

Susan's lips tightened. She pointed. "Why did you get this one wrong? You told me you studied each of these words last night!"

Franki's elation burst like a bubble pricked by Susan's sewing needle.

"But look, I got an A." She indicated the mark at the top of her paper.

"You lied to me! You told me this morning you knew every one of the words."

Tears welled in her eyes. "I . . . I thought I did. I . . . I got the rest of them correct."

"Not good enough. Tonight you will stay in your room and study these words until every one of them are ingrained in your brain."

"But what . . . what about Halloween?"

"Halloween is cancelled. Consider this your punishment for not telling the truth."

"I didn't lie! Please let me go!" Franki jumped up and down pleading to go out trick or treating. Susan remained resolute.

That night a brokenhearted Franki stood on her bed staring resentfully out her window, watching other costumed children giggling and shouting delightedly, racing up and down the street and going door to door, collecting their treats, while tears streamed down Franki's little face. She deserved to be out there trick or treating too. It wasn't fair. In utter defeat, she sat on her bed, hands cupped over her ears, trying to escape the noise of the doorbell ringing. All those kids were getting treats and she wasn't.

She hated Susan then. She hated her still. She had been chastised for not being perfect.

Abruptly, Franki turned away from the window and flopped down on her bed. She gave a deep sigh as if a knife had twisted deep inside. Here she was again many years later, this time being locked inside and having to watch others having a good time on the outside.

*   *   *

The morning snailed by while Franki's thoughts spun like a gerbil inside a wheel. Round and round they went, endlessly without resolution. Then she heard a clicking noise. Nurse Gertrude marched in like a knight from the old English army: stone faced and in white-suited armor.

"Morning, Mary Sunshine," Gertrude sneered. She plunked Franki's tray onto the rollaway table. A minute later, Sandy returned from the storage closet carrying a box of Kleenex.

"Hi, Franki."

"Take this poison away." Franki shoved the table, watching it zigzag across the room.

"Come on now, you need to eat. From the look of your medical chart, little buddy, you're in dire need of weight gain."

"Who cares? You keep me locked in here like some animal. And because you want me to eat, I'm supposed to believe you care about me."

"I do care about you. Yes, you are confined to this room, but remember how you got here. Franki, your blood count is low, and your protein count is dangerously low, which means your muscles are slowly deteriorating from lack of nutrition. Your body will soon begin feeding off your muscles to keep from starving to death. If you don't start feeding your body, you'll begin to lose your hair. That can't be an attractive thought. You haven't had your period in a month that I'm aware of. Work with me, Franki. We need to boost that immune system of yours with good healthy food."

"Thanks, but no thanks."

"Franki, you will get really sick if you keep starving yourself."

"So what? It's not like I'm going anywhere. I live in a box, Sandy. Don't you get it?" Franki's deep-blue eyes begged for understanding.

"Do you know what will happen if you continue to refuse to eat?"

"I'm just dying to hear this!"

"We will be forced to strap you down and put an IV in your arm and a feeding tube into your nostrils so your body will be fed necessary proteins, minerals, and vitamins. I know that can't be a pleasant thought, Franki." Sandy rolled the table toward the bed.

"It can't be any worse than the cell you keep me in. One goddamn window blocked with wire so I can't even look outside properly. And you come in here all high and mighty preaching I should eat. Do you know what I need, Sandy?" She stood with her hands on her hips. "I need to get out! Jesus, can't any of you see I don't belong in here? I'm not insane, damn it."

"Could have fooled me," Gertrude grunted from the doorway.

"Fuck off, you fat, ugly, frightening hag. Get the fuck away from me."

"Franki!"

"Get that fat bitch out of my personal space 'cause she ain't here to help me, that's for sure."

"Watch your mouth you insolent—"

"Give it up, you two. Enough is enough!" Sandy shouted.

"I'm telling you get this nurse bitch the hell out of my room. Now!" Franki screamed, blood rising into her face.

Gertrude crossed her arms. "I'm not going anywhere. If you want to, go ahead and throw a real good temper tantrum. It'll give me great pleasure seeing you strapped down again. Go ahead, make my day."

"Gertrude, don't make me say it again," Sandy said.

The nurse grinned, itching to go another round with the so-called tough street kid. It'd be rewarding to see the foul-mouth go down.

*   *   *

The law stated Franki had to be sixteen years of age before she could sign herself out of the institution. Sandy didn't have the heart to tell Franki that disappointing news. Since her arrival, Franki had lost three pounds, weighing only seventy-eight pounds. Virtually, she was down to skin and bones. A huge warning she wasn't doing well even in a controlled environment. It was obvious; she wasn't emotionally, mentally, or physically strong enough to take on life's simplest challenges. If only they had known the disturbing secret she was being forced to keep. The horrible events wouldn't have evolved . . . but . . . they did. And Franki suffered on account of their neglect to probe.

*   *   *

The medication was starting to take effect. Franki's fits of rage weren't as intense as when she first arrived. The scarring on her wrists was finally healing, but that was the only part of Franki's anatomy and psyche that was improving. The staff knew if young Franki were freed now, she would certainly take her own life. Clearly, she didn't believe she had much to live for at this point.

Sandy harbored a haunting past of her own. She understood Franki's painful emotions of not wanting to go on. Having won the struggle through her own troubled childhood, she knew that no matter what life throws at you, there is always a solution and taking your life is not one of them. She was living proof of that. Sandy believed Franki wasn't crazy; she was betrayed, hurt, and angry. Life had not been kind to young Franki, but to stop being a victim and become a victor in her life, Franki needed to stop resisting treatment.

Franki stood guarded, arms folded across her chest.

"Come on, it's time to eat," Sandy urged.

"And I told you, I don't care."

"I care," she replied softly. "Beneath your tough facade, I believe you do too."

Sandy's keen professional eyes took in Franki. Her eyes were red and swollen from crying. Her skin had begun to turn gray and dark circles hung beneath her eyes—a combination of over medicating, starvation, grief, and sleep deprivation caused by endless nightmares. Sandy slipped her arm around Franki's shoulder and guided her back to the bed.

Gertrude's lips pinched with disapproval. Placing her hand on her thick hips, she tapped her foot impatiently. "I don't know why you bother."

Sandy glared at her, ignoring her offensive remark. Franki gave up resisting. Somewhere in the back of her mind, Franki sensed Sandy was genuine. She reminded Franki of the same softness as her mother so many years ago. God, if only her mother were still alive, her life would have turned out so differently. Oh, she wanted her mother back . . . and her father. Damn it, she wanted her life back . . . The two sat silently on the bed until emotions calmed while Gertrude stood impatiently, sending out sighs of disapproval.

Finally, Sandy spoke up, "Gertrude, you can go if you like. I'll take the tray back to the kitchen when we're finished."

"Fine! If you want to throw your lunch hour away, it's your choice." She tossed the keys at Sandy and stormed out of the room.

"That old bitch doesn't look like she's missed any meals."

Sandy arched her eyebrows. "Now, now. Hey, after your lunch, want to go for a stroll down the hall, just me and you?"

"That Gert is a real piece of work. She doesn't belong in a place like this with that attitude. Hell, if I had to wake up to her ugly face every day, for sure, I would have done the job right." Pointing to her bandages. "She's one tall drink of crazy. And no, I don't want to go for a stroll so I can be reminded of the freedom I don't have."

"Franki, on this path of life, you are going to meet all kinds of people that you aren't going to like. That's a fact. The question you must ask yourself, little one, is how are you going to react? Maybe Gertrude is having a bad day."

"Give me a break. Every day is a bad day for that dirtbag. And you guys say I need professional help. Who in the hell is her shrink?" She shook her head.

Sandy tried not to laugh. She knew what Franki meant and had to agree. Gertrude lacked the right temperament for the job. Jail guard suited her no-nonsense personality.

"Now let's see what's for lunch, shall we?" She lifted the tin tray's lid: a burnt grilled cheese sandwich, french fries that had been cooked at nine this morning and left under a heat lamp, plus a small bowl of green grapes and two Styrofoam glasses, one ice water, one milk. The tray was decorated with a neon-bright notice that read No Sharps. Third-floor-ward patients weren't permitted sharp utensils like forks or knives. In a paper container were two little pills—one green and one white—to help stabilize the chemicals in her brain. No one liked seeing Franki short-circuit.

"I've seen better, but it beats eating out of a dumpster."

Franki picked up her glass of milk and took a gulp. Her face puckered as she sat it back down. "Wow! That is so disgusting!"

"What's wrong with the milk?"

"It's warm as piss and sour. Want a taste?"

"No, thanks." Sandy giggled. "I'll take your word on it. I'll run down to the kitchen and get you another glass. When I'm gone why don't you reconsider the walk I suggested?"

"Don't bother."

"I don't mind, Franki." Sandy locked the door behind her and headed for the kitchen.

Franki nibbled away until her sandwich was gone. She tasted a couple of mushy fries before slamming tight the lid. Then Sandy returned with a freshly poured glass of cold white milk and three chocolate chip cookies.

"I lost my appetite." Franki shrugged.

The nurse opened the tray and removed the bowl of green grapes. "Here." She placed it on the nightstand beside the cookies. "You might want a snack later. So, have you decided?"

Franki washed her pills down with the cold milk and then got to her feet.

"We better go now before I pass out in the hallway."

"Let's go, kid."

The two strolled slowly down the corridor.

"So, what were you thinking about when I came into your room?"

"My lousy existence."

"What about it?"

"It sucks!"

"It doesn't have to, you know?"

"Yeah, like I have control over what happens in here? May I remind you, I am doing time in a nuthouse."

"May I remind you that you won't be at River Edge forever. Instead of thinking of ways to destroy what's left of your life, why don't you try thinking up ways to better it? Use some of that feistiness to change your life for the better."

"How?"

"You said you like to read and journal. Why don't you start drafting up some short stories? If you don't like talking about your feelings, why not tell it in a story? It will help to heal some of your pain. The pen is mightier than the sword. It works for me."

"Yeah, right. Your life is so rough."

"Not now, but it wasn't always peaches and cream, kid."

"You were never incarcerated into a pill factory."

"Don't be so sure about that."

"Really? I don't believe you."

"A person's life isn't always how it is perceived to be by others."

"Hell, that almost sounded poetic."

Franki stopped and turned to the door to her left, hearing the loud moaning sounds coming from inside.

"Everyone has problems, Franki."

"Fuck, that's creepy, like something out of a Stephen King book."

"Tortured minds from which there is no escape."

Franki went silent for a moment; the moans of anguish clawing up her spine.

"How long do you people plan on keeping me in the prison cell?" She started walking again.

"The good news is you haven't had an episode in four days. Dr. Viewer will be in to see you this afternoon to reevaluate your progress."

"Keep that pencil dick away from me!"

"This is what I mean, Franki. You have to work with us here. The more you cooperate, the greater the chances are for getting to the second floor and outside."

"I swear, if he asks me one more time why I tried to kill myself, I'm going to stab him in the neck with his pen that he doesn't stop clicking the entire time he's in my room." She gritted her teeth.

"If you stab him in the neck with his pen, the chance of you getting to the second floor will be none." She gave Franki a lingering glance. "So why did you try and commit suicide?"

"Tired of struggling. A hooker's life isn't an easy one. It's not like fuckin' *Pretty Woman* where Richard Gere comes to save the day. That shit don't exist out there. Shame, pain, and fear gets tiring after a while."

"I'm sorry. And that's what you tell Dr. Viewer."

"It is what it is."

"Do you still think about dying?"

"Yeah and no."

"More yes or more no?"

"More no."

"Good answer." Sandy smiled. "Do you need to use the washroom before we start heading back?"

"Sure, why not, beats squatting over the bedpan."

Sandy stood outside the door so Franki could have privacy. Franki flushed, washed her hands, and exited. "Hey, I have an idea, Sandy?"

"Let's hear it."

"We seem to get along. Why don't you take me home with you, or was all the nice talk just bullshit?"

"Franki, I would love to take you home with me, but it's against policy. I'd lose my job."

"Is that the only reason?"

"Absolutely. Why do you ask?"

"Because no one ever seems to want me."

Sandy froze, her eyes expressing such remorse; it made Franki turn away. *No one,* Sandy was thinking, *should ever feel like they weren't wanted, especially this little girl.*

"I would take you home in a heartbeat if I were permitted. I'm truly sorry."

"It's cool. It's not the first time I heard a good reason for not wanting me." An invisible hand seemed to reach inside and squeeze her heart.

"It's not like we can't be friends, Franki. When's your birthday?"

"October 11."

"By then, you will see things in a different light. I promise."

"Keep on dreaming, woman."

They were back at the iron door. Sandy opened it. "It'll be a better day tomorrow. Hang in there, kiddo."

"Do you honestly think I'm like the other crazies that have to live like this?" She sank onto her bed.

"Professionally speaking, yes, you have to stay here. How long will depend on you. The reality of your situation is this: Yes, life has not been fair to you, but you haven't dealt with anything. You've allowed yourself to get submerged into a world of drugs, pain, and God knows what else. You gave up, Franki. I'm glad you didn't succeed in attempting suicide because, little girl, you have great potential. You can do great things with your life if you just believe in your abilities. You survived street life, and that takes great courage. You are a force to be reckoned with."

"But—"

"But nothing." Sandy knelt before her, taking her thin hand into her own. "Please hear me out. You are hiding a world of hurt under that angry mask you wear. Franki, people don't attempt suicide unless they are desperate. You have issues, justifiably so, and if you don't want to be in a place like this, then work with us and address what's driving you to that desperate despair. You need to help us help you, or you'll never be free of pain. I'm sorry you lost your parents, and if I could bring them back, I would, but no one can. That's a harsh reality, but it is reality. Destroying yourself won't bring them back either. Your parents would want you to have a good life, so make them proud and do what needs to be done."

Franki stared down at her hand tucked securely in Sandy's firm grasp. It felt warm and comforting.

"I'm not crazy, you know?" she murmured.

"I know you're not. It's time to show the doctors in charge that you are trustworthy. Most importantly, you need to learn that your life has value and purpose no matter what happens along the way. If you fall, get back up. Now, let's do what you need to do, deal?"

Sandy let go of her hand and stood gazing down at the crown of Franki's golden strands of hair.

Franki nodded.

"What? I can't hear you. Was that a—?" She cupped her ears.

"I'll do it. I'll make my parents proud, and I'll show everyone I can be trusted." Franki raised a clenched fist.

"Good to hear. I have another matter to discus. Yesterday I heard that you threw a book at Ethal. You know the nurse with red hair and freckles. Is it true?"

"Jesus, good news travels fast." She groaned.

"I take that reply as a yes. Why?"

"Yes, she pissed me off. One of you guys better warn her if she comes near me again with a fucking needle, she's going to get more than a book thrown at her, and I ain't kidding!"

"So you freaked again?"

"Hey! I was pretty comfortable sitting up in bed reading, minding my own business. Here's the book." She held up *The Trade Mission* by Andrew Pyper. "I mean, I look up and there's red storming in with a needle, saying that the injection was ordered. I told her I take my meds in pill form. She obviously didn't believe me, surprise, surprise."

"An injection of what?"

"The venom that instantly sedates me like a dart from a tranquilizer gun. The stuff they use when I'm acting all nuts."

"And you were just reading? Please tell me the truth." She stared into Franki's eyes, imploring her to be straight with her, looking for any signs of deception. Eyes that were unblinking and guileless held her own.

"I swear."

"Who ordered the needle, do you know?"

Franki gave Sandy one of her famous palms up and how-the-hell-do-I-know shrugs.

"I'll find out what's going on. But you, young lady"—she pointed—"no more using books as weapons. Or I'm afraid they will take away your privilege."

"Hey, I didn't start it. Let 'em try."

"I'll look into it. But in the meantime, Franki, you have to try to curb that temper of yours."

"What the hell would you do if some moron wanted to give you an injection for no reason at all? Not likely you would take it, and neither did I."

"I'm not sure what I would do. But no more firing shit across the floor, okay?"

This was the first time she'd heard Sandy swear. Franki laughed. *Not so perfect after all,* she thought. "I got it!"

When Sandy left and closed the door gently behind her, Franki fell onto her bed, feeling vindicated at last. "I'll show that doctor how trustworthy I can be! Here I come second floor." She smiled with a new confidence.

CHAPTER ELEVEN

Dr. Blake took the three patients' files from the gray metal cabinet, placing his first file in the middle of his desk. He looked up at the sound of the knock on his office door and then palmed his thinning salt-and-pepper hair and straightened his gray pinstriped tie. He opened the door. Gloria smiled incandescently and with open arms entered his office. Anticipation warming his loins, he closed and locked the door. He couldn't resist her hot body. Hands slowly moving down her back, he grabbed her ass and squeezed not too gently. A sly, satisfied smile crossed his lips at knowing he had fooled everyone into believing he was nothing more than a medical geek. If only his colleagues knew what deep perverse darkness lived inside the mind of a true psychopath.

*   *   *

Inside the doctor's inner office, known to Franki as the Monster's Torture Chamber. The walls were plain white, the tiled floor speckled in gray and black. A small countertop held tongue depressors, a plastic jar of cotton balls, facial tissue, cotton swabs, and culture dishes to be sent to the lab for tests. A box of latex gloves of course. Beside the examining table and at waist level hung a blood pressure cuff and sphygmomanometer, mounted to the wall. Next to it was an otoscope for checking ear canals, an ophthalmoscope with a special light designed for examining the muscles behind the eyes, and a stethoscope for taking a patient's heart rate.

Without hesitation, Gloria proceeded to Dr. Blake's inner office and began undressing as she'd done on numerous occasions. Clothes completely removed, she climbed onto the examining table and waited, barely able to contain her eagerness. Dr. Blake rechecked the locked door and then turned to Gloria, his eyes wild with lust and face flushing with expectation and excitement. Gloria had no idea she was about to become Dr. Blake's next victim in his dangerous game of Russian roulette. The wheel had spun, and she was the winning slot. She watched noiseless as he tore off his clothing and scurried over to her. He kissed her hard on the mouth; then lips and teeth nibbled down her neck. She moaned softly, unaware of the surging impact of pleasure this incited in his evil mind. His hands groped roughly at her breasts, forcing her nipples to stand erect. He sucked at them like a hungry infant trying to feed. His hands rushed along her body, reaching for his destination. He slid two fingers in and out of her hot moistness until he felt her shudder and then gush warm wetness. His hands gripped her tightly around her arms, pulling her off the table, directing her to kneel in front of him. He gripped her red hair, pulling her head toward his erect organ. Her mouth seized on it, tongue dancing up and down the shaft. The warmth of her mouth sucking and licking brought him within seconds of orgasmic explosion. Abruptly, he pushed back her head and lifted her up onto the table. Immediately, he climbed on top of her and thrust himself inside her. With one last groan, he spent himself completely. Their eyes met for a mere second as he hurried to get off her. Her eyes were lit with elation like two candles lighting the way into the darkness. She had beautiful big brown eyes with matching long eyelashes. Her red hair shone like oil. Her five-foot-four lean frame shimmered with droplets of sweat. Gloria always smiled with her mouth closed to hide the horrible shape of her teeth.

Blake strode to the sink, grabbing a bar of sanitizing soap and a towel from the hanger.

"Did that feel good?" he asked while washing up.

Gloria turned over on her side, her head resting on the palm of her hand.

"Oh, yes, yes. You really love me," she breathed.

"You're my special girl, Gloria." He grinned.

"Special girl, special girl," she sang.

Dr. Blake had been taking sexual advantage of Gloria for the last year, but now, he had a motive. It was far removed from pleasuring the woman who thought he loved her.

"Stop singing. You're annoying me now."

"So-rr-y."

They dressed muted beneath the humming noise of the frosty air-conditioning. The two had a spring in their steps as they entered his outer office.

"Now, when you go back to your room, what must you do?" He searched her brown eyes. She lowered hers submissively. "Take a shower. I remember. I will."

* * *

Gloria was so beautiful when she was a teenager. Everyone told her she was model material. Not only did she have a lovely face and great body but also she was highly intelligent. Without warning, all that changed. In her senior year of high school, she met a man not approved by her parents. When her daddy ordered her to never see that man again, she packed her belongings and ran off with him. It didn't take long—six weeks at the most—before Scott Mise, the local troublemaker who professed to love her, had her hooking on the street corners to support his very expensive three-hundred-dollars-a-day cocaine habit. Gloria hated sleeping with other men for money, but she did it because she loved Scott.

In spite of her attractiveness, when growing up, Gloria had been very insecure. Scott was popular, charming, and good-looking. She felt like the bell of the ball standing beside her man. At nightclubs, he introduced her to his friends as "his dream girl." She was so shy and quiet, never speaking out of turn; his friends couldn't understand what an intelligent pretty girl was doing with a sleaze like him. He was a real piece of work: the handsome bad-boy-type that women love and want to rehabilitate. Gloria wanted to prove her parents wrong about him. In the beginning, he spoiled her with jewelry, clothes, expensive dinners, and then shamed her into staying.

Gloria still couldn't give clear details of what took place on that horrible night a lifetime ago. She remembered the cold rain, driving winds, and darkness. She had been standing under her umbrella freezing, waiting for a trick to pull up. Four hours and three johns later, she called it a night. Chilled to the bone, she hurried back to their east-end apartment where Scott immediately started counting her earnings. Enraged at discovering she hadn't made her quota, he grabbed her by the hair and punched her in the mouth. Blood splattered against the wall. He picked her up and threw her across the living room. Her head struck the wall like a pumpkin being smashed to the ground. She felt terrified. She'd never before seen this side of Scott. She begged him to stop. He wrapped his fist around her hair and jerked her to her feet. Out of his mind for a fix, he dragged her backward down the two flights of stairs and out to his little red Toyota car. Once inside, she took several more slaps across the face. She could feel her eyes and lips swelling up like balloons. The bitter taste of blood swirled inside her mouth. Beyond scared and shock, she begged Scott to pull over. She pleaded with him to go back, promising to go out again into the cold night and make enough money for him. Finally, he pulled over to the curb about four or five blocks from their apartment. Scott jumped out of the car and dragged her out of the passenger side. She remembered falling to the ground and that's when Scott put the boots to her moneymaking frame. She tried to protect herself against his deadly blows by curling into a ball, wrapping her arms around her head and legs, but it was no use. He was too powerful and too fast.

That beating stole Gloria's high intelligence and maturity. All she could remember about the horrible event was she didn't bring him enough money and he was punishing her. After administering blow after deadly blow, Scott drove out to the country and dumped Gloria's broken body by the side of the road. Early the next morning, a farmer found her beside their bright red mailbox, barely alive. He called 911. She suffered multiple broken bones to her face, shoulder, and left leg, leaving her with a permanent limp. By the time the ambulance arrived, Gloria was hemorrhaging inside the brain. The doctors worked on her for six hours, relieving the pressure by inserting shunts for drainage. It was too late! She suffered massive brain damage and slipped into a coma. The doctors weren't sure if she would ever fully recover. Five months later, the prognosis remained the same. The specialists, Dr. Fernal Morgan and Dr. Julia Meron, thought it was time to pull the plug. Her mom, a staunch woman, wouldn't allow it and with an Irish Catholic background, believed in miracles. If her daughter were going to die, God alone would make that decision.

Gloria's mother thanks the Lord every day for keeping her faith. Nine months later, Gloria came out of her coma state. She did not know who she was or who were her parents. Unable to take care of herself, she was admitted to River Edge. Both parents worked nonstop to pay off the medical expenses and to take care of their daughter's ongoing expenses. Beginning with extensive therapy: speech, how to feed herself, how to walk again. After the bloodcurdling beating by Scott Mise, Gloria was like a toddler learning to walk and talk. Even to this day, her speech remained limited. That was fourteen years ago.

Dr. Blake was saying encouragingly, "Very good. What else, Gloria?"

"I'm your special girl."

"Yes, you are, but what else?"

"Secret, secrets don't tell." She giggled into her hand.

"No one!" He glanced down at her chart, changing the subject. "Teeth still hurting you?" She placed her hand on the left side of her face, demonstrating exactly where the area of pain was. "My teeth. This side."

"How bad does it hurt?"

"Sharp. Owe." She pointed to one of the five rotten teeth.

"They need to be extracted."

"Huh?" She tilted her head like a hound hearing the word *treat*.

"Pulled. They need to be pulled out."

"No!" She cried, cupping her hand over her mouth and shaking her head from side to side adamantly in protest.

"Don't freak. I'll give you Amoxicillin to clear up the infection and Tetracaine for the pain." He jotted a few notes in her chart, then continued, "I'll see you back in my office in a couple of days to make sure the medicine is working."

It was evident he would need to make a call to Dr. Rogen, the institute's dentist. Gloria's right and left molars were decaying; he doubted there was much to be done except extraction. The infection was making her breath rancid and a slight puffiness was forming along the left side of her jawbone.

Blake rose up from his chair, motioning for Gloria to do the same. He gave her butt a little pinch before opening the door. She put her hand over her mouth to hide her giggle as she strolled along the noisy corridor.

It won't be your teeth you'll need to be concerned about, sweetheart, he thought, slowly making his way back to his desk.

CHAPTER TWELVE

Psychiatrist Ellen Smith was now back to work after a four-week relaxing vacation at home with her adoring husband, Tom. Now it was time to get up to speed on the occurrences at River Edge. She was sitting at her desk reading the patient's file, awaiting her first appointment of the day. She knew a little regarding the patient's history, not only from reading the folder, but Sandy's updates as well.

This doctor shook her head. She disagreed entirely with Dr. Viewer's diagnosis of Franki Martin's mental condition. She took a deep breath and continued reading. *No wonder Sandy had unpleasantries with this idiot*, Ellen thought. Ellen hadn't picked her career because of any monetary or prestigious gain. She was a highly compassionate, committed, trained professional. And she was repulsed by the negligence of the medical staff handling Franki's care. Clearly, Franki Martin had been neglected at River Edge; Ellen just didn't know the extent, but she would. In fact, the girl had a good case for suing for malpractice at River Edge, but why hadn't anyone stepped in to help the poor girl? It wasn't as if the facility hadn't seen cases like Franki's before. Sandy had been doing all she could, but it wasn't enough.

The report documented Franki Martin had been spreading lies about the physical abuse she'd suffered at the hands of Susan Wilkins and her husband, Gary. A psychologist who in Ellen's opinion shouldn't be in practice wrote these reports. Dr. Viewer believed that while Franki suffered from slight depression, her violent outburst or temper tantrums were self-seeking and a strategy to get released from River Edge, a place she absolutely hated. Ellen wasn't buying any of it.

She flipped to the next page: Rev. Morton Doer at the Holy Mission Church. He claimed, Franki was nothing but a deviant who was on a self-destructive journey with no hope for redemption. She was a danger to anyone around her. He went on to state that in his judgment, Franki Martin was a manipulative thrill seeker incapable of gratitude, and that's why she ran away from her loving foster parents, Susan and Gary Wilkins's home. The Wilkins were strictly churchgoing, kind enough to take in a troubled Franki when no one else would.

The final shock came when Ellen read that Franki had an older sister, Beth. The girls were separated when their parents died in an automobile accident. Disgusted, Ellen pushed away the file and took a long swallow of tepid coffee. She could not comprehend how the so-called professionals running the social welfare system could have separated these siblings after such a tragedy, knowing they only had each other. To claim it was in the best interest of the children was absurd.

An hour had passed in studying Franki Martin's file. She swiveled her chair to face the summer's shine. She had a fair idea of what to expect from this upcoming visit: outburst of rage and self-mutilation were categorized under a number of disorders, bipolar, schizophrenia, and dysthymic disorders, but Dr. Smith thought it unlikely in Franki's case. Post-traumatic stress disorder was more the diagnosis. The child suffered inexcusably. Self-destructive patterns in abused children were common. It wasn't about gaining attention; it was about true suffering. It was their way of releasing the pain, by drug addiction, self-mutilating, and reckless abandonment of life. There was always an underlining in an emotionally disturbed person's Pandora's box. It would have been devastating for a little girl of nine to lose both parents and then be torn from the only person left in the world, her only sibling. Absolutely gut-wrenching. That's why Franki ran amok.

I don't know if I wouldn't have done the same thing, she thought. Before I finally retire from this facility, Ellen vowed, those two girls will be reunited.

*   *   *

A good day was dawning for Franki; she just didn't know it yet. She made her bed and then buzzed twice for a nurse to take her to the bathroom. Fifteen minutes went by, twenty minutes; finally her bladder couldn't hold it any longer, and she squatted over the bedpan. At seven forty-five, ward nurses Kathy and Alice arrived. Franki huffed that one of them had better empty her bedpan because she had no intention of smelling her own urine for the day. Alice disappeared with the full bedpan while Kathy ever so pleasantly delivered Franki her breakfast.

Sandy was the only one who could take Franki for a walk on her own. Franki was too volatile with the other nurses to be trusted. After breakfast, she was escorted down the hall to take a shower. Today, instead of a nightgown and a pair of rubber slippers, the nurse granted Franki light cotton pant pajamas with housecoat.

"Well, my ass won't be hanging out today now, will it?" She leered at Alice.

"Oh you." Alice flushed.

Franki's attitude was slowly changing for the better since Sandy talked to her. She didn't fling books across the floor, throw piss—or puke-filled bedpans at the nurses, or shred apart magazines for spite. She was eating three small meals a day and feeling better for it. The scent of rotting flesh had subsided, but the nightmares continued. The demonic voices were haunting but tolerable. When they would get too scary, she would curl in a ball and rock back and forth. It was better than ripping at her flesh.

*　　*　　*

The hot sun beamed through the holes in the screen as she sat propped against her pillows, reading the novel written by James Patterson. A few minutes later, she put it down and took another, a black-bound edition. She opened the pages of the Bible, turned to the First Book of Samuel, and read,

1: *My heart exalts in the Lord*
2: *My horn is exulted in my God*
3: *I have swallowed up my enemies*

"I have a few enemies you can have," she cried out and then continued.

4: *There is no Holy One like the Lord*
5: *There is no rock like our God*

Halfway down the page, Franki decided enough of this bullshit and was about to close the book when the door sprang open.

"Well, well. What do we have here?" Gertrude sneered.

"None of your business, evil witch." Franki slammed shut the book.

"You will come around, my dear."

"That's what you think." Franki glared, embarrassed.

"Let's go, smart girl. You have an appointment."

"Fat chance. I'm not going anywhere alone with you."

"It's a scheduled doctor's appointment, and all the nurses are busy. So let's go."

"What kind of doctor?" Franki's heart began to race inside her chest.

"You'll find out soon enough."

Oh, you bitch . . . you sure like playing head games, she thought.

"As long as it isn't jerk-off Blake."

"Watch that mouth."

"I'm not going anywhere alone with you until I know exactly where we're going." Franki tensed, ready for another violent confrontation.

Gertrude stepped closer. Franki leaped off the bed; she didn't want another smack across the face. "I guess I don't have a choice." She stood, waiting for Gertrude to grab hold of her arm. "Your own set of handcuffs would be great, eh?" Franki snapped.

"I don't need them." Her strong fingers cuffed her forearm.

"Right, you already have a good choke hold on my arm. Look, it's turning purple from you squeezing it so hard, you stupid cow."

"March, smart mouth."

Quickly, the nurse ushered Franki out into the hall. Instead of turning right, she went left. Franki felt relief. Right would have meant Gertrude lied, and she was going to the lion's den for another round of sexual torture.

The pair hustled through a maze of doors and well-lit corridors. *Holy shit! This part of the nuthouse, people are allowed to roam free,* she thought. There were none of the tormented cries she heard on her wing.

The two stopped in front of a white birch door. Franki began praying to whatever God might be listening that whoever was on the other side of that door was not going to be another Dr. Blake. She'd had all she could handle from that monster.

The door opened wide; a little gray-haired woman stood in the opening. The lines on her face were etched deeply from age, giving off a grandmotherly facade. The white overcoat contributed to Franki's heightened apprehension. *It's damned sad,* she thought, *when the only place I feel safe is in my prisonlike room.*

Ellen's pleasant voice was saying, "You must be Franki Martin? My name is Dr. Ellen Smith. Won't you come in, dear?"

Suddenly Franki imagined a wolf camouflaged in a dress, inviting Little Red Riding Hood into the cottage. She stepped back into the hallway. Gertrude immediately seized her by the wrist and squeezed hard. Lightning bolts of excruciating pain shot up and down her arm. She cried out and yanked her arm away from Gertrude's painful grip.

"Fuck! You stupid cow. Oh my god, this hurts! Ouch!" Franki held her wrist, jumping up and down, trying to rid the pain.

"Gertrude, that's enough!" Dr. Smith stepped between Franki and the nurse. "This sort of force on patients is unacceptable. Since when do we treat our residents like prisoners? We never use unnecessary force. Do I make myself good and clear?"

Could have fooled me, Franki thought.

"My humblest apologies, Dr. Smith." Gertrude's thin red lips curled. "I was just making sure she didn't run away." She folded her arms across her chest with attitude.

Franki wanted to yell, "Yeah, you finally got it, you old battleaxe!" But she refrained, knowing she'd be pushing her luck. Calling her a stupid bitch could have its consequences, especially if she was the nurse picking her up at the end of this session. No point in risking another fight with the bully on the block.

Dr. Smith dismissed the nurse, who closed the door with unnecessary firmness.

"Are you okay, Franki?" Dr. Smith asked, taking her arm into her hands looking for spots of blood on her white bandages. Luckily for Gertrude, the stitches, she thought, were still knotted together and weren't bleeding.

"I'll live." Franki shrugged and stepped further inside.

Franki's sapphire eyes quickly scanned the office. It was a large room with a window backing the huge pine desk and leather chair with two padded cloth chairs in front. Three industrial filing cabinets rested against the north wall. Pleasant black and white photographs, done by Annie Leibovitz graced the cream-toned walls. Between the leather chestnut couch and chair sat a two-inch thick plated glass coffee table. Luscious green plants lined the window adding peacefulness to the already brightly lit atmosphere. The scent of lavender filled her senses.

"This doesn't look anything like Dr. Blake's office," she muttered quietly to herself. The delightful aroma of brewing coffee made her taste buds water.

"Please make yourself comfortable, Franki." The doctor gestured toward the furnishing of choice.

Franki couldn't decide whether to lie down on the comfy couch set in the middle of the room or relax on its matching chair.

"Would you like a cup of coffee?"

"Yes, please," Franki replied politely.

"Have a seat and I'll bring it over to you."

"Where would you like me to sit?"

"Wherever you like, dear."

Wanting to see her reaction, Franki defiantly sprawled out on the sofa. Dr. Smith just smiled and set two steaming cups on the glass table. A silver tray held the creamer, sugar, and spoons. Franki doctored her coffee while Dr. Smith retrieved a folder from her congested desk and then sat in the chair across from Franki.

"Are you feeling tired, Franki?"

"Nope. I'm stoned, and I'm fucking bored to death, but thanks for asking. This place is a drug addict's heaven, did you know that?"

"Your report states you didn't come willingly?"

"Giving up my freedom wasn't on my priority list."

"Do you like it here?"

"What the hell do you think?"

She continued staring up at the ceiling.

"My guess would have to be"—she paused—"no."

"Point one for you genius." Franki gave attitude.

"So they tell me." Dr. Smith grinned then became serious. "You were brought to us by the police."

"Yep, another point."

"You consider yourself to be a badass?"

Franki hid her surprise at this shrink's grandmotherly-appearing language.

"I can handle myself pretty good."

"It shows."

"Minor setback is all."

"I hear you can get pretty angry at times?"

"You heard right."

"So tell me, Franki. How is your visit been with us so far?"

"I hate it. I get poked with needles from you animals, and on top of that, I'm choking down more drugs four times a day, supposedly to keep my brain chemicals in check and the worst is keeping me locked up like a prisoner. I've committed no crime."

"Sounds to me like you are still very upset?"

"You think." Franki's face scrunched like a tight fist.

"Made any friends since you've been here?"

"A nurse. She's not my friend, but she's cool to talk to."

"You've been here a while now, and you've made one friend." Ellen raised a brow. "How many enemies?"

Franki laughed. "How many does it say?"

"As far as I'm concerned, one is too many."

"Yeah. Where did you hire Nurse Ugly, from prison camp?"

"I'm assuming that would be Gertrude?"

"She'd be the one. A tall drink of psychotic, that one is."

"You don't like her?"

"She smacked me across the face. Did you know that?"

"No, I wasn't aware."

"Well, now you are. Going to do anything about it? Or are you like the rest of them and let it slide?"

"I promise it will be dealt with."

"I want proof when you're all done."

"What would you like to see happen to the nurse, Franki?"

"Fired."

"What about a suspension?"

"Take her off my ward so I don't have to look at her ugly face, that's a start."

"I'll see what I can do. How is that?"

"Finally, someone who knows what the hell they're doing in here."

"Other nurses not living up to your expectations?"

"What expectations. One is nice and the rest are like vamps."

"What's a vamp?"

"Vampire. Instead of long sharp teeth, these guys have long sharp needles."

"Can you tell me why they are rushing at you with needles?"

"Because I get out of control."

"And why do you do that?"

"I hate it in here. Why do you give a care?"

"Franki, I'm your new—what's the term?—shrink. We will be working together in hopes of finding a solution to your problems. How does that sound?"

"Just want to let you know, Doc, that my name isn't Dorothy, and I'm not traveling no yellow brick road. How does that sound to you?" Franki smirked.

"Sounds like we have a little work ahead of us."

"No kidding."

"So, do you like getting high?"

"Occasionally. It takes the edge off. Sometimes I feel like the world is crashing in on me, so I do a little whatever is available and it makes me feel better. No biggy."

"Types of drugs you have used recently?"

"Regular stuff. You know whatever is available, pot, pink panthers, and apple jacks."

"Often?"

"As often as I can. Scrounging dough is tricky business sometimes. I have to admit those injections are pretty cool."

"On a scale of one to ten, how high would you say you are right now?"

"Eight. Brain is one organ of fog."

"Do you feel you need that much medication?"

"I think you're the doc and you know best." Franki's answer surprised the psychiatrist.

"I think you're correct." Ellen smiled at the fragile girl now sitting across from her.

Dr. Smith quickly scanned the pages. "Wow! You're taking a mood stabilizer with an antidepressant and Thorazine." Ellen was shocked. Franki wasn't giving off any signs that violence was going to erupt. She wasn't incoherent, delusional, and irrational. She wasn't pacing back and forth, ready for a confrontation. To Ellen, the young girl seemed pretty unbended. If Ellen believed what she had read earlier, she would be wearing a full body-contact suit with six-foot orderlies at her side for protection.

"Doc, stabbing me with a needle so I'll sleep is getting on my nerves."

"No more injections, I promise. I'll start taking you down slowly off the antipsychotic medication. We don't want you to have a seizure from withdrawal. And by next week, you should begin to feel the brain fog lifting."

"One problem, Doc. I need something to help me sleep at night."

"Not sleeping well?"

"It's not falling asleep. It's staying asleep."

"Okay, I'll prescribe a nonnarcotic mild sedative."

Franki sat up taller like a debutante. Then, eyeing her name on the folder, her smile disappeared.

"Great, down for the count before I even get started." She gave a depleted sigh, pointing to the file in Ellen's hands.

"I'm not here to judge. Consider this a new beginning."

"What kind of crap do you want to know?" Franki leaned forward.

"Let me start by saying how sorry I am to hear about your parents. That must have been horrible for you to deal with at such a young age. Would you like to talk about what life was like when your parents were alive?" Dr. Smith inquired gently.

"My favorite subject, Doc. My parents were awesome," she began. "My dad worked in a coal mine and Mom at a local grocery store, part-time. We loved that she was at home after school, waiting for us. She always had some kind of goodies ready like milk and cookies, banana loaf, something home-baked."

"Franki, you mentioned 'we.' Can you tell me who 'we' is?"

"My sister, Beth, and me. What they did to us was absolutely disgusting. Anyway, let me tell my story." She took a deep breath. "I remember our house smelled of sweet baking every day after school. Dad would come home after work and take us up in his arms and kiss us with his hairy face till we screamed for mercy. We were his little princesses." Franki paused and took a sip of coffee. "We'd all eat dinner together and talk about our day and how it went at school and stuff. Our job was to make our bed and clear the table. We'd fight at times for who was carrying more dishes, but usual sister tiffs. Mom and Dad took turns reading us bedtime stories. I believe that's why I love to read so much today. Before I was imprisoned in here, I used to sneak into the library and quietly find a corner out of the way so I could get lost in the words while ignoring my own problems." Hot tears began to sting her eyes. She went on, lost in her memories, paying no attention to the notes Dr. Smith was taking. "We'd always had what my parents called 'family time,' especially on weekends. Time set aside to do something special like movies, summer camping, swimming, biking, always something fun. Dad taught us how to fish, but I didn't like it. In the winter, we'd go skating, sledding, or ski-doing. We'd all come home chilled to the bone. Mom made our favorite, cocoa. It took two hands to hold the mug. She'd add colored marshmallows. We were also into brownies one night a week. I can't remember now which day it was."

Dr. Smith interrupted. "Who babysat you girls when your parents were out?"

"Our next door neighbor, but only for special occasions, which was rare. My parents felt it was their responsibility to raise us, not anyone else's job."

"Hmmm," muttered Dr. Smith. "Please go on."

"That's how they died. I mean, 'tis the season to be jolly shit. They had gone Christmas shopping. On the way home that night, the accident happened. All I remember about that night is the police at the door, Beth crying, saying over and over that they're never coming back. Isn't the police report in the file?" She asked, looking puzzled to be talking about a tragedy that should have never happened.

"Yes, it is. I want to hear it from you," Dr. Smith replied softly.

"I see." Franki shrugged. "Well, later on, I found out that a drunk driver hit my parent's car head on. They didn't have a chance. The guy was speeding down the highway the wrong way. Thing is, that bastard walked away without so much as a broken bone, and later, I was told the gruesome truth: that the police couldn't find my mother's head. She'd been decapitated. My dad burned to death. The engine was on his lap when the car exploded. I still don't know if they ever found my mother's head. That's a nightmare in a child's mind. And to boot the system wonders why I have anger issues. The coffins were closed. Since then"—she leaned back against the couch—"my life has been one long ride into nightmare land. The shrinks label me this and that, but they don't know what is going on inside my soul."

"Why, sweetheart?"

"Pretty simple, Doc. I trust no one."

"Understandably so. Franki, no one has ever asked about the pain."

"They didn't care. They just shipped me off like I was a worn-out rag doll, without any attachments or feelings. To the system, I'm a paycheck." Her lower lip began to quiver.

"Franki, I am so sorry you lost your entire family. And . . . I am so sorry that the system you were supposed to trust failed you miserably. I am now validating you."

Franki couldn't believe her ears.

"What did you just say? I think I would like to hear those words again please."

Firmly Ellen repeated herself.

For a split moment, Franki's face lit up like a Christmas tree, then the plug was pulled.

"Thanks, you seem like a genuine person, Doc, but it's too late. I'm too far gone." Franki's chin fell against her chest.

"Like hell you are."

Franki's head snapped back up and then burst out laughing. "You're pretty cool for an old gal."

"Are you calling me old?" Ellen peered over the top of her metal-framed glasses.

"Not in a disrespectful way or nothin'." Franki smiled.

"Franki, I am surprised and proud of you. You have given me quite a bit more information than I was expecting. I could not have gotten the human side by reading a profile. Your life hasn't always been troubled. I'd say you came from a secure, loving, nurturing, respectable home before your parents died. And you can't forget what your parents taught you."

"Yep. We were the Cleavers."

"Do you still find it really painful to handle the loss?" Franki nodded in agreement.

Separation anxiety, Dr. Smith thought. "And Beth?"

"Fucking bastards. Don't get me started on that one."

"Too painful to talk about, Franki?"

"I want to destroy everything around me when I think of what they did to us. I begged to stay with Beth."

"Any relatives willing to take you and your sister in after the accident?"

She shook her head slowly, puckering out her lips. "No aunts or uncles. Mom and Dad were only children in their families. I never met my grandparents."

"That explains why you both were placed in separate foster homes."

"Doesn't make it right."

"Your file says—"

Franki interrupted. "That thing is a pack of lies, all bullshit! Don't bother reading that report. I ran away a lot, but what isn't in that report is why. I took off trying to search for Beth. I needed my sister, and no one would tell me where she was."

"What do you mean, 'trying to search' for you sister?"

Dr. Smith knew the answer already but needed to hear Franki's reenactment of the events.

"How in the hell was I supposed to know where she was? No one would tell me anything. I was flying blind. They split us up and that was that. I was expected to forget I had a sister. No address of where Beth was, no nothing. Beth just vanished without a fucking trace. There are no words to describe the level of rage I feel inside for what those losers did to the only family I had left. They should be grateful that I didn't turn out to be a psychopath, or I would have killed every last one of them."

"I'd say you are pretty angry."

"Wouldn't you be pissed if they kept you away from the only remaining person you loved?"

"Mmm," Dr. Smith said noncommittally, "any explanation as to why they separated you girls?"

"Answer my question first, Doc! Would you or would you not be very angry if they stole you away from the only person left in your world?" Franki leaned forward in her chair, eyes boring into Ellen's demanding an answer.

"I would be screaming mad, dear."

"Thank you, Doc. You don't know how many years I have been waiting for someone to say those words. I started to believe that I didn't deserve a friggin' answer to my question. I don't understand why they split us up. You already know, it's in the damn report."

"I want to hear your side of it. That's what counts here, Franki, not theirs."

Franki waited while Ellen poured them another cup of coffee, then continued.

"My parents had no will or money. They had enough saved to pay for the funeral costs and their debts. They weren't expecting to die that night either. The house went back to the mining company. Some know-it-all counselor told me it would cost too much money for one family to raise two growing girls. The system is screwed. So here we are, Doc." She tipped her cup at the psychiatrist. "End of story."

Ellen inhaled deeply and let a long sigh, heavy with sympathy, escape her lips.

"Franki, I am sorry that so far your life's journey has been the shits. It's been one tragedy after another. It angers me too that you've been so mistreated. As far as I'm concerned, the system that we put our confidence in should have done anything and everything to keep you and your sister together. Franki, from this day forward, I want you to know that I am going to do everything in my power to help you. I don't want to see you struggle through hardships the way you've had to so far. There are no words to measure the extent of your pain. I'm not saying your life won't be without challenges, but it will be a walk in the park compared to what you're use to. I would like to help you deal with the pain and anger of yesterday so you can have a better today. You can't have a peaceful mind if yesterday's bitterness is always in the way. I will not take away from how you feel. You're angry and hurt and justifiably so."

Franki sat speechless. This was the first time since her parents died that she had been given permission to be angry about the wrongs in her life. She hadn't even been allowed to grieve their loss. She'd been sent straight into a housing shelter without her sister and expected to cope silently. Her only remaining security and love gone.

"You, my dear," Ellen smiled gently, "have done amazingly well today. Be proud of yourself. It takes great courage to talk about devastating events that happened. Now"—she closed Franki's file folder—"let's leave our session as is and take care of other business, shall we?"

"What business?" Alarm pooled in her stomach.

"And you are in room—"

"Cell number 321, ma'am." She saluted the psychiatrist, who chuckled at her good sense of humor.

"I heard you weren't too happy."

"Heard correct."

"I'll have you removed off that ward and into a new room by the end of the day. All right, allow me to show you around." Ellen rose to her feet. "Time for the grand tour."

A waterfall of relief flooded through Franki. "Ready when you are." She gulped down the last mouthful of coffee. "Waste not, want not. Who knows when I'll get another cup of the real good stuff again?"

"How about every morning at breakfast, if you like."

"Oh, stop! I'm getting way too excited!" Franki winked.

Dr. Smith couldn't help but laugh. *Definitely a survivor!* she thought.

The doctor escorted her new patient around, showing her the television area and the recreational center. Franki was impressed with the variety of activities that were available to her. The pool and ping-pong tables were in use by enthusiastic players. Residents in wheelchairs were playing board games and listening to music, coming from the corner speakers. Snacks and juice were set out in the small kitchen area. Today there were pears and vanilla cookies, orange juice and ice water, tea and coffee. Decaffeinated of course. *Wouldn't want the nutcases restless,* Franki thought, *especially close to their bedtime.*

"This isn't so bad," Franki said. "I just won't stare at the people with the hollow eyes and drool dripping down the corner of their mouths."

"Franki, there is no need to fear. If an argument starts, it's broken up by an orderly on duty." The doctor patted her on the shoulder.

"That's good because fights usually find me. I don't go looking, honest."

The end of the tour brought them directly across from the nurse's station. Room 201. After being held prisoner in the horrible cell, this seemed like a piece of paradise. It was bright and huge with two single beds divided by an end table. Two numbered lockers sat side-by-side in one corner. A private bathroom she could call her own, no more disgusting bedpan for her. A real window she could look out and see clearly everything. She would finally feel the sun's warmth on her face. A light box secured to the wall at the front of the bed for reading. Landscape art graced the walls bringing the room to life.

"What do you think?"

Franki could only beam from her newfound freedom.

"There are two beds to one room. You, young lady, have no roommate as of yet. Who knows what tomorrow will bring." Ellen rolled her eyes.

"Ah, I'm so hard done by," Franki quipped.

"Franki, moving you to this room is conditional. In order for you to stay in this nice room, you are not allowed to put yourself in any kind of danger. That means, no mutilating or angry outbursts. And you must eat three square meals a day to feed that good brain of yours, understand?"

"Yes, ma'am."

"And one more thing, no destroying your room because you are pissed off. You hear me?"

"I hear you. What do I do if I get angry?"

"Try talking to someone like Sandy, okay?" Dr. Smith winked. She then took Franki's hands in hers and examined the bandages around her wrists.

"I know, no more slashing. Freddy Cougar days are over." Franki rolled her eyes.

"Thank you," Ellen replied.

CHAPTER THIRTEEN

Dr. Blake had begun his career in 1975, ten years after River Edge opened its doors. In a short time, James Blake had earned the respect of all his colleagues by working endless hours, doctoring the mentally sick. It made him feel like somebody. He called in sick maybe ten times, out of his thirty-some years in practice. He was what his peer's called "workaholic." He enjoyed his job very much, too much at times. He was relentlessly trying to better himself. On breaks, Dr. Blake was found with his head in a textbook, avoiding all human contact with his colleagues. Two of his favorite subjects were science and biology. He was absolutely, undeniably fascinated by the human anatomy. Blake was, without doubt, the shiest guy on staff. Socializing wasn't one of his strongest suits. He always felt he never measured up; others had a sense of self he craved. He was invited out for a night on the town on several occasions but always had an excuse, and eventually, they stopped bugging him. James Blake was a closet moth, not a social butterfly.

Dr. Blake's specialty was alcoholism. Maybe, his colleagues speculated, this had something to do with his home life. Patients who were admitted to River Edge suffered from mild irritation to delirium tremens. He had a gift with these types. It was as if he could read the road maps that were driving their tortured minds. He had held the hands of many an alcoholic assigned to River Edge in a state of absolute hopelessness. Blake delighted in the chronic cases; he'd been able to dry out the alcoholic enough to be returned to a sober life. Rarely was there a permanent recovery, but it did happen. The staff admired Blake's endless commitment.

In the beginning, the purpose of housing the mentally sick was to protect society and the criminally insane from hurting themselves and others. And other lost souls society had thrown away, like prostitutes. There were laws protecting the mentally ill from going to prisons, where they could and often did become targets of violence. There were few effective medications to treat their tortured minds. Those souls who could no longer do the simplest tasks for themselves like bathing then and still now occupied River Edge fourth floor.

The third floor also occupied patients who couldn't be trusted not to do harm to themselves: bipolar, dementia, schizophrenia, attempted suicides, and the ones deemed dangerous but treatable like Franki Martin. Family members had their loved ones committed for refusing to take his or her medication. Patients who were found roaming alone in incoherent states and agitation were picked up by police and brought to River Edge.

Depression is no longer taken lightly. Years ago, it was regarded a self-pity syndrome. Psychiatrist and psychologist often heard patients describe their depression as being locked inside the core of a vacuum with no way out. Second-floor patients were on the track to stability but not quite ready to challenge life on the outside. The first floor treated patients in follow-up care programs on an outpatient basis, which no longer lived inside the facility. They were coping with life, and River Edge was their lifeline.

Being employed at River Edge was not emotionally easy. Blake had to deal on a daily basis with patients suffering from withdrawal ranging from feelings of irritability and general malaise to tremors and intense anxiety, confusion, hallucinations and at times, convulsions, common colds, pregnancy and such. It was his job to assess the patient's physical condition upon arrival at River Edge.

Throughout his career, there'd been some chilling times on the wards, 3 and 4. The scariest was back about five years ago when they were bringing in a very dangerous convicted serial killer, Roger Taut, to the fourth-floor ward. This psychopathic male was unpredictable and, one day, demonstrated just how unpredictable he could be when he grabbed a nurse and put a nail file to her neck, threatening to cut her throat open if he weren't freed. It took a few tense minutes, but Blake somehow managed to talk Roger into putting the nail file down and releasing the nurse unharmed. After that almost fatal episode, no one was allowed to go alone into Taut's room, and that included the big, burly orderlies.

And there were patients who had to be restrained in straightjackets and confined to padded rooms. Each day the medical staff faced a number of emergencies.

Today, River Edge is no longer viewed as the Dark Tower. It's a place for the mentally distressed to get the help they need.

CHAPTER FOURTEEN

The morning after visiting with Dr. Smith, Franki opened her eyes, feeling a sense of freedom. A print curtain replaced the metal bars on the Plexiglas window. Graced on the fresh white walls were happy pictures. A boxed light secured above her head, along with an emergency bell. With the natural sunlight pouring in and the light above her head, Franki would have no trouble reading. She had a shower without eyes on her. This morning, she didn't even mind the hospital two-piece pink garb. Her body felt weak though. As much as she hated to admit it, surviving life on the street had taken its toll. Panhandling and selling her body in exchange for food and drugs was a high price. Trying to run from her emotional pain had been exhausting. But now, after talking with her new shrink and seeing the proof of her good intentions—she looked around the room—Franki felt hopeful as a hungry baby bird with its mouth open, expecting a nice juicy worm. Help was finally on the way. Maybe that black cloud would lift and she could become the person her parents would be proud of. Whoever that was?

She lay back on propped pillows waiting for her breakfast to arrive. She rested her hands behind her head, enjoying the scenery and serenity of her room. She no longer heard death screams from behind locked doors. All she heard outside her door were the scents and sounds of real life. The scent of coffee was a welcoming treat to her mind. Her stomach growled at the clang of trays sliding in and out of the food cart not far away from her room.

Her eyes swept over her new residence. The moveable table even looked different from the one upstairs. Beside the bed, stood a two-drawer metal nightstand. A small pine wooden built-in closet sat in her peripheral. *This room is going to suit me just fine,* she thought, and smiled.

*   *   *

Franki was finishing the last of her oatmeal and toast when she jumped at hearing her name boom into her room over the intercom. Dr. Blake was summoning her to his office. She knew what for. If she didn't cooperate and if he had the power he said he did, he'd have her moved out of there to God knows where. Oh god, what should I do? Franki liked being on the second floor. She stopped at the nurse's station to make sure her ears weren't deceiving her. Franki's heart fell to her ankles at hearing the answer. Slowly, she scuffed along the corridor as if she were kicking dirt. Franki half angry, half discouraged wanted the sexual abuse to stop. Hesitantly, she knocked on the door with the dreaded nameplate: Dr. J. Blake, MD.

Dr. Blake ordered her straight into his inner office. Silently, he sat down on the stool and began to uncoil the gauze, exposing the damage. It was evident that this wasn't the first time Franki had used a cutting tool on her wrist. The bruising and swelling had healed. Visible lesions like the ripple of ocean waves ran up her arms. Franki would wear the badge of what she had done to herself for the rest of her life. The only way of masking these scars was long sleeves. Taking a pair of tweezers off the metal tray, he plucked out the not yet dissolved threading. He lathered a thick coat of antibiotic ointment on to the healing wound before rewrapping her up in clean white gauze and took her blood pressure. Normal.

Maybe the abuse is over, she thought. He hadn't tried anything sexual. Franki thanked him as she rushed for the door. Then she heard the snap of his rubber gloves. She froze. Something told her not to turn around but did anyway. That's when his hand gripped her by the shoulder, spun her around, and pulled her to him. Dark eyes glittering with lust stared into hers. He licked his lips, mouth pursing to plunge. He wasted no time undoing the buttons on the pink pajamas provided by the ward.

Suddenly, Franki found the courage. Her heart beating furiously like it was going to rupture inside her ribcage; she knocked his hands off of her.

"You can't keep doing this to me," she yelled, pulling away from him.

His eyes went hard. She flinched. Was he going to hit her? Then he started laughing.

"I mean it." Her fist clenched. "If you don't stop raping me, I'm going to tell on you."

"Is that right?" He smirked. Without warning, he grabbed her by the throat and slammed her against the wall. His face only inches from hers, he hissed, "Look, you little whore. I'm the one in charge here!"

Franki fought hard to pry his hands loose, but he was too strong. She hated it that her lips began to quiver. Never did she want that bastard to see her surrender.

"If you do so much as breathe a word of this to anyone, you little sleaze, I promise I will make your stay here a living hell. Who knows? You may succeed the next time you decide to slash." He pushed her, and she staggered backward, gasping for air.

"Do you understand me?"

"Yes, yes . . . I understand," she sputtered.

Before she could scream or run, he grabbed her, yanked down her pink pajamas bottoms, and threw her down onto the examining table like she was nothing. He sodomized her. Making sure she understood how powerless she was to him. This predator was unstoppable.

When he was finished, he ordered Franki to pull up her pajamas bottoms and sit on the stool. Wincing, Franki swiped angrily at her tears and mouth and slowly sat down. Franki then went to a place in her mind where she felt safe. His squeaky voice sounded like an echoing from across the Grand Canyon. She pressed her legs together, trying to stop their trembling while Blake washed his face and hands and changed into his lab coat. *Somehow, someway,* Franki thought, *I have to get away from this sick pervert.*

He turned to face her. "Now I need a sample of blood."

Franki extended her arm across the cold metal table. He took a rubber band, tied it tight around her biceps, and waited for the brachial artery to swell.

"Only two vials this time."

She closed her eyes, expecting the sharp, piercing point of the needle. When it didn't come, she gazed up at him, taken aback.

"I can be gentle if I want to be. Remember that, and you and I will have great fun together."

Franki's stomach heaved at the acidic foam rising to the back of her throat made her gag.

She waited in the outer office for permission to leave. He walked out and nodded.

"Yes, you can go. Oh, by the way, enjoy the independence of room 201, good things around here don't last."

"How did you know I have a new room?"

"I know everything that goes on in this facility. The walls have eyes, Franki." He laughed.

Lowering her head, Franki walked away from the evil monster that hid behind a compassionate profession.

*   *   *

After scrubbing down and disposing of her blood-spattered bottoms, she redressed. She spent the rest of the day in her room, running and rerunning the mental tape of Blake sodomizing her. It made her sick to her stomach, yet she couldn't turn it off. She clenched and unclenched her fists. Somehow, someway, she must win the battle against Blake's sick savagery. It would never end unless she found a way to end it. But how? He was pure evil, insane. He was the worst kind of predator because everyone respected him, trusted him. Yet, she was branded the nutcase.

CHAPTER FIFTEEN

Around midnight, Franki jerked awake by an excruciating pain clutching her stomach like a steel fist. Moaning, she turned on her side and drew up her legs in a fetal position, desperately massaging her stomach in hope of relieving her unbearable agony. Suddenly, a warm fluid gushed from between her legs, soaking her bed. She fumbled for the light switch, flipping it up.

Blood! Her head began to swirl as the light commenced to dim. *Oh my god, what's happening?* She moaned for help, trying to make it to the bathroom, before passing out. The faint light in her eyes turned black.

*   *   *

Nurse Katie, on duty at the station across the hall, noticed the beam of light shining under Franki's door. *You're supposed to be sleeping kid,* Katie thought.

"Time to investigate," Katie spoke to Judy, pointing at Franki's door.

Opening the door, Katie's eyes took in the pool of blood on the starched white sheets and then followed the floor's trail of crimson leading to the washroom. Its door was sealed shut.

She knocked and called out, "Franki, is everything okay in there?"

The dead silence loomed thick in the air. The nurse knocked harder. "Franki, open the door. Franki?" Fear crept up her spine. She pushed against the door, managing to open it a small crack. Franki's body was heaped against the door, blocking the entrance. Katie had to get in there. She used her shoulder to push the door open wide enough to squeeze inside. Franki lay in a pool of her blood that was steadily trickling beneath her legs. Katie pulled up Franki's gown and drew in a startled breath. She'd lost an enormous amount of blood.

"Franki, dear! Franki, can you hear me?" Katie called her name several times. No response. Quickly, Katie took her pulse. It was seriously faint, and her skin felt cold and clammy against her hand due to inadequate blood flow to the body's organs. Franki's pupils were dilating. The nurse ran to the doorway and yelled to Judy to get help.

Two orderlies raced up the hall when they heard a distress call.

"I need a stretcher immediately," she ordered. "Judy, call Dr. Blake and have him meet us in emergency now. Time is against us!"

Orderly, Malcolm squeezed inside the bathroom, lifted Franki's lifeless body off the cold tiled floor, and waited for the second orderly to come with the gurney. There wasn't time to wait for the ambulance. Without warning, Franki began to shake like she had been left out in the winter's cold for too long. The stretcher arrived. Judy ripped a blanket from the unused bed and wrapped it tightly around Franki's little frame. The two orderlies then fastened Franki to the stretcher and rushed next door to Morial Hospital. Franki was going into shock.

"Hang in there. Come on, Franki, stay with us. Come on, Franki. You can do it," Katie coaxed, running alongside the stretcher. A few minutes later, Dr. Blake was suited and waiting in the operating room, along with surgeon Cecile Markeet.

*   *   *

At six thirty the next afternoon, Franki became conscious, but her mind was befuddled: Where was she? What had happened? The last thing she remembered was the stabbing pain in her gut, the blood, and the dizziness in the bathroom. She'd woken several times throughout the day but had no recollection. Her mind seemed to float in a fog that was devoid of form or substance. She started to doze again when an unfamiliar nurse entered her room.

"Oh, look who is awake." She smiled at Franki.

"Where am I?" Franki's tongue felt glued on to her palate.

"You're at Morial Hospital, dear."

"What? How did I get here?" She furrowed a brow.

"Franki, you were brought in late last night."

"Why? What's wrong with me?"

"Don't worry, the doctor will be in shortly to explain everything to you."

"What time is it?"

"Six forty-five. Can you sit up so you can sip some water? You must be thirsty."

The nurse assisted in propping her head and shoulders against an extra pillow. Franki wanted to gulp down the entire glass. Her throat felt as parched as if she'd spent days in the desert without water.

The nurse took the plastic glass from Franki's hand. "Slow down or you'll get sick again."

"I don't remember getting sick the first time!" Puzzlement spilled out of her blue eyes.

"Let me take your temperature." The nurse stuck the thermometer inside her ear. In seconds, the beeping noise announced the results.

"Good news, Franki. Your temperature is back to normal."

"My hand is stinging."

The nurse examined the needle piercing the dorsal carpal artery. Franki's arm felt too heavy to lift on her own.

"Franki, I'm going to remove this needle and replace it with a butterfly needle. It's a shorter needle designed for smaller veins like yours."

"Will it hurt?"

"It might sting a little, but it will help ease the soreness. It won't hurt as much after it's in. You're such a little bitty of a thing, no wonder your hand is sore."

"Why do I have this in me?"

"Rest, Franki. The doctor will be in shortly."

Jesus, what happened last night? Franki thought as the nurse left the room. It was all so confusing. Then she found herself floating again in the rolling fog. A short while later, the nurse returned to change the IV needle; just as she finished, the doctor emerged in her room.

Blake crossed the white-speckled floor to stand at the middle of the bed and kicked the steel spring located on the bottom of the rail. The barrier slid down, allowing him easy access to Franki.

"Hello, Franki, and how is my favorite patient?" His thin lips curved up in a smile.

"Weak and drugged. What happened, and why am I here?"

He rolled her pale-blue nightshirt to her breasts to check the hospital's thickly padded pants again overflowing with blood.

"She'll need to be changed as soon as I'm finished," he ordered the nurse.

"Yes, Doctor."

Dr. Blake pressed on Franki's lower abdomen.

"Stop, that really hurts!" She pushed away his hands.

"That's to be expected," he replied unsympathetically. "Your stomach will be tender for the next couple of days."

"Can someone please tell me what the hell happened? And why am I here instead of over there?" She jerked a thumb in the asylum's direction. "And why do I have a needle piercing my friggin' hand and what's the reason for those?" She pointed to the two bags hanging from a chrome pole positioned beside her bed.

"Franki, did you know you were pregnant?" Dr. Blake searched her face, watching carefully for her reaction.

Her eyes bulged with shock. "No. No!"

"Last night you miscarried. Do you remember bleeding excessively?"

"Yes. I felt like guts were being ripped out."

He nodded. "That's because you started hemorrhaging."

Franki's eyes widened with shocked disbelief. She turned to the nurse for affirmation.

The nurse patted her shoulder. "I'm afraid the doctor is telling you the truth."

"Surgeon Cecile Markeet had to perform a D and C: medical term dilation curettage."

She was afraid to ask but knew she must. "Am I going to be okay?"

"You'll be fine. And now you understand what happened? This clear bag hanging here"—he reached up, tapping it with his index finger—"is a strong antibiotic called Tegopen, preventing you from procuring any infection. The container of blood is to replace what you lost. Any other questions?" Half turned ready to leave.

"Yeah. That 'D and C' thing you were saying. What's that?"

"It's like a vacuum. It cleans the walls of your uterus. Nothing to worry about."

"Oh!"

"You'll bleed like you're having a heavy menstrual cycle, but after that, it'll calm down. Nothing alarming."

"Easy for you to say you're not flowing like a river," Franki grumbled. The nurse chuckled.

"Good night, Franki. I will look in on you tomorrow. The nurse will bring you something to help the discomfort and make you sleep."

"How pregnant was I?"

"Ten, eleven weeks. I'm guessing."

"Will I be able to have children?"

"Time will tell." He shrugged.

In the meantime, the nurse had left and returned with medications.

"Take this now, Franki. It will help with cramping so you can get a good night's rest."

She hadn't enough strength to argue. One swallow and the pill disappeared.

The nurse washed and changed Franki without too much movement. Franki liked this lady; she wasn't judging her for the sins of the past. Yet, when the nurse left the room, guilt and shame, thick as ether, seeped out of every pore. How could she be carrying a life in her own body and not know? Her mind waded through the mental mist to reflect back over the last eleven weeks. All of a sudden, the damned-up memories burst like the opening of rain clouds, and she saw clearly.

CHAPTER SIXTEEN

The day's wind carried with it a cold rain that seeped through to the bone. Franki huddled in front of the liquor store, panhandling for change. She was starving and needed to eat something healthy. Sparkie, her protector and friend for the last few months, had ditched her for a chemical high that would steal her away for days. It didn't upset Franki. That was the way street life was: every woman for herself when the pain of shattered dreams became too much to bear. Franki's stomach growled loudly. The food in the Dumpster behind Fongs Chinese Restaurant was making her ill. She needed real food and refused to go to the soup kitchen for fear a volunteer might call the cops if she was recognized as missing. There was no way she was going back into lockup. To Franki, this cement sidewalk was no worse than sleeping on a cell floor; even there she'd done sexual favors for clean clothes and a hot shower.

A forest-green Jeep Cherokee pulled up to the curb, close to where Franki was stationed. A man in his early twenties jumped out. He was gorgeous. He had a strong masculine frame, dark hair, and brown eyes. She still had mystery man etched in her mind.

"Sir, can you spare some change?" She looked up into eyes that could melt butter, unmindful of the big droplets of rain splashing against her face.

He stopped for a second, staring down at her with pity, then without a word walked on past. She thought, *Yeah, he's a good-looking guy and full of himself. Cheap bastard can't even spare a buck.* She shook her head. A few minutes later, Mr. Gorgeous emerged, carrying a brown paper bag. He stopped again and stared at her.

What she wanted to say she didn't. Instead, she mustered up the courage to beg again.

"Sir, can you spare some change please."

"If I give you money, what will you spend it on? Booze, drugs, what? Are you a junkie?"

"No! I'm not a junkie!" she lied defensively.

"What's the money for?" he asked sternly as if lecturing his little sister.

"So I can buy something to eat, as if you really care."

"This is the deal, take it or leave it. I'm not going to give you any money. I'll do one better."

"Yeah, and what's that?"

"Come with me, and I'll make you a home-cooked meal."

Rising to her feet, *Hell,* Franki thought, *I've given blowjobs for less.*

"Why not? It'll get me out of this miserable weather."

"Hurry up then." He motioned for her to follow.

"How do I know you're not some psycho?"

"You don't, but rest assured, I'm not." He grinned.

Franki's loud growling stomach was the deciding factor.

He opened the Jeep's passenger door, waiting for her to climb in. *Well, well,* she thought, *Prince Charming has finally arrived.* She rolled her eyes. He turned up the heater full blast, and she leaned back against the seat, basking in the warmth. The two made small talk while he drove down familiar streets to his house.

He opened the back door. Franki stepped inside, dropping her wet duffle bag and coat at the entrance. He led her three steps up into the kitchen.

"Would you like a coffee or tea?"

"Coffee would be great, thanks."

"Then coffee it is." He filled the filter with Folgers and filled the percolator.

The house, a little two-bedroom bungalow with basement, felt homey and cozy. Franki wandered into the living room. *This guy,* she thought, *is a real neat freak. Nothing seems out of place.* The tan leather couch and love seat went well with the light-beige carpet. A thick burgundy throw rug lay in front of the black and white marble fireplace. The walls were decorated with Egyptian art. Glass lamps sat on smoky-gray side tables. A corner wall unit housed a twenty-eight inch flat screen television and an awesome Panasonic stereo system.

Franki went to the picture window, stood staring at raindrops pelting hard against the pane. The grass was as verdant as the forest and well maintained. Steve sauntered to her side, handing her a cup of hot coffee and a chocolate chip granola bar.

"Here, this should tie you over till dinner."

"Thank you."

"I'm Steve Michaels." He shook her free hand.

She laughed. "Franki Martin. I guess it's only proper to know the name of the guy who rescues me from the cold blizzard out there."

"Well said, Franki."

They stood quietly, looking out into the dark, clouds almost touching the rooftops. There wasn't a ray of sunshine to be found.

"What kind of music do you like?" He walked over to the stereo.

"I'm not sure. It's been a while. What do you have?"

"Everything. I'm a big fan of music, helps soothe the soul."

"You pick." Steve put a disc into the player. "Do you know who this is?" He held up the disc's jacket.

"Can't say that I do."

"Greg Graffin. He's written books and seventeen albums. The man is a genius." He wiggled a brow.

"He sounds pretty cool." She went back to looking out the transom, taking polite nibbles off her bar.

"Here is the plan," Steve announced, fluffing her hair.

Her immediate gut reaction was, "I knew this guy wanted more then to cook me a meal!" She gave him the look.

"No offense, Franki, but you stink."

"You would too if you didn't shower for days."

"How do you do it?"

"The plan is to wear layers so when I get good and ripe, I just throw away the inner layer. Unfortunately, I've run out of layers."

"Are you serious?"

"Afraid so."

"Come on. I'll show you where the bathroom is so you can have a bath and warm up." She followed Steve down the hall to the bathroom. "Here is the shampoo, conditioner, and if you like, bubble bath." He gestured toward a shelf of bathing products.

"What's a macho stud like you doing with lavender bubble bath?" She arched her eyebrow.

Steve laughed. "Men like bubbles too. My robe is hanging on the back of the door. Once you've undressed, throw me out your wet clothes. I'll wash and dry them for you."

"Are you for real?"

Steve checked his face in the mirror. "Last time I checked. Oh, and one more thing, Franki. The coat you were wearing, is that your only coat?"

"Yep, that's it."

"This ugly weather is supposed to continue for the next couple of weeks."

She made a sour face. "Thanks for the news flash."

"I guess a new wardrobe is out of the question, eh?"

She laughed from behind the closed door. "Not on my salary."

Franki changed out of her wet clothing and handed them to Steve through the crack in the door. Then she closed the door and looked in the full-length mirror. Staring back was a complete stranger. Her sapphire eyes were hollow and sad. Her lips were dry and cracked, and her skin had lost its luster. She couldn't remember ever looking so bad. Suddenly, superimposed over that image was Franki from a long time ago when life was good. She had just taken a bath and her mother had come in to brush her hair . . . Franki shook her head and ran her hands over her face to erase the memory from the mirror. She couldn't afford to look at the past. She turned away and gave her armpits a quick sniff, wrinkling her nose at the putrid smell. He wasn't kidding, she thought. *One day, I won't have to live this way,* she vowed, trying to sound believable to herself.

The tub was filled with lots of bubbles. She closed her eyes and let her mind and body submerge under the white fluffy suds, escaping the realities of her life.

Moments later, it seemed, eyes sprang opened, startled by the Jeep's engine. Her first reaction was that Steve had gone to get his buddies for a good gangbang. "Nah." Then she shook her head. *He wouldn't do something that cruel. But if that's the case, he'll be in for the surprise of his life,* she thought. She smiled and closed her eyes again, resuming her mode of relaxation.

Franki awoke with a start. She'd fallen asleep not knowing how long Steve had been gone; time was unimportant living on the street. Hearing the Jeep pulling up the driveway, she washed quickly, shampooed her hair, and rinsed away the lather. Her scalp tingling with energy, she repeated the procedure with conditioner. She glanced in the mirror. Her blond wavy hair was once again clean and shiny. Gosh, she'd forgotten how good it felt to be clean. The sweet fragrance of Irish Spring clung to her skin. This was like a wonderful dream from which she didn't want to awaken. Or was it a nightmare into which she carelessly walked?

After toweling dry, she wrapped Steve's thick terry cloth robe around her. Taking a deep breath, she opened the door. No one lurked in wait. Hearing the loud clanging of pots and pans, Franki made her way down the hall toward the racket in the kitchen. Mr. Gorgeous was preparing dinner.

"How old are you?" he asked, making conversation.

"Fifteen, why?"

"I was going to offer you a drink, but you're underage, I don't supply minors."

"A guy with a moral compass?"

"You got it."

"But you're going to have a couple?"

"Yes. Would you like a pop?"

"Sure, since you won't to share the real good stuff." She laughed.

"Does it bother you?"

"Hell no. I appreciate everything you've done." She took a sip of her pop.

That evening, she devoured a plateful of baked stuffed pork chops, mashed potatoes and corn, and still had room for dessert of Black Forest cake. Finally, she sat back against the chair, patted her stomach, and smiled. "That was so delicious, Steve. Thank you."

"I'm glad you enjoyed it. It's not the best, but it's better than french fries in the cold rain. You didn't believe that I was going to cook you a meal, did you?"

"French fries in the rain would have been a luxury compared to the scraps in the Dumpster behind Fongs Chinese Restaurant, but no, I thought you were up to something. No offense."

"Do you still feel that way?"

"I don't know how I feel about you. Weird, I never had anyone pick me up and bring me to his crib without a motive. If you know what I'm saying."

"Well, Franki, I'm happy to be the first."

Steve's eyes expressed sympathy. Franki's life made him grateful to have what he had. A loving family and wonderful friends he could count on. He had never been homeless, nor did he want the experience. It was a real shame: Franki Martin was a very beautiful girl. Even hiding behind that angry, protective mask, he could see a soft vulnerability. He left the table to return with a coat he'd purchased for her at Sears while she was taking a swim in his tub.

"What do you think? Do you like it?" He showed her a warm, waterproof light-blue coat.

"It's very nice. Is it for your girlfriend?"

"No. I bought it for you."

"Shut up!" Her eyes lit up with surprise.

"It's for you, honest. I told you earlier that the ugly weather wasn't going to let up for another week or two. This will keep you warm and dry."

"Wow! I don't know what to say!" She grinned from ear to ear.

"Thank you usually works." He laughed.

"Thank you so much." She stepped forward and stopped herself from giving him a hug. "I so appreciate this."

"You're welcome." He handed over her new coat.

Excitedly, Franki struggled to pull her new coat over Steve's thick terry cloth robe and then burst into giggles. "What an idiot. Obvious, it'll fit better over my clothes once they're dried."

Steve grinned. "Good idea."

*　　*　　*

After she and Steve did the dishes, they retired to the living room to sit in front of a roaring fireplace. Steve sipped his Keith's Pale Ale while Franki enjoyed a hot delicious mug of cocoa topped with marshmallows, restoring warm earlier memories of her family.

Franki wasn't one for opening up to strangers, but Steve made her feel safe. At his prodding, she told him what happened to her parents and the events leading to her life today. At first, she'd been totally unprepared to survive on the streets, but she'd learned how to keep herself safe most of the time. Foster homes had proved to be the most dangerous. She'd been mistreated and even sexually assaulted by foster parents, who wanted only the government funds for looking after their wards. Group homes held to the same standards, only this time, older and tougher kids did the abusing while the so-called counselors turned a blind eye to the visible pain.

At least on the street, Franki felt disentangled from the confining powers. Sure, it had its disadvantages, especially on days like this. She didn't have the frill of brushing her teeth or taking a shower when she wanted. Of course, she longed for a warm safe place to sleep at night. But you do the best with what you got. She'd learned how to be street-smart. She'd come to accept she'd never have the opportunity to get educated. The worst part of survival on the street was being raped, robbed, and beaten up. Then she'd met Sparkie, a local street kid kind enough to take her under her wing and show her the ropes of survival. Sparkie had turned out to be the one person Franki could count on.

Sparkie had taken to the street because step daddy couldn't keep his hands to himself, so she split from her poverty-stricken family life for a life without having to sit across the table from the pervert she knew would come into her room and steal what innocence was left. After Franki had been raped in a darkened alleyway, Sparkie taught her to stay away from certain paths that were calling cards for human violation.

Franki made it abundantly clear that she was not looking for pity. Steve had asked, and Franki was telling.

Steve listened attentively, trying to picture himself struggling to hang in there day by day. He admired Franki; she had more guts and courage than anyone he had ever met. He wasn't sure he had what it took for the street life. And here this kid was toughening it out day by day. How could he not feel sympathy and respect for her? My god, look at what she had been through . . .

Franki began telling one of her many scary events on the street. "This one time, I wasn't so sure about what to do or where to go. It was cold but bearable. I could sleep outside with my roll-up blanket." She took a sip of her cocoa. "The moon was the fullest I've ever seen. I was hiding from the cops because if they caught me, I was going back to juvenile hall. They spotted me on Thundell

Drive. When I saw the squad car stop, I took off running like a madman. I ran three blocks to Maple Park and hid behind a big oak tree. That night, I should have let the police catch me. I'm here to tell you. I would have been better off. So I crouched down behind the tree for a long time to catch my breath and make sure the coast was clear. I thought I was safe. I shook my pack off my shoulders and put it on the ground so I could rest my head. Being stupid, I fell asleep. Suddenly, I felt this incredible pain shoot under my rib cage. I jolted up, second mistake, grabbing my side, and trying to breath. I'm not sure how many were there because it was dark. I looked up in time to just make out the next boot coming at my face. I tried to block it with my arm, but the boot was faster. I fell back hard against the ground, my cheek burning and my lips split wide open. Man, did it ever sting. I thought my jawbone had shattered; I was booted that bloody hard. The inside of my mouth tasted like copper. I was bleeding pretty badly. A few stitches in my lips wouldn't have hurt, but I was afraid the doctor would call the cops. I felt fucked, excuse my language. Then, my head was yanked back by my hair so I couldn't move. She, I think it was a girl, sure sounded like one, demanded I hand over my backpack. I struggled to grab hold of it, but she only yanked harder on my hair. I thought I was going to have a big bald spot from the hair she tore out. My ribs felt like they were broken. I was spitting blood from the boot to my face. With no other choice, I surrendered my bag, begging for the only pictures I had left of my family. The bitch rifled through my pack, throwing the photographs on the ground in front of me like garbage and laughing. Oh I wanted to kill her. She told me that the park was her territory and if I were found there again, I would get a beating I would not soon forget. Then they took off. I managed to get to my feet. Hanging on to my side and spitting blood, I staggered to the nearest alleyway to hide and puke. I was hurt, cold, and exhausted. That night, I thought I would freeze to death; they'd stolen my roll blanket. So I sat shivering in the dark, praying for daylight. Sparkie wasn't around that night or those bitches would have never gotten my pack and I wouldn't have gotten a beating."

"Where is your friend now?"

"She sometimes disappears for a few days to do some crack. As soon as you get going on that stuff, you don't want to stop until the body gives out. She's likely trippin' right now. Anyway, the next day, I saw my reflection in the store window. My cheek was swollen, black and blue. My lips were caked in dry blood and twice the normal size. I looked like something out of a horror movie. I don't think my own mother would have recognized me."

Steve's handsome features tightened in horror. "My god, you've been to the abyss and back. Could you not have stayed in a youth shelter?"

"No, I didn't trust that they wouldn't rat me out."

"Why are you still on the street?"

"Evil foster parents and no place to go."

Steve shook his head at Franki's incredible story of survival. "Franki, I'm not so sure I could keep going under those circumstances."

"You'd be amazed at the human spirit. You do what you've got to do, right?" She laughed and ran a hand through her silky dry hair. "Now you know about me, what about you, Steve?"

He sighed and got to his feet.

"I would love to sit up all night and talk with you, sweetheart, but unfortunately, it is now one thirty in the morning. I have to be up in six hours to go to work."

"Oh, I'm sorry. I shouldn't have kept you. I forget people have real lives. Thank you, kind sir. Dinner was great."

Quickly, Franki changed into her clean clothes Steve had left in the bathroom. When she approached the living room; he had a wrought iron shovel and was placing the hot embers that were still glowing red into a metal bucket. Her eyes swept over the lovely, cozy room, heart hurting with longing. *This sucks,* she thought, *I don't want to leave this place, and Steve . . .* Before she broke down and cried, she hurried to Steve and wrapped her arms around his waist.

"You're wonderful. Thank you for everything." She slid her feet into her sneakers, slung her pack over one shoulder, and ran out the door before Steve had the chance to change her mind.

Well, well, Steve thought, chuckling. He strolled back into the kitchen to prepare coffee for morning. This had become his nightly ritual, nothing like fresh brew in the morning. He shut off the light and headed down the hall to his bedroom. He stopped at the sound of the doorbell and chortled, knowing who would be standing on the other side of the door. Sure enough, Franki stood in the downpour, cold and shivering.

"Does that offer still stand?"

"Get in here before you get soaked. Did you think I'd feed you and then turn you out into this deluge." He smiled warmly at her.

"I promise I'll be out of your hair first thing tomorrow morning."

"Relax, tomorrow isn't here yet."

Taking her cold hand, he led her to the guest bedroom. "This is where you'll be sleeping."

"I can't remember the last time I bunked out in a clean bed."

Greeting her eyes was a double-sized bed with a blue-and-white-checkered comforter, with matching shams and big fluffy pillows. A white eight-drawer bureau stood in the corner, a lace runner covering the top. On it were some athletic trophies of Steve's proud moments from childhood. The room smelled of fresh flowers in bloom. She closed her eyes, taking the pure, clean scent deep into her lungs.

Steve handed Franki one of his flannel shirts to sleep in, presuming she had none. He couldn't supply pajamas because he slept in boxers or nothing at all. Franki sat in the middle of the bed, eyeing Steve.

"Something the matter?"

"Sort of. Why are you helping me?"

"Everyone needs a break, Franki."

"No. Tell me the real reason. I'm sure you don't go around picking up girls begging for change, feeding them, and allowing them to stay the night."

"You're right about that. You are the first. To be honest . . . there's something real special about you, Franki. And when I figure out what it is, I'll let you know. Tonight, I know you're safe and can live with that." He gave her a half smile.

"That's fair."

"Sleep well." Steve left, closing the door behind him.

For the second time, she changed out of her clothes. Briefly, she sat naked, rubbing the blue flannel shirt gently against her face. She inhaled deeply. The sweet scent of laundry soap and fabric softener took her back to the simple comforts she once enjoyed so long ago. An overwhelming sense of loss and loneliness swept over her, threatening to drown her in longing. She clenched her fists, fighting the yearning seeping its way into the marrow of her being. What she had with her parents was gone. She couldn't let what she didn't have eat away at her. Nothing could turn back the pages of time. This was her life now. It was more than a new chapter. It was a whole new book. Franki dressed in the flannel shirt and wiggled herself beneath the sheets, pulling the comforter up to her chin. She smirked contently basking in the moment; tomorrow was hours away. She reached out a hand and turned off the lamp.

* * *

Steve was stretched out on his back, his hands resting behind his head, asking himself why. Why had he brought Frank home? He'd never before brought a street kid back to his house. Was it pity, compassion, kindness . . . her beautiful sad eyes? The innocent trusting way she looked up at him? He couldn't understand it. He grabbed his book off the nightstand and began reading *The Last Juror* by John Grisham. He needed to distract his attention to something else other than the beautiful young girl in the next room.

Franki was also tossing and turning, unable to sleep. She fantasized about falling in love with a guy like Steve. He was so kind, gentle, and drop-dead gorgeous. She wondered why a fine catch like him hadn't been scooped up. He wasn't gay, at least she didn't think so . . . Finally, restlessness drove her out of bed, and she wandered down the dark hall to his bedroom. She didn't know if he would be sleeping or not, but there was only one way to find out. She drummed her fingers quietly against the door.

"Come in," he answered.

She peeked her head around the door. "You busy?"

"Yes, trying to force myself asleep. What's up? Can't sleep in a real bed?"

"Yeah, something like that." She laughed.

"What's wrong?" He put his book back on the nightstand.

"All that talking about my family and my life is making me feel pretty lonely." She strolled over to his bed, sitting down beside him. Her heart fluttered like a small bird trapped in a cage when their eyes locked.

He succeeded in keeping his distance throughout the evening, for Franki's attractiveness was undeniable. Until now he had resisted, telling himself this was so wrong. She was just a kid. An underaged kid at that. But at that moment, Franki perched beside him on his bed, and her sapphire eyes offering an unmistakable invitation. She was all woman. He felt himself weakening to the ageless stirring.

"You shouldn't be in here, Franki," he said, his voice hoarse.

She leaned over him, pressing her lips against his. At first, he pushed her away, whispering, "No, Franki, this is wrong." She ignored him, unfastening the buttons on her flannel shirt. It slid off her shoulders, exposing her hungry flesh. Her rosy nipples, hard and erect, were begging to be fondled by his mouth.

"Franki, please, you don't have to do this!" he cried, feeling his own rush of desire mounting.

"Steve, I've never needed anyone the way I need you right now."

As though in a dream, he found himself moving over to the other side of the bed, allowing her room to climb in. They kissed and touched, exploring every inch of each other's bodies, until they both exploded into a greedy climax. Afterward, Steve held her gently in his arms. To be held the way Steve held her was a first for Franki. After sex and payment, she was usually discarded like a piece of trash. To be held felt amazing.

After caressing her back, he abruptly lifted her head off his chest.

"What, need a smoke?" she teased.

"Franki, let me see your back."

"Why?" She looked like a deer caught in the headlights.

Steve leaned sideways to steal a peek. It was a peek he'd not ever forget in this lifetime: visible markings of torture marred the skin.

"What happened to you?" He couldn't control the slight tremor in his voice.

"Evil foster parents."

"Come again."

"This was how these so-called nice foster parents punish bad kids like me. At least on the street, I have some sort of control."

"Sweet Jesus." Steve fell back against this pillow. "Do you want me to take you to the authorities so that you can press charges against those monsters?"

"The authorities already know, Steve." Franki resettled her head upon his chest.

"What do you mean, they know? What did they say?"

"They didn't say anything. They just brought me back. But I left not long after. It doesn't matter now. What's done is done." Tears welled in her eyes, spilling down on to his chest. Impatiently, she brushed them away. She never let anyone see her anguish.

"I'm speechless."

Franki sniffed and forced a laugh. "Steve, let's enjoy tonight. I don't want to ruin this moment by thinking about what happened yesterday or what the hell is going to happen to me tomorrow. Deal?"

"But, Franki!"

"I don't want to talk about this anymore, Steve. Please."

"I'm sorry. I didn't mean to upset you . . . but, Jesus Christ . . ."

"I understand." Franki moved up so her lips were on his, taking pleasure in the moment, then paused, and looked deeply into Steve's brown eyes. "So, you want to go another round?"

*　　*　　*

Steve lay awake for over an hour, wrestling with the unexpected dilemma he now found himself facing. He could not, would not, let Franki go back to live on the mean streets. There could only be one recourse. He would ask her to stay with him. He would surprise her over breakfast. He stroked her soft hair until he heard faint little snores coming from her open mouth. He felt honored that Franki felt safe enough to fall asleep in his arms. Steve couldn't wait to see her expression when he told her tomorrow morning. He couldn't let her go to be gobbled up by the crime in the street. At that moment, he wanted to be her hero, to make everything better. How could he be so involved in one day, hours even? It didn't make any sense. It wasn't like he hadn't dated women his own age. But Franki, she was extra special. She had a strong and fighting spirit that wouldn't quit. The kid deserved a break.

*   *   *

At five the next morning Franki laid awake watching Steve sleep. He looked so handsome and peaceful. She wished he would wake up, take her into his protective arms, tell her that he'd fallen in love with her and would protect her forever.

She hated awkward good-byes. Quietly, she slid from under the warm covers and tiptoed into the spare bedroom, where she dressed quickly. At the door, she put on her new coat, tossed her backpack over her shoulder, and vanished into dawn's drizzle.

CHAPTER SEVENTEEN

A heavily sedated Franki couldn't comprehend the strange noises coming from the doorway to her room. She tried to move but couldn't. She was strapped to the bed with restraining belts around her wrists and ankles. The hospital room was engulfed in darkness, making it difficult to see who was standing in the archway only a few feet from her bed.

"Who's there?" she cried out.

No one answered. Like a disembodied spirit, the silhouette floated silently across the floor until it reached her bedside. A cold chill ran up and down Franki's spine. It was worse than any hallucinations she had at River Edge. It was Gertrude, the nurse she hated and feared. Why was she in her hospital room? What did she want? Franki tried to scream, but no sound escaped her mouth. Gertrude leaned over her. Even in the dim lighting coming from the hall, Franki could see the malevolence shining in her eyes. Franki tried to recoil, but she was paralyzed by fear. Gertrude extended toward Franki a white towel soaked in blood.

"Look what I have for you, my sweetness." Gertrude's breath fell cold against Franki's cheek.

Gertrude flung open the towel and brought its contents to within inches of Franki's face. She gasped at the sight: the remains of a fetus ripped savagely apart as though by a wild animal. Mangled flesh hung from its tiny bones. Franki screamed from the sheer horror of the hideous sight before her eyes and screamed again and again. Doctors and nurses rushed forth into the room. She didn't recognize any of their faces. She started shaking uncontrollably. Sweat dripped off her face. The nurse standing at the opposite side of the bed held up a clear plastic vacuum tube. Franki's heart began to dance rapidly. She pushed the tube into Franki's face so she couldn't escape seeing the contents: fragments of tissue, bone, and blood cleaved to the sides of the plastic container.

Franki couldn't catch her breath, yet screamed on and on in horror and shame for what she had done. She didn't mean for this to happen, not to a precious baby child. Not the infant she carried. In her hysteria, she hadn't noticed Steve. He was staring at her from the foot of the bed. Tears streaming down his cheeks.

"Why did you do it, Franki? I would have taken care of you both. I would have given you and my son the life you deserved. How could you not have trusted me? I brought you in, fed you, and loved you. And now our child is dead because of you. You selfish bitch, you killed my boy! How could you?"

Blame and humiliation flooded every fiber of her being. There was no escaping this anguish.

"I'm sorry. I didn't know. I'm sorry. Forgive me. You've got to believe me. Please, Steve."

Steve's icy stare froze her out of his former love and gentleness. Her lips kept apologizing, but not a sound was audible; only the misty breath escaped her lips. Steve just stood there, head bowed, their combined weeping louder and louder.

Franki struggled to depart from the madness, but the straps held her firm against the leather bonds. Now the nurses and doctors were chanting, "She is the devil's daughter. She is the one who should be slaughtered. She is the devil's daughter. She is the one who should be slaughtered."

Franki let out a primal scream that could be heard to the end of the corridor. The two nurses on duty came rushing to investigate the loud shrieks. Jean, the first one in, quickly assessed what had happened. She placed her hand on Franki's shoulder, trying to wake her. Luckily, the side rails were up, or Franki would have fallen to the floor. The young girl was beside herself.

"You've had a bad dream, dear, that's all," Jean, said loudly enough that Franki's eyelids flew open, and she bolted upright to a sitting position.

"No, no, she was here, she was in my room!" Franki's eyes darted back and forth. "She butchered my baby."

"Who was in your room, dear?"

"That nurse, Gertrude."

"No, dear, nobody is here but Margaret and me. Come on, lie back down," Jean coaxed. "You had a horrible dream, that's for sure. We're here now, and nothing is going to happen to you. I promise."

Franki's face, hair, and gown were drenched with perspiration. The nurse grabbed a cloth from the bathroom and washed her face, then replaced the wet gown with a dry one.

When finished, Nurse Margaret reinserted the butterfly needle that had been pulled loose from Franki's frantic thrashing. The bruising on Franki's hand was a psychedelic purplish green.

Jean turned to leave when the young frightened girl began pleading for her to stay.

"Please, please don't go. She'll come back and get me. I know she will." Jean motioned Margaret to go back to the nurse's station. She would stay beside Franki until she fell asleep.

Hell of a nightmare, Jean thought, as she stared down at the frail girl, stroking Franki's damp blond hair. She sighed; Franki Martin was her daughter's age.

CHAPTER EIGHTEEN

Franki hadn't remembered the window behind Dr. Smith's desk the last time she was there. The sun lit up the entire room like a magic glow. A large bouquet of fresh orchids, violets, daffodils, and roses sat on the coffee table, their sweet aroma masking the ever-prevalent odor of hospital disinfectant. Franki inhaled a lungful of the light breeze, blowing in from the side windows. Franki left the window and took her seat on the couch as the coffeepot gurgled it was ready.

"Care for a cup of coffee, Franki?" Dr. Smith held up an empty mug.

"Sure, if it's not too much trouble."

"No trouble at all. What do you take?"

"One sugar, one cream."

Franki sat admiring the multicolored bouquet and leaned forward to touch the velvety soft petals. As Dr. Smith handed Franki her coffee, she at once saw how tense she appeared this morning. The muscles in her face were strained, her lips tight. Dr. Smith went to move the arrangement off the table when Franki abruptly grabbed her wrist. Ellen didn't show any alarm. Franki didn't have any intention of harming her. She needed a few more minutes to admire the beautiful flowers chorused in the vase.

"Leave them where they are, Doc."

"I need to push them aside so I can see your face when I talk to you."

"I'll do it." She slid the vase to the corner of the table, demonstrating she needed some sense of control.

"Is that better?" Franki asked.

"Much better, thank you. Do you like flowers?"

"The colors. The feel. The different shapes. Yeah, you could say I love flowers. Something that represents life."

"My husband is an excellent gardener. He'd be out in the backyard doing his thing from morning to evening, if I let him." She gave a little wink.

116

"What kind of flowers?"

"Every kind imaginable."

"Love to see them sometime."

"That could be arranged." The doctor gave a warm smile.

"You're looking at me a little weird, why?" Franki asked.

"Am I? I don't mean to be, dear. Now with the weird stuff aside, how are you?"

Franki shrugged her shoulders.

"I hear you had a horrible ordeal over the weekend. Do you want to talk about it?"

"I was pregnant, aborted, end of story."

"That was said without feeling."

"Do you want to see tears, Doc? Sorry to disappoint you, no can do. I have no regrets." She shrugged.

"You don't sound like it. And you sure don't look it either."

"What is it you want me to say? I'm sorry? Well, I'm not. It's over and life goes on. Like I would have won Mother of the Year Award? I don't know if you've noticed, Doc, I'm in a nuthouse." She slapped her hand down against her thigh.

"Well, that's a start. Accepting where you're at is a good thing. Do you know why you were brought to River Edge?"

"Because everyone thinks I'm crazy."

"Give me your definition of a crazy person, Franki."

"You want me to tell you what 'crazy' means?"

"No. I said tell me, in your own words, what is a crazy person?"

"A person that has lost touch with reality?"

"Correct. Now, are you crazy?"

"Guess not. I have enough reality for six hundred people," she moaned.

"So, crazy you're not. I believe you have some serious issues, but nothing that you and I can't handle. You've just been carrying around too much real pain for far too long."

"Why does everyone else have a different opinion? 'You tell lies, Franki.' 'You're this and that, Franki.' 'Be responsible, Franki.' Bullshit!"

"I don't care what others think. I'll form my own opinion, thank you. And that's why they pay me the big bucks." Dr. Smith gave a sly smirk.

"Is that right?" Franki hesitated and then returned her smirk.

"I will give you my professional view of what I believe to be true. Ready?"

Franki's instant reaction was to lean back against the seat and fold her arms across her chest. Franki had no idea what clues her body language was telling the doctor: she was shielding herself against attack, was fearful and defensive all rolled into one.

"Fire away, Doc."

"I believe you know right from wrong, which means medically you're pretty sane. Insane means that you are not mentally sound. You, my little one, are not unsound! You don't trust anyone, with good reason. Your whole world fell apart the night your parents died. The only person left for you to lean on and love was Beth, and she vanished. Desperately, you long to feel some sense of closeness, comfort, and familiarity. You cover up your hurt three ways: sarcasm, anger, or humor. Everyone in some way has betrayed your trust, and right now, you are not about to let anyone else take another shot at you. It won't matter what acts of kindness they show, you believe they have a hidden motive. You appear tough on the outside, fragile as eggshells on the inside. You want to feel safe. You want to make yourself feel better, but you don't know how. It's like being lost. When the pain becomes too difficult to bear, you try and numb out with drugs. When that doesn't work, the other alternatives are cutting for release and suicide. Suicide is a permanent solution to a temporary problem, Franki. Everything that is in you, all the torment, pain, loss, and suffering, is buried beneath your tough exterior. But the suffering is growing stronger, and it's about to explode out of you—and God help the consequences if it does. The only solution I see is to deal with the problems, past, present, and future.

"Now, this is where I get to come in, aren't you the lucky one?" Franki laughed. "Together, we can defeat this painful shit. You will learn to deal with situations that you thought were hopeless and beyond your control."

"How, Doc? I trust no one. Remember? Besides, how am I going to dig through years of betrayal and bullshit? My whole life is one huge mess, and we both know it. I'm not sure I even want to get fixed. It doesn't do me any friggin' good. If anything, stepping back into my past only makes me want to rage or get high, whichever comes first."

"With a big shovel?"

"What? What are you talking about?" Franki screwed up her face, lips puckered, and eyebrows wrinkled high on her forehead.

"With a big shovel," Dr. Smith repeated. "Your shovel is being open and honest with me about what took place in foster care. Franki, the more you talk about what has happened to you, the more power you regain. The less control it will have over your life. The bad stuff doesn't have to define who you are."

"No way! That demon will hunt me down and torture me to death. And I don't see the point."

"Well now, she can't do anything worse than you haven't already done or thought about doing to yourself."

"Oh, I underestimated you, Doc. You are good."

"Told you that's why they pay me the big bucks."

Franki unfolded her arms from across her chest, taking a sip of her creamed coffee. She gave Ellen a smirk. At that moment, Dr. Smith visualized a couple of bricks crumble off Franki's wall of stone.

"It doesn't matter to me, Franki, what is written in any report about you. I will form my own professional view. Now, without any defensiveness, how are you?"

"You mean the weekend?"

"We can start with that if you like."

Franki took a deep breath and then described how afraid she was waking up in pain and then the gush of blood that came out of her without warning. How she felt waking up alone in the hospital, seeing two bags hanging from a pole. The horrific dream about a mutilated baby—her baby. The awful feeling surrounding the loss of her child that she had no idea she was carrying.

"I feel sad, Doc, but we're both better off. Like I said earlier. I wouldn't have won a Mother of the Year Award. I know I wouldn't give my child up for adoption. I might be mentally screwed up, but I'm not heartless. So all is well."

"Do you know who the father is?"

"Of course I do. I'm not a full-time whore. I sell sex only when I have to," she huffed.

"I wasn't calling you one, young lady. I never asked in fear of offending you. How close are you to this person?"

"We're not anymore. I don't even know where he is," she lied.

"Would you like to find him?"

"No."

"Why?"

"It was a one-night stand. He was good, I have to say."

"How did you meet?"

"I was panhandling at the liquor store when he rolled up. I asked him for change, and he told me he would do one better." She smiled recalling the memory. "Invited me to his place for dinner."

"Weren't you afraid he could harm you?"

"It was cold and raining. I was starving. I didn't have anything to lose."

Ellen shook her head. "What if he had turned out to be a killer?"

"Then you and me wouldn't be having this conversation now, would we? And besides, I asked." She laughed. "He told me he wasn't, so I got in the Jeep."

"Then what?"

"Oh, you want the dirty details, do you?"

"The whole story is all."

"He took me to his place, fed me dinner. Let me have a bubble bath. Washed my dirty clothes and gave me a new coat."

"You slept with him obviously."

"Sure did, and I would do it again in a heartbeat. He was gorgeous, and he treated me real nice. I went to Steve, not the other way around."

"Did you think you owed him something?"

"No, just needed to be close to someone that gave a shit."

"That's fair. Did you ever go back?"

"Why would I?"

"Like you said, because he gave a shit."

"One night only, Doc. I live in the real world remember? It's not like *Pretty Woman*, where the hunk falls for the hooker. It is what it is: a good memory I intend to keep."

"I'm sorry it ended."

"I believe you, Doc." She sighed and put her head down, recalling the good feelings the fantasy of being Steve's girlfriend.

Ellen crossed her legs for more comfort. "How is your room?"

"Great. Beats cell 321 for sure."

"What do you think of Dr. Viewer?"

"Arrogant asshole comes to mind. Why?"

"I heard you two didn't get along."

"Heard right. He didn't do anything for me. He'd rush into my room and poke me with a needle. And then to add insult to injury, he said, I was having freak-outs because I was an attention seeker. I didn't ask to come here. He's a goof."

"You don't seem to like too many people?"

"Keep asking me these bullshit questions and you'll be next on my list."

"Is that right?"

"Are you challenging me, Doc?" Franki placed her elbows on her knees and leaned forward. Quick to anger and fight, Dr. Smith observed. "No. Let me set the picture straight. You are assigned to River Edge to get help. I am the one who can help you. It would be in your best interest to lose that tough, nothing-bothers-me attitude and trust me. I know it won't be easy. I have no ulterior motive. I stand to gain nothing but a paycheck for helping you and others like you. I love my job, and its perks are watching residents get better so that when they leave here, they can have a decent life. A tortured mind can't be fun. So, if you and I are on the same page, that's good. You need help and I'm offering. The street is not where you belong. It won't be easy for you to trust me, but please—give me a shot at proving myself."

Franki's face flushed. "I didn't say I didn't like you. I just hate it when so-called therapists pick and dig for stuff I don't want to talk about. It makes me mad."

"Why don't you try getting mad at the ones that have already damaged you rather than the ones who sincerely want to help you?"

"Bullshit. Like you said, I'm just a paycheck."

"Franki, I get paid whether I help you or not is what I mean. If you don't want me as your doctor, I could arrange for you to have someone else."

"No, I'll take my chances with you, if you don't mind."

"Don't mind at all. The one requirement I ask from you is you give it your all."

"And what the hell is that supposed to mean?"

"Start talking about how you were treated while in the care of the Wilkins. There are some heavy damning accusations being thrown around about what happened to you in that house."

"I'm not going there. All I will say is those twisted monsters should never ever be allowed to foster kids. Monsters, pure evil."

"I can't stop them from doing to other children what they did to you unless you give me some facts to hang them with, Franki."

"Doc, you can't stop that madness even with an army behind you. They won't believe me. I'm just a troublemaker to them. No one fucking believed me back then and I had proof. What makes you think they'll believe me today?"

"We have to have faith and believe that justice will prevail. And besides, you have me on your side."

"Faith my ass."

"Tell me what happened and let me judge for myself."

"Ooh, Doc . . . do I have to?" Franki squirmed in her seat. "Just one?"

"That's all. Just one memory." Ellen smiled warmly.

"Get that pen and paper ready because I'm not saying this shit twice. Deal?"

"Deal. For today! Remember what I said—the more you tell, the less power these ugly memories—and monsters—will hold over you. Let me assure you this: there isn't anything you could have done that could warrant such brutality."

"Sure." Her voice held little conviction.

Franki sat quietly for a long moment, sifting through her unwanted keepsakes of ugly memories. Finally, she began, "I was ten years old when they found me a foster family, the Wilkins. I had been to two-dozen other foster 'homes' prior, but they never worked out. I kept getting into fights with other kids, rebelling against house rules, and running away. In the beginning, the Wilkins—Gary and Susan—were nice to me until the first time I ran away on them. That's when hell opened up for me. To them I was ungrateful and selfish. I thought they of all people would understand my running away. I wasn't trying to be disrespectful; I was searching for my sister, Beth. I mean, no one would tell me where she was. I needed to know if she was okay. At ten and not too smart, I didn't get very far. They found me hitching on the side of the highway a few blocks away from the house. Where I was going I had no idea. I was on a mission. I was brought home by the pigs and escorted up the stairs to the front door. After that, all privileges were no more. No television, music, nothing. I was allowed to school and home again. Majority of the time, I spent alone in my room or locked in a closet."

"Why did you run away?"

"To be defiant, what do you think?" Franki glared across at the doctor. "I told you, I was trying to find Beth. I wasn't allowed friends because they might influence me. I was no longer trusted, but I didn't really care. It's not like this treatment was all new. I had attitude. I was made to do chores and thorough cleaning on weekends and read their damn Bible. I was treated more like Cinderella than a wanted foster child. They told me, I lacked discipline, and in God's eyes, it was their job to straighten out children like me. To show me the right path, I had to get down on my knees and pray two horrible hours a day. Every Sunday, I was forced to go to church. If I dared to disobey, I was whipped on the ass with a leather belt. I got that corporal punishment a few times. I didn't even get to choose what to wear. Independence gone. She would place this hideous yellow-and-pink frilly dress on my bed every Sunday morning faithfully. It wasn't humiliating enough that I had to wear the dress, but Doc, I swear every Sunday morning, they would parade me off to church like I was the prize pig. It really pissed me off. The Reverend was useless. A big old, fat, balding dude that smelled like mothballs. He would ask me, 'Are you being a good girl in the eyes of the Lord?'

"I wanted to shout in his face, 'No, you fucking idiot! Are you?' Instead, I would nod my head yes. Susan always showed affection in front of the pews of religious nuts. Always flapping her gums about how blessed she was to have a sweet girl like me. Bullshit! She was a coldhearted snake. The nice family bit was all fake. When the money check came in the mail for taking care of me, it became a different story. She rarely used the money on me. I wore secondhand shit. Most of the time, she made my clothes, and they were uglier than the ones from the church rummage sales.

"But, it wasn't about the stupid clothes or the ugly stuff she made." Franki looked away from the doctor, wringing and unwringing her hands resting in her lap. In barely a whisper, she said, "It was about leaving me alone in the house with that pervert. While she went off to the bingo parlor to gamble away my goddamn money . . ." Franki stopped wringing the sweat from her hands.

"Franki, what happened to you after she left?" the doctor asked softly.

"Unspeakable acts of . . . oh . . . fuck!" Franki bent over at the waist, wrapping her arms around herself for protection. "Doc, why are you making me relive this shit? Don't you know it rips me apart?"

"Yes, I do Franki. And I'm very, very sorry that you have to go through this in order to heal."

"C'mon, Doc." Franki shuddered. "I do drugs so I don't feel this pain, and now you're cutting me open like it's going to help. Okay, you really want to know?" She stared defiantly at the doctor. "The second she was out the front door, I would run and hide in my bedroom! I knew what Gary wanted because of the way he would leer at me. He would make some excuse to get me back into the living room to sit next to him on the couch. The only reason I went was so I could watch television, which she wouldn't let me do. The bastard lied." Dr. Smith's heart wrenched at watching Franki struggle to set free this memory of abuse. Franki rocked back and forth on the sofa, her emotional pain worse than any physical pain she could possibly endure.

"The first time it happened, she was out to bingo. He took my hand and put it on his crotch so I could feel what a 'real man' felt like. You know, for future references. He unbuttoned my shirt, putting his hand inside my training bra, playing with my nipples. I didn't even have boobs, for Christ's sakes. I was ten years old!" Tears streamed down her cheeks. "At first, it felt weird and scary to be touched like that. I didn't understand what was happening to me. With his free hand, he cupped it over mine that was on his crotch, teaching me how to rub him up and down until he got good and hard. He unzipped his pants and forced my hand inside his underwear. He wouldn't stop moaning this gross, pathetic sound. He started rubbing outside my pants before pulling them down along with my underwear. He made me stand in front of him while he played the 'hot game,' as he called it. I know what the sick perverted game means today. I kept telling him to stop, but he wouldn't. He threw me down, pinning me to the couch. I knew then that I was done for. He climbed on top of me. He put his fat ugly fingers inside me. I told him it hurt, and he stopped. Then out it came. He tried to get his dick inside, but it was too big—or so I thought. I started crying, begging and pleading for him to get off me, that he was hurting me. He slapped me across the face and told me to shut my mouth. The first time, he said, is always the worst. He wasn't kidding. He picked me up in his arms and brought me to my bedroom. I remember being so terrified all I could do was shake. We know what took place then." Franki's voice dwindled to a whisper.

"What did he do to you?"

"He stuck his dick in me and raped me!" Franki said through clenched teeth.

"What happened after that?"

"He made me take a bath and get into my pajamas like a good girl while he changed my sheets because they were stained with blood and sperm. That was Wednesday night. Saturday, he took me shopping for new clothes at the mall."

"How long did it take before Susan found out?"

"About three or four months, I'm not sure. She was becoming insanely suspicious and jealous over how nice he was treating me. Buying me stuff and helping me with house chores and, let's not forget, homework. I earned everything I got from that monster."

"How did she find out he was having sex with you? What did she do?"

"It was another bingo night. She'd left but realized she'd forgotten her lucky bingo dabber and came back to the house to get it. She got more than her lucky bingo dabber that night. Neither one of us heard her coming down the hall until it was too late. She caught him on top of me. She beat on him a little bit, and I was stripped of all my clothes and locked down in the basement. 'If you're going to act like Jezebel, you're going to be treated like a harlot!' were her exact words. I was ten years old."

"Did he try and help you?"

"No. He was her little bitch after that. All bark and no balls. If she told him perform a trick, he did it, no questions asked. That night, I got a beating with the belt, and she didn't care which end struck my skin. I had deep welts all over from that weapon." Franki rose up off the couch and pulled up her hospital pajamas shirt to show Ellen the ugly scars that the evil hell hag left behind.

"Sweet Jesus, Franki." Ellen gasped at the sight of Franki's frightful mess of scars.

"And the authorities sent me back there to live after they saw what she had done to me. And they wonder why I have trust issues. I wasn't allowed to eat with them. I went to school and back home again. If I had homework, I was permitted to do it at the kitchen table only. Once I closed the books, I would have to strip down and go back down the basement. I ate there, slept on a little piece of foam, smaller than the size of a crib mattress. I had one pillow and one see-through blanket. I was allowed out to use the bathroom and go to school, but that was all. I always had to be naked. I mean talk about sick."

"How long did this go on?"

"A while . . . I'm not sure. I lost track of time. She stopped going to bingo so there were no extras like a before-bedtime snack. He wasn't allowed near me. Oh, and every Sunday, that revolting piece of cloth she called a dress was washed, pressed, and waiting. She threw out all the things he bought me. I was allowed no makeup. My hair had to be tied into a ponytail. Then one day, I'd had enough. This time, I wasn't running to find my sister. I was running to be free because I believed if I didn't, that one day, she would go too far and I'd end up dead. I wasn't dying at the hand of that bitch. And no one can tell me that what she did to me wasn't abuse because my parents never treated us like that. The law eventually found me again, and I was brought back to Wilkins."

Franki shook her head in disbelief of the memory coming forward to proclaim its horrible reality.

"That night, I received the whipping I would never forget. To the darkened dungeon I went. This time, she was ready for me. A rope was slung over the beam. Tied to the end of the rope was steel pair of handcuffs. She shackled my wrists and pulled my arms into the air. Once she finished whipping me with the belt until I bled, she left me standing with my arms suspended and shackled.

Franki was panting from emotion, her hand shaking as she took a sip of warm coffee.

"She was a sick bitch. A while later, she came back down the stairs and released me. My arms fell like deadweight. She rubbed ointment on the welts that were bleeding and laid me onto the piece of foam. Telling me the whole time, this was for my own good. 'Spare the rod and spoil the child' mumbo jumbo from the Bible. The next couple of days I spent suffering. I knew at that point I had to tell the authorities what was going on. It took a week before I could wear a shirt and go back to school. I was supposed to abide by the rules and be a good girl.

"That morning, I dressed for school, but I didn't make it. Instead I took a detour. I reported the Wilkins to the police. After taking my statement, they put me in the back of the police car. I was relieved, thinking they were taking me someplace safe. Instead, the two officers drove me to 444 Mill Drive, the Wilkins. Doc, my mouth dropped wide open. I thought, 'I'm dead! She's going to kill me now for sure.'"

The doctor made no attempt to hide how she felt about what Franki suffered at the hands of those evil perpetrators. Tears of outrage and sympathy coursed down her cheeks.

"The one officer rapped on the door. Susan answered politely and invited them inside. I was praying they were there to get my stuff so I could get the hell away from them. They disappeared into the house for a short time, but it seemed like an eternity. I was still in the backseat of the cop car. The cop opened my door, and for as long as I am alive, I will never forget what he said to me, 'Young lady, it's not very nice to tell lies about people who are trying to love you like a daughter. These nice people want you back, Franki. This is your home, young lady. So no more wasting time with false allegations, you hear me?'

"Doc, my eyes went blurry, my mouth dry as cotton, and I heard this weird ringing in my ears that I never heard before. I thought my heart was going to leap right out of my mouth. I thought of bolting but knew it was useless. What could I do? I was screwed and I knew it. I walked to the front steps as if I was sentenced to the gas chamber. To my surprise, I didn't get a beating or get yelled at. Nothing. I had my room back. I was allowed to eat at the table with them, not that I wanted to. There was one thing missing: trust. Fear of being beaten, raped again, or brutally murdered became my every waking thought. A month later, it was a beautiful Monday morning. I took my shower, dressed and ate breakfast, and hugged Susan good-bye. I never made it to school that morning or any other morning after that. I was determined to never again return to the Wilkins torture chamber."

Franki sank back against the cushions. "So, there is a memory, Doc. Sick bastards." She ran a trembling hand through her blond hair and managed a weak smile. In spite of the terrible events she had just narrated, Ellen noticed with relief that her face was drained of its earlier tension. Franki almost looked relieved.

"Franki, do you know why the two officers came back to the car and told you that it wasn't very nice to tell lies?"

"I assumed she told them I was all messed up, why?"

"You're right, kid."

"I knew she told a bunch of lies, but why they believed her, I will never understand."

"Did anyone see the scars on your back?"

"Yeah, some lady from the services or something. Why?"

"The story you told me, was it the same one you told this woman?"

"Yeah."

"Susan lied and told the officers you had those scars before you came into foster care."

"Son-of-a-bitch!" Franki screamed and jumped off the couch. "You know when I get out of here, I am going to make her pay for what she did to me."

"Franki, you don't want to take matters into your own hands, honey. It'll only backfire." Dr. Smith peered over her wire-framed glasses.

"Got any bloody suggestions?" Franki hollered from across the room.

"First, I'm going to send you over to the Morial Hospital next door for a complete examination. And then they will take pictures of your back and document everything. When that is all done, they will fax me the information so that we can go forward legally. The Wilkins will be brought to justice. You don't have to let anyone get away with abusing you ever again."

"The courts will drag me through the dirt, and that makes me a little scared. It's not like I've done everything right in life." Franki flopped back down, rubbing her palms together.

"If the system hadn't failed, you wouldn't have had to use skills to survive. I'll be right beside you the whole time. You have more than enough evidence to prove your allegations of abuse. And this time, someone is going to stand up and listen."

"Promise, Doc? I mean, swear."

"With all my heart. I will not abandon you." The doctor went to Franki and sat on the sofa beside her. She wrapped her arms around the girl and hugged her. Ellen wasn't surprised that Franki tensed and then gradually relaxed. Trust was an obstacle that could be hurdled, and she was doing it by allowing herself to be held if warily.

Dr. Smith determined right then and there to see this thing right through to the end. She would do everything in her power to see Susan and Gary Wilkins jailed. The heinous acts of cruelty bestowed on Franki Martin were absolutely nauseating and unacceptable. Ellen would also ensure that Franki would be compensated for the physical pain and sexual torture and emotional suffering she endured at their hands. Franki would seek and get justice the right way!

Chapter Nineteen

After the session, Franki and Dr. Smith were strolling back to Franki's room with her own bouquet of flowers, which she handpicked, from River Edge's Three-Mile Garden.

"Next visit, Doc, can we have our session outside?"

"I don't see why we can't."

"Great! I need one more favor from you—if you can, of course. I need clothes. I don't want to wear these prison pajamas things anymore. They're good for sleeping in, but everyone on this floor is wearing normal trash."

"For starters, what is 'trash'?"

"Oh, Doc, you really need to learn the lingo. 'Pack my trash' means my clothes. My duffle bag is in my room, but I can't wear those clothes." She made a face.

"I understand." Dr. Smith smiled.

"I have those granny pannies, courtesy of Morial." Franki laughed.

"I'll see what I can do. I'll make sure you have new panties that fit you." Ellen winked.

"Thank you. You're pretty cool for a shrink."

"Remember the big bucks," Dr. Smith quipped, continuing down the corridor.

Franki couldn't help but laugh.

*   *   *

Although Franki felt good about her first real session with the doctor, uprooting the past had left her emotionally drained. But she knew Dr. Smith was correct. If she didn't unearth what happened in that house of horrors, it would continue to haunt her. Franki gave a big yawn. She placed the flowers in the vase then lay on the bed, eyes closed, trying to escape the nagging cramps that came every few minutes. She exhaled deeply still feeling the lingering love Dr. Smith had given her. She liked Doc.

Franki returned from the bathroom and was pleasantly surprised to find Sandy, clad in casual attire, sitting on her bed. She envied her clean jeans and yellow shirt and white tennis shoes with not a scuffmark on them. Outside of that drab nurse's uniform, Sandy had a pretty fit body.

"Hey, you clean up well. Day off and nothing better to do than hang out with the crazies. You really need to get a life, Florence Nightingale."

"And hello to you too. Yes, I have a life, thank you."

"Then what are you doing here?" She asked, trying to mask her excitement.

"I came to see how you're doing. I heard you had a rough weekend?"

"Good news travels fast around here." She rolled her eyes.

"Is it true?"

"Yep."

"I decided to bring along a friend to help cheer you up."

Sandy brought her hands from behind her back and extended a stuffed white teddy bear, soft and white, with a little pink nose. A pink ribbon tied around its neck sported a perfect bow. The glass eyes were gentle brown, reminding her of Steve's. Franki was speechless. It had been a long time since someone had done anything this special for her. Sandy had no idea how much this unexpected token meant to her, especially to be given anything in this place.

"Shut up. Mine, really?" She pointed a finger at her chest.

"It sure is, kiddo. And here is an iPod so you can listen to music."

"Oh, wow! She put the buds in her ears. "How did you know I like country?"

"Good guess."

"You really shouldn't have."

"Yes, I should, Franki."

"How will I ever be able to thank you?"

"Believe in yourself as I believe in you. And one more thing." Sandy handed her a hard-covered handbook with a picture of a little girl standing in the middle of a meadow of flowers. A diary can be a girl's best friend. And here is my published book of poetry. I think you will be able to relate."

"Jesus, anything else, Ms. Surprise Me."

"Told you, I have a life." She smirked, tilting her head to the side.

Franki quickly scanned the pages of written poetry before hugging and squeezing the teddy bear, rubbing its softness against her cheek. It looked just like the one her parents gave her after having her tonsils removed.

"Thank you, but . . . why?" Franki's eyes narrowed suspiciously.

"I like you, Franki, in spite of what you may believe. Come on over here and sit down beside me." She patted the space next to her. "I'll tell you a little story. A long time ago—and I know you probably won't want to believe me—but I once was where you are now. I too tried to kill myself and ended up in an institution like this and in a ward similar to yours."

Franki hugged her bear and listened attentively to Sandy's every word.

Then Sandy extended both arms to show Franki the scars of proof. "Attempted suicide happens to all kinds of people, kiddo."

Franki studied the faded marks on Sandy's wrists. "Why you? What was wrong with your life?"

Sandy pointed at her face. "I had a very difficult time trying to cope with this scar. I couldn't hide it. And it wasn't from lack of trying, that's for sure. I tried powders and cure creams and foundations in every color imaginable."

"What did happen to your face?"

Sandy inhaled deeply. "My parents were very abusive toward one another. They fought all the time. At times, the arguments escalated into violent altercations. You know, slapping, pushing, and throwing objects. This day, I happened to be standing in the wrong place when my father grabbed the coffee percolator from the stove and threw it at my mother. She moved out of the way. I didn't. The coffee exploded in my face. The right side got burned the most. That's why the scar is so purple."

"Oh, shit. That had to kill." Franki winced, grabbing the side of her own face.

"You better believe it. I screamed and danced around the room clawing at my face. It burned clear through each layer of skin. I was rushed to the hospital and immediately placed upstairs: fifth floor, burn unit. I was in intensive care for a couple of months. They kept my face wrapped in layers of white sterile dressing, but they couldn't save the skin tissue."

"I thought I had it rough!"

"Don't minimize your own suffering. Pain is pain, no matter how you size it up. For us, it's different circumstances. I was released from the hospital two and a half months later into the care of my granny. She became my legal guardian. The scalding was nothing compared to the teasing I received from kids at school. They called me names like Scar Face, Elephant Girl, and Fugly."

"What's 'Fugly'?"

"It's short for Fucking Ugly," Sandy whispered in Franki's ear. "I became estranged from everyone, especially at lunchtime. No one would eat with me because I was too hideous to look at. I started isolating, and it got worse and worse until the day I broke apart a razor blade and began slashing both wrists, trying to kill the pain. Didn't work, of course. I only added more pain onto the one I already had. I did get better. I healed inside and out, but it took time. This is why I know you'll be okay because you're strong, Franki. You're in good hands in here, buddy."

Franki shook her head, dubious. "You really think so?"

Gently, Sandy took Franki's face in her hands and looked long into her eyes. "Listen, kiddo, if I can survive my ordeal, you can too. Try and remember: the more you talk about the hurt inside, the faster you will heal."

"I had a good talk with Doc today. It's funny that you should mention that, about talking out my problems, because she said the same thing. For an old gal, she's really cool."

"I love her, Franki. You will never meet another Dr. Ellen Smith. She is one in a million. And believe her when she tells you that she cares. She'll go to the end of the earth and back with you if you are willing to help yourself."

"I'm trying. I know someone else that is in the same category as Doc," Franki added.

"Who's that?"

"You, dork!"

"Oh, so now I'm a dork, and the doctor is cool?"

"I didn't mean it like that."

"I'm just teasing. Thank you for the compliment, kiddo, and yes, I'm here to help you in any way I can."

Sandy leaped off the bed with a prideful landing stance, making Franki smile with delight.

"Isn't that your medication you're supposed to be taking?" Sandy pointed.

"That's all I do, take friggin' pills. A pill for this a pill for that. It makes me sleepy. I'm sick of taking all these pills."

"Next visit with Dr. Blake or Dr. Smith, ask them about cutting back on your meds."

"Doc already said that she would do something about my meds. But that Dr. Blake—he's gross," Franki said this deliberately, testing the waters of trust.

"Tell me, why don't you like Dr. Blake?"

"He creeps me out," she lied.

"I know he's a little different."

"It's not what he looks like Sandy, he hurts me."

Sandy's expression went from happy to real serious in a nanosecond. "Do you mean when he examines you?"

"Never mind. Forget I said anything."

"You can tell me anything, you know that, right?"

"Yeah. Thanks, it's nothing, honest." Franki looked away from Sandy.

"Are you sure it's nothing?"

"Yeah, positive. I'm feeling tired, and when I get tired, I start getting all weirded out. It's nothing. Doc hasn't had the chance to change the dosage I'm taking yet, I guess."

"I'll remind her for you the next time I see her. She's been swamped with work since coming back from holidays. Okay, kiddo, I'll get out of your hair. Hug her when you feel tense or lonely and she'll help keep you company. Oh, and by the way, you look better already since you were brought downstairs."

"You need glasses."

"Franki, you are very beautiful."

"Yeah, yeah! Whatever, Nurse Nice."

"Well, I think you're pretty, even if you don't."

"Everyone is entitled to his or her own opinion."

"And opinions are like assholes, and everyone has one, right?"

"You got it, Florence. How long did you spend in med school?"

"Get into bed and try to behave!"

When Franki and her new little friend slipped under the covers, Sandy said, "Have a good sleep, and I'll see you tomorrow. Remember what I said: you can tell me anything."

Franki gave her best smile. "Thank you, Sandy." Then she snuggled up to her new friend, closed her eyes, and in a blink, was fast asleep.

CHAPTER TWENTY

The next morning, Franki awoke feeling as though her mind and limbs were paralyzed. Waves of nausea washed over her. At first, it felt like a real bad flu. Franki couldn't remember if she dreamt it or not. Did Dr. Blake really come to her room last night and stab her in the arm with a needle, or was it a nightmare she'd had? She had difficulty keeping her eyes open. This was better than any heroin she'd tried on the street. How could she have felt so good yesterday and so bad this morning? She struggled to sit up, but her limbs would not cooperate with her fogged-out brain. Why did she feel so languorous but could feel her heart fluttering so wildly?

Dr. Smith was just entering the building, stopping at her office first, before heading to Franki's room to pass on the good news. She would be receiving a donation of clothing that fit. Or as Franki called it, 'trash.' She wasn't going to let it slip that Sandy and she sprang for the bill, including new panties. Self-esteem was paramount on the journey to emotional recovery.

The nurses at the station were doing room calls and handing out medication to patients. Gertrude was assigned to breakfast trays. She stood in the doorway of Franki's room and found her still sleeping. She was supposed to be washed, dressed, and ready for breakfast. That damned girl was being her willful disobedient self. The last write-up stated Gertrude was to be nowhere near Franki Martin unsupervised, ordered by Dr. Smith and signed by Sandy Miller. A rule not to be disobeyed: unless Gertrude was willing to pay a consequence. However, something snapped inside Gertrude's head like the breaking of a light bulb.

"I'll show you what happens to girls who break rules!"

Gertrude stomped across the floor, slammed down the breakfast tray on the table, grabbed Franki's pajamas top, and yanked her out of bed. Franki, so lethargic, couldn't comprehend nor defend what was happening. The young girl stood swaying, held upright only by Gertrude's strong hold. Gertrude grabbed a handful of scrambled eggs and hash browns, forcing the food into Franki's mouth. She choked, struggling to get away from the big woman's iron grip. Franki fell facedown onto the bed, gasping for breath.

Gertrude didn't hear Dr. Smith entering the room. She gasped, then, "What in the hell do you think you're doing?" Dr. Smith bellowed.

Gertrude jumped, swiveling her head toward the doorway. "She won't eat. I was just trying to—"

"Get off of her at once!" Dr. Smith ordered through tightly gritted teeth.

Gertrude plummeted down from her power trip as if on a kid's slide. Cheeks flaming scarlet red, eyes darting like a frightened shoplifter caught with the goods in hand, Gertrude backed out of the room one quick step at a time. Why Gertrude hated Franki Martin so much no one knew the answer, but all the nurses attested to the fact. Sadly—and fortunately—now Dr. Smith had been a firsthand witness.

Slamming the file she carried onto the dresser, the doctor immediately began assisting Franki. She stuck her fingers down Franki's throat, attempting to remove any food lodged in her windpipe. When that didn't work, she performed the Heimlich maneuver until Franki's airway cleared. Ellen Smith's voice thundering throughout the ward alerted Nurse Nancy, who was just coming out of a patient's room. Hearing Ellen's distress call, she charged into Franki's room.

"Nancy, get a washcloth and puke bucket," Ellen ordered.

Nancy held the gray plastic container under Franki's chin just in time for her to throw up. Then she began slowly recovering and able to take in short breaths. Nancy quickly checked Franki's pulse. It was rapid but likely from the attack. Taking a fresh washcloth, she wiped away the food and perspiration from Franki's face and neck.

Dr. Smith found Gertrude four doors down.

"Gertrude, you are dismissed."

"How long this time?"

The doctor could not believe her ears. "I don't think you understood me correctly. You're fired. Now pack up your belongings and get out of this institution before I throw you out myself."

"You can't fire me," Gertrude hissed.

"I just did."

"You'll be hearing from my lawyer."

Dr. Smith laughed. "I look forward to it. Now get lost." She jerked a thumb and walked back to Franki's room.

Nancy had changed Franki's bedding by the time Dr. Smith returned.

"I'm sorry, Franki. This should have never happened, and I promise you it won't happen again. Gertrude has been permanently discharged. She won't be returning ever." Franki's eyes stared unblinking at the wall. Her breathing was normal, but she was still shaking from shock. Nancy fetched warm blankets and wrapped them tightly around Franki. When her shivers subsided, Dr. Smith and Nancy got Franki into the shower, dressed in a pair of fresh pajamas, before tucking her under clean sheets.

"That done, please page Sandy," the doctor directed, "and ask her to come and stay with Franki until I come back."

Then Ellen stormed out of the room.

Nancy returned just in time to find Franki trying to get out of bed. Too weak, Nancy caught her just before she crashed to the tiled floor. Nancy couldn't understand Franki's drugged psychosis state. It made no sense. She hadn't been this lethargic yesterday. She would check her chart to make sure she wasn't given the wrong medication or too much of it. Nurse Nancy knew this: even without looking at the chart, Franki Martin wasn't supposed to be this drug induced.

*   *   *

Several minutes later, Sandy arrived back at Franki's room.

"Hey, what in the world happened here?" Nancy had one arm secured around the girl's waist and was trying to help her sit up.

Sandy rushed to the bed. "Dr. Smith told me you're to stay with Franki until she comes back."

"Not a problem." The two nurses tucked Franki back under the covers. "Franki, honey, it's Sandy. I'm right here. I won't leave you."

Nancy wrapped the stethoscope around her neck.

"What's happened to Franki?"

Nancy rolled her eyes and scowled, "Gertrude."

"She had strict orders not to be near Franki without another person being present."

"She snuck in at breakfast while I was up the hall with another patient. She's been sent packing."

"Where is Dr. Smith now?" Sandy asked, taking Franki's cold hand into hers.

"I have no idea. She stormed out, saying she would return."

"I'll get the details then." She turned her attention to Franki, calling out her name repeatedly. She didn't answer. "Nancy, did someone give Franki an injection of something? She's like a limp little rag doll."

"Not that I'm aware of. I know something doesn't fit. I'm going to check her chart to ensure she received the right medication and the proper dosage."

"Please, because she's really out of it."

"Blake . . . ," Franki breathed.

"What, honey?"

Franki passed out again.

"Nancy, we may have to order blood work. This is not normal."

"Back in a second."

Sandy tried prompting Franki to tell her what happened, but she was too far-gone to make any sense. Nancy reentered carrying the chart.

"Sandy, according to this, she should be up and running. The medications have been rived in half."

"Hmm," Sandy murmured. *Something is very wrong here.* "Okay, thanks, Nancy."

"Want me to call Morial?"

"If you don't mind."

"Not at all." Nancy headed back across the hall to the nurse's station.

A few minutes later, Nancy returned with the news. "The medic will be here at one thirty this afternoon."

"You're the best."

"Anything you need?"

"Answers." She gave a look of real concern. "I'm going to sit with Franki until Dr. Smith tells me otherwise."

"I'm off to do rounds then." Nancy gave a wave as she exited out the door.

*   *   *

The doctor could not remember the last time she had experienced such fulminating anger toward another staff member. There were times Dr. Blake and she had their differences, but never were they this explosive. The veins in her neck pumped furiously as she stomped down the maze of corridors to the staff room. Inside, arms crossed, she leaned next to a row of lockers on the north wall.

"May I ask you something, Gertrude?"

"Ask me what?" the nurse barked, continuing to put personal items into her blue vinyl knapsack.

"Have you treated all of our patients with such brutality, or was it only Franki Martin you targeted?"

"That girl has been nothing but trouble since the first day she arrived here. She has secrets. And if you can't see that, Dr. Smith, then you must be blind?

She's manipulating all of you with her sad stories. But that whore knows what she's doing, and one day, you'll see I was right."

Ellen took a deep breath, trying to remain controlled. "So holding . . . a patient down while you force-feed her until she begins to suffocate is a better and more effective way to take care of patients like Franki Martin?"

"You have to show manipulative bitches like her who's in charge."

"You sure showed her, didn't you?" The doctor shook her head. "The only thing you showed Franki Martin is that some nurses are monsters who are on power trips. But people like you are cowards who pick on the people who can't defend themselves."

"Go to hell." She grinned.

"You are a pitiful excuse for a professional. I ought to press charges against you for assaulting a patient. What do you think, Gertrude? Should I?"

"No! I mean, don't bother. I'm leaving quietly."

"I am placing a restraining order against you. If I find out you're ever near this facility again, I will have you thrown in jail. Do I make myself crystal clear?"

Gertrude grabbed her bag and purse, flew out of the room, and down the hall to the exit sign. Dr. Smith followed her every step. Only when the nurse climbed into her old beat-up station wagon and sped out of the staff parking lot did Ellen take a deep breath of relief. She slapped her hands together as though removing unwanted dirt from her palms.

Dr. Smith took a walk around the Three-Mile Garden to calm down. She was mortified by what she had just witnessed. Pissed off too because this would mean more paperwork to be sent to the board explaining Gertrude's permanent dismissal. Odd though that Franki didn't try and fight off the nurse's attack. She was tiny but feisty, and no way she would have let anyone assault her that way.

A half hour later, Ellen was back at the nurse's station and ready for what needed to be handled. She was sifting through a stack of files when Nurse Judy from the night shift entered.

"Hey, aren't you supposed to be sleeping?"

"Yeah, I had to take my son, Jack, to school this morning so I could pay for his science trip, but when I got there, I realized I had forgotten to grab my purse. So here I am." Judy watched Dr. Smith perusing Ms. Martin's chart and noticed how disturbed she appeared.

"Dr. Smith, is something the matter?"

"I ordered Ms. Martin's medication to be halved, and this morning, I walk in and she is out of it. She was fine yesterday. I'm baffled."

"Dr. Blake went into her room last night around three."

"Did he say why he was there?"

"I'm afraid not."

"You've been a great help, thanks."

She placed the chart back on the peg. *What is going on around here?* She had some unfinished business to discuss with Dr. Blake. Did he administer medication without her authorization? If so, why was it not logged in the patient's medical chart?

"I asked him if he needed the patient's chart, but as usual, he dismissed the question. Sometimes I wonder who he thinks he is. It's as though he's above medical protocol and nurses are of no importance."

Dr. Smith placed a hand on Judy's shoulder.

"Judy, your job is just as important as ours, if not more. Nurses are the ones that provide the information we physicians need. We couldn't get along without you. It's a team effort."

"Well said." Judy laughed. "I have to get out of here so I can pay for my son's trip. And get some shut-eye before the day is gone."

"Sleep well. Thanks again, Judy. You've been a great help."

"Glad to assist." Waving, the nurse disappeared down the corridor.

Chapter Twenty-One

Dr. Smith stood at her colleague's door, taking a couple of deep breaths and trying to regain her composure. Every nerve in her body was dancing to a different beat as she waited for him to answer.

"Ellen, this is a nice surprise. I didn't realize you were back from holidays. Well rested, I hope?"

"Yes, thank you."

"So, what brings you my way? Or did you just miss me?"

Ellen studied the doctor. His mannerism was completely out of character, overly familiar. She never considered him to be one of her close friends. Ellen wondered if there was a full moon on the horizon because Dr. Blake sure wasn't acting like his usual unapproachable self.

"Hate to burst your bubble. No, James, I didn't miss you." She smiled. "Concern for my patient, Franki Martin. She was admitted to our facility when I was away."

"I can't place her." His eyes slid away from hers. He meshed his fingers together, hiding the sweat forming in his palms.

"She had a miscarriage on the weekend. Ring a bell? James, you were seen going into her room last night."

"Oh, yes. Yes, Ms . . . Martin. Poor thing, she's had a rough life." He gave a loud whistle and shook his head. "The poor dear, losing her parents that way."

"She's the reason I'm here."

"Sounds serious?"

"It is."

Anxiety sent his heartbeat into overdrive. He could feel the wetness forming on his upper lip. Dr. Blake dug for the puffer in his suit pocket and took in a couple of deep breaths. *What does she know?*

"So what . . . is it I can do for you?" He walked to his desk and began straightening the papers and folders on his already meticulous kept desk.

"It's her medication."

"What about it, Ellen?"

"I was told you were seen coming out of her room early this morning. Today, she is so lethargic. She can't hold her head up. I need to know if you're responsible for her condition?"

"I checked on another patient last night and slipped into Ms. Martin's room to see how she was faring. Being pregnant came as quite a shock to her, I'm afraid." He drew back his shoulders. "Why, are you questioning my credentials regarding this matter?"

"I'm not."

"Is there a problem I'm not aware of?"

"What were you doing in her room last night?"

"I've already told you."

"Do you have any explanation as to why she is so apathetic today—and that's putting it mildly?"

"Are you asking if I injected her with an opiate?"

"Yes."

"My answer is no."

"Sandy has ordered a toxicology screen today. I want to know exactly what's in Franki's system."

"Why?" He tried not to appear alarmed.

"Because something is physically wrong with the girl, that's why."

"You do know what medications she's taking?"

"Of course, and I ordered the cutback."

"You are aware of everything that is wrong with this girl, aren't you?"

"Fully."

"And that she flies into psychotic episodes. You do know that she has violent outbursts, not to mention she is into self-mutilation? In my opinion, I believe you're making a mistake. She's a danger to herself, the other patients, and even the staff."

"I appreciate your concern, James, but I've been in this business long enough to know how to treat patients. She is under my care now and not Dr. Viewer's."

"Ellen, please hear me out. You were away when she was wreaking havoc on everyone."

She waved her hand in the air dismissively.

"James, please do not undermine my ability to do my job."

"That's not what I'm trying to do. Okay, if you don't believe my word, have you had the chance to read Dr. Viewer's report? That should shed some light on this subject."

"Yes, I have, and once again, I disagree."

"What about the violence?"

"I will take care of my patient's welfare. Franki might once have needed Haloperidol but not anymore. Medication is not a cure. It only helps the procedure."

"I think you're making a big mistake." The doctor shook his head.

"You have a right to your opinion. You still haven't answered my question as to why you were in her room last night."

"I told you the reason."

"Did you administer any kind of sedative?"

"Now that I think about it." He paused, playing with the puffer still in his hand. "Yes, she said she couldn't sleep."

"Why wasn't it documented in her chart?"

"Never felt the need," he shrugged.

"You are treading on thin ground here, James. From this moment on, you are not to give her anything without my written consent. And not entering the meds on her chart might even be viewed as malpractice. Is that clear?"

"Christ, she couldn't sleep. I helped her. What's the big deal? She's already a drug addict."

"I don't care what she is. If she needs something, I'll prescribe it, not you."

"I'm justified in what I did last night. If she needs a fix to keep her calm, I don't see what's the big deal. Ellen, Franki Martin, contrary to your belief, is a violent girl. Obviously, she's pulled the wool over your eyes, but I've seen what she's really capable of. I can't believe you're willing to take this kind of risk. What happens if she loses it on one of the other residents, then what? I can tell you, this place will be sued to the ground."

"And I can't reach her when she's incoherent. I thank you for taking her on when I was away, but I'm back. I'll resume her care from here on."

Blake's heart skipped a beat. Somehow he had to keep Franki quiet. His reputation and career depended on it. If she came out of her stupor and told about his sordid little secret, he'd be finished. Dr. Smith's success was outstanding for bringing patients back from what was regarded as hopeless state of body and mind. It was only a matter of time before Franki trusted Ellen enough to confide in her. What should—what could—he do and get away with it? He beat at the question like a ball hitting a brick wall. Finally, he came to the obvious solution. He would have to silence her.

Blake rose up out of his seat and began pacing the carpet.

"Sorry, Ellen, but as far as I'm concerned, Franki isn't just your concern."

"Tell me, please, how am I supposed to help her get better?"

"I don't know. Perhaps she's not ready for your type of therapy."

"Excuse me? I have an excellent reputation with all my patients, and you know it! If I find out you've administered anything else to Franki or my other patients, the next time we see each other, it will be in front of the medical board. And you can take that to the bank."

"She's a violent menace, it's charted right here!" He grabbed the folder, shaking it in the air.

"I won't dispute that she's angry. She's been pushed way past the limit for what any human being should have had to endure. She has been raped and emotionally tortured. Christ, she lost her whole family in one shot at the ripe age of nine. A little PTSD I believe. I know I would be angry as hell at a system that took my only remaining loved one. She comes from the street, yes. That anger is what's pushed her into surviving this long. Thank God, she's a survivor. She doesn't lash out at others. She inflicts pain on herself. I assumed you doctored her wrists? That kind of behavior is internal, not external."

He flopped back into his chair, tossing his pen into the holder. He molded his mask into one of dejection and sighed.

"Fine, Ellen, she's your responsibility. I'd advise you to keep the haloperidol handy. I've a feeling you're going to need it."

"So, when the toxicology report comes back today, it will show screens of haloperidol, correct?"

"Yes. I hope you're right about this patient or both our asses will be in a sling."

"Nothing's going to go wrong. Have faith." Ellen made for the door and then turned to face the doctor before leaving. "One more thing, I almost forgot to tell you."

"What now," he groaned.

"I fired Gertrude. My report will be on your desk before the end of the day."

"Pardon me?" He pulled his glasses down to the tip of his beak and peered over the rim.

"You heard me."

"Fired for what?"

"I caught her manhandling a patient by forcing food into her mouth. Luckily, I walked in when I did or she might have choked to death."

"Who was this patient?"

"You figure it out." Ellen closed the door behind her.

Blake leaned his head against the back of the cushioned chair. "Franki Martin, of course." He sighed noisily.

*　　*　　*

Dr. Smith walked briskly along the hall toward her office, feeling quite satisfied. She was nothing to mess with, and now Blake knew it. If she saw an injustice within the facility, she fixed it and didn't care whose feelings got hurt in the process. If she needed to go to the board about a situation, she did. There was something odd going on here, and she was going to keep a much closer watch on Blake.

Ellen was rounding the corner when Sandy eyed her coming toward the nurse's station. Sandy waited with bated breath for the report on what horrible event took place this morning.

"How is Franki doing?"

"No change. She's resting now."

"So, the same?"

"Out cold. What happened?"

"I caught Gertrude on top of Franki, shoveling mounds of breakfast food into her mouth. Franki was choking and gasping for air when I entered. I caught the bitch right in the act. Why Franki couldn't fight back, we can thank Dr. Blake."

"Dr. Blake?"

"Judy saw him coming out of Franki's room last night. He told me he gave her something to help her sleep."

"What did he give her?"

"An injection of haloperidol."

"He went against your orders, Ellen!" Sandy threw her hands up.

"He won't do that again. I told him Franki is my concern now, not his. He fears Franki could freak out and be a danger to herself and everyone else. I told him I don't believe that will happen. And Gertrude obtained her permanent walking papers. She's no longer an employee at this facility."

"You fired her?" Sandy's eyebrows shot up to her hairline.

"Yes, I did. No one has the right to mistreat any of our residents. These people are here for help, not abuse."

"It doesn't surprise me, Ellen. She hated Franki from the get-go. I wrote her up a couple of weeks back and gave her a warning." Sandy leaned in closer to Ellen. "She really is a crazy bitch," she whispered.

"The good news is, Franki won't have to worry about that psychopath anymore. And Blake knows where he stands. Now everything can get back to normal." Ellen folded her arms across her chest.

"That's good news." Nancy joined Ellen and Sandy. "Franki hated the old battleaxe, she called her." Sandy chuckled.

"They battled." Sandy sighed.

"And Franki finally won a war. Okay, I'm off, page me when Franki wakes up. From now on, everything gets logged into her chart. Who goes in and out of her room, her moods, and her physical limitation—I mean every detail as of right now. I'll pick up the report at the end of each day. We're all in agreement?"

"No problem." The nurses smiled.

"If anyone of you sees Gertrude in this building, I want to be notified instantly. I'll call security. If she doesn't want to go to jail, today's the last we've seen of her."

"Amen to that," Sandy cheered.

"Doctor, I had no idea Gertrude was even in that room! We all knew she wasn't supposed to be alone with Franki because of the way the two rattled each other."

"None of what happened to Franki is your fault."

The doctor patted Nancy on the shoulder, and her face lit up in relief. "Thank you. I appreciate that," Nancy beamed.

CHAPTER TWENTY-TWO

With Gertrude gone, Franki seemed be turning into a new person. She had Dr. Smith's permission to be outside. Franki took advantage each morning as she made her way along the Three-Mile Garden and played pool on a regular basis with Jazz, a boy her age. He'd been admitted for lighting fires. His parents feared he was turning into an arsonist psychopath. He told Franki he did it for attention. His parents worked all the time. When they were home, they lectured him on how he could improve in school, his room wasn't tidy enough, his hair was too long, jeans were too baggy, and the list went on and on. So, Jazz started lighting fires to give his parents a real reason to complain. Franki liked his flamboyant streaked-colored hair and thought he was cool to hang out with.

One day while playing pool with Jazz, an ex-hooker who thought herself superior to everyone else, decided she wanted to play. Franki rolled her eyes at the way she fawned over Jazz, but he loved the attention. She bragged about how the oldest profession in the world had been so good to her. But how great was it that she too tried to end her life by overdosing on crack cocaine. A fellow junkie found her and dialed 911.

Franki spoke only when necessary to the other residents. "Head cases," as she called them, creeped her out. She cherished her solitude and being alone with her iPod. It helped escape memories of Blake's sexual assaults. Ellen's return made it harder for him to get at her. Twice a week, she had regular scheduled visits with Dr. Smith. Franki, for the first time, was now trying to face the terribly painful loss of her parents and sister. Her earlier rage had turned to sadness. Her hair began to shine again, the color in her face had returned, and she weighed ninety-six pounds. The second-floor staff was thrilled with her progress. They rewarded her with special treats. Franki was becoming everyone's favorite. She gave up smoking. She captivated the nurses with stories of life on the street.

Before having the luxury of being outside, Dr. Smith had Franki sign an affidavit promising she would not run away. Most sunny days, Franki could be found taking long walks around the Three-mile Garden, stopping occasionally to admire its splendor. Now and then, she watched a little television to abscond into a world that was not her own. Her passion to write stories far exceeded other priorities, except therapy with Doc. She no longer used the street life as an excuse for not learning. She wanted knowledge to better herself. School wasn't about survival; she already knew how to do that. Education would lead her down roads to success. Sandy still had reservations whether Franki would ever completely trust anyone again and have a normal life filled with peace, love, trust, and happiness. Faith in others would take time, and everyone knew it, but they commended her effort.

Sandy loved spending time with Franki, helping her to perfect her talent as a writer. Franki wrote the heart wrenching stories, and Sandy sent them away to be published. It didn't take long for the writing world to notice they had a rising star. Franki earned a little money from her short stories, published in *Reader's Digest*, *Bayou*, *Bellingham Review*, and *The Bitter Oleander* magazines. Her talent to articulate was mind-bending. It took little effort for her to create two or three stories a day. She had life experiences to draw from. There was no drug more powerful than writing. The rush was unbelievable. Although her spelling and grammar needed work, Franki wasn't a quitter. If she needed a word she took the time to find it in the dictionary. When she needed assistance, Sandy was there to lend a hand. Sandy was a tyrant when it came to finishing her correspondence courses. The fifteen-year-old decided the only way to shut her up about getting educated was to do it. She hadn't steered her in the wrong direction so far. Sandy, with Ellen's permission, bought Franki a desk for her room. She was becoming quite the celebrity on the second floor. Just for fun, Franki jotted lines of poetry. It was a quick release for her bottled-up hurt. She was at her desk, rereading the poem, she'd just written. It was to Steve.

WARMTH OF A FLAME

Come on in out of the cold
Sit by the fire and warm your toes
We can relax by the flame and talk
Have a seat and back and forth you'll rock
Here is a blanket to take away the chill
And you are? My name is Bill
So here we are to enjoy the night
Watching the glow of the fire burning bright

My intention is only to help a cold friend
I have a soft heart and time to lend
Your eyes show that you've had it rough
Yet you pretend to be tough
Now I must ask, why all the pain?
Or has life's path led you astray
There is a thing I've heard called hope
Or do you like walking the tight rope
From one friend to another
Unleash the scars of so much sorrow
Never give up and please continue to try
Don't let happiness pass you by
Give life and yourself one more chance
Who is to say you won't find true romance
So let us relish this special night ahead
You'll always know in your heart I am your true friend.

Franki Martin
Dedicated to Steve Michaels and our baby, Adam.

Even though Franki had lost her unborn child, she'd still named him, not really knowing if it was a girl or boy. It didn't matter what anyone thought. This was her life, and impressing others, those days were over.

With a big smile on her face, Sandy entered the room carrying a long white envelope.

"Hey, how is my favorite girl doing?"

"I finished my poem."

"Is there anything you can't do when it comes to writing?"

"I guess not." Franki giggled. "What's up?"

"I came to give you something."

"What?"

"Oh, just a letter from a *Bellingham Review*," Sandy shrilled, waving the envelope high in the air.

"Are you shitting me?" Franki's eyes lit up like a Christmas tree.

Sandy placed her hand on her hip. "When are you ever going to trust me, kid?"

"I trust you. Now, hand it over!" Sandy tossed her the envelope. Franki snatched it in the air, excitedly ripping it open. Quickly she scanned the letter and then let out a loud whoop.

"Come on, don't keep me in suspense here. What does it say?"

"Holy shit! They want to publish my story 'The Night of Darkness.'"

"Franki, that's great news!"

"Yeah, and they're going to pay me three hundred bucks. Holy shit!" Franki jumped up and down with joy. Sandy gave her a hug, and together, they jumped for joy.

"So, are you going to give them permission?"

Franki stopped. "Are you on glue?" She arched her eyebrow.

"I take that as a yes."

"Yes, yes!" She whooped with laughter.

"When?"

"Next month."

"I am so darn proud of you, girl."

"I couldn't have done it without you, Sandy. Thank you so much."

"You are welcome, my friend. Well, I would love to stay and enjoy your prosperity further, but I have a guest coming for dinner."

"Guy or girl?"

"None of your business, nosey parker."

"Sandy has a boyfriend," she chirped. "Sandy has a boyfriend," Franki teased, dancing silly around the room.

"Believe what you want, my dear." Sandy grinned.

"So, guy or girl?"

"I'm not telling you." Sandy laughed as she headed for the door.

"Hey, that's not fair."

"Deal with it."

"Fine." Franki held her palms out. "I know when to mind my own business."

"A guy." Sandy disappeared.

Franki flopped on her back, holding up the letter of acceptance. She felt a pride never before known. It was wonderful. And no one was going to wreck this moment of glory.

CHAPTER TWENTY-THREE

Franki had deliberately built a concrete wall around her for self-protection. Brick by brick, those walls were tumbling down. As hope and trust replaced the mortar of despair and suspicion eventually, cautiously and ever so timidly, Franki let Doc and Sandy enter behind her fortress of stone. Yet, there remained that ugly fear holding Franki back from telling the truth about Blake.

If the two women she trusted didn't believe her, if he somehow convinced them that she wasn't telling the truth, it would finish her. Their total acceptance of her was the only good she had to cling on to in the whole rotten world.

*　　*　　*

Franki had traveled a great distance to heal but still had a long way to go. She still flew off the handle, not yet knowing how to articulate her raw defrosting emotions. Instead of trashing her room, she battered the staff with imaginative choice of profanities. "Go fuck yourselves" was one of the unpleasant verbs she loved throwing around. No way she'd follow a regular routine like exercise or following an order. It didn't take much to set her off. A simple hello from an innocent bystander could ignite her like a firecracker or being told to do something she didn't want to do.

Everything Franki did was documented, from the time she opened her eyes until she closed them again at night. Ellen noted a significant pattern: these episodes always followed Franki's health sessions with Dr. Blake. But why did she harbor so much resentment toward him? Whatever the reasons, Ellen decided to do some careful probing into Franki's attitude. It was time for Franki to practice tolerance in all areas of her life, starting with people she didn't like. And Dr. Blake was a good beginning.

Ellen started preparing Franki for the psychological attitudes necessary to equip her when she returned back to the real world. Franki was going to encounter all kinds of people that wouldn't view life as she did. The tantrums had to stop; she wasn't always going to get her way. The big concern was her escaping problems by hiding in the drug world. Life isn't always emotionally comfortable. She had to learn how to play by society's rules.

*   *   *

The nurses assigned to Franki's care could see the bizarre pattern developing whenever Blake was involved. Today just happened to be one of those days. It started first thing that morning.

Franki was sitting in her chair, reading a book. She looked up when she heard her name announced over the loud speaker. She didn't have to ask who was summoning her. She knew who and what he wanted.

This time, she was going to try something different. She'd act as if she wanted to be with him. If his motive was power, this should throw him off his game. She would be less challenging and more compliant. If the skills she used on the street to stay alive were good enough to con the johns, why wouldn't it work on Blake? She wasn't strong enough to challenge him physically, but she sure could mess with his mind.

She had star qualities as an actress. Franki smiled and moaned like she was enjoying every second of what he was doing. Dr. Blake jerked away as though being burned by hot coals. When she came up behind him, wound her arms around his waist, and began kissing his bare back. He whipped around speechless. That terrifying trepidation he enjoyed seeing so much was no longer there. She was smiling sweetly, batting her eyes like he was the love of her life. Confusion, not cruelty, stared back at her.

"What's wrong, baby?" Franki cooed and cocked her head seductively.

"Go over there and get dressed." His mind raced. Was she playing him, or was she really falling in love with him like Gloria Shelby?

Mentally, his fingers flipped through the pages of his psychology book and stopped at the chapter on patient's emotional transference to their doctors. Of course, he had heard of such cases although never experiencing the phenomenon.

"What's the matter, you don't like me anymore?" She crooned seductively, stroking her fingers along his jaw line. But he'd dealt with too many mental patients to be that easily suckered. He swatted her hand away from his face as if swatting at a mosquito.

"I told you to get dressed. Hurry up."

Franki walked away, smiling. Now she had him right where she wanted him. He was no longer going to be in control. Blake finished dressing in silence, his thoughts whirling like a potter's wheel. She couldn't be falling for me? No, they're all whores, nothing more. And so was she. His mother told him never to trust women. Her voice boomed in his head, *They'll hurt you, James. They'll rip out your soul and get what they want. Don't believe her, James. She's a stupid little tramp.*

Of course, his mother was right. And yet . . . and yet . . . he pushed his mother out of his mind. Maybe he was being confronted with a full-blown transference.

He turned around, with a boyish smile, tugging at his lips. "So you are starting to enjoy our time together, are you?" He held his breath.

"What do you think?" Her eyes would have melted butter.

"You've never been this affectionate before today."

Franki shrugged. "What the hell. I like sex too, you know. If the only way I'm going to get out of this funny farm is to stop fighting and cooperate with you, then so be it."

He stared at her, amazement washing any suspicion from his mind. A sweet satisfaction glinted from his eyes.

It's time, thought Franki, *to wipe that boyish grin off his ugly face.* She took her stance, folding her arms across her chest and burst into laughter. He staggered backward as if pushed, bewilderment crumpling his face like a deflating loaf of sour dough.

Her loud braying laughter held no humor.

"What . . . what's going on here?" He gasped for breath.

"Oh, you really want to know how I feel about you?" She winked and blew him a kiss.

His expression lit up like a survivor pulled from a wreck. He placed his hand on his chest, relieved for a second.

"You fucking repulse me! You make my skin crawl at the sight of your naked body. I could throw up when I look at the pleasure you have raping me."

Blake felt the blood drain from his face. The shock of her words pelted at him like hail. He put his arms up to shield himself. Franki reveled in the pain she was causing him. Seeing him shatter was like basking in the sun's warmth for the first time. Blake's eyes darted around the room looking for escape. The glare of examining room's light overhead seemed to be beating down on him like a spotlight. To Franki, the room suddenly felt very cold, like evil had entered. She tensed every muscle, bracing herself for impact of him going ballistic. He astounded her by grabbing his clothes and striding into the office, slamming the door behind him.

The cold, hard truth of his mother's words striking at him, like the lashing of a whip. "How could you be so stupid to believe that dirty little whore?" he seethed. "What's wrong with you? Get a grip, go back in there, and show her who's in charge. Do it!" Then, "No. No. No. Stop yelling at me." He cringed from his mother's verbal assault, covered his ears with his hands. It was a futile effort, for her words were locked inside his head. There was no key to lock him self away from them.

Franki thought she could hear him rambling. She leaned her ear to the door, but all was quiet again. She shook her head, thought, *This guy is a total nut bag.*

Then the door opened. Blake had redressed into a fresh lab coat.

"Come over here. I need one more blood sample." His voice and demeanor were professionally low-keyed and calm.

"Why? Did you give me a disease or something?"

"Don't be silly." He smiled reassuringly. "I'm sure your blood count is correct. Don't worry it's just a precaution. I do this to all my female patients who are coming down off medication. Remember, you are a little addict, so we want to make sure the drugs you're using are prescription only."

"You said all your female patients. What about your male patients?" Franki argued.

"Stop making a big deal out of nothing."

"If my blood cell count was normal last time, why wouldn't it be the same this time?"

"You ask too many questions for your own good," he growled.

"Let me stick you with a needle and see how you like it."

"I'm making sure your liver count is orderly. That's why it must be done once a week." Dr. Blake rolled his eyes and sighed like she didn't deserve an explanation.

If bullshit were worth money, Franki thought, *you'd be a millionaire.*

"I feel fine. I don't like you poking me every week."

"I'm doing my job. I'm sorry if it's uncomfortable for you."

"Yeah, I bet you're sorry." She mumbled under her breath.

"You're mumbling again."

"I was talking to myself."

"You do know that's a sign of insanity?" He snickered.

"Very funny. In case you've forgotten, I am in an asylum."

"All you do is complain, 'Doctor, I don't like this'"—he mocked—"'Doctor, I don't like that. I don't like the way you bend me over the table the way you do.'"

"You're disgusting. Get this over with."

"Yes, then you'll be out of my sight." He plunged the needle into her radial artery and watched the barrel fill with her blood. "Done." He yanked the needle free and placed a cotton ball over the tiny hole.

"Can I go?"

"Yes."

Franki saluted and walked out, slamming the door behind her, feeling vindicated. *I'm going to send this guy to his grave one day,* she vowed, striding quickly along the halls toward her room. *But I'll need to have the steps down pat if I'm going to dance with that devil. This morning's performance was only the beginning. I'm going to teach him a lesson.*

*　　*　　*

When Franki arrived in the doorway, she lost it, seeing Nurse Carmen taking one of her magazines.

"Hey, what do you think you're doing, stealing my trash?" She swiped the magazine from Carmen's hand.

"Franki, I was just borrowing it. A patient down the hall wanted something to read."

"I don't give a shit. I didn't tell you that you could take my trash, you stupid cow. Don't touch my stuff again, you thief. And get of my room." She pointed to the door.

"Stop being such a brat."

"A brat? You come into my room and steal my stuff and I'm the brat. How would you like me to go across the hall and steal your purse and give it to someone else, you stupid bitch?"

"You are not allowed behind the counter. And don't talk to me that way."

"Then shut your pie hole and get out of here."

Nurse Carmen stormed out.

Franki was very protective of her belongings. Those so few items, her family photographs, special gifts given to her from Sandy, her rabbit's foot, a folder of letters from publishing houses, and of course, her stories and private thoughts she'd journaled were all she had left of her own. Everything else had been stolen from her. She hated people coming into her room uninvited, especially touching her stuff.

Five o'clock that afternoon, Franki was still in a miserable mood. She'd declined a game of pool with Jazz. Mad that Sandy hadn't stopped in to see if she were okay. Feeling sorry for herself, she lay with the iPod cranked, staring out into the abyss. She had no idea that Sandy was on her way to Dr. Smith's to ask a special favor.

The weather was still hot, with a warm breeze blowing through the air. Dr. Smith looked at the door when she heard the knock. "Come in," she called out. She never stopped doing what she was doing; yelling "Come in" had become a trademark of hers. Sandy poked her head inside.

"Do you have a minute?"

"For you, always. Come in and close the door." Ellen turned off her computer screen to give her undivided attention. Sandy sat in the beige-cushioned chair in front of Ellen's desk.

"What's up?"

"I was wondering if I could get permission to take our star patient out for a drive?"

"Does she have group therapy this evening?"

"Nope, her schedule is clear. I checked to make sure."

"I don't see why not."

"Great! I'll treat her to a banana split or a hot fudge sundae. The most we'll be gone is a couple of hours max."

"I'm jealous." Ellen stuck out her bottom lip like a pouting child.

"You're welcome to come along."

"Thanks, but as you can see, my desk is piled high with patient's charts. I now remember why I never took extended four-week holidays."

"Sorry to hear that, but rumor has it, that's why you get paid the big bucks." Sandy joked.

Ellen rolled her eyes, grinning. "I've been reading up on Franki's progress. How do you feel she's really coming along?"

"I think she is doing incredible. Her writing career is in flight. Ellen, you didn't see how closed off she was when she first arrived. It was almost scary. I thought we were going to need a chisel and hammer to break through the layers of brick. She has done a 360 in my opinion. She is so funny sometimes. The things she comes out with just floors me. And smart as a whip. Still has a temper problem, but hey." Sandy shrugged. "Physically she is getting stronger. The girl is beautiful if only she could get her head wrapped around that message. I just love her."

"How can you not?"

"At times her survival instinct is something to be desired, but the street is ingrained into her soul, I'm afraid."

"What do you mean?"

"It really bothers me that after each visit with Dr. Blake, she rages at everyone that comes within a thirty-mile radius. I mean she's argumentative, tosses things around, and curses at the nurses, demanding that they get the hell of her room. Today for example, I read that Carmen went to borrow a magazine to lend to another patient, and Franki freaked out. The magazine was from the sitting area, but Franki felt it was hers. Carmen logged the incident into Franki's file. The emotional switch is like night and day. She's even thrown me out of her room when she's in one of her moods. She pushes me away, trying deliberately to hurt my feelings. It doesn't work, but she doesn't know that. Has she been that way with you, Ellen?"

"You better believe it. It comes with the territory. I'm the one digging into dark graves of her life that she doesn't want unearthed. It causes her pain she would rather keep buried. They're too frightening to her. She rolled up a magazine one time and threatened to beat me over the head with it if I didn't shut the fuck up."

"What did you do?"

"I changed the subject long enough to get her to calm down, and then I began digging again into that painful vault. I notice how her eyes grow cold like there's a black fog moving into her brain. You're correct in thinking that she is trying to push you away because that is exactly her intention."

"She's at her worst after appointments with Dr. Blake."

"I know she has a strong dislike for the man, putting it mildly."

"It's more than mood swings. She hates him. And the names she has for him. A deep-seated hate."

"What names?"

"The 'predator,' 'creep,' 'fucking jerk-off.' That's one of her favorites. She's called me a couple of choice words too, but it's never said with the same spite and viciousness."

"And this is after her visits with him?"

"Seems to be. And what is puzzling to me is Gloria rushes to his page like a bouncing kid at Christmas. Something just isn't adding up. He always sees his female patients longer in his office than his male ones."

Ellen held Sandy's eyes. "Are you asking me to look into this matter?"

"It might be an idea."

"It just may be that Franki hates him and wants to sabotage his career. Survivors sometimes unconsciously sabotage because the person reminds them of a past hurt. I haven't changed doctor-patient relationship yet, because I want to find out how Franki will cope with people and situations that aren't always comfortable. I'm testing her limits because I don't want her to leave here and find out months down the road that she's back on the street or, worse, dead. She needs to learn how to cope with troubling situations."

"Sounds like a good plan."

"Her birthday is in two months, and it will be hard to keep her here after that. Her progress needs to continue growing rapidly if she is going to make it. She's begun talking about her past, but I can tell she still struggles between reality and fantasy. It's not easy dealing with pain. The brain is a wonderful mechanism. It can hide the details of the most incomprehensible abuse. If I can keep probing into the dark places she doesn't want me to visit, I feel the best is yet to emerge from Franki Martin."

"I totally agree." Sandy nodded.

Ellen placed her pen back into its holder. "I think I might have located Franki's sister, Beth. I'm just waiting to hear back from the agency." Ellen crossed her fingers.

Sandy almost leaped out of her chair. "What? Where?"

"Edmonton, but I'm not 100 percent."

"Oh, wow! That's wonderful news."

"I've just submitted an application to the Family Together Agency. After that, it will be up to Beth whether she wants to be reacquainted in her sister's life. If it's the right location."

"I can't see why Beth wouldn't."

"I can't either. But just in case, please don't say anything to Franki. I don't want her to have to deal with any more disappointments and rejections. That heartache would take her out of the game for good."

"Oh god. The hairs on the back of my neck are dancing," she gushed.

"Remember, not a word."

"Mum's the word." Sandy pressed her hand over her mouth.

"Are you taking Franki now?"

"Shortly. I have a couple of things left to do."

"Then get going. Franki awaits." Ellen laughed.

"I'm going. I'm gone. Don't work too hard. Remember, you have a wonderful husband at home waiting to take you for ice cream." Sandy gave a little jump of joy outside the door before heading to Franki's room to tell her they had the green light to go out for a treat.

*   *   *

Franki was sitting on her bed with a huge scowl on her face when Sandy walked in.

"Hey, you."

"Hey." Franki didn't smile back. She had that stormy look in her eyes that said, "Go ahead and say something that I don't like and see what happens."

"Is something bothering you? You look pissed, kiddo."

"I am. Hate this fucking place and everyone in it."

"Do you want to talk about it?"

"No!"

"Okay, I can respect that. I have something to tell you that I think will cheer you up. Guaranteed to put a smile on that pretty face."

"Oh yeah, like what?" She narrowed her eyes.

"How long has it been since you pigged out on a banana split or hot fudge sundae?" Sandy beamed.

"Hell if I know." Franki shrugged.

"Good. Then get ready. I'll come back in twenty minutes to get you."

"No way! Really?" She swung her legs over the side. "You're not playin' me? I really get to get out of here?"

"I'm not kidding. What do you take me for, a monster?" Sandy looked at her, hurt that Franki could believe she would lie to her.

"I've been screwed over a few times, remember?"

"Well, not by me, and you know that. We'll have to stop at the nurse's station to sign you out."

"And you said this wasn't a prison. How did you spring me?"

"We have a fairy 'Good Mother.'"

"Doc gave it her stamp of approval? God, I love that woman!"

"Okay, I'll be back in twenty minutes, make that fifteen now. Be ready to go, kiddo." Sandy gave her favorite patient a wink and left the room.

Franki dashed to the bathroom to take a shower. There was no way she was going to let the real world see her in an old sweatshirt and torn sweatpants. She was so delighted she could barely contain her excitement. Her anger vanished. She hadn't stepped outside the iron fence since she arrived. Quickly, she showered, brushed her hair and teeth, and pulled on a pair of white cotton shorts and matching T-shirt. She giggled at her mismatched toenail polish, showing through her open-toed sandals; every toe had a different color. She wrapped a sweater around her waist in case the weather changed and then took a fast look in the bathroom mirror. Sandy kept telling her that she was a natural beauty; she didn't need to cake her face in makeup.

The feeling of depression, anger, and being ensnared vanished. This was what it was like to feel fully alive. She'd almost forgotten. Franki opened her journal and began scribbling the words on to the blank piece of lined paper that were reeling from her head.

MY MASK

There are many masks I wear
Because I'm afraid that you won't care
It's hard for me to open and reveal
My masks help to hide what it is I feel
I wear these masks to protect myself

To make you think I don't need your help
I wear these masks each and every day
To lead you to believe I'm functioning okay

The many masks can hide my pain
To make you believe I'm not crazy, I'm sane
It's only the pain I pretend to hide
My masks hold in my anxiety and fears
Though my heart is filled with a river of tears
I fight to hang on to such little hope
As I balance life's tight rope
I have to wonder if that day will come
When the mask on my face will turn to one

Franki Martin

Franki was truly grateful for everything that Sandy and Doc were doing for her. And at times guilty, for she believed she had nothing to give back. Although she couldn't articulate her emotions, they knew the kindness inside her soul. She had just finished the last line when she felt the breeze of the door opening.

"Ready to get out of here?" Sandy asked, smiling.

"Let's go!" Franki leaped off the bed.

The two laughed and giggled like excited schoolgirls as they rushed across the parking lot.

"Where's the car?" Sandy finally stopped at her black Beamer.

"Shut up! No way! *This* is your car?"

"No, I stole it. Yes, it's mine. I am a cool chick, you know." Sandy laughed.

"I always thought—"

"You thought I drove a station wagon?"

"Something like that." Franki giggled. "Minivan."

"That'll teach you. Never judge a book by its cover."

"Proved that theory, haven't you?"

"More to come, kiddo."

"What do you mean by that?" Franki looked puzzled.

"I mean, let me into your heart. I think we could have a lot of fun together."

"I can't argue with a cool chick who drives a Beamer, now can I?"

"Good answer."

"No offense, but I thought you were a bit of a geek."

"I'll take 'cool,' thank you."

"Called a 'ncrd' when you were younger?"

"And much more." She rolled her eyes before covering them with her Ray-Ban shades. "I'm glad you think I'm cool."

"My pleasure. Now are you going to let me in?"

Sandy just grinned, pushed the button, and hearing the beep, unlocked the door.

Franki closed her eyes, loving the feel of the warm breeze blowing against her face as they drove over to the Dairy Queen and took a table outside.

Franki's sapphire eyes were like two sunbeams as she gobbled down her banana split. Sandy was just delighted watching her enjoyment, thinking, *This is how Franki's life was supposed to be: ice cream, girl talks, and sunshine evening drives* . . . Afterward, Sandy asked Franki if she wanted to drive to the beach to watch the sunset?

Without hesitation, Franki stood. "Well, what are we waiting for?" She ran for the BMW.

Sandy was pleased as she glanced at the energized girl enjoying every second of the ride. On the way, Franki sat tall with pride, waving and blowing kisses at the good-looking guys as they drove on.

They pulled into the parking lot and made their way across the warm sand, coming to a huge log that had recently washed up on shore. Perfect for sitting on. Neither spoke. They sat in awe, staring out at the breathtaking view. The sunset painted the sky a pallet of pastels with the mountains stretched in all its glory. Franki sat motionless, mesmerized by its splendor. The waves softly pushing toward the shoreline, sounding like a soft melody never before heard. The scent of kelp and salt water drifted through the air, tingling their sense of smell. Empty crab shells littered the sand left from the seagulls' feast. Franki closed her eyes, burning the unbelievable scenery on to her mind.

"You can't buy this kind of peace," Franki finally murmured.

"We have been so blessed. And yet a lot of us take our planet for granted, including myself. To watch a sunset, to hear the rush of waves . . . wow! And all that's asked of us is that we respect what we've been given. Too often we don't even do that."

"If this so-called God of yours wanted us to have such a wonderful life, then why all the pain and suffering in the world?" Sandy glanced at her to see an unexpected tear sliding down Franki's cheek.

"The only way I can answer that is to say God doesn't make bad things happen. Bad things happen to good people, Franki. Then it becomes our responsibility to do the best we can with the hand we're dealt with. I believe God gives us the strength to cope. We have the freedom to choose between right and wrong. Unless you're a certified psychopath devoid of any human feelings and not even then do we have an excuse. Not everyone makes the right choices. Understand?"

"Good versus evil, and sometimes good doesn't win. My parents never did anything wrong and look how they were taken out. Doesn't make sense."

"I didn't say life is fair. Sometimes it just sucks, and we don't have the answers. I'm sorry you lost your parents, buddy. If I could bring them back for you, I would."

"I believe you, thanks."

"But there are decent people still left like you. Look at Doc. She is the true essence of love. Being around positive people helps to stay in a positive frame of mind. Look at my face. I should be a Bitter Betty, but I'm not. Each morning, I wake up and ask for the strength to face another day. It's not like I don't see the weird looks I get or the whispers, but I don't let it consume me. I'm too busy giving back to others. It keeps me from feeling sorry for myself."

"Yeah, well, you and Doc are a different breed of animal."

"Different because we choose the side we want to be on."

"What do you mean?"

"We choose to be the good guys. Good versus evil."

"You're so cool. I hope I can get to where you're at one day. I'm still pretty pissed at this God you hold up on a pedestal. My life hasn't been that great, if you know what I mean." Franki frowned; shoulder slumped forward.

"It's okay to be angry, Franki. It's not okay to take it out on those who don't deserve it, though. As far as getting to where I am, you will. You have a big heart, Franki Martin, and that's all you need."

"You know more than me."

"You're a pretty smart cookie. Give yourself some credit."

"Thanks for the positiveness and all, but I'm like an old dog with two dicks."

Sandy did the double take. "Girl, what am I going to do with you?"

"No clue."

"Give me a hug?"

She couldn't just wrap her arms around the young girl at random. This minute was good, but there were days when she couldn't get within ten feet of the girl. Tonight, Franki was feeling safe.

They sat quietly, occasionally glancing at each other, exchanging ear-to-ear grins. *If I'd had a daughter,* Sandy thought wistfully, *I couldn't love her more than I do Franki. If I could hand her the world on a silver platter, I'd do it.*

"Sandy, I have to tell you something, but you can't tell anyone, including Doc."

Sandy tried to hide her surprise. "I thought you liked Doc?"

"I love her. Now promise me, Sandy."

"Franki, you're asking me for my word before I know what you're about to say. Why would you want to keep a secret from Doc?"

"Forget it. You're right. I can't trust that you won't tell her." Franki dug her toes into the sand.

"Now, you have piqued my curiosity."

"Don't sweat it. It's really nothing."

"Franki, are you in some kind of danger?"

"Why would you ask me that?" Her eyes narrowed suspiciously.

"An observation. I see how you get physically sick after visits with the doctor."

"Which doctor?" Franki countered. "I don't know what you're talking about."

"Honey, I think you do. You get so upset after each visit with Dr. Blake."

"He's gross, and I don't like the asshole, so what?" Franki said, trying to sound convincing and nonchalant. "It's nothing really."

"It sure doesn't sound like nothing to me, especially if you won't let me tell Doc."

"She's my shrink, that's why?"

"Then what am I?"

"I thought you were my friend."

"I am your friend, but I am also employed at River Edge, so if there's something bad going on inside the Edge, then I'm obligated to report it. You do understand that, don't you, kiddo?"

"I said forget it, didn't I?" Her tone raised a couple of decimals higher than necessary.

"I won't drop it, Franki. I need to know if you're okay?"

"No, Sandy, I'm not all right, and I'm not going to be all right as long as that fucking jerk-off is there."

"I need more information than he's a fucking jerk-off. We all know how much you hate him. You've made that perfectly clear. But what I want to know is how come?"

"I can't tell you now because you'll tell Doc and then Doc will go to him and then . . . oh never mind. Forget I even brought up the dip shit's name."

"Franki, if Dr. Blake is doing something he shouldn't be, we need to know, understand?"

"Sandy, drop it!" Franki got to her feet. "I want to go dip my feet in the cold water."

That kid's a real expert in shutting down, Sandy thought, sighing. If she didn't want you to know her private thoughts, you didn't. She could change a subject faster than you could blink an eye.

Sandy didn't push. There was something intolerably wrong between Franki and Dr. Blake. Danger crept up her spine as she remembered the first time she retrieved Franki from Blake's office. There was a warning flashing in Franki's eyes to which she should have paid closer attention. Now more than ever, Sandy was determined to uncover the truth. Whatever it was had to be very serious.

Sandy kept her distance, watching Franki from the log. Franki was rushing into the salty surf and out again before the cold could touch her designer toes. It reminded Sandy of a small child thrilled to be at the beach for the first time.

Her laughter exploded into the sea air, the wind carrying Franki's unabated joy with its currents.

"Hey, Sandy, thanks." Franki yelled, racing toward the log. "I can't remember when I've had so much fun."

"My pleasure, kiddo."

The warm sand felt good on Franki's cold feet. When the golden crystals began to dry, she took her index finger and scraped at the sand from between her toes. Cautiously, Sandy placed her hand on Franki's shoulder, giving it a gentle shake.

"What is going on between you and the doctor? Honey, I can't help you if I'm in the dark."

"Drop it, I'm fine. End of story."

"I have to respect your wishes, but I don't have to like it."

"I never said you had to like it," Franki snapped. "Remember, life's not fair."

"Said like a true professional."

The sun had disappeared into the sea, and sadly, it was time to go. Franki asked that the Beamer's top stay off until she was dropped off at the institution known as her "home." Franki rummaged through the CD collection searching for the Black Eyed Peas. Sandy put in the disc for Franki and cranked it loud. The speakers boomed from the back as they moved to the rhythm, belting out the lyrics at the top of their lungs.

*   *   *

In the report, Sandy described Franki as exciting, honest, gifted, humorous, sensitive, and very loving when she wasn't battling one of life's demons from her past. She wasn't fooled by Franki's rough exterior. This girl had all the star qualities to do great things with her life. Sandy knew she could have a fulfilling career ahead of her as a writer if she stayed committed.

They'd rolled up to the red light on Broad Street when Franki noticed a Jeep pulling up alongside the BMW. She stopped dancing, recognizing who was beside them. Her mind froze. She didn't know what to do. It was Steve Michaels, with a beautiful brunet in the passenger seat. Franki loved to live on the edge of defiance and decided to throw caution to the wind. It might throw a little chink into the lover sitting beside him. She started jumping up and down like a lunatic trying to get his attention.

"Steve, Steve it's me. Remember me, the girl in the rain?" He looked and looked again. There was a glint of recognition in his eyes. The last time Steve saw her, she'd been homeless and eating out of Dumpsters to stay alive. Here she was, a passenger in a BMW. He waved, not really knowing what to do.

The light turned green, and Sandy drove on; Steve turned left, heading for his place on Dunner Road.

"Does he have a name?"

"One of those nice guys that comes along once in a million years."

"Is that the gentleman that found you in the alley?"

"No. You remember me telling you the story about the guy who rescued me from the rain? He's the baby's daddy, Mr. Gorgeous himself—Steve Michaels."

"Should we go after him?"

"No. We're not on the same page in life, if you know what I mean. It's not like he can pick me up for a date at Hotel Insane."

"You'll find the right guy in time."

"Where, the nuthouse?" She laughed shrilly.

"You won't always be there, Franki."

"I sure hope not."

"You won't be. Promise."

"I can't wait to have a place of my own."

"You'll still have to watch for what triggers you."

"I know that. I'm not going back to the street again. I'll kill myself before I let that happen."

"Don't say that. I don't want you even entertaining those thoughts."

"Chill out! I mean I've had enough of surviving that glamor's lifestyle." She smirked and tossed her head back.

"You worry me."

"Useless emotion, my friend." Franki reached across the dash, cranking up the volume.

Sandy's subtle cue the conversation was over.

CHAPTER TWENTY-FOUR

That night, Sandy's mental clock chimed every hour on the hour. It bothered her that Franki didn't trust her or Doc enough to confide what was troubling her. This went far deeper than what could be considered "normal resentment." With Franki's background, she understood some of what could provoke hostility, especially with authority figures that tended to be autocratic, like Blake. Real or imagined, what could he have done to her? Was their trusted colleague the monster Sandy saw in nightmares? This situation was not only frustrating but also frightening. She glanced up at the wall clock: three thirty. Finally, a hint of dawn lightened the bleak sky; she stretched her tired bones, placed her coffee-stained cup in the sink, and headed for bed. She was powerless to help Franki this time of morning. Five minutes later, she was fast asleep.

*　　*　　*

Sandy arrived for work an hour earlier than usual. Evidence of a not-so-restful sleep hung dark smudges beneath her eyes. Her gut instinct told her that Franki was in real, not imagined, danger. Guessing was driving her crazy. What was young Franki trying not to say at the beach? Franki was obviously scared of Dr. Blake. Did he remind her of someone from the past? She needed answers, and fast.

Glancing at her watch, Sandy decided to take a walk down to the nurse's station. She checked through patients' charts trying to occupy her mind. Every few minutes, she found herself looking across the hallway at Franki's door. *This is useless,* she thought.

"I'm going to stretch my legs," she told Judy.

"Are you bothered by something?"

"Didn't get much sleep, that's all."

She headed to Ellen's office and stopped midway, relief filling her tired eyes. There was Dr. Smith rushing up the hall toward her.

"Hey, just the person I need to see."

"Good morning." Ellen smiled.

"Do you have a couple of minutes to spare right now? It's important."

"Sounds serious?" She said, unlocking her office door.

"I think it could be."

"Whom in particular are we talking about?" Ellen gestured to take a seat as she made it for her chair behind her desk.

"Franki."

"Something happened last night?" Ellen stopped in her tracks and turned. Sandy's face was unusually somber. "By those dark suitcases under your eyes, one of you didn't sleep much last."

"Right again. Do you have time for this?"

"Unfortunately, no. I'm running kind of late as it is."

The nurse groaned. "Can I come back later?"

"I've a lecture this morning and meetings all afternoon."

"Oh, darn!" Sandy felt like stomping her feet; she was so frustrated. She couldn't contain herself a moment longer. The words burst forth like an unplugged dam, "I think I know what is hindering Franki's progress!"

Ellen studied Sandy's face. Clearly, whatever it was had to be serious. But what to do?

"That grave, uh?"

"I'm sure I know."

"All right. I'll page you when I have a couple of minutes to spare. I can't tell you when it will be though."

Tension drained from Sandy's face. "Thank you so much. I wouldn't be this intrusive if I didn't believe this was important."

"I know that."

The doctor snapped shut her briefcase and headed out of her office. "Call you when I can," she called out over her shoulder, rushing down the corridor to the lecture room.

*　　*　　*

In addition to her administrative duties, Ellen Smith's passion for psychiatry propelled her to teach classes one day a week in the lecture room of River Edge. Her seemingly endless supply of energy prompted Sandy and the rest of the nurses to call her the Bionic Woman. Women half her age couldn't keep up to Ellen in a twelve-hour period. Med students working toward degrees in psychiatry came to River Edge for hands-on training by one of the best. That was Dr. Ellen Smith. She believed in giving her students facts. You can learn knowledge from a textbook, she told her students, but experience was the key to unlocking a patient's mind. Being a psychiatrist wasn't about sitting in a comfy office listening to patients talk about their problems. It went way beyond theory. The brain has many appellations, which control different functions of the body. Frontal Lobes control the body's movement, speech, and some aspects of the patient's personality. As well as the gyrus modifies behaviors. It was imperative to know this information when dealing with a diseased mind, such as dementia and schizophrenia; you needed to be on guard for the unforeseen danger, especially patients housed on the fourth floor. The criminally insane, although intriguing to study, could be very life threatening. She knew this for a fact. Ellen was the only psychiatrist privileged to interview the notorious serial killer housed on the fourth floor named Roger Taut.

Dr. Smith rushed in to find all thirty of her students' noses glued to their textbooks. She liked giving her pupils surprise quizzes. Being alert at all times, in this unpredictable field, could save your life. Working in institutions such as this had unforeseen crises, and she wanted them prepared.

"Sorry, class, for my tardiness this morning. I got held up." She placed her briefcase on a long marble table in front of the room. Her eyes scanned the room's vastness.

"I've got good news: all of your test papers are marked." She chuckled at the usual moaning and groaning.

"You can all exhale now. Well done! You were all paying attention. The lowest score was 92 percent. I am impressed." Dr. Smith gave them a proud smile.

Shouts of "Hooray!" filled the air. Dr. Smith handed back each student's test paper, giving them time to review their results before continuing on with the next chapter.

Then the class was ready to press on.

"Open your texts to page 234: 'Consciousness and It's Severed States.'"

Mavern, one of the class clowns, shouted across the room to another classmate, "You should know all about this subject, Ken." Everyone roared with laughter.

"Come on, now," Ellen chastised, hiding her own smirk, behind her hand.

"Can't shame me, you were at the same party, buddy," Ken bellowed back.

"How can I forget? That place was rocking." Mavern quipped.

"Okay, gentlemen, since you both seem to be experts on the subject, Ken, why don't you read the first page and Mavern you can finish on the second page."

"How come?" Ken looked flushed.

"You heard me, Ken. Please begin reading."

The doctor smiled as Ken began.

"Drug Dependence. All of the drugs we have discussed have profound effects on the central nervous system, and an individual can become psychologically or physically dependent. The fact that students as young as eleven and twelve years are experimenting with drugs is of concern, not only because of possible damage to their still-developing nervous system, but because early involvement with drugs predicts a more extensive use of drugs later on."

"So, is that what happened last night, Ken?" Mavern quipped.

"Mavern, save it for later. You're in my class now, and I tend to take psychiatry very serious." Ellen peered over her metal frames.

"Sorry, ma'am." Mavern put down his head; eyes back to the page.

"This does not mean that the use of a particular drug invariably leads to the use of others in sequence. Only about one-fourth of the students who drank hard liquor progressed to marijuana, and only one-fourth of the marijuana users went on to try such drugs as LSD, Amphetamines or Heroin. The students stopped at different stages of usage, but none progressed directly from beer or wine to illegal drugs without drinking liquor first, and very few students progressed from liquor to hard drugs without first trying marijuana." (Kendal 1975; Kendal et al 1986)

"Let's stop for a second," Dr. Smith interrupted. "How many here believe that these statistics are correct?" A row of hands went into the air. "Jake, would you care to answer?"

"More."

"Could you elaborate on 'more'?"

"I mean, it's really sad, but there are way more addicted people than what these surveys have predicted or ever could predict. Not everyone gets clean. Nine—and ten-year-olds are drinking and drugging and having sex. Pleasure sensor located in the frontal lobe, which activates memory, which is also located in the temporal lobe. Ten-year-olds are showing up in AA and NA rooms all across the world. We have institutions like this one filled with patients that are trying to get clean. We've seen them wandering down the halls and strapped to beds because they're in the core of hallucinations. I believe alcohol and drugs given to an underdeveloped brain causes mental disease and long-term damage."

She smiled. "Jake, if I asked you to prove to me what you proclaim is true, how do you think you could do that?"

"Grab a blanket, Dr. Smith, and you and I will hang out down by the river on Blanch and Blue. You'll see what statistic are truly all about. There are the unfortunate ones that don't make it to the help line because they're too far-gone. Fine to read, sure. We sit here and get educated, but you said it yourself, until you're able to step inside the patient's mind, to explore what that person has experienced, then no matter what knowledge we have regarding the functions of the mind, we'll still be in the dark."

"How do you know this stuff?"

"I'm a recovered addict. Started at the age of ten by stealing my parents booze, then tried a little marijuana and that led to hard drugs. I couldn't get enough of the euphoric feeling. So now I spend my weekends down at the river trying to help some of these kids get clean."

"Thank you for sharing."

"Anytime."

"Mavern, finish it up for us, if you please."

"No, single personality type is associated with drug use. People try drugs for a variety of reasons such as curiosity or the desire to experience a new state of consciousness escaping from physical or mental pain or as a relief from boredom. However, one trait that is predictive of drug usage is social conformity. People who score high on carious test of social conformity, who see themselves as conforming to the traditional values of American society, are less apt to use drugs than those who score low on such a test. The nonconformist may be either a loner who feels no involvement with other people, or a member of subculture that encourages drug use. A study of teenagers identified several additional traits relating to social conformity that are predictive of drug use. Eighth and ninth graders, who were rated by their classmates, as lacking in ambition and having poor work habits were more likely to smoke, drink alcohol and take drugs. They were also more likely to start using these drugs early and to be heavy users twelve years later as young adults. (Smith 1986)

"Newcomb and Bentler (1988) have conducted a major study on the effects of drug use on young people. They concluded that a lifestyle that involves regular use of drugs also includes nonconformity to traditional values, involvement with other deviant or illegal behaviors and involvement and individuals engaged in such behaviors, poor family relations, few educational interests, experiences of emotional turmoil and feeling of alienation and rebellion."

"Thank you, Mavern. Homework. I want you to write a ten-page essay on the horrors of drug use and why. It can be from a personal experience or an educational side, your choice. Jake, I would write about what you know based on experience. This disease touches everyone. We have a ward full of patients that have overdosed one too many times and the result is permanent brain damage.

"So they have brain fry," Janet stated sadly.

"Yes."

"This assignment should be a breeze. I'll just use Ken's experience from last night." Mavern snickered.

"Don't you utter another word? At least I sort of remember being at the party. From what I hear, you were doing things last night you wouldn't want your mama to find out," Ken wisecracked.

"Dr. Smith, is there an open bed on that ward because—get ready—Ken is on his way!"

The students roared with laughter, including Dr. Smith.

"Okay, people"—she held up her hand for attention—"your assignments are due next Friday."

Students began waving good-bye to Dr. Smith as they left the lecture room in single file.

In the quiet, Ellen had just enough time to prepare for her next meeting with the board of directors. *No rest for the wicked,* she concluded.

* * *

Sandy tried to keep busy, but the previous evening's scenario at the beach kept replaying over and over in her mind. The barely suppressed danger in Franki's voice, the fear in her eyes . . . She'd have had to be dead and blind not to recognize the girl's torment. It was the same fear as the day she came to get Franki from Blake's office hours after she arrived. She wished now she'd shut up and let Franki tell her what was bothering her. She stopped dead in her tracks at hearing the sweet sound of Dr. Smith paging her to come to her office. Quickly, she finished with a patient and hurried to Ellen's office.

She knocked and walked in without waiting.

"I've got time for a quick coffee," said the doctor, holding up a cup. "Want one?"

Ellen filled the mug while Sandy sat in the cushioned beige chair in front of Ellen's desk.

"Actually, just hooking me up intravenously would be better, but a cup of caffeine will have to do."

"You sure look like tired today."

"I am."

"So, what's going on?"

"I'll start at the beginning and then you can tell me what you think."

"The beginning is always a good place to start."

"Franki didn't do anything wrong yesterday. We enjoyed ice cream at the Dairy Queen and went to the beach to watch the sunset. Loves my car, by the

169

way. We had the music blaring in the car, you know, like teenage stuff. I've never seen her so happy. Here comes the tricky part. She wanted to tell me something about Dr. Blake, but first I had to promise not to tell you. She was suppressing a whole lot of hurt and fear."

The doctor's eyes opened wide with alarm. "So . . . did you promise not to tell me?"

"No, I didn't. I told her if something was happening to her, it was my ethical obligation to report it. She completely shut down. I tried to make her understand that I have a legal responsibility for her well-being. That turned her right off. She told me to drop it, and she meant it."

"She retreated behind her impenetrable concrete wall again?"

"Yep, that's exactly where she went. What bothers me the most is why she wouldn't want you to know. Ellen, as far as she is concerned, the sun rises and sets on you. But when trying to get her to discuss Dr. Blake, I saw actual fear in those blue eyes. This goes way beyond an average resentment or hostility."

"And she did not want me to know?"

"Exactly. Why is beyond me."

"I know she hates to unearth those skeletons."

"It might be because of that."

"I believe I would know if she were playing me, trying to fool me into believing she's making progress so she can get out of here, seems absurd."

Sandy shook her head. "She's not playing you, Ellen. Franki's hiding a big dark secret that concerns Dr. Blake. Maybe she doesn't want to open up because you and James work closely together. It's a safety issue."

Ellen rubbed her forehead. "This does not sound good at all."

"How well do you know your colleague, Dr. Blake? I mean, what do you really know about the guy?"

"I know he's a good doctor with a respected reputation for bestowing the best medical care on patients. Outside the institution though, no one seems to know him. He doesn't socialize."

"Why not?" Sandy pressed.

"Likes to keep to himself. Although he donates a lot of money, he declines all invitations to social events. Professionally, he is a brilliant doctor. His bedside manner could use a little work at times, but for the most part, he seems to be professional and an all-right guy, though a little on the strange side." Dr. Smith chuckled. "But come on, we all get a little wonky working here. After a long time, this place can make anyone of us a little strange. I'll talk to Dr. Blake. Maybe he can shed some perspective into what's going on. Stop worrying, Sandy, Franki will be just fine."

"I hope you're right. The mere mention of his name sets her off."

"If something unethical is going on, I'll find out, promise. I don't want you losing anymore sleep over this. It doesn't look good on you. Sandy Miller, you are such a worrywart when it comes to little Ms. Franki Martin."

Sandy didn't reply, but her smile said it all. She loved the kid and wanted to protect her. Franki had enough emotional damage to deal with; she didn't need any more.

Chapter Twenty-Five

Once again, Dr. Blake made the journey up the dry dusty steps. He'd brought prepared meals from home so as not to cause any suspicion. His mother loved her food. He opened the door, trying not to inhale the bitter, familiar stench that made him retch every time. Even the open window didn't help this morning. He grabbed the bottle of Glade tough-odor eliminator and gave the room several long squirts. In bed, his mother lay motionless. He knew there was no way she could be sleeping with the load of excrement she'd accumulated down below. He softly touched her shoulder, giving her a little shake. She didn't stir. He shook her a bit more roughly the second time. No movement.

"Mother, it's time to wake up. I have your favorite breakfast: blueberry pancakes."

Nothing. *I'll pinch her and that'll end this silly little game,* he thought, squeezing her arm. Alma still showed no movement. Instant panic flooded through his veins, sending butterflies whirling around inside his stomach. Quickly, he searched for his puffer, taking two quick puffs. The last injection of his experimental drug must have backfired.

"Mother! Mother, come on and open your eyes," he pleaded. He placed his palm against her forehead. She was cool. Frantically, he searched for a pulse. None. He couldn't believe it. She was gone. He'd accidentally killed her while experimenting with the fatal toxin. Time of death, he suspected, was early last night. Rigor mortis had come and gone, meaning she'd been dead about twelve hours. Bodily fluids discharged from the corpse had stained the sheets with poison. She had peacefully passed on into a new world. He fell back into the wheelchair, sobbing into his hands, broken. She'd been right all along: he was nothing. A failure. Agony swept over him with an intensity he had only felt once before—when he watched his mother brutally stabbing his father to death. Now powerlessness clawed again at his soul, and he leaped to his feet, paced the floor, and pounded his fists against the sides of his skull. There was no escaping the painful wrath of failure.

The doctor had no idea how much time had lapsed; he was so lost in guilt, shame, and glory. He'd accomplished what no other scientist had even thought of using, knowledge not to save life but to destroy it. Some might call him a madman, but he knew he was brilliant. No one had created such a deadly poison merely from tree bark.

For what would be the last time, the doctor advanced to the dresser and took the items from the drawer. Mother would not be wearing a hospital gown today. This wasn't the first time he'd witnessed the stench of death, but it was one to which he would never get accustomed. Sometime during the night, her bowels had given way, painting her in foul excrement from the waist down. Tenderly, he began washing his mother, remembering the first time he'd caressed her body this softly. He brushed her frizzy white hair, setting a mauve butterfly barrette at each side. Then, he clad her in her favorite purple dress with the sheer sleeves and flowers embroidered across the chest. He struggled with zipping up the back of her dress, but he managed. Lastly, he forced open her mouth to insert her false teeth.

He would have to get to Morial sometime today. He needed the formaldehyde, methanol, and ethanol among other solvents used to embalm her body. It wasn't likely he could bring her downstairs. And he sure couldn't take her out to the yard for a burial. This room would be her resting place forever.

The room held an eerie silence as though a dark vapor were rolling in from nowhere. He stood over his mother, staring down at her bluish complexion, tears escaping his bloodshot eyes. This woman who had haunted him for all these years was gone. It was all over now . . . Then emotions began feeding upon him with the ferocity of vultures, ripping at the meat of their prey. His mother would never ever witness the applause of scientists the world over for his grand achievements. He clenched his fists, barely able to contain his fury. How dare his mother go to her death believing her only son was a failure! His soul shattered, he slumped back in the wheelchair, only inches away from the dead body. After some long moments of reflection into his pathetic past, he finally collected himself and got to his feet.

"Well, Mother," he said, planting his lips against her cold forehead, "what goes around comes around. Kill and be killed. Shame." He shrugged, walked out, locking the door behind him.

*   *   *

It was now one thirty in the afternoon; James Blake cancelled all his appointments for the rest of the day, using the excuse he was coming down with a bug. He stressed that he would not be available under any circumstance. For the first time, he shut off his pager. No members of staff found it odd that he had taken sick. It was that he remained in his office and never went home. That was what they found odd. He remained in his office engulfed in blackness, lights off and blinds drawn tight. The only sound was the low hum from the computer. He sat slouched in his big leather chair, eyes closed.

His mother's death triggered ugly memories of the past. The videotape played on in his mind: the verbal and physical violence between his mother and father, brutal. His father was a peaceful man. He only once retaliated against her. He enjoyed a drink of rye after a hard day of work. It was his father's way of escaping life with Alma. James sided with his father. The man could do no right in Alma's eyes. She despised anyone relaxing or having fun. Someone having a drink after a hard day in the mining pit was a low-down drunk. James wondered if it was the drink she hated or his father. She was a jealous, pitiful human being. She measured success by material gain. If the neighbors purchased something new, Alma had to have it too. Albert bought her nice things when he could afford it. Each time she was given a gift, it usually ended up on the floor from her fits of rage. When Albert couldn't take anymore, he retreated to his shop for some peace. There, he tinkered with building boats as a hobby.

August 1, a day James never would forget. Each anniversary sent shivers racing throughout his body like spiders spinning webs. Something that horrific could never be forgotten.

It was early Sunday morning, around seven thirty. His mother's voice boomed as she strode into his bedroom. She marched to the window and pulled wide the deep-blue curtain. James threw his arm over his face to protect his eyes from the blinding sunlight. There was no such thing as sleeping in late under Alma's roof.

"Get up," she growled. No, "Good morning, son, how was your sleep?" Just "get up." He leaped out of bed, rubbing his eyes. As he made his way to the bathroom down the hall, he could smell the sweet aroma of sausages and bacon wafting through the air. When he entered the kitchen, he could taste the tension in the air like sour milk. The steam rising from the stove made him think of rolling mist in a scary film, right before the evil Jason claims another victim.

His dad was sitting at the table drinking his morning brew. He gave his father a hug. His father's big mining hands patted his back and tousled his hair.

"Sleep well, son?"

"Great, Dad. Do you want to do something with me today?"

"It depends on what you want to do."

"Maybe you could help me throw the baseball better."

"Yep, we can do that." His dad smiled and gave him a high five.

"There is work to be done around here first," his mother countered.

"Like what, dear?" He winked at his boy.

"The lawn needs mowing, and the fence needs fixing."

"I just mowed it two days ago. And yes, I will fix the fence. Alma, relax woman. You're too tense."

"You didn't do a very good job on the grass," she spat.

"Okay, dear. I can mow the grass again just for you." He rolled his eyes, making James giggle. His dad quickly put a finger to his lips.

James knew why his mother was in a bad mood. It started last night. As a coal miner, he often worked late, and one of those days was yesterday. Alma didn't like that her pot roast had to be reheated in the microwave because she believed he was out having an affair with the floozy down the block. Being late only brought out the beast in her. As if his mother weren't enough to deal with, without his dad trying to juggle another woman. When he arrived home, all he wanted to do was to have a drink and unwind in front of the television, watching a little baseball. Alma had other plans. All of a sudden, she needed him to fix the spring in the toilet tank and the lock on the garage door. Sometimes his father refused. Couldn't she see how physically exhausted he was after digging coal for sixteen hours. His dad had warned James that if he ever took his side, he'd better not do it openly. He didn't want him being punished for coming to his defense when he wasn't around to protect him. She'd proven that in earlier arguments.

That morning was no different. James sat with his hand on his cheek, trying not to cry as the tension rose in the air like the dark clouds waiting to burst. Then she turned on Albert, nagging about the broken lock on the garage door, the unkempt yard and fence. Getting no rise from Albert, so she started screaming about money.

"Do you have money for the mortgage or have you spent it on that tramp down the road?"

"Alma, you know I have money. You ask me the same question every single weekend, dear."

"If you weren't such a drunk, I wouldn't have to ask." She slammed the cast-iron frying pan down on to the back burner.

"Now don't be like that," he said wearily.

"Like what?" she snapped.

"Alma, behave yourself please."

Her eyes bulged from their sockets like they were about to explode. She whirled around like a possessed demon.

"Don't you dare tell me how to behave? I live with a lazy, good-for-nothing, womanizing drunk. All you do is drink and screw that woman down the road. Nothing ever gets done around here."

"That's horseshit and you know it!" Albert rose up from the table; he'd had enough and was about to walk away when she pushed him hard almost knocking him over the chair.

"Woman, I am sick of you. You're mean and nasty all the damn time. I'm going out for a while."

"Like hell you are." She smacked her husband across the face.

"That's it. I have had it with you. You're like a rabid dog."

"Don't you dare call me a dog, you two-timing drunk."

Albert tried to leave the kitchen when he heard her crying. He stopped momentarily before carrying on. "It's not going to work this time." He walked out the door, slamming it hard behind him.

Alma marched into the living room, grabbed the Chinese vase from the coffee table, and hurled it at the television set. It smashed into a million shards of glass. Surprisingly, the television didn't smash.

Albert, still in the garage, hurried back into the house when he heard the crash.

"Now what did you go and do that for?"

"Because I damn well felt like it," she screamed.

James had sat silently at the table, wishing he were invisible. If he moved or made a sound, she'd turn and strike him again. He turned, seeing his father in the door, his face perplexed. James hated seeing his dad treated so badly. One time, he'd asked his father why he put up with it. Albert admitted the painful truth that her violent spells were getting under his skin. He wanted to walk out, but he stayed for James's sake. That answer made James feel awful like he was the one responsible for his dad's sadness. He was afraid to ask why he and his dad couldn't run away together.

"Alma, let's start over this morning. This fighting isn't doing any of us a lick of good." He walked back to the kitchen where his son was hiding his head in the crook of his elbow.

"Sorry, son."

James lifted his head, tears brimming.

"It'll be okay James." He rustled his hair again. "After we're finished, we'll play ball, promise."

James wiped his nose on the sleeve of his truck pajamas. "Okay, Dad."

Albert poured himself another cup of coffee and sat down again at the table to have breakfast. The peace didn't last long. Alma returned to the kitchen with a dustpan filled with shards of glass.

"Look what you made me do." Egging him on.

"You did that."

Albert refused to be drawn into another violent spat. In complete silence, James and his dad gobbled down a healthy plate of sausages and scrambled eggs before hightailing it outside. Father and son worked side by side, enjoying their moment together. He did not know it would be his last.

* * *

James's memories were free-flowing now as he sat in the dark, tears streaking his face. About a week later after that incident, his parents decided to go out for an evening of dinner and dancing put on by the Miner's Club. The occasion was a total disaster. A couple of hours after they'd left, Alma arrived home from the party alone. She stormed into the house slamming the door so hard James and the sitter jumped half out of their skin. She paced back and forth, ranting and raving about her husband's drinking and inappropriate socializing with the whore down the block. Sixty to seventy hours a week digging coal underground didn't give him the right to have a good time. There was no pleasing her, but it wasn't from lack of trying on his father's part. The one thing he was adamant about was not giving up his drinking. That was his only way of coping.

Albert was James's hero. As a young boy, he prayed to God every night that things would change. His prayers went unanswered. Things got worse and worse. The arguments grew louder and lasted longer. More things around the house got deliberately broken during his mother's rages. And James didn't understand why God wasn't listening to him. He was trying to be a good boy and do as he was asked. Why were he and his father made to suffer this cruel madness?

Albert was a hardworking, decent man. Quiet, never bothering anyone, was well liked by his neighbors and his buddies at work. He would stop to help anyone. The guys he worked with stopped by from time to time and have a little nip with Albert—out in the garage of course. The wives of the other miners didn't like Alma and thought her to be a mean-spirited person. They saw how Albert endlessly tried to pacify his wife. She gossiped about everyone while Albert never spoke an ill sentence against anyone.

James, at his wits end, begged God to strike down his evil mother. "Make her die," he implored, "because she's mean and hateful." She didn't love him or his father. At night as he lay in bed pretending to be asleep, he would fantasize being the hero that would save him and his father from the wicked witch. In his mind, they took amazing adventures and had such fun battling villains and winning. But with his mother around, no one could have any fun. He and his father were caught in the devil's web.

Then a wave of guilt would come to sit heavily on his shoulders. No matter what she did, she was his mother, and it was his loyalty as her son to love her. He remembered his father telling him that once a long time ago . . .

Now James's mind slid back to that awful Sunday morning. He and his father were sitting at the kitchen table eating their breakfast, laughing and joking like guys do. Alma was in the living room, cleaning up from another night's argument. Alma marched into the kitchen with the remnants of one more cherished gift she'd destroyed in a fit of rage.

"What are you two laughing about?"

"Just planning our day, dear." He winked at James. He had earlier told James that no matter what, he wasn't going to argue this morning. Today was going to be an enjoyable day spent with his son. Alma didn't appreciate his calm, indifferent reaction.

As the seconds ticked on, she became madder than a wet hornet. They were enjoying themselves while she had to clean up her mess. Just as his father lifted the cup to his mouth, she flew across the kitchen and smacked the cup out of his hand. Steaming hot coffee splashed down his shirt and on to his pants. Albert jumped out of his chair as hot coffee burned his skin layer by layer.

"What in the hell is wrong with you? You could have burnt the boy. No more, Alma. No more!" he screamed at her. He was so angry the veins stood out on his neck like cords of rope. James sat frozen to his chair. He had never before seen his father so furious. His mother stood with her hands on her hips, ranting and screaming horrible obscenities at his father, hurtful stuff that wouldn't be forgiven by a simple "I'm sorry." James couldn't stand it anymore. He yelled at her to stop. She lunged forward and smacked him so hard across the face, his head rocked.

His father took James by the arm and pulled him to his feet. "Get dressed, son, we're leaving." He marched them out of the kitchen.

"You stay right where you are," his mother ordered.

"No, James. Come with me and get dressed."

"I said stay where you are!" Alma grabbed James by the scruff of the neck and threw him onto the floor. He crawled for cover under the table as his mother tried to grab him. That's when something inside his father snapped like an explosion. His hardworking large hands wrapped around her thick neck and pushed her back against the fridge. Again and again, he smashed her head against the door. James peered out from his safe place beneath the table. His father's grip was like a vise. His mother was clawing at his father's strong hands, struggling for air. James yelled for his father to stop. Jolted back to reality by his son's tormented scream, his dad released his mother, and she sagged against the kitchen counter, spent.

James winced at recalling the next scene. It all happened so fast. His mother grabbed the five-inch butcher knife in the draining board. Back and forth, the blade whizzed through the air, cutting his dad deep across the back of his left hand and forearm. Blood gushed from the gaping wounds. James tried to scream, but nothing came. He wrapped his arms around his chicken legs and wanted to borrow his head against his chest so as to be spared the horrible events unfolding before his eyes. Alma went mental over and over as she plunged the blade into her husband's body. Blood was sprayed everywhere, the wall, the floor, her face, hair, and clothes. The coal miner who was his father—strong, kind, and gentle—slid silently down the wall to the floor. His mother brought down the knife one last time, thrusting the already stained blade deep into his heart.

James watched the blood trickling out his father's mouth. Her chest heaving hard, his mother turned to glare at James. Her eyes were as cold and intense as a cobra, eyeing a trapped rabbit. *You don't have a heart or a soul,* James thought. *You're a real monster sent from the other side like the evil bad guys in my comic books.* At that moment, his life changed forever. He was suddenly cold and shivering, and then realized he was sitting in his own urine. He couldn't remember wetting himself, but he must have because there was a yellow puddle streaming toward the chair. He tried to control his ragged breathing. He wanted to touch his daddy to see if his hero was still alive, but if he reached out, maybe his mother would chop off his arm. James couldn't remember any nightmare being as terrifying as this. He stared into the eyes of a cold-blooded monster; his heart was beating so fast and hard, he feared it would rend out of his chest. Then, his eyes jerked away and locked on to the knife sticking out of his dad's chest.

The sound of his mother's voice reeled him back. He was to get out from under the table and go get a couple of old sheets from the linen closet upstairs to wrap up what she called "a sack of shit." He wanted to scream at the top of his lungs, "Why did you kill my daddy?" Terror held his tongue. Even in death, she couldn't leave his father alone. Expressionless, she gave his father a final kick to the ribs, sending blood spurting from his mouth.

As ordered, James fetched and returned with two sets of sheets. By the time he came back down the stairs, his mother was already returning from the garage, carrying a blue plastic tarp. The knife lay on the floor beside his dead father. The monster that was his mother spread out the tarp. James stood watching as she rolled his dad into it. Taking the sheet, she spread it over his blood-soaked body. Then she had James helped roll the body over and over, encasing the body within the sheets. Next they wrapped the tarp around tightly before tying it with yellow-knotted rope. His mother positioned on the chest side, and he at the feet; they lugged the body to the garage. It hit the cement floor with a dull thud. James stared down at the sad heap containing his father. His hero was gone.

"Soon this no-good bastard will stink because of the summer heat and decomposition," said his mother. Their secret would be safe for another couple of hours; the garage was a couple degrees cooler than the house.

"We'll get rid of him at nightfall."

"Why, Mama? Why did you do this to Daddy?" Tears were streaming down his cheeks. Scowling, she walked over and slapped him across the side of the head.

"Straighten up or you'll be next. Now you'll do exactly as you're told. You won't be getting away with nothing now."

"Yes, Mama." Head bowed, he brushed away the tears with the sleeve of his pajamas.

They headed back inside through the side door.

"No one will see anything come nightfall. If those snooping neighbors just happen to peek over the fence, we're burying the family pet."

Back in the kitchen, James could not only smell the bitterness of blood cloying in the air, he could taste it.

"Help me clean up this mess." She demanded.

Armed with a few rags, sponges, and buckets of hot soapy water, the two went to work. The hot water mingling with the blood turned pink, swishing large smears of foamy pinkish blood across the floor. Bile rose to the back of James's throat, and he stifled gagging, wanting to puke. Covertly, he wiped his tears. His ear was still ringing from the last smack. In circular motion, James washed and rinsed away his hero's blood. Two hours later, the entire kitchen smelled and sparkled of Pine-Sol and Javex Bleach. The secret of this gruesome crime was washed clean. No one would ever know.

She told James to take a shower. He knew it wasn't to freshen up; it was to wash away the evidence of a murder. While standing under the warm spray, suddenly, his whole body began to tremble, and he leaned over the drain, puking. He clenched his hands into angry fists and sobbed. He should have tried to save his father. He should have tried to do something; instead, he'd huddled beneath the kitchen table, afraid, a coward . . . Scrubbing frantically at every inch of his skin with a nailbrush, still he could not wash away the guilt.

He was told to put his soiled pajamas into the paper bag left on the countertop. His mother had her shower after him. The blood-soaked clothes went into the fireplace, leaving absolutely no trace of a crime. Three things were destroyed that morning: his father, soiled clothes, and his fragile mind. James knew it then as he knew it now: he would never be the same.

Covered in a terry cloth robe, his mother approached him as she came out of the bathroom.

"Tell no one, James. If anyone asks where your daddy is, you are to tell him or her, he ran off with another woman. Say it, James. Let me hear you say the words."

"My daddy ran away with another woman." He coughed the words from his throat, fighting back his anger.

"That's just fine, son. Now go and play in your bedroom for a while. Mommy needs to lie down for a rest."

That night, they dragged his father's body out to a wooded area in the back of their house and buried him in a shallow grave. James could never let go of the guilt and shame. Animals had better funerals. What happened was never talked about again. When his mother was away working, James would sneak out to the unmarked grave and sit beside a heap of dirt. He could smell the rotting. James didn't tell his mother that he had to keep throwing more dirt over the grave because of the animals digging and feeding off the dead carcass that had been his father.

James never forgave himself for his father's death. He still felt responsible. *I was a coward,* he chastised himself for not jumping into save his father's life. Nothing could convince him otherwise.

Year after year, he was haunted by the same nightmare. He could see his father struggling to claw his way out of the dirt. James could hear his father's anguished cries for help like a soughing on a cold wind. He stood beside his father's makeshift grave; his feet felt rooted to the earth as though the tendrils were wrapping themselves around his father's corpse. His mind would scream, "Do something!" Then he would suddenly wake up drenched in sweat.

* * *

Around midnight, James made his last journey up the dust-covered steps to embalm his mother's body. This would be the evil one's final resting place.

CHAPTER TWENTY-SIX

A couple of days after embalming his mother's body, James willed himself back into his work, trying to forget. He was sitting at his desk, carefully reviewing the prognosis of one of his patients when he was startled and then annoyed by the knock at the door. He wasn't expecting anyone. He crossed the room and opened the door.

"Hi, do you have a couple of minutes?" Ellen asked.

"I'm in the middle of reviewing charts, Ellen. Why, is it important?"

"It might be. I'm not sure."

He stepped aside so she could enter.

"Can I offer you something to drink?"

"No, thank you." Ellen settled into the visitor's chair in front of his desk.

"So, how can I help you?"

"It's about Franki Martin, I'm afraid."

"Has something happened?" His muscles tensed. What she had on him could ruin his career and his life.

"I had a conversation with Sandy, Franki's primary caretaker. The topic of concern that was brought to my attention was you."

"What about me?" James could feel his stomach muscles constricting into one large knot.

"The mere mention of your name triggers a violent reaction in her."

"Such as?" He frowned, his face mystified.

"Extreme anger, fear, and language that would top men's locker rooms. I am here to find out why. I was hoping you could shed a little light on this for me."

James leaned back in his chair, looking thoughtful. "I know she doesn't like men or authority."

"What makes you think that?" Ellen asked.

"It's not what I think, it's how she behaves around me."

"Is there something about how she behaves that's disturbing to you? I haven't received any report from you regarding this perplexity."

"I didn't feel I needed to write a goddamn report every time a patient exhibits antisocial behavior. That's why they're in an asylum! They're all nuts!"

"James, take it easy."

He took a few deep breaths, wiped away the beads of perspiration forming on his forehead, and looked chagrined.

"I'm sorry, Ellen."

"Are you all right?" Ellen looked bewildered.

"I'm tired, that's all. Anyway, Franki says whatever is on her mind. Maybe it's the shock value she enjoys. Like the one time she asked me how she could go about getting special favors, if you know what I mean?"

"I'm not entirely certain I do know, James. Why don't you explain to me what it is that you do mean?" Ellen kept the alarm out of her voice.

"Of course. I was taking a cell count to make sure her liver enzymes were normal when she started making sexual advances toward me. I ignored it, and when I was finished, I sent her back to her room. Ellen, surely you don't believe I would . . . do something so disgusting and unprofessional as to lay my hands where they don't belong? Is that what she is accusing me of? If it is, I deserve to know this instant." He leaned forward, face flushed.

"Calm down, James. No one is accusing anybody of doing anything. I'm just trying to find out what is going on. And why she hates you so much?"

"She's a miserable brat who's never had any nurturing discipline. That's why she doesn't like me. My god, Ellen, she's little more than a child who has been running amok since her parents died."

"Yes, Franki Martin has problems. I agree."

"Whew, for a minute I thought—"

"Okay, so it's nothing you've said or done. Now it's time to talk to the source. Sorry for the intrusion, James. But next time one of my patient makes an inappropriate action toward you, I'd appreciate knowing. All aspects of their behavior and treatment must be recorded. You know that."

"Ellen, there's no reason why you should bring this up to Franki. The poor girl has had plenty of problems to deal with. I understand why she's the way she is. That's why I didn't bother entering the misdemeanor. There was no harm done. Franki was just using drastic measures to get out of here."

"You're probably right, but—"

"If it happens again, I'll tell you, and we'll both talk to her. Okay? We must do whatever is necessary to help this young lady move forward in her life."

"Thank you, James." Ellen rose to leave, then, "James, you haven't given her any extra doses of sleeping aid, have you?"

"No! You made it quite clear, Franki Martin is your patient."

"This morning when I stopped by to see her, she was again very withdrawn and morose. More than usual."

"That's odd. Her tox came back normal, correct?"

"The reason I'm asking is because you were seen coming out of Franki's room again. I just wondered why you were there."

"Stopped in to say hello. I am her medical physician too."

"I need to ask you to stay clear of her until I get to the bottom of her hatred. Something still isn't right here." Ellen walked out of his office, closing the door behind her.

*   *   *

Ellen was on her way to confront Franki when her name blared over the PA system to come to room 332. It was an emergency. She would have to talk later with Franki at her three o'clock appointment. At the moment, Franki was either in-group or sleeping. Ellen couldn't remember. Her caseload of 150 patients at River Edge, group therapy for her outpatients' program, and her students from university who attended her weekly lectures kept the doctor enormously busy. The demands of her job seemed to be growing higher, and there weren't enough hours in a day.

But in spite of her workload, Ellen resolved to continue searching to find answers to Franki's bizarre hatred toward Dr. Blake. Like Sandy, she felt Franki was special. Victims of sexual abuse have on-the-edge licentious behavior patterns. With Franki's streetwise history, why shouldn't she believe her colleague? Hustling was a huge part of Franki's history. Franki and Jazz were close buddies. On good days, Franki was seen joking around with male nurses and orderlies on the second floor. The girl had a natural ability to pull people in, especially males. There were never any hints of anything sexual going on, just harmless flirting to make the time pass more quickly. But according to James Blake, Ellen had overlooked something. She doubted it. Victims of sexual, physical, and emotional abuse had certain risky behavior patterns. Perhaps Franki was so angry with Dr. Blake because he rejected her, as he claimed. Yet Franki displayed no such pattern with anyone else. Obviously, Blake wasn't Franki's type. In fact, Ellen chuckled to herself; Blake was no one's type!

The steel doors slid open, and Ellen stepped out on to the third floor. She entered the room 332 in time to see two orderlies struggling to restrain a young muscle-bound man named Luther. Something had spooked him. According to the quick report, Luther had suddenly gone ballistic. He'd clawed and punched the screen window until the tips of his fingers and his knuckles turned raw. His head was split open from bashing his skull against the cement wall. Luther managed to do this much damage deliberately and undetected until noted by the nurse on rounds.

Ellen ordered the male orderlies to strap him down so she could administer 5 cc of Diprivan. Ellen poked him with the sharp needle and waited a few minutes until the sedative took effect. Five, maybe six minutes later, they wheeled him down to Blake's office. Ellen walked alongside the stretcher, applying pressure to his head—trying to stop Luther's profuse bleeding. Blake worked his magic, stitching the wounds quickly and efficiently. A half hour later, Luther was back in another room, closer to the nurse's station.

* * *

No one would have guessed the cordial and cooperative James had a growing resentment against Ellen. Inwardly, he seethed with fury at the betrayal of both bitches. Ellen was not only a nosey busybody; how dare she question his professional integrity and tell him what to do as if he were an errant schoolboy. Franki had done the unthinkable. She had told on him.

He'd warned Franki what he would do if she squealed on him. Now she would pay. He began plotting how he would permanently silence her. Indeed, she left him no choice. If Ellen continued with her probing, she just might begin to doubt him and start to believe Franki. That couldn't be allowed. Absolutely, not a hint of suspicion must fall on his shoulders.

This was all Franki's fault. All she had to do was shut her mouth and take it like the whore she was.

* * *

Franki, having a nap in her room, was totally unaware of the kettle of fish that was brewing. Nor did she know the wheels were in motion for someone to pay the ultimate penalty for Sandy's indiscretion.

Chapter Twenty-Seven

That afternoon, Ellen and Sandy made a scheduled time to meet in Ellen's office. She assured Sandy that Dr. Blake didn't know why Franki hated him. Ellen told her about the sexual advance Franki intentionally made. Sandy flat out refused to believe Blake's side of the story and vowed to prove his allegations were false. Ellen understood how emotionally attached Sandy was to Franki. That degree of closeness could cloud her judgment. Sandy was adamant that Franki did not and would not make a pass for special favors. Ellen had to admit not only did the story seem farfetched, but therapy pointed complete contrary to what Dr. Blake was contending.

*   *   *

At three o'clock, Franki was reminded she had an appointment with Dr. Smith. Her brain felt sluggish as molasses, and she really wasn't up to discussing her life. Franki headed slowly down the hall, scuffing her feet the whole way in her nightgown and slippers. She hadn't the energy to get dressed.

Ellen greeted Franki like always, with a big smile and eagerness.

"Care for a glass of iced tea to take outside with us?"

"Nothing, Doc."

"Are you sure, sweetheart?" Ellen noted the lack of emotion on her face.

"Yeah."

"Let's take a walk outside then, shall we?"

Ellen believed Franki's spirit would brighten once she hit the summer breeze. The sun was gleaming bright, with a light wind fluttering the foliage. The two started down the cobblestone path of the Three-Mile Garden. A quarter way around the trail, Franki stopped, asking to take a seat on one of the wooden benches. The heat was already at twenty-seven degrees Celsius. They decided to sit on a bench, shaded by a big maple tree, whose canopy would protect them from the direct rays. Newscasters warned people of the dangers of melanoma, a skin cancer caused by overexposure to the sun's rays. It was hard to believe, Franki thought, that something so beautiful could do such damage.

Franki turned to face Ellen. "What is it you wanted to talk to me about?"

"First up, how are you doing, kid?"

"I'm okay."

"How was the evening at the beach?"

"Great! Sandy is so cool. She drives a real hot car too."

"A BMW." Ellen smiled. "So how are things without your pal, Gertrude?"

Franki laughed. "How do you think, Doc?"

"Better?"

"Yes. I'm not looking over my shoulder waiting for the snake to strike."

"I'm sorry about the way she treated you, Franki."

"At least you did something about it. Trust me, I appreciate it."

"Behavior like that is unacceptable and calls for immediate dismissal."

"Yeah, and it should be!"

"Franki, if you were being threatened by someone, would you tell me?"

"Depends, Doc, I have a lot of respect for you, so don't get me wrong, but there are certain evils that you can't protect me from." Suddenly, a window seemed to shut in her eyes.

"Like what?"

"I don't know." Franki shrugged her shoulders and fiddled with the loose thread on her pajama's hem.

"Franki, I need to ask you something."

"Shoot."

"How is your relationship with Dr. Blake?"

Franki stiffened and looked away. "He's an asshole."

"Besides that. Specifically, what is it you don't like about him?"

"Doc, what in the hell did Sandy tell you?" Franki's eyes were hot as coals when they met Ellen's.

"What makes you think she told me something?"

"Because you've never asked me about that asshole before, that's why?"

"Okay, I'll be straight with you."

"Up front is how I work."

"Sandy came to me with some concerns about your relationship with Dr. Blake. She believes it goes deeper than a simple resentment. But I haven't found anything in our sessions that indicates how deep this resentment goes."

"Pretty deep. Why did she have to open her big mouth? Christ, I trusted her, and she goes flapping her gums to you."

"You say you respect me?"

"Of course I do, Doc."

"And when I found out what Gertrude had done to you, did I not do something about it?"

"Yeah."

"So why would you believe that if something not right is going on between you and Dr. Blake that I wouldn't do something again to protect you?"

"I never said that."

"In so many words, yes, you did."

"Whatever." Franki held up her palm. "I'm tired. I want to go back to my room."

"Nice try. I have you for another thirty minutes."

"What do you want from me?"

"The truth."

Dead silence filled the air between them while Franki's heart brimmed with fear. Doc was getting too close to the truth about Blake raping her. If she told Doc, for sure he would kill her, and there would be nothing Sandy or Doc could do to stop it.

"The truth about what?"

"Why don't you like him?"

"Cause he creeps me out. Sandy is making a big deal out of nothing."

"I went to see Dr. Blake earlier."

Franki's heart leaped into her throat, and her eyes stung in their sockets. "Why? Why? Jesus! And you guys wonder why I trust no one. You went to see the jerk-off without talking to me first?" She got up from the bench and paced.

Ellen remained seated. "I need to know, young lady, if you are safe?"

"I'm fine!" Franki yelled.

"That doesn't sound 'fine' to me."

"If everyone would just fuck off and stay the hell out of my business when they're not invited, everything would be fine. Got it?"

"It's my job to be in your business, young lady. So, I don't have to bugger off."

"I don't even have to talk to you."

"No, you don't, but I know you want to get better."

"I will get out eventually, you know."

"Yes, I know. Are you going to tell me what's going on, or do I have to give you his version?"

"Fuck, fill your boots. You seem to know everything anyway."

"Did you make a pass at the doctor to try to get out of here earlier?"

Franki started laughing. "What? Are you shitting me?"

"No, I haven't lied to you yet."

"I wouldn't make a pass at that ugly prick with your body."

"Thanks a lot. I don't think I just received a compliment from you."

"You didn't. Doc, he told you I made a pass at him?"

"That's what he told me."

"Holy hell. More like the other way around."

"Want to repeat that."

"I said nothing. Can I go back to my room now?"

"Twenty-two minutes." Ellen tapped her index finger on her watch.

Franki told herself that no matter what she had to keep her cover. It was better to dance with the devil she knew than the one she didn't, and telling Doc the truth would be risking dancing with the devil she didn't. She could live with Blake sexually violating her, but she couldn't live without Ellen, her mentor and friend. But getting honest with people in authority had always cost her big-time. As pissed off as she was at Sandy for opening her big mouth, she wasn't prepared to let go of the only two friends she had in this place. Jazz was just a nice temporary distraction. They were only passing through each other's lives.

"So nothing is going on that I should be concerned about?"

"I'm okay, honest."

"Talk to me, Franki. Please. I can see something is wrong."

"The only thing that's wrong is you guys thinking that something's wrong when it's not. I don't like the idiot, and it's my right to like whoever the hell I want. I don't always need a fucking explanation for feeling however the hell I want to feel, Doc. Now change the subject or I'm going back to my room, twenty-minutes or not."

"Guess I just got told."

"Yeah, you did." Franki offered Ellen a hand up "I'm ready for a walk now."

"Let's finish the path, shall we?"

"That should take the rest of the twenty minutes."

"You're a brat." Ellen took Franki's hand. "Before I forget, I have more clothes for you in my office."

"Wow, thanks! You do know I appreciate all you do for me, don't you?" She cocked her head to the side.

"Yes I do."

The two women strolled along the path, taking in the warm sun and beautiful surroundings.

Minutes later, Dr. Smith heard the faint sound of sniffling.

"Want to talk about what's upsetting you?"

"I miss my parents."

"It's healthy to grieve such a devastating loss, Franki. You were yanked out of a safe, loving home and thrown into a nightmare with strangers."

"Yeah, but crying won't change a damn thing." She swiped at her tears with the back of her hand. "My parents are still dead, and I'm living in a nuthouse."

"Franki, no one can change yesterday's tragedies and that really sucks."

"Yeah, it sure does, Doc. My whole goddamn life sucks. I want my old life back."

"I know your parents would be proud of you for trying to make your life better. Franki, only you can control your destiny."

"How in the hell do I do that?"

"Remember the shovel."

Dr. Smith always had a way of making Franki laugh.

"You can do this. Get rid of those ghosts that keep haunting your peace of mind. I have faith in you. Sandy has faith in you. Look at what you've accomplished so far. I bet when you arrived here, you didn't expect to be getting educated, let alone your writing published, did you?"

"No." Franki laughed. "I knew I could tell a story, but no, I never expected a publisher to buy my work. Hell, I'm just telling stories about my life. I never thought it was worth shit, and they're paying me money for it."

"Life has a way of surprising us when we least expect it."

"No argument there, Doc."

"Your parents are so proud of you, Franki. I hope you know that."

"I guess I do."

Franki strolled quietly beside Ellen, rummaging through her past for one more story of horror to share with her shrink.

"I guess you want to hear another gory story?"

"Can't hurt you." Doc smiled.

"One question before I get started, okay?"

"Shoot."

"Do you get off on this stuff?"

"Oh yeah, I love it." Ellen rolled her eyes.

"Just asking. This was when I was living at the Wilkins. Susan, foster bitch; sewed together a pair of pants—bell-bottoms, they were called. At lunchtime, she had me try them on to see if they fit. It had been raining that day, so the ground was pretty muddy. After my lunch, I skipped back to school wearing my new bell-bottom pants, proud as a peacock. After the bell rang, we all lined up to go back inside. This bully girl asked me where I got my pants. I told her my foster mother, Susan, made them special for me. She laughed like something was funny, which I thought was strange. Like not all her dogs were barkin'. Anyway, she intentionally jumped in a mud puddle, splashing mud all up the side of my pants. I wanted to kill her, but I knew I couldn't take her physically. She was way too tough. I asked the teacher for permission to go to the washroom. I tried washing the mud out, but the more water I splashed on my pants, the worse the stain got. Now it was all smeared into the fabric."

Franki's eyes clouded over. The memory was still painfully fresh. "After school, I went home to show Susan what the bully did. If I had known what that bitch was going to do to me, I would have never gone home. Without warning, man, she grabbed me by my ponytail, pulling me to the bedroom. She slapped me across the face, I don't know how many times, before demanding I strip down. She threw old clothes at me, screaming the whole time about how ungrateful I was, that I didn't deserve nice things. She grabbed my soiled clothes off the floor, throwing them at me. Manhandled me all the way to the laundry room in the basement. I was so upset. I couldn't stop sobbing. I tried to tell her how sorry I was, but she wouldn't accept it.

"We had one of those old-fashioned washtubs beside the real washing machine. She filled the tub with scalding hot water and forced me to wash my pants by hand. The entire time yelling at me about how selfish I was. I could hardly see from the tears streaming out of my eyes. The water was way too hot to stick my hands in. Seeing me struggle, she walked up behind me, grabbed both of my arms, and shoved them into the scalding water. I remember screaming as I fought to pull my hands back out. After that, she beat me all over and told me to get to my room. She didn't need to tell me twice. I ran them steps as fast as my legs could carry me. That night, I went without dinner. You know, Doc, she was right. I had no business wearing those pants without permission. But I wasn't the one that splashed mud on myself. Does that make any sense to you?"

"Franki, do you feel responsible?"

"I should have asked her first."

"Did she give you any indication that you were not supposed to wear your new pants that day?"

"No!"

"Well then? What she did was not discipline. She tortured you, sweetheart. She put your little hands into scorching water. Making you feel unworthy of nice things was wrong. Dead wrong!" Dr. Smith's lips tightened in emotion.

"Doc, why did she hate me so much?"

"I don't believe it had anything to do with you. Some people are pure evil. I don't believe you were her first victim either."

"Doc, this is going to sound pretty twisted, but knowing that I wasn't the only victim of her hatred kind of makes me feel better."

"Why do you say that?"

"I wasn't the only one that hell hag hated."

"I can understand that. No child deserves to be raped, yanked, jerked, shoved, kicked, slapped, pulled, burned, beaten, sworn at, or talked down to at anytime."

"She told me so often how I made her sick. I started to believe it."

"Susan Wilkins is a black widow spider, and you were the fly stuck in her web waiting to be its next meal. It wouldn't have mattered how good you were. She would have found a reason to hurt you. There is absolutely no excuse for what she and that pedophile did to you."

Franki's eyes filled with tears.

"What would you have done under the same circumstance?"

"If you were really muddy, I would have brought a towel to wrap around you while you changed out of your dirty clothes at the door. That way you wouldn't track mud through the house. Then I would have asked what happened and would have believed what you said. Taking your dirty clothes to the basement to be washed would follow that. Just like your mom would have done, Franki. When you get confused about right or wrong, allow what your mom or dad would have done to enter your mind."

"I tried that, but they told me I was a spoiled brat that needed to be shown the righteous path."

"I'm telling you now, you're a great kid! Loved deeply by those who know you, hint, hint."

Franki smiled through her quivering lips. "I know my mom would never have done any of the things that miserable hell hag did to me. Really, you wouldn't have thought of spanking me, Doc?"

"You didn't receive a spanking, Franki. You were deliberately beaten. You didn't cause the mud on your pants. Even if it had been your fault, for god's sake, it was only wet dirt. You didn't murder anyone. No, I would not have spanked you."

The windows in Franki's eyes were opening. Ellen saw hope.

"Those two are as sick as they come," the doctor continued. "Normal minds don't whip a child until she bleeds, not to mention sexually torture a young, vulnerable girl. He's a sick pedophile that should be incarcerated for the next hundred years or until therapy has proven to work."

"Is that why you're pushing me to sign that affidavit paper or whatever you call it?"

"Yes. It's about time those two are held accountable for what they did to you. Jail will look good on both of them. Franki, we have laws to protect our children against predators like Susan and Gary."

"Those are really nice words, Doc, but the law didn't save me then. I wasn't protected the way I should have been, was I?"

"No, you weren't, and you have no idea how much that upsets me. Franki, you hold the power if you sign that paper. You can put them away for a very long time."

"How long?"

"Long enough for them to know who's in charge of her own life. How would that feel?"

"Pretty damn good."

"That's my girl." Ellen patted her shoulder. "You will have to go to court and testify, but no worry. Sandy and I will be right there the whole way. With us on your side, you're guaranteed to win the war. You, my dear, will be walking into the light, and Susan and Gary Wilkins will be crawling into a dark hole where they belong."

"Yeah Doc."

"Franki, you have to know there is nothing I wouldn't do for you."

"Get me out of here then."

"When you're healthy enough to leave, freedom will be knocking at the door. In the meantime, you're going to do everything in your power to help yourself."

"When will court be?"

"The process will start within the next couple of months. The prosecutor has already arranged the paperwork when you're ready to sign, that is." Ellen smirked. "Witnesses will have to be called. I believe you are not going to be the only one on the stand telling your story. Patience, my friend, these things take time."

"I have enough of that."

"Have you heard the expression, 'What doesn't destroy you, makes you stronger'?"

"I should be super girl then." Franki smirked.

"There is nothing that can break your spirit, Franki. I've heard what disasters you've been through, kid. You have what it takes. Remember, you survived on the street, and you will survive this too." The doctor took Franki's face into her aging hands and wiggled her face gently.

"Can we go in now?" Franki asked, wanting to shy away the subject.

"Certainly, lead the way."

Along the beautiful Three-Mile Garden's pathway came the flower bed; full of roses in every color, along with white lilies, deep violets, orange carnations, tall sunflowers, tiny daisies, and flowers Franki never heard of before, but planned to relieve her curiosity by finding the answers. The garden was absolutely breathtakingly winsome.

"May I?" Franki asked.

"Go ahead, pick whatever flowers you like."

Choosing a yellow rose, Franki caressed its softness against the side of her cheek, inhaling its intoxicating scent.

"Am I ever going to be normal?" She gave Doc a sideways look, afraid of the answer.

"There is no such thing as 'normal.' All I can tell you is that one day, you'll be living life on your terms. You'll decide how you want to live, be owner of your own soul."

Franki gave a little grin. "I have dreams, you know."

"I'm happy to hear that. I believe you're already living your dream, Ms. Author."

"Sometimes I lie in bed going over every word in the letters I've received from the publishing places even the ones that reject my stories, and I can't help but laugh out loud like some crazy girl."

"Why? Because you just can't believe something good can happen to someone like you?"

"Something like that. It's weird. All of a sudden, an idea will pop in my head, and it doesn't leave my brain until I get it down on paper. Like a haunting ghost with a twisted sense of humor."

"I think that's excellent."

"If it weren't for 'big mouth,' I would never know I could write."

"So you think Sandy has a big mouth." Ellen chuckled. "And a big heart when it comes to you, don't you think?"

"Yeah. I just wish she'd lighten up."

"She would be belly-laughing if she heard you say that."

"Probably."

"She adores you, kid."

"The feeling is mutual."

The two were a football field away from the door.

"Franki, where can you see yourself, say, in five years?"

"I want my fairy tale to come true."

"What's that consist of?"

"I want to be married to a real nice guy, have a career and two children. I would never treat them mean in any way. I call it the perfect life like you read in those romance novels. We would live in a fair-sized home with three or four bedrooms and a beautiful garden. I don't want a picket fence though. I've seen enough fences to do me three lifetimes. The man I marry is going to look like Steve. You remember me telling you about the baby's father, Steve? A sensitive, good-looking, warm-spirited man. He would love me no matter what. Two kids, a boy and a girl. If we couldn't have our own, we would adopt from foster care. We would love them like they were our own. I would protect them like a mama bear protecting her cubs." Franki paused, looking for Doc's reaction. The doctor nodded approvingly.

"Well, I'd drive a hot car like Sandy's. Writing books all day would mean I'd be home for my kids. My man would be in construction. Like they say, opposites attract. I would find my sister, and we would never lose touch again. She'd buy a house next to us, and we would live happily ever after."

"And if you're not careful, Franki Martin, you just might get your dream."

Franki looked puzzled before catching on to what Doc meant. She started laughing. "I hope you're right, Doc."

"You are so gifted, young lady. I have had so much pleasure working with you. But, in your dream, you forgot to mention that you would be meeting with my family once a week over dinner."

"Thanks, Doc. I hope one day I can feel the same about myself as you see me. And, of course, I'll have you and your husband over to the house for dinner. Is it really . . . possible?"

"I believe it is. All you need is faith, you already have the talent."

Dr. Smith glanced at her watch.

"Out of curiosity's sake, Doc, why didn't you trust me before to be outside by myself?"

"The fences around this place aren't high enough."

"What do you mean, not high enough?" She smirked.

"I didn't trust that you wouldn't find a way to scale over the fence in a weak moment and hightail it out of here."

"Like running away?"

"Yep."

"I wouldn't have run away from this palace, Doc. I like it too much."

"Who are you trying to kid?"

"The day I leave this fine establishment, it won't be high-jumping a damn fence. It will be through the front gate, walking out on my own to a newfound freedom."

"Yes, you will. Come on, let's go and get your clothes from my office."

"Can't wait, Doc."

On their journey back to the office, Dr. Smith suddenly turned to Franki at the door and rested her hands on her shoulders.

"My dear, sweet child, I wish I could show you at this moment what you can become in the future. The sky is the limit. I promise, Franki, if you deal with the demons of the past, no one will be able to rob you of your future. I believe in fairy tales. Dream big, learn large, stay strong, and you will make it. But most importantly, love with all your heart and trust with all your soul, and life will be filled with unimaginable joy." Dr. Smith wrapped her arms around Franki like a warm security blanket. "The owner of your soul."

"You're getting soft on me, Doc."

Excited, Franki carried her box of clothes back to her room.

*   *   *

Ellen closed the door behind her and sank into the chair behind her desk. Absently, she tapped her pen against Franki's file folder. She wished her intuition felt as confident as her words. Franki was doing so well, beyond all expectations. But she was withholding something from herself and Sandy. That meant it had to be serious. Franki's emotional state was still fragile. It wouldn't take much for the Big Bad Wolf to blow her house down and shatter her progress.

What could she possibly be hiding?

CHAPTER TWENTY-EIGHT

Back in her room, Franki wandered aimlessly around her bed. She wanted to be mad at Sandy for opening her trap but couldn't. Sandy had been too kind to her. She felt guilty for not telling Doc the truth, but how could she? Blake was unpredictable evil. He had threatened to do serious harm if she squealed. All he had to do was inject her with something untraceable that would make her a vegetable or, worse, dispose of her body and say she'd run away. It could be so easy for him. Her mind spun horrible image after horrible image. Franki plopped onto the bed and flipped through the pages of *The Best of Women Quotations*. Even it couldn't hold her attention. She rummaged for a piece of paper and sat at her desk. Words began forming on the page like sprinkles of magic. Her deepest thoughts were coming to light, no longer buried in shallow graves of darkness and confinement.

The Cage

The body on its own is very shallow
A broken heart isn't so hollow
My scars run as deep as an ocean
The pain inside of torn emotion
The stonewall is collapsing in
The depth of misery I have nothing to give
Alone, I wonder why?
Hearing the screams of anguish, I cry
Outside the wall is a fiery hell
Filled with pain and suffering I have felt
How do I break through these steel bars?

Who will mend all my many scars?
In this cage, screaming to get out
My brain is saturated with so much doubt
No one understands what I see inside
Only broken promises and angered lies
I dwell here in my cagelike box
Please pity me, undo the lock
I need out of my suffocating cage
To walk free outside my rage
This time, I will not fail
Don't leave me to become bitter, old, and frail inside my emotional jail.

After writing her poem, Franki lay back against her propped pillows, arms folded across her chest, satisfied with what she had just expressed, but those were just words. In the real world, she had two good friends, but nothing else in her life had changed. She was still being abused by an authority figure. The man with the many changing faces whom no one knew, but her. He was the secret puppet master of her life—and how many other patients? He'd pull a string, and she danced to his liking. This place was her cage.

Oh, she was so grateful for Sandy and Doc. She knew she would never have gotten this far without them. It was because of them, she learned to respect and love. She had not learned forgiveness. Never would she forgive the horrible people that deliberately hurt her. It baffled her how someone could feel two emotions from the opposite spectrum of life in the same time frame.

She had to get out of her own head. Putting her poem into the desk's drawer, Franki decided to wander the halls in search of something positive to write about. It was emotionally draining always writing about her darkness. She still wasn't the social butterfly that some of the nurses expected. Franki liked the safety in solitude. She avoided looking into the hollow eyes and the haunted faces of the lost souls that couldn't change even if God performed a miracle. No plan in mind, she would let her feet lead the way.

Sandy had invested in paper, scribblers, pens, pencils, and everything a writer would need. It didn't take long before Franki's pages were half full of ideas, dreams, tortured emotions, and hope. Franki spent hours rereading her poems and validating her emotional pain. Franki knew she had some kooky thoughts, but she damned well wasn't crazy. The one character trait Franki did believe about herself was that she had a huge heart like her mother. She and Sandy shared conviction in their poetry. Poetry made her feel like she was in control of her own mind. No one could violate her thoughts; that's why she shared a special bond with Sandy. The spirit of positive thinking rang loud and clear when they were together.

As she strolled along the corridors, a moment of absolute clarity struck her like a lightning bolt. She no longer had to suffer at the hands of anyone, including Dr. Blake! It was time to tell. For the first time, Franki was suddenly willing to go head-to-head with that monster. She was done suffering. It was time to stop Blake from hurting her and anyone else. Dr. Smith needed to know what her trusted colleague was doing, if she was going to help her get better. Franki needed to tell if she was ever again going to truly trust another human being. At that moment, Franki felt flooded with that faith Doc talked so much about. She finally had the magic key to unlock her cage.

Her mind cartwheeling, Franki's pace quickened. Doc and Sandy were right; she was no longer alone. She pushed fear aside, felt strength coursing through her veins. She had survived the big bad street for months at a time. She could deal with that deranged pervert. Control was about taking back what was rightfully hers. Franki felt anxious and excited at the same time. Two emotions colliding against a force, she knew in her heart, she could win against. The sexual abuse was over. She would tell Doc right away. She walked quickly along the corridor, basking in the idea of Blake the Monster getting fired. It happened to Gertrude; it could happen to him, too. *Time to clean house,* she thought. She tried to imagine what it would be like to live without constant fear. A smile crossed her lips; she was ready to learn. Franki looked down at the hard-covered book Sandy had bought her. The smiling girl on the tome looked like she felt. Today, she would have a beautiful ending to a horrible beginning . . .

Without warning, Franki was jerked backward, the force knocking the book out of her hand. Shocked, she spun on her heels to see who had put their hands on her. There stood one of the mental patients. As Franki bent down to pick up her book, the woman shoved her down and grabbed it from her hand. Franki stared up at a grin that was devious, not friendly. She was taller than Franki, and her dress revealed a toned slender frame but, missing two teeth, one on the bottom row and one top front tooth. The rest were yellow with decay along the gum line. The woman taunted Franki by swinging her book almost close enough to catch it. Franki rose to her feet and extended her hand to retake possession.

"Give it back? It's mine." Trying to sound assertive.

"No, mine." The woman clutched it tightly to her chest, rocking on her heels.

Although at times explosive, Franki hated confrontations. This nutcase seemed pretty scary. Franki wondered if she was going to go off like a total lunatic. *Stand for something or fall for everything,* she thought, willing strength into her soul. Again, she reached out for her property. The woman's eyes told secret stories that Franki didn't want to know. *She might have brain damage,* thought Franki—whether from an accident or birth—from the way she looked, spoke, and acted. Franki held out her hand a third time.

"Give me my book back. It doesn't belong to you. Get a book from the sitting area. That one's mine." Franki's voice went up a decimal.

"Now mine. Holds secret powers." She held up the book, taunting Franki some more. Franki's patience was wearing thin.

"Give it to me, now!"

The woman held out Franki's book as if she were going to hand it back, even letting the cover of the book touch Franki's fingertips. Before Franki could take it, the woman snatched it back, grinning like the Cheshire cat; only it had a mouthful of sparkling clean teeth.

"That's it! If you don't give it back this instant, I'll smash the rest of your rotten teeth down your throat, you ugly bitch."

The woman bolted. Franki didn't hesitate; she charged after her, full speed.

"Stop, you stupid bitch!" Franki yelled.

The woman was rounding the corner when Franki tackled her to the speckle-tiled floor, landing with a loud thud. Over and over, they rolled, Franki landing a couple of good punches to the woman's rib cage. Then the tables turned, and Franki was pinned beneath. Mouth gaping wide, the woman looked ready to take a huge bite out of Franki's face. *She's not human*, Franki thought. Squirming her hips, Franki managed to throw her off before the woman had the chance to sink her rotting teeth into her face. Franki closed her eyes and launched a full-on punch that landed in her opponent's face. Franki heard bones break, not knowing if it was her hand or the psycho's face. At that moment, she didn't give a shit either. The woman was about to eat her face like Hannibal Lecter. The impact of Franki's punch knocked the woman flat on her back. Her primal scream of pain resonated throughout the corridor. The patient's hand flew over her nose, blood gushing like a tiny red waterfall between her fingers. The second she saw the blood; she started wailing like a wounded cat caught in a mousetrap.

Franki got to her feet and waited for the cavalry of nurses and orderlies to show. No point in running. The psycho would tell, and she sure as hell wasn't going to lie to Doc or Sandy. Besides, it wasn't her fault.

She swiped the book off the floor and began wiping at the bloodstains.

"Stupid bitch. I told you to give it back. Fuck! How could you be so stupid as to believe it had powers? It didn't have to end like this. All you had to do was give it back. Jesus, you must be retarded or something."

She suddenly froze. His voice came from behind her. Instantly her heart pounded into a full gallop. Every inch of her wanted to make a run for it. But she knew it would do her no good. They would find her.

* * *

Franki had no way of knowing that Dr. Blake had arranged for this to happen. This would prove she was violent and out of control. Franki watched Dr. Blake examining the woman's bloody face. A red stream was running down her chin and through her fingers. *So much blood,* Franki thought. *She must be a bleeder.*

Blake turned and glared at Franki before pressing his expensive silk handkerchief to the woman's face.

"What did you do to Gloria?"

"I hit her 'cause she wouldn't give me back my book." She glared back at him, holding up her tome.

"She hit me," Gloria squealed.

"You shouldn't be stealin' my shit that don't belong to you. It wasn't your fucking book." Franki turned back to face Blake. "And she tried to take a bite out of my face like some mental defect." She held Blake's gaze and refused to be the first to look away. She was prepared for his anger but, not the cool amusement that appeared in his eyes and lifted the corners of his mouth. In that instant, Franki knew without a doubt, she'd pay dearly for this incident that wasn't her fault. That somehow, Blake would manipulate things to his advantage. He had her by the short hairs, and they both knew it!

"Go to your room. I will deal with you later."

Franki left the scene as the doctor helped the crying woman to her feet. Passing Franki going the opposite direction rushed a nurse and an orderly. The orderly went up the hall to retrieve a wheelchair while the nurse assisted with applying pressure on Gloria's nose to slow the bleeding. Franki wanted to roll the bitch right off the face of the earth. Instead, she marched back to her room.

Halfway, her march turned into running the rest of the way to the nurse's station. She slid to a stop and burst into tears.

"Hey, what's wrong, dear?" Nurse Allan asked.

"Where's Doc or Sandy?"

"Sandy is making rounds right now, Franki. Dr. Smith might be in her office. I'm not sure."

"Can you please page either of them for me please. It's urgent!"

"Is there anything I can help you with?"

"I just told you, are you deaf? Page Sandy or Doc and hurry up! It's a matter of life and death!" Surprised, Nurse Allan just stared open-mouthed at Franki.

"Fuck! Will you, hurry up!" Franki hollered.

"Franki, that's enough of that intolerable language. Now please go and wait in your room. I'll try and page Dr. Smith."

"Do it and hurry up or I am – so dead!"

"Is there anything I can do just in case I can't locate Dr. Smith?"

"No no no please, you've gotta get Doc or Sandy." Shaking her head in desperation, Franki crossed the hallway to her room.

Franki sank onto her bed and wrung her hands. Dr. Blake sure as hell had her now, and there wasn't anything she could do about it. Unless someone found Doc or Sandy before he got to her, it would be checkmate. The only way she could win now is if angels dropped down from the sky and carried her away on their magical silver wings. *Wishful thinking.* She fidgeted on the bed, trying to come up with something. Then it dawned on her, and it was so simple, she almost laughed. Run as fast as she could to Doc's office. She leaped off the bed and tore down the hall as if pursued by a dangerous, slobbering pit bull. Patients stared wide-eyed as she raced by.

Upon reaching Ellen's office, she banged as hard as her fists could stand, heart pumping like a jackhammer. Only silence answered her knock.

"Where are you? Where are you?" Franki called out again and again. No one answered. No one came.

The core of Franki felt a peculiar weakening in the fiber of her soul. The threads that held her together were unraveling. She was, pure and simple, screwed.

*　　*　　*

Back in her room, Franki paced back and forth, pissed off at herself. Why didn't she just get help when psycho stole her book? Why did she have to take matters into her own hands? It all happened so fast; she didn't have time to preplan the outcome. And she sure as hell wasn't expecting Dr. Blake to be lurking around the corner. *He probably watched the entire fight,* she thought. Or was she nutso for even thinking that? Christ, she must be going psychoparanoid . . .

Then came the dreaded sound of his voice over the PA system. She considered hiding but knew it would only make things worse for her. Judy came in on the second page.

"Franki, did you not hear Dr. Blake's page?"

"Yes, I heard his fucking page."

"What's wrong with you?" Nurse Judy rolled her eyes and shook her head.

"Have you ever heard the expression, 'I'm fucked'? Well, guess what? I'm fucked."

"Is there anything I can do for you, Franki?" Consternation became concern.

"No, it's too late." Franki shuffled slowly across the room and stepped out into the corridor.

"Franki, I just tried again, and Dr. Smith isn't answering. I'm sorry." Nurse Allan said from the nurse's station.

"It won't matter now," Franki murmured, barely above a breath.

*　　*　　*

Sandy was with a male patient when she heard the second page. She suddenly felt a cold chill clawing up and down her spine as goose bumps spread up her arms. The nurse expediently finished her checkup and then left his room. She headed quickly to the nurse's station. What was going on? Blake was not to have anything to do with Franki's care.

"Judy, did Franki acknowledge the doctor's page?"

"Yes, she did." Oddly enough, Nurse Allan said, "Franki came to the station earlier in a big panic and demanded she get you or Dr. Smith immediately."

"Why did she need one of us?"

"Not sure." She shrugged. "After the second page, I asked her if there was anything I could do to help. She told me she was dead—and fucked—and that it didn't matter. Sandy, she looked scared."

"Did you page Dr. Smith?"

"Yes, but according to this schedule, she's out of her office for the rest of the day."

"Damn. Why didn't someone call me?"

"We knew you were busy, Sandy, with that rather difficult patient. I was reluctant to interrupt you. We all know how every once in a while Franki has these little meltdowns."

"Not this time."

Judy's eyes widened with alarm. "I'm sorry. I thought she was, you know—?"

"No, what? Playing?" Sandy shouted.

Judy sank back against her task chair. "Yeah . . . sort of. Sometimes, Franki gets wild when she doesn't get her way." Her pretty face crumpled in bewilderment. "Is there anything I can do?"

"Pray! And keep trying Dr. Smith. Just by chance she happens to show up."

"And if we connect, what is it you want me to say?"

"Tell her to get back here as fast as she can. Franki's in real trouble."

*　　*　　*

Franki walked into Dr. Blake's office, slowly and methodically closing the door behind her. Two male orderlies stood on each side of the door, arms across their broad chests. From their stern expressions, they might have just arrived from military boot camp.

"Have a seat, Franki." Dr. Blake instructed.

"I'll stand."

"I said, sit down." He pointed at one of the two visitor's chairs in front of his desk.

Franki plunked herself down.

"Franki, you have been a very bad girl."

"I . . . I . . ."

"No more excuses. I don't want to hear them."

Franki kept glancing over her shoulder, both intimidated by the two men blocking her only exit to freedom and relieved by their presence. Blake wouldn't dare try anything harmful with them in the room.

Blake cleared his throat, fingered the knot on his perfectly aligned royal-blue tie and began. "We do not tolerate any form of violence at this facility. Dr. Smith has gone out of her way to defend you to me. She tried to convince me that you could be trusted. I told her that I knew differently. She did not accept my expert opinion. Your attacking Gloria today is my professional vindication."

Never in her entire life had Franki felt so demoralized. Had there been a hole in the floor, she'd have gladly jumped into it.

"I'm not violent. I was trying to get my book back don't you get it? That mental defect is a thief. She was the one trying to pick the bloody fight."

"Don't you speak to me in that tone, young lady. You need a lesson in how to respect other people. Do you realize the damage you've done to Gloria's face?"

"Gloria?"

"The woman you beat up in the hallway. You really are trying to play dumb with me, aren't you?"

"I'm not playing anybody, man. I didn't know her friggin' name, okay! But . . . please, will you just listen to me for a minute? I didn't start the fight. She pushed me down and stole my shit. What was I supposed to do, just let her have it?"

"So you decided to beat the tar out of her over a lousy book of poems. I hope it was worth it?"

"They were my special poems. I wrote them. And they're good poems, not 'lousy,' you moron. You write a friggin' poem and tell me how easy it is." What the hell? There was no point in trying to talk nice to the son of a bitch. He had already made up his mind; it was all her fault.

At the knock on the door, Franki swiveled in her chair to see a wonderful sight—Sandy's face peering into the room.

"Doctor, sorry for the intrusion. I'm looking for Franki Martin. She must have forgotten she has an appointment with me and—"

Relief flooded through Franki. She rose from her seat and tried to catch Sandy's eyes, but the door wasn't opened enough to allow Sandy to look fully around Blake's office. But Franki knew Sandy had seen her.

Blake interrupted promptly. "She's busy. Cancel her appointment," Dr. Blake said, motioning the orderly to close the door.

"But—" The door slammed in her face. Astonished, Sandy stood staring at the closed door. Something was wrong. Why else would Blake be so rude and shut her out like some vacuum salesperson. She had to find Ellen, and now!

*   *   *

Blake walked around his desk and positioned himself on its corner.

"That was interesting." He looked toward the door.

"I have an appointment with the nurse," she protested. "You're in deep shit when Doc finds out you cancelled my appointment just because you wanted to yell at me over some stupid fight that I didn't start."

"I don't like the way you behaved today. It really displeases me when one of our resident goes around jeopardizing the safety of others. We do not tolerate premeditated acts of aggression."

"Premeditated my ass! She started the goddamn fight!"

Blake shook his head. Looked at the orderlies and tapped his temple. *She's nuts.* The orderlies nodded like mechanical robots.

Franki relented and shrugged in defeat. What was the use of trying to defend her side of the story? The doctor gestured, and the orderlies rushed to her side, one orderly to her left side and the second orderly to her right. Franki glanced apprehensively from one to the other.

"Hey, what is this?" she cried out.

The larger of the two orderlies held out a straightjacket. Franki's body began to shake in alarm.

"No way! No, get away from me!" she screamed. She wiggled and struggled and fought with all her might, trying to prevent them from restraining her. "Please, I didn't do anything wrong. Don't believe this bastard. Please don't do this to me, I beg you!"

The orderlies were efficient and quick. Before she could have recited "Jack and Jill went up the hill," Franki was laid out flat on the doctor's carpeted floor. One orderly held her shoulders, the other her feet.

Dr. Blake kneeled on one knee, removed a needle from his doctor's jacket, and stabbed the point into her perforating artery. Silently, the curare drained from the barrel. Franki threw back her head, ready to scream, when what Blake said next knocked the breath right out of her. He whispered in her ear, "I told you what would happen if you told."

"No, I didn't," Franki sobbed. "You've got to believe me—"

"Okay, gentlemen, take her to the fourth floor. By the time you get her there, all the fight should be gone, right Franki? Gentlemen, don't forget you have my order to follow and see it through, no matter what!"

Franki went wild, kicking and hollering all the way to the elevator. A couple of nurses came out of their patient's rooms to see what the ruckus was all about. Nurse Lisa looked shocked at seeing Franki in a straightjacket being dragged down the hall by the two orderlies while screeching at the top of her lungs for someone to help her. Her flushed face was drenched with sweat like she just stepped out of the shower.

By the time they reached the fourth floor, Blake was correct, Franki had no fight left. She looked almost catatonic. The orderlies carried Franki along the corridor until they reached and entered the assigned room, ordered by Dr. Blake.

"What are you doing, man? Take off the jacket at least," said the smaller of the two orderlies.

"Hey, soft heart, I'm following orders," the larger man countered.

"This isn't right, Bruce. Look at the condition she's in. She couldn't hurt a fly. This is so wrong."

"You're new here. You'd be surprised what a small little thing like this could do if given the chance. Better toughen up, Gerry, if you're going to keep working here. Remember, man, these people aren't right in the head and can snap at anytime. I've seen it. A girl, a few months back, no bigger than this one, stabbed a nurse right in the arm. Man, there was blood everywhere."

"I refuse to believe that this little girl is capable of anything real bad."

"I know differently."

The two men strapped her chest and ankles securely to the bed. Franki was silent as they went to the door. Gerry glared at Bruce and voiced another objection before leaving the room.

"I still don't think what we were ordered to do is right. Strapping her down fine, but the straightjacket . . . I don't know, man."

"You want to go argue with the doctor's decision?"

"No. Don't make it right. She isn't some kind of animal. Look at the size of her. What is she a size zero?"

"Don't know, don't care. In case you haven't noticed, they're all head cases in here."

"That's cruel. They're human beings getting treatment."

"Don't get too attached. This job will work you over good. Block it out of your mind."

"How?"

"Mind your business."

There came the metallic clank of the door being locked, and the room fell silent in which Franki was the sole occupant.

The ride down to the first floor was also quiet as Gerry pushed the ugliness of Franki Martin strapped to the bed, encased within a straightjacket, from his mind.

Chapter Twenty-Nine

Sandy was livid at the doctor's gall. How dare he shut me out like that! Hadn't even let her finish her sentence! She no longer suspected that Franki was in danger; she knew it. This was not legitimate professional behavior. This was a person who had something to hide.

Judy didn't have to ask. From the furious expression on Sandy's face, bricks were going to hit the fan. Good ol' sweet-tempered Sandy was totally pissed.

"I haven't stopped checking for Dr. Smith," she said at once.

"Please don't. And if you do reach her, please page me right away."

"So what happened? You did go to Blake's office, didn't you?"

"Yes. I told him, I had an appointment with Franki, and the door was slammed in my face even before I could finish my sentence."

"He did what? Why?"

"That's what I would like to know. Dr. Smith will be informed about this, I assure you."

"What a jerk."

"I don't think that's all he is." Her eyebrows creased. "I mean, what harm would it have done to let me speak to her? I saw her trying to make eye contact. Anyway, I have rounds to make. Let me know if you hear anything please, Judy."

*   *   *

Sandy checked periodically throughout her shift to see if Franki had returned from Dr. Blake's office. When she hadn't, Sandy was completely mystified. Five o'clock and her shift had finally ended. Sandy had a good mind to go to Blake's office and give him a piece of her mind. She decided against it. He was one of her superiors. Better to let him and Ellen lock stethoscopes over this. Ellen was guaranteed to win the battle. Sandy's worry thermometer hit red when she heard nurses from the first floor up to second had not heard or seen Franki either. Sandy decided to take a walk through the Three-Mile Garden. Maybe Franki was out there somewhere, cooling off. No such luck! She wondered if she might have run away but then dismissed that thought just as fast as it came. She'd bet a week's wages; Franki was not willing to risk the respect she'd earned. Taking one last search of the second floor, reluctantly, Sandy left for the day.

The sky was beginning to cloud over; the city was in for a good downpour. Driving home with the top up and the Dixie Chicks cranked, she tried to surrender to their upbeat tempo. Even they couldn't drown her concern. She'd call the second floor later on to see if Franki had returned to her room. But why didn't Franki come when she paged her? Maybe she was just making much ado about nothing. Franki was probably fine, had to be fine. Why wouldn't she be? Sandy wanted to call Ellen at home but, knowing how draining those board meetings were, decided against it. Ellen deserved time with her husband to do what couples do.

Upon closing the door to her house, Sandy's nose picked up on the stale smell of last night's dinner of fish and chips. She opened all the windows and went overboard with the Tangerine Febreeze. After eating leftover salad, she stood at the patio doors, eyeing the sky. Bruised clouds were scudding across the expanse, heavy as a cast-iron skillet. In the far distance, thunder rumbled and lightning snapped. Nature emulating how she was feeling. She downed the last of her vodka and orange juice and reached for the phone, dialed 555-1298, and pushed aside her wild imagination. The worst-case scenario was Dr. Blake had sent Franki back to the third floor. Ellen would reverse that in short order.

A male voice picked up.

"Hello."

"Hi, Trey. It's Sandy."

"Sandy, how are you? It's been a while, girl."

"Been real busy. You sound like you were sleeping?"

"Sorta."

"Busted."

"What's up?"

"Have any plans for the night?"

"Is this an offer I won't refuse?" Trey joked.

"Get real."

"Whoops, sorry. For a second, I forgot I was talking to the sexually repressed Ms. Miller." He laughed.

"So, do you have plans, smart-ass?"

"You mean like building an ark? Have you seen it outside? Batten down the hatches, a mean storm is on its way."

"It's a little rain, wus. Want to go for a drink?"

"One?"

"Doubt it."

"Sure. Can I drive your car?"

Sandy busted a gut. "Why is it every time I ask you out for a drink, you want to drive my car?"

"I won't even dignify that with an answer. You've seen my beaten-down Toyota with a mind of its own."

"Buy a new one."

"Sure, right after I go to the bank and get a big fat loan that I can't afford to pay back."

"I told you, I would lend you the money."

"No, I don't borrow money from respectable friends like you. So . . . are you going to let me drive your car?"

"Yes, if you move your lazy butt off the couch to come out with me."

"Nothing gets by you."

"Shut up and go brush your teeth, splash a little cold water on that sweet face, and be ready."

"How long are you giving me?"

"Fifteen minutes."

"Yes, ma'am."

Sandy hung up, grabbed her purse, quickly applied lipstick, and ran a hand through her shiny brunette hair. She stopped at the front entrance, contemplating her umbrella. Trey was right; it was nasty out there. Raindrops the size of pennies splattered on the concrete. To hell with it—she dashed to her car, trying to dodge getting soaked.

CHAPTER THIRTY

The next morning, Sandy awoke with a double-whammy boomer of a headache from too little sleep and the pitcher of Piper's Ale. She and Trey closed the Mile-High Pub at around one forty-five. Time flew and before she knew it, the bartender was yelling last call. She enjoyed the company of her friend more than she cared to admit. Because if she did, that would mean she would have to acknowledge how lonely she was. The two had met in med school. Sandy went on to finish her nursing, but Trey couldn't handle the pressure and went on to be a free-spirited artist and bartender at Legons, a popular spot in the middle of the city. He said it wasn't such a polarity. Doctor's mixed pharmaceutical cocktails; he mixed booze. He considered himself somewhat of a shrink. Who better than a bartender to listen to the sad tales of woe, night after night, as the clientele staggered up to the bar in search of solutions to life's problems, and not charge a dime?

Sandy staggered to the shower, plucking sleep out of her eyes. She stood under the cool spray longer than usual, hoping it would help freshen her mentally and physically. Her tongue felt as if it were stuck to the roof of her mouth permanently. She opened her mouth wide, letting the cool spray rinse away the taste of last night's stale beer. Donning in her pink-flowered uniform, she quickly slurped down a glass of orange juice. Hearing the click of the toaster, she grabbed the slice of whole-wheat toast, smeared it with blueberry jam, and headed off to work.

The weather had changed drastically since last night. The grass sparkled like diamonds in the morning sunlight. It was already twenty-four degrees Celsius. Sandy thought about taking down the car's top, but this morning, it was too much like work. Taking another bite of toast, she slid into the driver's seat and sped down the road. Luckily this morning was a quiet ride; her head hurt. Looking into the mirror, she licked the smeared jam off her lips and reapplied a fresh layer of pink lipstick.

The instant her nurse's practical shoes stepped through the facility's glass doors, Sandy felt a knot tighten in the pit of her guts. It wasn't last night's careless fun either. She tried to push the fear aside, telling herself she was being silly. She would find Franki nestled safely between the sheets.

The air-conditioning felt cold compared to the outside's climbing humidity. Tossing her belongings into her locker, she didn't squander any time heading to the nurse's station.

"Where is Franki?" she asked immediately after checking her empty room.

The two night shift nurses Ruth and Selma did not give her the answer she needed to hear. Panic tightened around her throat and squeezed like a boa snake.

"Not sure, Dr. Blake never said. He stopped by here last night, telling us that we wouldn't be needing Franki's chart."

Sandy's heart began to pound wildly. "Did anyone think to ask him why."

"No," Ruth said, with an edge to her voice. "I didn't know we were supposed to challenge a doctor's decision."

"I only found out Franki wasn't in her room when I made my rounds," Selma explained. "When I came out, Dr. Blake was behind the counter, taking her chart. We could hardly tell him he couldn't have it."

"And he never said why?"

"No. He just held up the chart and disappeared down the corridor."

"Why, Sandy?" Ruth questioned.

Sandy shook her head and held up her hand. "Later, okay? Right now, I want you to page Franki to come to the second-floor nurse's station. If she answers the page, call me. If one of the nurses on a different floor happens to answer the page with any information, inform me immediately. Understood?"

"Sure, Sandy, but what's going on?" Selma asked, eyebrows closing into a unibrow.

"I don't know yet. I'm going to the third floor to check with the staff there. I can't press upon you both how imperative it is that we find Franki somewhere in this facility, today."

"Sandy, this is sounding really scary." Ruth's eyes were growing wider by the minute. "I'll start searching on this floor."

"Good idea. And Selma, you safeguard the phone in case someone calls with information to the whereabouts of Franki Martin."

"Got it! Sandy, the next shift should be here in about twenty minutes. I'll ask if anyone knows anything about Franki Martin. Someone should know something. I believe the worst case circumstance was that she was moved."

"I hope you're right, Selma. If you hear . . . anything—"

"I'll let you know pronto. Promise."

Sandy rushed to the elevator. Hearing the bell, she stepped inside the steel trap and pushed button number 3. Once the doors slid open, Sandy hurried to the enclosed workstation, where its monitors viewed every room on the ward. Nurses Karen and Stewart looked up from their paperwork. It was their responsibility to make sure the shift coming on duty knew what to expect: Who was highly agitated, who was calm, who received what injection of what and who was ready for the second floor.

"Hey, what brings you to this floor?" Stewart Marcel smiled. "Needing a fix of real action?"

Sandy didn't return his cheerful greeting. "Any paperwork on Franki Martin?"

"No new faces came in last night. One gone MIA?"

"Yes, a Ms. Franki Martin."

"Isn't that the little blonde who was transported to the second floor some weeks ago?"

"She's the one."

"Then why would she be brought back here?" Stewart and Karen exchanged glances.

"It's a long story."

"We've got a couple of minutes, girl. Sandy, you don't look that great."

"I don't feel like myself."

"So, what's up? Has the young girl split, and you're not suppose to tell us?"

"Nothing like that, Karen. Franki never showed up here last night, at all?"

"All monitors, darling, say no-show. Sorry, hon."

"What's the scoop?" Stewart pressed for information, getting comfy in his chair, anticipating the dirt.

"Who was the last to see her?" Karen inquired.

"Dr. Blake."

"Why have you not asked him, woman?"

"Long story."

"Ah, someone resents the good doctor."

"Call it personality conflict." Sandy grinned. "Do me a favor and ask the next shift coming in if they'd seen or heard anything. If they have information, please have them inform me." She turned to leave.

"Gotcha. Oh, Sandy—" She looked back at them.

"Stop worrying. Franki Martin is fine. She might be in the company of a good-looking boy. Did anyone think of that logical explanation?" Stewart winked. "Boys will be boys."

"Thanks for the tip, Stewart. I'll check."

Sandy searched every crevasse of River Edge, starting with the third-floor stairwell and worked her way down. She searched stalls in bathrooms, broom closets, rec rooms, and outside along the Three-Mile Garden. Then she asked Jazz and his pals if they'd seen her. No one had seen Franki Martin since yesterday morning. The situation was looking grave. Everything inside of her told her that it was about to get a whole lot worse.

Stopping at the first-floor nurse's station, she received the final news she didn't want to hear: no one had seen hide or hair of Franki. Sandy decided to check out the fourth floor. She had to be somewhere in this facility. Residents didn't vanish without a trace. Sandy and Franki had a strong bond; she'd promised to always be there for the young girl. She intended to keep her promise.

*   *   *

The fourth floor had an eerie, empty feeling. The only people roaming its highly lit corridors were janitorial staff. Security was a number 1 priority on the special and unpredictable ward. Doctors and nurses worked inside the plastic bubble for their own protection. Two licensed guards with Browning 9 mm strapped to their hips stood watch at the exit. Sandy choked down a swallow of dry air and forced her feet to keep moving. In one sweep, the guards took her in with precise x-ray vision. *They probably,* she thought, *know the brand name of my unflattering underwear.* She scanned the area; no one was working inside the bubble. They were all out on rounds. She then came upon a two-inch-thick iron door, bolted for security reasons. Important security reasons, because the patients behind this big iron door were highly dangerous and not to be trusted. So, who was manning their post? She was just about to venture back to the second floor when an orderly came striding toward her. A pictured nametag dangled from around his neck.

"Excuse me. Do you have a key to open this door?" She pointed.

"Sorry," he shrugged. "No one is allowed in there without a permission slip, written up by Dr. Blake or one of the psychiatrists."

"Do you know if anyone has been admitted in there within the last twenty-four hours?"

"Sorry, I don't know that either."

"What do you know?" Sandy snapped. "Oh, I'm sorry, I'm searching for someone who's missing. I need to know if she is behind that big door."

Her concerned tone didn't faze him. Again, he shrugged his thick shoulders.

"Fine. Who else do I see about getting in there?"

"Dr. Blake is the only one I'm aware of. As to the other shrinks, I don't know what their schedules are. Now if you'll excuse me, my shift is over."

"Thanks anyway." She walked away, discouraged but not hopeless.

"Sorry, I couldn't be of any help." He yelled, heading toward the elevator.

"Not your fault, you just work here," she muttered.

She took the stairs back to the second floor. She was in desperate need a cup of coffee. Maybe that would kick-start her sluggish brain. She checked her watch: seven fifty-six; Ellen would be in her office in a few minutes—she hoped.

*   *   *

Reaching for yesterday's paper left in the staff room, Sandy quickly scanned the news, but nothing diverted her mind from Franki's disappearance. She stared blankly at the black ink scrawled along the newspaper, fingertips drumming the table's surface.

Then came a pleasant thought. She imagined herself storming into Blake's office, grabbing him by his nicely pressed shirt and tie, and shaking the living daylights out of him until he fessed up to what he'd done with Franki, her little pal. She knew the ramifications of doing that, but the image pleased her mind.

Time was passing ever so slowly; each minute felt like five. She couldn't sit idle any longer. She'd taken her coffee and chance it that Ellen would show up early for work. It happened on occasion. She knocked a couple of times. Silence answered her question as it had for Franki the day before. Sandy leaned against the wall, sipping at her coffee while she waited. Franki's disappearance was far too grave for Ellen not to be notified immediately even if it had to fringe on her private time. If she didn't arrive soon—

Approximately, five after eight, Dr. Smith's quick light steps came around the corner, heading for her office door.

She raised her eyebrows, surprised to find Sandy hovering at her door.

"Good morning. Is that a cup of coffee for me?" Dr. Smith asked, eyeing the Styrofoam cup in Sandy's hand.

"I'm afraid not." She showed Ellen the empty cup. "I really, really need to see you."

"I have until nine thirty before my first appointment of the day arrives. This must be your lucky day."

"Ellen, she's missing," Sandy blurted, almost in tears. "I can't find her anywhere."

"You're going to have to be more precise."

"Franki! She didn't come back to her room yesterday, and this morning, she still hasn't shown. I've searched everywhere, inside and out. The last to see Franki Martin was Dr. Blake. I know she was in his office. I saw her and then the door slammed in my face—"

"Have a seat. Tell me everything you know from the beginning."

Sandy sat down inhaled a couple of deep breathes. "Yesterday," she began in a trembling voice, "I heard Dr. Blake paging Franki over the intercom."

"What time was that?"

"It was about two thirty."

"That's odd. Franki Martin has been removed from his caseload until further investigation as to why she has such a huge resentment against him."

"Well, I think there is a whole lot more going on. I believe he's being deceitful about Franki making a pass at him. Come on, look at her, and look at him. I refuse to believe she would run away despite her past record. Yesterday, I talked to Nurse Judy at the nurse's station, and she informed me that yesterday, Franki demanded Nurse Allan get a hold of you or me right away. Allan tried, and when the second page went out, Judy went into Franki's room to tell her in case she was sleeping. Franki was visibly upset. And when Judy said she would keep trying, Franki told her to forget it, it was too late, she was 'fucked'—excuse my language. Something has happened to her, something bad. I mean, she never answered my page, and no one has seen her since yesterday. I can feel a real sense of dread like she's calling out to me. I know it sounds ridiculous. This morning, I talked to Selma and Ruth, and they told me that Dr. Blake came by last night, took Franki's file, and said they wouldn't be needing her chart any longer."

"Damn it, he was told to stay away from Franki."

"Ellen, I've checked for Franki on every floor, in every room and broom closet, bathrooms, stairwells. She is gone, vanished. I have asked all the nurses. No one knows where she is. I even went up to the fourth floor, but the orderly up there knew less than I did."

"Why did you go to the fourth floor?" Ellen tapped her pen against a stack of papers crowding her desk.

"To search for Franki."

"You do know you're not allowed to be up there?"

"I went anyway."

"Before we take this into panic mode, let me call James and ask if he knows where our young lady may be. He might have moved her to another room. But why he would go against my orders—"

Ellen picked up the phone and called Blake's office. Sandy closed her eyes, counting seconds. Ellen replaced the phone onto the receiver and shook her head. Sandy's heart shriveled in disappointment.

"He isn't answering. You should not have gone up to the fourth floor without letting anyone know where you were going. It's such a dangerous ward, Sandy."

"I know, but—"

"But nothing. That ward is strictly to house the criminally insane and patients with severe dementia."

Sandy practically jumped in her seat. "Ellen, please, we have to look there first. I know she's behind that iron door. I feel it, Ellen, as sure as I have green eyes. Something is very wrong. Franki would not have run away. Please, please, trust me on this. I know I sound like a raving lunatic, but truly, I'm not."

"Let's put both our minds at ease. Shit. I haven't even had my morning coffee."

"I'll get you one later. To the fourth floor!" Sandy waved at Ellen and was already at the door.

"Hold your britches." Dr. Smith unlocked her desk drawer, taking out a round key ring the size of a coffee mug. From it dangled an assortment of key sizes, shapes, and colors.

*   *   *

The elevator ride to the fourth floor was devoid of their usual chatter. Sandy was praying that they would find Franki, and Dr. Smith was praying that they wouldn't. She was hoping that whatever happened to Franki was all just a misunderstanding. It would have to be one hell of a misunderstanding to warrant a search of the entire institution, especially the fourth floor—one had to be dangerously psychotic, a physical threat to others. Franki Martin didn't fit that description.

Sandy anxiously waited for the steel doors to slide fully open. She stepped out first. Ellen grabbed her fearless friend by the shoulder to slow her down.

"It's not policy for you to be allowed here," she whispered. "Only staff with authorized name tags. I'm warning you, what you're about to see isn't pretty."

"I'm fine. I took lots of psych courses. I can handle it." She managed a tremulous smile.

The guard made his way toward Dr. Smith.

"Morning, Dr. Smith. Is there a problem?"

"Good morning, Dominic. Why would you ask?"

"This nurse was here earlier, and I didn't see an authorized name tag."

"It's okay, she's with me, Dominic."

"Need an escort, Doctor?"

"Not this time, thank you."

"Okay, then." He stepped back to his post.

Ellen Smith slid the key into the metal lock and slowly turned the key counterclockwise, waiting to hear the familiar clunk indicating that it was ajar. She yanked hard on the door until it was spaced enough for her and Sandy to enter. One foot inside the doorway, Sandy stopped suddenly at what could only be called spine buster screams coming from the rooms along the corridor. An instant of absolute terror wrapped its arms around her, but she inhaled deeply and shook it off. Nothing was going to stop her. She had to find her little friend. Door by door, she peered through the thick, shatterproof windows. It surprised Sandy to see men and women of a variety of ages and race sitting placidly on the edge of their bunks. All of them appeared to be quite harmless until about the fifth door down. Sandy stopped, eyes searching as with the earlier five rooms, then gasped, and leaped back from the window. Inside was a seven-foot giant of a man running butt-naked at the door like a linebacker on a football team. Ellen took her by the sleeve, and they moved onward.

Another patient was a very good-looking gentleman sitting upright in bed, reading a romance novel.

"He looks so mild mannered," Sandy mentioned to Ellen.

"Yes, he does. Don't let appearances deceive you. Unfortunately, he has a fondness for killing women."

"A psychopath?"

"Mmhmm." Ellen nodded.

Sandy shuddered. She now better understood the doctor's caution about the fourth floor. No wonder it was off-limits.

"You okay? Do you want to go back to the second floor?"

"I'm good. I just wasn't expecting a naked quarterback to come charging at me or to meet our resident psycho who loves killing women. He looks a bit like Tom 'Good-looking' Cruise."

A few doors down another horrible sight stood gazing out from behind the thick shatterproof window. In her eyes radiated an evilness that Sandy had never before encountered. Without warning, the old woman threw back her head, let out a raucous, blood-curdling scream and began ripping fistfuls of gray hair from her scalp. In only seconds, blood clotted her hair. Sandy froze but was quickly moved aside by a duo of orderlies. She hadn't even heard their approach above the woman's spine-bending screams. The men unlocked and entered the room; quick intervention was necessary. The woman would be bald if they didn't restrain and sedate her.

Sandy and the doctor continued on. By now, they'd almost explored every room along the corridor. There was only one room left. Dr. Smith peered through the window. This room appeared vacant. She unlocked the door anyway, and Sandy stepped inside, her hand searching for the wall's light switch.

The two women stared in shock. They'd found Franki Martin. She was strapped onto the bed, restrained within a straightjacket.

Whoever ordered Franki to this room in this manner did not expect her to be found easily. Bricks would hit the fan now. It was hospital policy that no patients, no matter the circumstances, were to be strapped to a bed still restrained in the straightjacket. One or the other. but never both. This was considered unethical and illegal.

"Oh my dear Lord. Sandy, how did you know?" Dr. Smith looked at her in disbelief and then rushed to Franki's bedside.

"Instincts. Let's untie these straps."

Franki was alive but incoherent. This could occur when a patient deliberately shut mental acuities down to protect oneself.

"Sandy, please retrieve the wheelchair from the corridor."

In seconds, Sandy returned, and together, they lifted Franki out of bed and into the sturdy chrome chair. Hastily, Sandy unfastened the buckles on the straightjacket. Franki was finally freed. Her head fell forward. She had no muscle control in her neck and shoulders like a newborn baby. Sandy cradled Franki's head with her nurturing hands while the doctor wheeled her out of there. At the elevator, the two women stared at each other. Words didn't need to be spoken; their eyes conveyed their feelings. Disgust and anger gripped the doctor's heart and squeezed. This facility was to help people, not harm them. How could anyone at River Edge have done such a horrible act to a patient, to another human being?

"I'm glad she was placed on her side at least." Sandy voiced.

"She should not have been in that damn room at all. But yes, Sandy, I do know what you mean."

"What happens now?"

"For the first time in my career, I'm not sure."

"The last one to see Franki was Dr. Blake."

"Oh, this will be taken care of, Sandy. I will find out exactly what has gone on. You can bank your money on it!" Ellen smiled, but her eyes were hard as flint.

"Now I know why he wouldn't let me talk to her yesterday and why the door was slammed in my face. The bastard had planned this."

"Slammed the door in your face? What do you mean?"

"I told you most of it. When I heard the page, I decided to do a little investigating. I know it wasn't my place, but I had such a bad feeling, I just couldn't ignore it. I even had goose bumps, that's how eerie his page hit me. I went down to Blake's office to try to get Franki. I lied, telling him she had an appointment with me. He wouldn't let me in the room. Told me to cancel the appointment, and an orderly slammed the door in my face before I had a chance to finish my sentence. If that's not the action of a guilty person, then I don't know what is. I know it was Franki. I caught a glimpse of those magnetic blue eyes."

"It's okay, Sandy. Your instincts were correct, yesterday and again today. James had no right to shut you out, no matter what. Blake's going to get burned at the stake for this one."

"I'll light the match! I was never fond of the guy, but now, I know why. He's an evil man," Sandy spoke matter-of-factly.

*   *   *

The nurses watched wide-eyed as Dr. Smith wheeled Franki past the station and into her room. "I'll talk to you later" was all she said to their immediate questions.

Sandy changed Franki's soiled clothes and dressed her in a clean nightgown. Franki remained unresponsive. Dr. Smith ordered a variety of blood work to assess any physical damage. When Franki was safely tucked under the covers, she didn't nestle up to the bear. Sandy placed it beside her. Franki's eyes were wide and empty as if her soul had been sucked out of her body. Sandy could have wept to see Franki this way. Only hours ago they'd been laughing and talking about Franki's bright future . . .

"I knew she was there, Ellen. I just somehow knew it. Why did he send her up there, for Christ's sake? What happened?" Sandy rambled. "I mean . . . why did he do this to her? Oh, Ellen, I am so pissed off right now, I could just spit!"

"I don't have the answers yet, but I sure as hell intend to find out. I want you to perform a physical, including a vaginal smear. And have someone deliver it straight away. I need to know if he's been doing the unthinkable. Don't allow anyone into this room until further instructions. I will inform the nurses at the station of my decision on my way out."

Sandy went through the entire rape exam, taking saline swabs from both Franki's vagina and anus. Then combed her pubic hair and examined her hymen, cervix, and vaginal walls for any abrasions. When it was over, she placed all collected swabs into their assigned containers and placed them in a plastic evidence bag. Then moved on to her skin, making sure there were no visible markings of abuse. There were discolorations on her arms and torso from struggling against her captors. Sandy took photographs. Her vitals, other than slightly low blood pressure, indicated nothing alarming. After documenting every detail of Franki's being, Sandy handed the plastic bag to the lab technician and watched her disappear out the door.

Sandy sat beside her on the bed, caressing her forehead and blond hair, hoping for some kind of response, but none came.

"I'm here now, kiddo," she murmured. "Nobody is going to come within five feet of you, sweetheart. I promise. Franki, please, please believe me. You're safe now."

She felt almost frantic at the thought of losing this girl whom she considered a daughter. Franki just had to recover. Sandy had to tell this child how much she loved her.

CHAPTER THIRTY-ONE

Slam! Dr. Blake almost jumped out his comfortable leather chair at the unexpected explosion of his door hurling shut, when Ellen Smith stormed into his office. If she wasn't so angry, she could have laughed at his instant pallor and protruding fishlike eyes. *Yeah,* thought Ellen, *that just about scared the shit right out of you, didn't it, little turd!*

The loud bang could be heard echoing all the way down the corridor. Staff members stopped what they were doing and stared toward its origin, wondering what was going on.

"Ellen!" The glare of her hostility let him know why she was there. He opened his mouth, mind reeling, trying to think of something to say. Ellen raised a hand. "Don't, James. I'm in no mood."

She'd found Franki Martin up on the fourth floor.

She marched across the carpet to his desk and stood glaring at him, hand on her hips.

Dr. Smith was nothing to mess with, and everyone knew that, including Blake. But she was fair. He also knew, she did not tolerate insubordination from her colleagues, and sending her patient to the fourth floor without her consent was being insubordinate.

So now he would use the oldest ploy in the book; indeed, it was used by many of her patients—counterattack.

"I take it you found your star patient." He affected a smug tone.

"You're damn right I did. I demand an explanation! Who made the order?"

"I issued the order."

"And who in hell gave you permission to send my patient to the fourth floor without my authorization. Damn it, I told you to stay away from her. How dare you—"

"You weren't here to sign, so I took it upon myself to have her taken to the fourth floor, and with good reason."

"Do you know how I found her?"

Blake flapped his right hand in the air, signaling clearly to her that he wasn't interested.

"Oh, you will hear what I have to say, James. My patient, Franki Martin, was strapped down with belts, still wearing the jacket you restrained her in. Which tells me why her jogging pants were wet with urine. The goon squad you ordered—Oh, Jesus, I am so pissed off at you, I can hardly speak." She blew out a deep breath. "Were you hoping no one would find her? Did you order that too?" Her eyes drilled into his deceptive pools of evil.

Blake looked away.

"Answer the damn question—yes or no?"

She was right in his face now, so close he could feel her hot breath shoot up his nostrils.

"Did you or did you not order her to be kept in the straightjacket?"

"Yes!" he yelled, inching away from the fire in her eyes. "Yes, damn it. I ordered it all!" *Careful,* he cautioned himself. *Don't blow this.*

"Then, Doctor, you better have one hell of an explanation to justify the cruel abuse I just witnessed. As far as I'm concerned, this is ground for your immediate dismissal. And by the time I'm done with you, you won't be able to get a job at a fast-food restaurant."

Blake sighed deeply. "This perfect patient of yours had one of her violent outbursts yesterday."

"Elaborate."

"I warned you this would happen, but you didn't want to believe me."

"And I don't believe you now," Ellen barked.

"Maybe you'll be convinced after I tell you what she did."

"I doubt it, but go on." She plunked down in the visitor's chair, folded her arms across her chest.

"I was on my way to my office when I noticed I had the wrong patient's file in my hand."

"I don't care. Get to the point."

"Fine." He narrowed his eyes, recalling the incident. "I saw Franki beating up another patient."

"Who was this so-called patient?"

"Gloria."

"Gloria Shelby?" Her voice heightened with surprise.

"Ellen, Franki was hammering on her. I had to pull her off before she did anymore damage."

"I still find this story pretty hard to fathom."

"Well, maybe you can fathom this: Franki broke her nose while she was hammering the hell out of the woman's face."

"Who started the confrontation? Obviously, I can't ask Franki her side of the story because she's catatonic. You've managed that for the both of us now, haven't you?"

"Gloria said she was looking at a book when Franki jumped her from behind."

"No way. Please page Gloria, pronto. I'll judge for myself on the merit of what she has to say."

Dr. Blake took the phone and requested Gloria to come to his office. Ellen remained quiet; she was still too angry to be civil. About four minutes later, the redheaded patient, wearing a white bandage across her nose, appeared in the doorway. The swelling below her eyes indicated that her nose was broken since swelling precedes the bruising.

Dr. Blake invited Gloria to come in and take a seat next to Dr. Smith.

"Hi, Gloria. I want to ask you about the fight you had yesterday. Is that okay with you?" Ellen spoke gently, containing her anger she felt for Dr. Blake.

"Said I stole book. It's mine. Holds secret powers." She swayed back and forth.

"Who beat you up, Gloria?"

"Blond mean girl."

"Do you know her name?"

"Fran-Frank-Franki." She stammered.

"What kind of book was Franki trying to steal away from you?"

Before Gloria could answer, Blake interrupted. "Dr. Smith, your proof is right there, in front of you. Look at Gloria's face. She obviously didn't punch herself in the nose."

Ellen gave James a shut-your-mouth stare.

"What kind of book did Franki try to steal from you, Gloria dear?"

"Don't remember."

"Drop it, Doctor. She doesn't remember the book."

"Thank you, Gloria, for coming to talk to me. I hope you feel better. You can go back to your room and rest now." Dr. Smith patted her arm and smiled.

"You're nice. Are you a real doctor?" Gloria asked as plain as day. "No, you're not?"

Nervously, she stuffed her fingers into her mouth and suckled.

"Yes, she is a doctor. Her name is Dr. Smith, remember?" His eyebrows furrowed.

The redhead smacked the palm of her hand against her forehead, sending ripples of pain to her nose. Her eyes began to water. "Ouch!"

"Go back to your room now, and I'll check on you later," Blake said.

"Pro-mise?" Flirtatiously, she twirled her red hair around her index finger. Ellen could feel the white hairs on the back of her neck begin to stand at attention. She'd never before seen a female patient act in a sexual manner toward Blake. This unusual incident was one she intended to store in her memory bank.

Gloria left, leaving Ellen to battle it out with James. She sat in silence, collecting her thoughts. This was one for Blake; Franki had indeed broken Gloria Shelby's nose. Ellen's responsibilities were to protect the safety of all the patients at River Edge, not just one. Dr. Blake sat back in his chair, one leg crossed over the other, a faint slow smirk formed on his lips. *You arrogant bastard*, thought Ellen. *I might have lost this battle, but I will win the bloody war. You're hiding something, Doctor, and I intend to find out what that is.*

Ellen rose to her feet. "James, I'm telling you right here and now that I am scheduling a hearing in front of the board. I'll start with reason number 1: misuse of power and abuse causing bodily harm. By the end of the day, I want on my desk the names of the two orderlies who took Franki upstairs. If you want to counter this, please be my guest. You know as well as I do that Ms. Martin should not have been taken to the fourth floor. I expect the report will explain why you ordered her to be taken there rather than to the third. And don't forget to put in that report that when we found her, she was still in a straightjacket, strapped to the bed. If there was anyone else involved, I suggest you document that as well. And as far as having the door slammed in Sandy's face, you can bet I'll also be writing that incident in my report. What you have done is so disgraceful. I'm embarrassed to call you my colleague."

"What . . . what the hell?"

"Don't say it out loud, James. Write down your excuses."

"Ellen, you can't be serious. The girl is a menace."

"Save it for the board of directors."

Before she left, she made sure James understood that Franki was to remain on the second floor. Her medication would be increased and decreased if she sought fit. He was to have nothing to do with her care, pending the board's decision. James didn't argue; he knew he was on shaky ground. But he'd bluff it through. He always did.

Prior to stepping into the corridor, she remembered one more thing.

"Where is Franki's chart? You took it yesterday evening."

"Right here."

"Hand it over. 'You won't be needing it any longer,' quote unquote."

"Fine." He walked over to his filing cabinet, retrieved it from the top drawer and handed it over.

"I am not going to forget the insufferable condition I found my patient in, and I will make damn sure that the board doesn't either."

"Don't you think you're overreacting a bit?"

"Get ready to take a long holiday."

"I don't believe it will come to that."

"Don't bank on it." Ellen slammed the door behind her, letting off steam and letting Blake know this was not over by a long shot.

Dr. Blake leaned his head back against the chair, hands resting comfortably behind his head.

"I'm sure going to miss our fun, Franki."

*   *   *

Back in her office, Ellen made for the phone. She needed to call her good friend Bill Cobie, president of the board. Ellen advised him what she found on the fourth floor. Both sides were to present their case, and then it was up to the board of directors to decide what course of action would be taken. She hoped they would fire his ass. What he did to Franki was cruel and unforgivable. A couple of weeks without pay would not substantiate the unscrupulous brutality, he'd ordered on a defenseless child. She hoped Bill and the other members would feel the same way.

After their phone conversation, Ellen went to see if there were any changes in Franki's condition; there weren't. Sandy was sitting in the chair next to the bed, reading a book. She'd stayed the entire time, hovering around Franki like a mother bear protecting her cub, checking her vitals every half hour, stroking her blond hair and assuring her, how much she loved her. Ellen told Sandy what had transpired with Blake and asked her to write a statement, telling what happened yesterday and what she found this morning up on the fourth floor. Sandy was happy to oblige. After Ellen checked Franki's vitals, in her opinion, Franki was in shock, caused by induced trauma. Ellen was upset, but not overly concerned. Franki should be back to her old self in a couple of days, she assured Sandy. In the meantime, she was going to assign only three primary nurses to Franki's full-time care: day, afternoon, and night shifts. Sandy volunteered to do round-the-clock care, but Ellen wouldn't allow it. Burning the candle at both ends wasn't healthy; she needed rest too. Nancy agreed to take the afternoon shift with Franki. All she had to do was check her vitals every hour and make sure no one else went into that room. Ellen called Ruth for the night shift before leaving her office. Everything was a green to go.

CHAPTER THIRTY-TWO

Ellen left her office just after five. Her muscles and joints begged for a long soak in a warm bath; her mind's synapses and neurotransmitters were short-circuiting. She needed to get home and distance herself from the stresses of River Edge. All she wanted was to walk into her house and throw her arms around her husband. Tom was the life raft that kept her afloat, reminded her of the essential goodness and sanity of the world. Her job was highly satisfying, but very demanding. No matter how professional she was, everyone needed some TLC. Today was one of those days.

She had Franki's file in her briefcase to study this evening. She wasn't wrong about Franki's prognosis and by rereading it; she would doubly prove it. She needed to ensure there was nothing she'd missed. She was convinced that Franki did not start that fight. Tonight, she would unearth every fact to back up her prognosis. She had no intentions of stepping into the board meeting unprepared. Bill Cobie assured her that disciplinary action would be taken. He agreed: Dr. Blake had no business sending Franki Martin to the fourth floor because of the altercation. The third floor yes, but not the fourth.

Ellen wanted to know the names of the two orderlies responsible for taking Franki there. And what were their orders? She snapped shut her briefcase, making sure the coffeemaker was off and the windows were secured. One last glance around the office space, she turned off the light and closed the door. She left it unlocked. The janitorial service was scheduled to do a seasonal spring-cleaning of her office later this evening.

*   *   *

Sandy had already clocked out at four, gone home, changed her clothes, and returned to the facility. Nancy wasn't too surprised when Sandy, wearing a comfortable pale-blue tracksuit, reappeared. She gave Nancy the polite boot. She was going to stay with Franki. Nancy didn't balk it. The nurse knew Sandy was webbed in Franki's life, more perhaps than she should, but no one said anything. The kid really needed to be loved, and Sandy volunteered. She pulled up a chair next to Franki's bed and began reading poetry aloud from her own handwritten collection of poems. The rails were already up for Franki's safety. This was their thing, sharing ideas and discussing literature. Writing in any form knitted the two together like matching mittens. Sandy would read romantic poems, and Franki would talk about falling in love with a guy like Steve Michaels. Sandy countered with a story about a boy she'd met in med school, but it hadn't worked out. The rat only got close so she would tutor him. There was more healing going on between them and within themselves than they were willing to admit. But tonight, Sandy read, and Franki remained silent, locked in an unreachable world.

*   *   *

On her way to her car, Dr. Smith paused. "One last check," she said aloud. She turned and walked back to check on Franki. Opening the door, she stopped midstep seeing Sandy sitting there. The nurse looked up from the book, smiling.

"Hi. What are you doing back here?"

"Couldn't stay away."

"I figured that. Don't you get tired?"

"I could say the same thing about you."

"Then I guess we're both guilty."

"What's with the briefcase? Has it become a permanent extension of your arm?"

Ellen lifted her briefcase in the air. "You might have a point." She laughed.

"I don't see other shrinks taking their work home with them."

"That's other shrinks. Anyway, look who's calling the kettle black."

"Isn't that the pot calling the kettle black?"

"Smart-ass. I guess I am tired." Both women laughed.

Ellen put down her briefcase and stepped up to the bed for a closer inspection. "Any sign of cognizance?"

"Nothing yet. I put a catheter in. If she hasn't improved by tomorrow, I think she should be admitted to Morial."

"Sweetheart, she'll only be transferred to the psych ward there and, then in a few days, passed back to us. And besides, I think when she does come to, Franki will want to see familiar faces, plus surroundings."

"You know your stuff, Doctor."

"I do."

"I wish she'd wake up and tell us what happened yesterday."

"I have no doubt she'll wake up and be madder than a hornet. Have you checked her vitals?"

"Every hour on the hour. Her pupils are dilated, but her pulse is normal."

"Nothing's changed."

"Same as when we found her."

Ellen borrowed Sandy's stethoscope to listen to Franki's heart, then took out what looked like a miniature flashlight. She shone the light directly into the pupils. "No movement."

"None?" Sandy questioned.

"Nope. I'm certain this is the result of aftershock. When a person faces too many traumas in their life, sometimes the mind makes the body shut down. It's a way of giving its flesh a break. The brain can only handle so much stress before it says, 'To hell with you!' I think this is what's happening to Franki."

"I hope that's only what it is."

"Don't worry, Sandy. All of her vitals are normal. Her heart sounds strong. Her pulse is normal. If her pulse becomes rapid and eyes start flickering back and forth, then we have a problem. If there's no change in her condition by morning, I'll order an in-depth tox screen, just to make sure what's prescribed is in her blood and nothing that shouldn't be. CT scan will tell us how well her brain is functioning. If nothing shows up there, then I'll order an MRI."

"Ellen, patients with severe head injuries become catatonic."

"And some violent. Franki has suffered a grave trauma. She was taken away and placed in a strange room by two goons. I bet she didn't even know. Franki might also be feeling separation anxiety, PTSD, and sometimes, this is how it rears its ugly head. The mind will shut down when it needs to. This condition results in abnormal loss of self-awareness and of one's surroundings. I believe unconsciousness, in this case, is going to be brief. Franki Martin is strong, but this goes to show, everyone has a breaking point. This young lady has experienced situations in her life that I wouldn't wish on my worst enemy. Let's not forget that she is a strong survivor."

"I hear you. She just looks so friggin' fragile."

"How long do you plan to sit here?" The doctor peered over her glasses, expressing concern.

"Don't worry about me. It's not like I have men beating down my door for dates." Sandy grinned.

"If you stayed home once in a while, you just might be surprised who'd knock on your door."

Sandy gave her a funny smirk. "Fine, I won't worry then."

"If there is any change in her condition, please don't hesitate to buzz me at home."

"Sure."

"I'm going home to my darling husband."

"It's about time." Sandy glanced pointedly at her watch.

"I'm leaving. Bye, Sandy." Ellen stopped at the entrance, looking over her shoulder. "Don't be here all night."

"I thought you were leaving?"

"I'm gone." She closed the door.

Sandy sat down beside Franki, opening the page where she'd left off.

CHAPTER THIRTY-THREE

The minute Tom, the newly retired meteorologist, greeted his wife at the front door, he could see she'd had one hell of a hard day. Ellen couldn't hide anything from her husband. Her hazel eyes said it all. He kissed her on the cheek and took her briefcase.

"You look like you could drink a tall glass of ice tea."

"A stiff drink is more like it."

"That bad of a day? What would you like?"

"A good dose of Chivas Regal."

"Here, sit back and relax. I'll get it."

"I love you." She smiled warmly at Tom.

She adored him as much now as she did when they first married. She leaned back, resting her head against the back of the chair, trying to empty her mind of the eventful day and what was yet to come.

Tom came back into the living room carrying a crystal tumbler of Scotch on the rocks. He handed his wife the glass. "Here, this should help." She relieved him of it graciously.

He lifted Ellen's legs from the footstool, removed her shoes, and began massaging her feet. Soft moans of pleasure escaped her mouth as Tom gently applied pressure to her sore, tired feet. Ellen appreciated Tom's wonderful treatment after she'd had a long and grueling day.

It wasn't long before she began to relax.

"I thought this might help loosen the tension."

"You thought right, my darling."

Tom watched as her facial muscles relaxed while her feet began tingling with renewed energy. Slowly, Ellen opened her eyes and smiled brightly.

"Thank you, honey." She wiggled as life surged into her toes. "What is that yummy smell?"

"That, my dear, is roasted garlic chicken, Greek salad, mashed potatoes, and fresh mixed vegetables from the farmer's market."

"I am the luckiest woman alive to have a husband like you."

"I know!" He laughed. "Bring your drink to the table, dinner will be served in ten minutes."

"Lead the way, my darling." Hand in hand, they strolled into the kitchen.

"Anything I can do to help?"

"Yes. Sit in the chair and finish your Scotch."

"Tom, really, let me help you," she begged. He patted her backside and pointed to the dining room chair.

"Do you want to talk about it?" Tom asked, never pushing.

"No, but yes. Crap from River Edge."

"Average crap or worse?" he asked, before putting a forkful of potatoes into his mouth.

"Do you remember me talking about Franki Martin?"

"The kid from the street?"

Ellen nodded.

"You said she was making baby steps of recovery."

"That ended yesterday."

"Ended, why?"

"Apparently, she got into a fistfight and broke a resident's nose. Blake witnessed this fight and sent her to the fourth floor."

"Is the allegation true or false?"

"I'm afraid it's true. The woman's nose is broken."

"What brought this on?"

"A book. A bloody book."

"And you believe that?"

"That's where it gets tricky. There are some accusations on Blake's part that aren't adding up. Sandy is furious at him. Yesterday, when I learned he'd paged Franki to his office, she went to get her. The door was rudely slammed in Sandy's face in the middle of her sentence. He's still in deep shit over that, but that's a horse of a thousand colors. The worst is he sent the young girl to the fourth floor without my authorization. Now here's the whammy: the two orderlies restrained her in a straightjacket, strapped her to the bed, and bloody well left her there overnight. If we hadn't found her, God knows how long she would have been left there, undiscovered. This morning, Sandy was waiting outside my office door, fit to be tied. Franki was missing. She hadn't come back to her room all night. The last one to see her was Blake. Then, she was told Blake had taken Franki's chart from the nurse's station, saying they wouldn't need it any longer."

"So she didn't run away?"

"No, but my suspicions tell me that's what he wanted us to believe. For the life of me, I cannot fathom how he could do such a thing. Before I arrived, Sandy had done her own search for Franki. The only floor left was the fourth. And only Blake, a few others, and I have authorization to be there. Tom, you should have seen Sandy. She was really scared. She told me she somehow just knew that Franki was on the fourth floor. So we went looking, and sure enough, she was there."

"He's finished, I bet. Why would he do such a horrible thing? She's your patient, isn't she?"

"Yes."

Ellen went on to tell Tom about the incident with Gloria that led up to this fiasco.

"But Blake absolutely had no right to treat Franki—or any patient in that manner. I hope they fire his sorry ass."

"Well, they should."

"And his crap excuse was, I wasn't there, so he saw fit to make the decision. He's not the only one in hot water. The two goons that took her upstairs and just left her, ordered or not, should be slapped with a nice suspension. Tom, her gray track pants were soaked with urine. No one went into that bloody room all night. That tells me, he didn't want anyone to find her."

"Ellen, this sounds like a total misuse of power."

"You bet. I lost it on him today. I stormed into his office madder than a wet wasp. He justified every single one of his actions. 'It's the institution's responsibility to protect all our patients' was what he threw at me. Not just one! I would have smacked that smug look off his ugly face if I'd thought I could have gotten away with it."

"I'm glad you didn't get into a fistfight." He smiled.

"Yeah, but it sure would have been self-gratifying. Finally, around three thirty, Bill called back, telling me he'd scheduled an emergency meeting tomorrow morning. The good news is Bill doesn't like Blake much and never has. So as it stands, Sandy is with Franki now. I'll buzz her later and find out how Franki is doing, but for now, she's holding her own. No one is allowed in that room without my permission, and that includes Blake."

"Wow, honey. What a day." He kissed the back of her hand. "How was the young one doing when you left?"

"She's catatonic. I believe it's from the trauma she'd endured. Her vitals are fine, so there is no cause to worry. I'm hoping she'll be up cursing a blue streak by morning."

"If she is as strong-willed as you say she is, she'll be good and pissed off tomorrow when you go to visit her."

Ellen laughed. "I can hear the profanity now. Not that I blame her."

"With a shrink as caring as you, how can she go wrong?" He patted her age-speckled hand.

"My halo's getting tight, darling. I'll call later."

"If there's anything I can do to help, you just let me know. Now enough about work, finish your meal, and that's an order!"

"Yes, boss." Ellen playfully saluted her husband.

*   *   *

At eight thirty that night, Sandy got called out of Franki's room to answer the phone.

"Sandy, it's Ellen."

"I've been expecting your call."

"How's Franki?"

"No change."

"Maybe I should come in?"

"No. Her blood pressure is normal. Her eyes are wide and ridged though."

"I want you to put two drops of Visine Dry Eyes, every four hours so her tear ducts don't dry out. And put that in the report for Nancy."

"Got it. I've just ordered warm blankets from down stairs. Her body is cold from lack of movement."

"If you like, you can exercise her arms and legs. That will keep the circulation flowing."

"That was my next step, thanks."

"Sandy, Franki should be better by morning."

"I'll stay a little longer. If she gets worse, I'll phone in another doctor, from Morial."

"It's your call. If there are any sudden changes, please contact me. Otherwise, I'll check on Franki first thing in the morning. And you leave within the hour!"

"Good night, Ellen, and thanks."

It was quarter to eleven when Sandy dragged herself away from Franki's side. She wanted to pick her up and carry her home where she knew she would be safe from harm, but she knew it wasn't allowed.

She gave Nancy a list of instructions that were also to be passed on to Ruth when she arrived. Both were to immediately call Dr. Smith or herself if there were changes in Franki's condition.

CHAPTER THIRTY-FOUR

Tom awoke around three o'clock to find his wife not in bed. He rolled the covers down and slipped into his robe. Rubbing at his unshaven face, he staggered down the hall to the den. He spotted a sliver of light shining from underneath the door. He rapped lightly, not wanting to startle Ellen. He poked his head in a crack. There, she was, sitting at her oak desk, scanning intently the words on the pages of an open file. She looked up and smiled at her husband as he came through the door. His gray hair lay flat on the right side of his head. His robe opened revealing his gray chest hair and black silk boxers. His legs still bulged with muscles, from years of working out. Tom was just as attractive now as he was when Ellen first met him. Even after thirty-plus years of marriage, seeing his manly body still gave her an electric zap.

"Hi, what are you doing awake?"

He rubbed his eyes. "I should be asking you the same question."

"Franki Martin." She pointed to the file.

"What about her?" He yawned. "What have you found?"

"Nothing, Tom. I have been reviewing her file, and there is nothing that indicates to me she's as vicious as Blake contends. There's no substantial proof to his absurd allegation. No proof whatsoever. Tomorrow, the board is going to know exactly what I believe is going on based on my medical findings."

"Like what?"

"Franki Martin embraces pain like it's all she deserves. She doesn't strike out unless she's seriously threatened. Something Gloria did caused Franki to lash out. What, is the question. I believe Franki was defending herself against Gloria."

"Maybe Gloria was the one to strike first?"

"Exactly, Tom. Why did James send Franki to the fourth floor? It's almost as if he wants to keep her quiet. She hates him and calls him really rude names

I'd rather not repeat. A few days ago, he told me that Franki made a pass at him. Sandy refuses to believe it. I've seen Blake. He sure isn't Franki's type. I have scrutinized every word of her past, and nothing shows me she's violent. She flees from confrontation and pain, and that's why she ran to the street. She was looking to be left alone. If Franki Martin is to remain on the second floor, I have to prove that she's stable. I have to prove she didn't start the fight. How can I do that when the only two witnesses say she's responsible? And his saying, Franki made a sexual pass at him for a special favor is only going to make her appear more like a deviant. I can only hope she's awake tomorrow morning so she can tell her side of the story."

"Or you have some fancy talking to do." Tom scratched his head.

"Let me read this report to you."

"I'm all ears."

"In the first three years of life, the brain undergoes tremendous enlargement. At birth the brain weighs four hundred grams. Most of our growth occurs in the first three years. A major factor in this enormous growth is the development of connection synapses between nerve cells. During this period, the brain's hard wiring is established. The psychosocial environment is largely responsible for the maturation of the brain during this period. Tom, according to this, there is not a thing medically wrong with Franki's brain. It is healthy. The reason I know this is because she was with her real parents at its time of growth. Her parents were nurturing and very loving. The abuse occurred subsequent to the growth of her brain's development. Franki was physically and mentally tortured after her parents were killed, not before. I think also what I am going to have to do if she hasn't recovered fully by tomorrow is order an MRI scan. That will prove my theory beyond a shadow of a doubt. But that will be too late. The board meeting will be over, and the decision made."

"Can you explain to the board that you've ordered the test?"

"Yes, I could, but—"

"The test will prove scientifically that the young girl has a healthy brain with no malfunctions or enlargements. The MRI scan once completed cannot be disputed by anyone, including Blake. Right?"

"Correct. I'm determined to win this, Tom. Now listen to this one case of child abuse at its finest."

"Do I have to?" Tom slumped back against the leather couch.

"No."

"Go ahead, honey. I just hate hearing about a child being hurt by a person in power. I get angry, that's all."

"Listen." Ellen smiled.

"My beautiful wife is now playing detective."

"Shhh. One of the many times Franki was sent to the hospital. It is documented she suffered from nicotine poisoning. She was seen after school with a couple of girls from her class smoking a cigarette behind the building. This next-door neighbor, Mrs. Mockey, squealed to Susan, Franki's foster mother. When Franki came home, she was immediately confronted. Franki, like many frightened children, lied to save her skin. Keep in mind this woman is a sociopath. Under the same circumstance, I would probably have done the same thing and lied. She made Franki go to her room while she slipped out to the store. Now remember, Franki is ten years old.

"Let me guess: she bought a pack of smokes?"

"Yes, Export, with no filters. She made her smoke ten of the cigarettes before she puked and was sent to her room. When Susan went to check on her a half hour later, Susan couldn't revive Franki. She had to call an ambulance. The child had gone into anaphylactic shock. Franki had an allergic reaction to nicotine. She was literally poisoned. They had to give her a blood transfusion in order to rid her little body of chemical toxins. Her blood was poisoned.

Tom's eyes sprang wide at the unbelievable horrors this girl suffered. "Why didn't they remove her then? It's not like they didn't have good reason? Franki Martin could have died from this woman's stupidity. What is wrong with these idiots?"

"It makes me mad too. Blind eyes, less work for the caseworkers, who are understaffed. Not to mention, Susan lied and said it was Franki who did the smoking without her permission."

"That woman is a horrible person. So many wonderful people wanting to adopt, and yet there are still cases of severe child abuse. I will never understand."

"Tom, before you get all worked up, why don't you go back to bed? I think I've told you enough to upset this night's sleep."

"It's too late for that, I'm already worked up, but I am going to go back to bed. Ellen, it's four o'clock in the morning. Why don't you call it a night—or rather, a morning?"

"I have a few more pages to review and a report to write, then I'll come to bed. Promise."

Tom leaned over the back of Ellen's chair and kissed the top of her gray head. "Good night, my love. Don't be up all night."

"I won't, darling." Hearing the door to the den close softly, Ellen resumed her work.

*   *   *

Sandy was at her kitchen table, sipping at a cup of hot chocolate. Her grandmother used to call it hug-in-a-mug. Her body sagged with exhaustion, but her mind wouldn't quit. The haunting image of Franki strapped down to the bed, wearing a straightjacket, wouldn't vanish from her mind. She tipped up her mug and swallowed the last mouthful of sweetness. Maybe a warm bubble bath would help relax her tensed muscles enough to fall asleep. She had called over to River Edge for the last time. The diagnosis was still the same. Sandy wished it were seven o'clock so she could go to see Franki. An hour later, she finally crawled under the covers; she asked God if he were listening, and if so, would he please make Franki better. With that, Sandy floated into a deep well of slumber.

CHAPTER THIRTY-FIVE

At six o'clock the next morning, Dr. Blake stood on the path of the Three-Mile Garden, staring at the flowers that interested him the most: a patch of white lilies that were rooted beside the red roses, swaying back and forth in the morning breeze. He bent forward and picked three of the largest and most attractive lilies in the bunch. The light-green leaves sprouting from their stems gave the physician an overwhelming satisfaction. With anxious anticipation, he slid gently his index finger along the leaves, rubbing off the tiny specks of dirt particles. Their smooth-as-silk petals virtually beseeched him to be grounded into a fine powder of lethal poison.

Tenderly, he carried the three lovely lilies across the grounds to Morial's laboratory. The parking lot was near empty except for the staff vehicles. Ambulances were parked, in wait of the day's unexpected emergencies.

Pattie just happened to glance up from her computer in time to see the familiar face scurrying the receptionist counter, flowers tucked beneath his doctor's coat. He was gone before Pattie had time to wish him a jolly good morning. Although she was curious as to why he was in the hospital again at this time of the morning, she didn't have time to entertain the thought for long when the phone rang.

The doctor unlocked and entered the lab. The fragrance of disinfectant loomed heavy in the air. Chrome sinks and faucets sparkled brilliantly. Fluorescent bulbs generated a luminous, shadowless glow. Accuracy was very vital. A low humming resonated throughout the lab. Dr. Blake stood at the front of the room, pondering where he would be most comfortable. He made his choice. Firstly ensuring the door was locked, he then strode to the back of the room.

The doctor plunked himself down on the stool and placed the beautiful lilies on the tabletop before him. Reaching into his doctor's jacket pocket, he pulled out a vial containing a yellow liquid. Holding it between his thumb and index finger, he gently rocked the container back and forth, watching the tiny air bubbles gather at the top of the vial. Then, he carefully sat the vial down in front of him. One by one, he raised each flower to his nose, inhaling the raw scent deeply into his already constricted airway. One at a time, he plucked the stamen from the lilies. He leaned sideways to the drawer, opened it, and brought out a sterile empty culture dish and scissors. From his other pocket, he removed a flat miniature kitchen shredder. One flower at a time, he shredded the stamen into a fine powder. When all three were grounded into fine particles of dust, he picked up the vial, carefully sucking out the liquid with an eyedropper, and then released six drops into the fine powder. He smiled as the dust liquefied. Pouring carefully the liquid back into its original vial, capping it before shaking it well, he held it up and smiled again. The liquid changed magically into neon orange. "This should keep the bitch from squealing." He placed the vial into his doctor's coat. Before leaving, he took a couple of sheets from the paper towel rack and cleaned away any trace of his ever being there. Discarding the residue of lilies into a plastic bag, Blake then locked the door behind him. He felt pleased. Another mission completed.

Pattie only felt the breeze of his passing. She didn't bother looking up from the computer.

Dr. Blake stepped into the now warmer morning air, whistling a merry tune as he crossed the grounds to River Edge Institution. He chucked the bag into a large trashcan just outside the front door. The contents would be taken to the dump at three o'clock today. All evidence of his clever plot would be gone.

Now the doctor was heading straight to Franki's room. He had a job to finish.

*   *   *

Ruth had just gone on a quick bathroom break when Dr. Blake entered Franki's room. The nurses had strict orders from Dr. Smith that the only person allowed in that room was Sandy, Nancy, or Ruth, who was assigned to Franki's care. That left Judy the sensitive job of telling the doctor what he could and could not do.

"Dr. Blake! Doctor!" Judy yelled after him.

Dr. Blake turned and glared contemptuously at Judy, continuing to walk and ignoring any acknowledgment.

"Doctor, no one is allowed in that room. It's Dr. Smith's orders!" Judy sought after him.

Blake entered anyway. He believed he was above everyone and everything in this facility, including Dr. Ellen Smith. By the time Judy left her seat and crossed over to Franki's door, Dr. Blake was coming out.

"Sorry, Doctor, but it's Dr. Smith's strictest orders."

He smiled. "No harm done." He strode away to his office. The second he stepped over its threshold, he vented his rage. With one hand, he cleared everything off his desktop, including the only picture of his parents.

"James, you are so goddamned stupid!" he yelled. "Why didn't you fill the syringe? How could you be so stupid? Stupid! Stupid! Damn you!" He stomped his feet like a three-year-old."

Finally, he fell into his chair, sweat bubbling on his forehead and upper lip. Chest heaving. Closing his eyes, he slowly began to calm down, taking calculated breaths. When he opened his eyes, he was shocked at the mess on the floor. Immediately, he leaped out of his chair and began tidying the items, he had thrown about in his fit of anger. Once everything was back in place, he sat back in his chair and pondered the situation. He could wait to visit Franki another time. *No harm done,* he convinced himself. She was still catatonic from her first injection of curare—a highly lethal drug that was causing her catatonia. He was safe for now. Curare would take days to find in her bloodstream.

Blake reread the report he'd prepared for the board meeting this morning. He didn't know what was going to happen, but he felt confident. Whatever the board decided, at most, he wouldn't get more than a mild reprimand, a mere slap on the wrist. In view of the stakes, he held the winning hand.

*   *   *

Judy ran back to the desk and documented the exact time, Dr. Blake entered Franki's room and her two ignored requests for him not to do so. Judy wanted Dr. Smith to know this information. Something wasn't right with this guy. Even the nurses on the second floor were beginning to dislike Blake. In the staff room, they'd commented they were seeing subtle changes in Blake's behavior. He seemed, well, strangely . . . preoccupied.

*   *   *

Ellen Smith was back inside the doors of River Edge at seven, with three hours of sleep under her belt. She placed her first cup of coffee on her desk, opened her briefcase and retrieved Franki's file. She sat comfortably in her chair, reading the last few pages that she had been unable to finish last night. A couple of sentences into the paragraph, Ellen stopped. This paragraph showed clearly what Franki was capable of when under extreme duress. How could she have missed this important information? Then again, sleep deprivation could do that to a person. She read on. Great! A sigh of relief freed the tension around her mouth.

The situation was in self-defense, according to the gist of the school's report and Franki's statement. The report stated: Franki was in the sixth grade. It was a Tuesday morning, late October. Tuesdays were assigned library days for her sixth grade class. In her usual hurry to get out of the Wilkins house, Franki forgot her library books on her bed. She didn't say anything to the teacher, partly embarrassment and for fear of chastisement. She went to the library with the other children. The teacher, Mrs. Page, noticed Franki sitting alone at the far end of the room with her head resting on her elbows while the rest of the children were busy picking out new books for the week. Mrs. Page approached Franki, "Why aren't you getting a new book?" she asked.

"I'm not allowed," Franki had replied.

"Why not?"

"I forgot my books at home."

"Franki, you know every Tuesday is library day."

"I didn't mean to. I just forgot." She shrugged.

"That's no excuse. Get yourself out of that chair and go stand in the corner."

"I didn't mean to forget my books, okay?" Franki's tone was argumentative.

"You heard me. I said the corner, now!" Mrs. Page pointed to the wall.

"No." Franki retaliated. She folded her arms aggressively across her chest. She would not budge.

Mrs. Page reached out to take a hold of Franki's arm. Franki pulled away. Mrs. Page again tried to take her by the arm. The teacher's second attempt hadn't worked any better than the first.

"I'm not going. The kids will laugh at me," she'd said.

Mrs. Page's last attempt ended in a physical altercation. The moment Franki felt the teacher's cold hand wrap around her arm, she jumped up from her seat and punched the teacher square in the jaw.

"You go stand in the corner, you stupid bitch!" Franki screamed and then fled the library. By the time Mrs. Page recovered from the shock of being assaulted in the face by her student, Franki Martin was nowhere to be found. She had taken off down the road. After running three blocks from the school, she found shelter in the woods. Following a frantic search, a team of police officers found Franki Martin approximately four hours later.

Franki's punishment was a three-day suspension from St. Lutheran School. Leaning back in her chair, Ellen mused aloud, "I'll bet that was worse punishment than a guilty man walking his final steps to be executed. Three straight days and nights with Gary and Susan Wilkins would have been a living hell. I can't imagine what kind of torture Franki endured within those three days." Ellen took a gulp of coffee. "This does not prove to me beyond a reasonable doubt that Franki Martin is as violent as Dr. Blake insists she is. I know now that I must order that MRI scan this morning. What time will it be done? I have no idea. But that will be all the proof I need!" she whispered into the sunlight streaming across her desk as she closed the file.

After coffee number 2, Dr. Smith finished her report:

> Excess Guilt Identification . . . the threatening or punishing aspects of this person (Franki Martin) with whom we identify may seem so strong that we feel as if we (Franki Martin) are 'bad' inside. This kind of excess guilt, a feeling of wickedness, is seen at its most extreme in some forms of depression and may feature in the sort of suicide that occurs when a person believes he/she doesn't deserve to live any longer.

> My hypothesis is that foster parent Susan Wilkins suffers a form of psychiatric illness projection so marked that the patient feels persecuted by the wickedness of others and makes violence of her supposed enemy (Franki Martin). It can take form of a delusion, that is, a false belief, which is not open to reason and cannot be accounted for by prevailing social or culture conditions.

> Projection and displacement is one of the most common forms of preserving an internal sense of comfort. It is easier to see the badness, destructiveness, or rapacity in others than in oneself. Child abuse was suffered by and at the hands of Susan and Gary Wilkins, foster parents of Franki Martin.

> With all the information I have viewed, my conclusion is that Franki Martin is not a vicious patient. I was away on the day in question, the day this confrontation happened between Gloria Shelby and Franki Martin. Sending my patient, Franki Martin, up to the fourth floor was abuse in power and protocol by Dr. James Blake. Nurse Sandy Miller and myself found Franki Martin on the fourth floor on the morning of July 12. Ms. Martin was strapped to the bed, still wearing a straightjacket ordered by Dr. Blake. The girl's condition was reckless and inhumane. Her gray sweatpants were stained and wet with urine, indicating that she was left alone for the entire evening, which goes against the rights of the patient. In my opinion,

we were fortunate to find Franki when we did. She is now in a catatonic state due to the trauma suffered in isolation. This type of insubordination is brutal and atrocious. River Edge's mandate is to treat our patients with the highest regard. I feel Dr. Blake along with two orderlies he instructed to perform this heinous act should be disciplined to the fullest. Whatever Dr. Blake's reason is, it could not possibly justify his actions. They are morally, ethically, professionally, and legally unacceptable. Dr. Blake had options other than sending Franki Martin to the fourth floor, which is strictly for the criminally insane and those with severe dementia, which Franki Martin has not been diagnosed. We have different floors to treat different types of mental illness, and they should be used accordingly. The third floor is where the doctor should have sent this patient until her primary psychiatrist, myself, could have appraised the situation and treated the patient accordingly. Under no circumstance is mental or physical cruelty, including leaving a young vulnerable girl strapped down to a bed wearing a straightjacket and isolated for more than twelve hours unsupervised, be inflicted on any patients. I feel strongly that Dr. James Blake deserves immediate dismissal.

Thank you with regards to this critical matter,
Dr. Ellen Smith

*   *   *

Now, Ellen needed to get in touch with Veronica Winston, Franki's lawyer. There was no way Franki would be well enough to attend court this week. She was still way too traumatized for such a stressful ordeal as facing her adversaries. Ellen took a deep breath before dialing. Today was supposed to be Franki's day in court. Ellen was angry. This was to be the beginning of a newfound strength and freedom toward her future and absent from an abusive past. And here she was, facing another injustice.

Rape of a minor and physical and mental cruelty and endangerment of a child were only the beginning of what she wanted the lawyer to start with. Ellen had confidence in Veronica Winston. She was a tough attorney when it came to criminal conduct against children. She felt it was her responsibility to team up with children who had the courage to come forward and tell their unforgettable ordeals of abuse. As far as she was concerned, Franki Martin was overdue to get justice. Those two deranged psychopaths, she vowed, would never have the opportunity to hurt another child, not as long as Veronica had anything to say and all thanks to Ellen. Dr. Smith was a woman who cared enough about one girl to help her find the courage to press charges against two vicious criminals that shouldn't have liberty. Veronica admired that in the woman.

Ellen heard the phone line on the other end begin to ring.

"Veronica Winston, please."

"May I ask who is calling?"

"Dr. Smith from River Edge."

"Just one moment."

Ellen waited, thumbing her fingers on the top of her desk.

"Veronica Winston."

"Veronica, it's Ellen Smith."

"Dr. Smith. How are you?"

"I'm good, but our star patient, I'm afraid isn't. Reason I'm calling is to inform you, Franki Martin won't be showing up this afternoon for her court appearance."

"And why is that?"

"It's a long story that I'd rather not get into at this time. The long and short of it is Franki Martin is catatonic."

"Catatonic?"

"Yes. Can you get the case remanded until further notice?"

"I can try. Can you give me something to use?"

"Yes. Franki was found in a catatonic state yesterday and hasn't recovered yet, I'm afraid. I have hope. Would you like me to fax a letter to Judge Denac?"

"No, I don't believe that will be necessary, but the judge may want to call you, if that's all right?"

"I'm in a meeting all morning, I'm afraid. This afternoon will be a better time to reach me."

"Sorry to hear about Franki, Dr. Smith. She's a great kid."

"That makes two of us. Anyway, Veronica, I have to scoot, but I will keep you updated on her progress."

"The two monsters will just have to remain in jail, that's all. No great loss as far as I'm concerned."

"I couldn't agree more. Thanks again, Veronica. Sorry for the inconvenience."

"No problem. I'm on my way to the courthouse right now. I'll have a meeting with Judge Denac as soon as I arrive."

"Thanks again, Veronica."

"Keep me informed."

"I will."

"Talk to you soon." Ellen hung up the phone.

Chapter Thirty-Six

Ellen gathered up what she needed before checking on Franki. Taking the last swig of coffee, she headed out the door. She was well equipped to nail Blake's ass to the wall on this one.

*   *   *

Blake was getting nervous as he primed for the meeting. He knew no matter how prepared he was, he would be reprimanded, for sure. There was no way of getting out of a consequence for placing a patient on the fourth floor without just cause. He buzzed for the two orderlies to come to his office, pronto. Dr. Blake wanted to make sure they were all on the same page. And to make sure they all said the same thing: Franki Martin was out of control. If they did not sing the same song, he was screwed.

*   *   *

Ellen suddenly remembered she had one more thing to do before going to check on Franki. She looked at her watch: twelve minutes past eight. Immediately, she picked up the telephone and dialed Morial Hospital.

"Good morning, Morial Hospital. Can you hold one moment please?"

"Yes."

Ellen tidied her desk, waiting impatiently for the cheery receptionist to come back on line.

"Yes, how may I help you?"

"Can I have radiology, please?"

"Just one moment."

"Good morning, can you hold please?"

"I don't have the patience for this, this morning." Ellen whispered into the mouthpiece. She impatiently checked her watch.

"Yes, how may I help you?"

Ellen forced her voice to remain calm.

"Good morning. This is Dr. Ellen Smith next door. Is Dr. Flank in please?"

"Just one moment."

"Here we go again," she grumbled.

The doctor wanted these procedures done to see if there were any abnormalities in Franki's brain that could only be seen by CT or MRI scans. Brain scinitigraphy would provide information on the adequacy of blood to the cerebral cortex.

A few more minutes of drumming her fingernails on her desktop, and finally, she heard the doctor's familiar voice.

"Ellen, how are you?"

"I'm good, Charlie, and yourself?"

"Can't complain, I guess. What can I do for you?"

"How busy are you over there?"

"Really busy, why?"

"I need an MRI, CT, and EEC for a patient of mine today—yesterday, really."

"Ah, an emergency?"

"Catatonic emergency, Charlie."

"I'll fit you in at nine thirty, no later though."

"Thank you, Charlie."

"Oh, Ellen, don't forget to tell that old fart of a husband of yours that I said hello."

"I won't forget, Charlie, and thanks again."

"You owe me big-time for this favor."

"What do I owe you, Charlie?"

"Dinner with Ethal and me."

"Deal! Let's say Saturday night at six thirty?"

"Six thirty it is!"

"Bye, Charlie. You truly are a lifesaver, and I don't mean the candy!" They both hung up their phones, chuckling.

Ellen didn't squander any more time getting to the second-floor nurse's station, praying the entire time that Franki's prognosis would be greatly improved. But something told her that there was no change or she would have heard from Sandy by now. Franki's door was closed, keeping out the excess noise of the busy hallways.

At the nurse's desk, she asked, "Doris, any news on our little one?"

"Sorry, Doctor, she is the same. Sandy is in with her now."

"Thank you."

Ellen made her way across the hall to Franki's room.

"Hi, Sandy."

"Good morning." She shook her head. There'd been no change in Franki's medical condition.

"I've ordered an MRI, EEC, and CT scan at nine thirty this morning, and you are the elected one to take Franki across to the hospital."

"Not a problem."

"Good. With any luck, we should have the test results back later today."

"I thought you were going to order blood work?"

"I will, but I need those brain scans first."

"Why the scans?" Sandy's forehead puckered.

"Let's say, I'm covering all the bases." Ellen smiled devilishly. "I'm ready to kick ass at this meeting."

"Good because Blake doesn't belong in this or any other institution after what he did to Franki."

"I agree, my dear, and I am going to do whatever it takes so this type of abusive conduct never happens again."

"Here's my report." She handed it to Ellen.

"Thank you very much." Ellen grinned like she had already won.

"Ellen, I thought you said this catatonic state wouldn't last."

"This is temporary. Sandy, remember that Franki suffered grave fears yesterday from being locked up on that ward. She is taking extra time coming back. If there's anything abnormal, Dr. Flank will find it. Don't worry please. It isn't helping anyone."

"You're right. When we come back, I'd like to hook her up to an intravenous drip."

"Good. After the scans, bring her back and hook her up. I'm not sure how long she'll be like this, I'm afraid."

Ellen moved to the side of the bed to check Franki's vitals. When she shone a penlight into her eyes, she could see Franki was still not present. It tugged at Ellen's heartstrings.

"Am I scheduled to stay on with her today?"

"Yes, same as yesterday."

"Fine by me."

"Good. I didn't think you would have a problem." The doctor spoke with great confidence in Sandy.

"Thank you."

"Didn't get much sleep last night, I see."

"Should I say the same about you?" Sandy countered.

"I'll sleep when I'm dead."

"If you don't get some proper sleep soon, Doctor, I'm afraid that's coming faster than you think."

"From one workaholic to another. Don't worry, I'll sleep tonight."

"So, what time did you really get to bed?" Sandy pressed.

"I'm running on three hours sleep, and you?"

"About the same."

"Our little buddy has to get better soon. These late nights are killing us."

"Take it easy today."

"I might sneak a sleep right here this afternoon."

"Great idea."

"Okay, so nine thirty, it is."

"No problem."

"I'm off to the board meeting. This is when Dr. James Blake gets a hard kick in the rear end. Insubordination is not taken lightly around here." Ellen grinned.

"That was fast. I am happy to hear that someone's ass is going to get kicked over what has happened to Franki. What's the worst that can happen to Blake?"

"He is removed completely from Franki's care. And he'll get a few days off without pay."

"The orderlies?"

"They could lose their jobs, I'm afraid. The two of them will have to prove their actions were on Blake's orders."

"Sounds like you have a battle ahead of you?"

"A good one." Ellen winked. "I have a couple more things to do before the meeting. I'll be in touch sometime today. If anything unusual comes up, have Charlie notify me immediately."

"Got it. Ellen, thank you."

"For what?"

"I know it isn't easy going against someone you had respected."

"*Had.* That's the operative word now. Talk to you later."

*　　*　　*

Sandy gave Franki a warm sponge bath and changed her into a clean nightgown. She checked her catheter and replaced her almost full bag with an empty one. Good sign; Franki was still hydrated. Pulling the chair next to the bed, she began reading one of Franki's favorite authors C. S. Lewis, *The Lion, The Witch, and The Wardrobe.* Then it was time to take Franki over to radiology for her scans with Dr. Flank. Sandy got Franki prepped and ready to go, then called for Tommy to come and assist. Together, they transferred Franki gently onto a stretcher bed and wheeled her across the attractive grounds to Morial Hospital.

Franki never uttered a sound.

CHAPTER THIRTY-SEVEN

Bill Cobie buzzed his secretary and told her he was sorry for not asking her yesterday to have the conference room ready for this morning's meeting and that she had to hustle. She looked at her watch; she had fifteen minutes. Rosa shook her head and laughed. Trust Bill to forget. It would be done in time, she assured him. She hurried to the staff room to get the coffee and goodies ready for Bill's guests.

Bill had decided late last night that he'd be the only one conducting this morning's meeting. He would gather all the facts from both sides and then determine if he should call in the other board members. He hoped that the situation could be resolved without calling in the other reinforcements. Bill confessed to himself, he did enjoy calling the shots on some of the decisions regarding the welfare of River Edge.

Rosa walked in carrying a silver tray with a shining chrome coffeepot and a teapot and a clear crystal pitcher of ice water. Placing the tray at the head of a twelve-chair oval redwood table, she left and returned a few moments later with another silver tray topped with an array of cake slices, cookies, napkins, and forks. She opened wide the beige-colored drapes, and sunlight filled the room. She inhaled deeply. This room always smelled new, not like the rest of the facility that reeked of disinfectant. You could tell this was an important room, where important people made decisions of importance. *How exciting,* thought Rosa, *to be one of them.* Dust particles bounced in the sharp rays of sunlight. She watched in awe for a couple of seconds, thinking even the dust comes to life with the warmth of the sun. Rosa stood in the open doorway, her eyes sweeping over the room to ensure everything would meet her boss's approval. She nodded and left.

Rosa enjoyed working for Bill. His orders were always clear and direct. She couldn't remember being yelled at for any accidental mistakes she'd made.

When she needed time off, Bill was always accommodating. Rosa admired and appreciated her boss, so anything he needed to make his job more productive, Rosa never minded lending an extra hand. It was a pleasure, not a chore to come to work.

*   *   *

Ellen had all she needed tucked under her arm, secured with a rubber band around the white file folder. The determination to right a wrong electrified her every nerve. She understood that Bill's decision was completely out of her control but trusted Bill explicitly. He had admirable morals and values, but above everything, he sought justice for all, including the patients who couldn't speak for themselves.

She waited impatiently for the elevator to take her to the fifth floor. Rosa looked out to see Dr. Smith when the elevator doors opened. Rosa showed her into the meeting room and invited her to sit. The two women shared a few pleasantries before Rosa returned to her desk. Ellen set the file on the table, opened, and read through it word by word. Her lips pressed tightly together in concentration. Not a punctuation mark escaped her eyes.

At nine fifty, the two accused orderlies, Gerry and Bruce, entered the room. They both sat as far from Ellen, down the table, as possible. That was fine with Ellen. Gerry's face was pulled down by guilt. He reminded Ellen of a hound dog caught munching on a steak he'd stolen from the table. But Bruce's smirk announced this meeting was nothing more than a joke. Ellen would have loved to smack that smug grin right off his face. Gerry kept his head bowed.

Finally, Bill made an entrance. He strolled around the table to where the two men were sitting, shook their hands, and told them to help themselves to a cup of coffee and goodies. Then, he made his way to the top of the table where Ellen was sitting. He leaned down, kissing her cheek. He never kept hidden from anyone his loyalty and respect for Ellen. She did her best for River Edge. If that meant ruffling a few feathers, so be it. She was honest and up front about everything that went on between her patients and staff. Bill knew how many long, grueling hours Ellen worked in a day. Many times, he'd reminded her that she had a home and a loving husband waiting for her. Bill poured Ellen and himself a cup of coffee and then took his place at the head of the table. Rosa walked in carrying a folder, placing it on the table in front of her boss. Bill checked his watch: ten on the dot. The meeting should have gotten underway, but they were missing one person: Blake.

"I'll give Dr. Blake five more minutes before I have Rosa call him."

"Good idea."

The foursome sat chatting about the beautiful summer they were having, trying to keep the room's atmosphere light. It would get heavy soon enough.

* * *

James Blake knew he had a very important appointment upstairs, but an emergency had risen. Now he was waiting for a patient. He put the special needle back in his drawer, locking it. This little token of appreciation wasn't for this expected patient. At the knock on his office door, Blake summoned for Simon to enter. He was holding his hands to his throat.

"What is it I can do for you today, Simon?"

"My throat is killing me."

"How long have you had this sore throat?"

"It was a little scratchy yesterday, but today, it hurts so bad, I can't even swallow. It feels like I'm swallowing glass."

"Come with me. I'll take a look in the back of your throat."

Dr. Blake placed his two hands an inch down from Simon's ears, pressing to see if his glands were swollen.

"No swelling there."

"That's a relief, I think."

"Open your mouth as wide as you can."

Simon did so, and Dr. Blake swabbed the back of his throat with what resembled an extra long Q-tip.

"I can't make a prognosis, but from the puss cupules, I'd say you have strep throat, my friend. I'll prescribe an antibiotic for you. Amoxicillin should do the trick. The nurse will give you your first pill just as soon as we are finished here. I'll give you this antiseptic spray to coat the back of your throat. It should help with the discomfort until the antibiotics begin to work."

"Thanks, Dr. Blake. I really hate being sick."

"Don't worry, you will be better in no time. It states in your chart that you will be leaving us to go home tomorrow?"

"Can't wait. I am feeling so much better about myself, thanks to Dr. Smith. Wow, she is the best!"

"She certainly is." Just saying those words made his own throat feel like he was swallowing glass.

"I've prescribed enough medication to last ten days. Hand this over to the nurse at the second-floor station. If the soreness persists, I suggest that you go and visit your own doctor. I'll call you if your throat swab comes back abnormal, but I really think that you have strep throat. My guess is that you will be as good as new in a week."

"I really hope it's nothing more."

"Don't worry. Even if it isn't strep, the antibiotic I have prescribed should clear any infection within the next ten days."

"Thank you, Dr. Blake. As of tomorrow at noon, I'm a free man."

"Good luck, Simon."

Simon shook hands with Dr. Blake before he left the office. Dr. Blake phoned the nurse's station to ensure that Simon had his first pill of Amoxicillin and for the nurse in charge to fill his prescription before he left the next morning. Dr. Blake had just ended the call when his phone rang. He knew who was calling even before he picked up the receiver.

"Blake here."

"Dr. Blake, it's Rosa. Mr. Cobie is expecting you in the conference room."

"I'm on my way."

"I'll tell him, Doctor." He hung up without so much as a thank-you or good-bye. Rosa rolled her eyes at his rudeness.

Blake grabbed the folder off his desk and rushed out of his office. He didn't wait on the elevator. Instead, he took the stairs, two at a time; it would be faster. He rushed past Bill's receptionist to the conference room, where everyone else was waiting for him to show.

"Glad you could make it," Bill stated, raising his eyebrows.

"Sorry I'm late, but I had a small emergency."

"No other doctors available who could have taken care of the patient?"

"Not really." Blake settled into his chair.

Bill moved around in his chair, getting comfortable for the next couple of hours ahead. Ellen did the same.

"Coffee is in the middle of the table if you want some, James," Bill offered.

"No, thank you. I'm fine."

"Okay, we all know why we are here this morning. Let's begin, shall we? Who would like to start this process?"

"I would like to go first, Bill, if that's okay with everyone?"

"Anyone opposed to Dr. Smith stating her case?"

"No, no, no," chorused the room.

It took Ellen about three-quarters of an hour to present her defense for Franki Martin. Bill Cobie took notes as his colleague clearly and precisely stated her facts. He jotted down questions and waited until Ellen finished speaking before he asked the big question: why was Blake in charge of her patient to begin with? Ellen explained she had been away on holidays when Ms. Martin first arrived at River Edge.

Dr. Smith's presentation was as professional and thorough as Bill expected. Her case was unshakeable as far as he was concerned, and Blake knew it too.

Next up were the two orderlies. Bill was curious to hear what these two had to say in their defense. They both told Bill that Dr. Bake ordered the young girl to the fourth floor and that she was to be left without being released from the straightjacket.

Then it was Dr. Blake's turn. He stuttered and stammered as he reread the report he had written the previous night, beginning with the fight between Gloria Shelby and Franki Martin. Bill stopped him several times to ask questions, which visibly agitated Blake, throwing him off course as he tried to maneuver between any faultfinding on what had taken place and, most importantly, why.

When Blake was finished, Bill informed the group they would have his decision by the end of the day. But he did state that as far as he could tell, there had been a gross injustice committed against Franki Martin. He did not say, but everyone knew, if this were true, there would be repercussions on Blake's professionalism. Bill reassured Ellen that she was right to have reported this incident. Precautionary measures would be taken against ill behavior like this. It would never happen to another patient at River Edge.

Ellen was anxious to know the outcome now but trusted the necessary process. She hoped she judged correctly Bill's tone toward James Blake. If so, dismissal could be on the horizon for Blake and the other two ignoramuses who took Franki Martin to the fourth floor, for leaving her in such inhumane conditions.

CHAPTER THIRTY-EIGHT

It was midafternoon, and the hallways were quiet. Patients were in their rooms, napping or reading. At the nurse's station, a couple of nursing students were chatting about their night out at the bar. Their bloodshot eyes and drained giggles could be heard all the way down the long corridor.

"I could not believe that poor woman last night. Man, was she ever drunk."

"I know. I wouldn't want to have her head on my shoulders today. Jeez, I don't want my own aching head." Nurse Lander sighed.

"Why, what happened?" Sharon one of the older nurses, asked.

"We were at a karaoke bar, and there was this woman, all dressed more like a dinner date. Not bar material, if you know what I mean?" Kaylie said.

"I didn't realize she was that drunk until she stumbled up on the stage, trying to get the crowd's attention. She received the attention all right, but it wasn't a positive one. Everyone at the bar was laughing and making jokes as they waited for her to start stripping out of her clothes," Lander explained.

"I wanted to go up and help her off the stage, but she probably would have told me to go to hell." Kaylie shook her head.

"That's true. There's nothing that impresses the boys more than a good catfight on the stage."

Sharon nodded. "You two aren't going to bars trying to find men, are you?"

"Kind of, sort of," Lander admitted. "You should have seen the blonde following Kaylie all over the bar."

"What blonde? I didn't see any blonde."

"By the end of the night, you didn't see too much, did you?"

"She really is a bitch. Did you know that?" Kaylie raised her manicured eyebrows quickly up and down. "Besides, if my memory serves me correctly, you were just as inebriated as I was."

"I didn't pound back the shooters the way you did."

"What! I had three shots of Sex on the Beach. That's nothing!"

"What is Sex on the Beach?" Sharon inquired.

"It's a sweet shooter. Don't ask me what's in it."

"Sounds nasty." Sharon placed a finger in her mouth.

"It does the trick, and it's good."

"By the look of your bleeding eyes, girl, it does more than just a trick." Sharon scowled.

"Good point. But I didn't drink that much, honest."

"Whatever!" Lander put up her palm. "You don't even remember the puppy dog blonde."

"Got me there." Kaylie shrugged.

"The place was seriously packed with good-looking men, that's for sure," Lander proudly announced.

"Are you two serious about finding a nice man in a bar?" Sharon questioned.

"Yes. And besides, stranger things have happened." Kaylie laughed.

"No, I don't believe we will find our knight in shining armor," Lander disagreed. "But the eye candy is sure good for the soul."

"Which bars do you girls go looking?"

"Eddies and the local pub on Blue Street. Sometimes we head out of town but not very often. We didn't last night."

"Eddies? Not that hole in the wall over on Madzen? You gals are way too classy to be in a dump like that."

"Thank you," Lander said, looking surprised, but pleased.

"That's a very nice compliment. But that's where everyone hangs out," Kaylie stated defensively.

"But . . . my mom keeps telling me, I'll find my dream guy in some grocery store." Lander said rolling her eyes.

"What aisle, squeezing the melons or buying feminine products?" Kaylie's contagious laugh started everyone around her.

"You won't find a nice guy down at Eddies, I can assure you both."

"Don't be so sure." Kaylie spoke out.

"Who knows, Sharon? Have to be positive," Lander jumped in.

"You girls should go bowling or something."

Lander and Kaylie looked at each other and then at Sharon. "Isn't that what old people do?" Kaylie asked.

"No offense, but that is an old people's sport. My mom bowls."

"You two are hopeless. Hopeless I say," Sharon said and went back to filing a patient's chart.

Just then, Sandy and the orderly came down the hall, pushing Franki on a gurney back to her room. Sharon offered to help, but Sandy told her everything was under control.

"Back to my loyal duty of sponge bathing and bedpans," Lander piped up.

"It's that time again," Kaylie followed.

"I'll stay here and finish up." She winked as if to say, "Serves you both right for getting drunk last night."

*　　*　　*

The phone rang; on the other end of the line was Dr. Blake calling the desk to make sure Simon received his prescription of antibiotics. He was told yes, again. He hung up the phone and rested his head on the back of the chair, closing his eyes. His mind reviewed the meeting in the boardroom. He had worried but knew he wouldn't be dismissed permanently. The institution needed every available doctor; with Franki being in a comatose state, he had time to finish what he started. His plans were presently delayed, nothing more.

*　　*　　*

Dr. Smith was busy catching up with her cancellations from the previous day. She left a note at the front desk notifying everyone that she would not be available until four forty this afternoon, unless Bill called. At four forty-five on the dot, the doctor's phone rang.

"Dr. Smith, speaking."

"Hi, Ellen, Bill here. Are you in the middle of something?"

"I just finished up with my last patient."

"Want to come upstairs please?"

"I'm on my way."

*　　*　　*

Dr. Blake was filing a patient's chart when his phone's ring broke the silence.

"Dr. Blake."

"James, it's Bill. I have made my decision. Please come to the conference room."

"Will do." Blake hung up the phone and looked down at his hands. Perspiration gloved his palms. He tried to imagine what the outcome was going to be by the tone of Bill's voice but couldn't. He walked out of his office, heart pounding hard inside his chest. *Calm down*, he chided himself. *The worst that'll happen is a reprimand. No problem. Then back to plan A.* As he stood waiting at the elevator, his two accomplices arrived. They too had received Bill's summons.

"Do you think we're fired?" Gerry asked the doctor.

"Nothing to worry about." Bruce smirked.

"Pretty sure of yourself, are you?" Blake countered.

"It wasn't my order, man. It was yours."

The man's a moron, thought Blake, *not worth a retort.* The elevator doors slid open, and a few seconds later, all three stepped out on to the fifth floor. No one greeted them. The threesome slowly made their way to the conference room, where they would hear the final fate of their jobs. Blake opened the door, and the two orderlies entered first. Bill and Ellen were already seated. This time, Bill didn't move around to shake anyone's hand; there were no coffee or goodies to eat.

"I have made my decision," Bill announced without preamble. "I would first like to say that I am thoroughly disgusted by all three of your actions. We have special people in this facility with special problems. This isn't a place where abuse is seen as something acceptable on any level. As far as I am concerned, there has been proof of abuse. Dr. Smith's report read that Franki Martin, in fact, was making steady progress. That was until you screwed it up, James. Now this young girl is in a catatonic state. Dr. Blake, I find what you did to be cruel and unprofessional. You have never before, that I am aware of, sent a patient to the fourth floor, unless deemed by the courts. And as long as I'm running things around here, you won't send another unauthorized patient."

"As far as you two are concerned—" He glared at the orderlies. "I am . . . not at all pleased with your performance. You never should have followed Dr. Blake's order. Gerry, against your better judgment, you still violated Franki's human rights by leaving her alone and restrained for such an unprecedented amount of time. However, this time, I have decided to be lenient with you both because you unwittingly followed an order Dr. Blake gave you. You now have written warnings on your records. If I ever get wind that either of you have placed one of our patients in jeopardy again, you will be fired immediately, no questions asked. You both are free to leave." Bill watched silently as the two men rose and expressed gratitude for not getting fired.

The room fell silent. Dr. Blake rubbed his perspiring hands together, waiting nervously for the verdict.

"James, Franki Martin is no longer one of your patients."

"But . . . but . . ."

"But nothing. You will have no contact, period, starting from this moment on. You are to hand over any medical files pertaining to Franki Martin to Dr. Smith. I understand River Edge has a no-violence program, but what you ordered was just as violent, if not more so than the two women having a fight in the corridor. What you did was unprofessional, unethical, and maybe even illegal. I am suspending you for the next five days without pay. I hope you have learned something from this. You've had an outstanding record since you've been here, and may I add, if you hadn't, your ass would be dismissed with severance pay and out the door. All I can say is let this be a lesson. Next time, you won't be so lucky. If you decide to file a grievance against my decision, feel free do so, after your return."

"In my defense, I was only doing it for the safety of all patients that have to reside here."

"I'm afraid you went about it wrongly. River Edge's concern is for the safety of all our patients, including Franki Martin. This meeting is over."

Silently, Blake rose from his chair, anger tightening the lines on his face, and strode from the room. Had it been possible, Ellen and Bill could have seen steam rushing out his ears. Ellen was glad he hadn't said anything else. She didn't want to listen to anymore of his excuses. Ellen stared at Bill, a relieved smile lighting her face.

"Thank you very much, Bill."

"It was the least I could do. How is our Franki Martin doing?"

"Still comatose."

"How long do you think this comatose will last?"

"Not sure. Depends on how deeply she was traumatized while up on the fourth floor. She has what medical mystery calls a sleeping sickness. She has checked out, so to speak, giving her body and mind a rest. Her vitals are normal, which is a very good sign."

"Stupid bastard. Blake, of all people, should have known better. I wanted to fire his ass. Trust me, I did. But this round, I did only what I was permitted under board of ethics."

"True enough. I believe you made your point though."

"It had better been received loud and clear because if I ever get wind of something this inhumane again, he will be standing in the welfare line. I'll boycott him from ever practicing in another mental facility anywhere. What he did is incomprehensible. His ego got the best of him."

"I think it's more than ego, Bill."

"Ellen, when Blake returns, if possible, I want you to try and keep an eye on him."

"Are you saying to get the nurses involved?"

"If you have to, yes."

"I don't believe that will be necessary. When he left, I am convinced he understood the full implication of his action."

"It's your call."

"Thanks again, Bill." Slowly, Ellen made it to her feet. "Now I am going to my wonderful husband."

"Good idea."

"Could use a stiff drink right now, but a few more minutes of waiting won't kill me."

"Could use one myself. Glad it's dart night with the boys."

"Have a celebratory one for me."

"I'll do just that."

He smiled as he watched Ellen saunter out of the room. *Hell of a gal,* he thought.

CHAPTER THIRTY-NINE

Ellen had a fun evening with her husband. She told Tom all about the meeting, and how pleased she was with the result of James Blake being suspended for a week without pay. She knew herself that there was no way Bill could have fired the doctor. His record up to this point was squeaky clean. That evening, she and Tom entertained friends by playing bridge until eleven. Then Ellen called it a night and went to bed.

The next morning, she felt more rested than she had in days. A sense of relief and peace filled her very soul. Franki was suffering, yes, but in Ellen's medical opinion, this episode of sleeping sickness wouldn't last too much longer. She enjoyed her morning coffee on the sundeck, before taking her shower and getting ready for work. She kissed her loving husband at the door and drove off down Coble Road.

*   *   *

She smiled at the nurses, doctors, and residents roaming the corridors as she made her way to her office. While organizing her work for the day, the phone rang.

"Hello, Dr. Smith speaking."

Ellen had been taking files from her briefcase, scheduling the program for Franki Martin. There were three nurses assigned for the weekdays and six nurses for the weekend. All of them were trustworthy in this next endeavor. During the week, Sandy would be on from eight to four. Nancy worked her already scheduled afternoons. Judy, Ellen believed, was quite competent for the night shift. Pam, Jean, Lisa, Donna, Mary, and Sarah worked weekends. It would not matter to the schedule if there were any interruptions in the calendar. Sandy was always present, ensuring there was always someone with Franki.

She planned to drop it off at the nurse's station, the moment she had the chance to get off the phone.

"Hi, Ellen, it's Charlie here."

"The test results are in, I hope?"

"Sure are."

"Good or bad, Charlie?"

"Do you have a minute to stop by? I'll explain everything to you. Not that you probably don't already know how to read the prognosis yourself."

"Thank you for the vote of confidence. I first have to drop off a schedule at the nurse's station. Can you give me about ten minutes?"

"See you when you get here."

Ellen didn't want to keep Charlie waiting long. As the chief radiologist, Charlie was a busy man. She stopped at the nurse's station with the new schedule. After posting it, she immediately went into Franki's room to let Sandy know she was on her way over to the hospital.

"Hi, Sandy."

"Ellen, hi."

"How is our star patient?"

"The same." She let out a sigh.

"I'm on my way over to the hospital for the results of Franki's scans."

"I hope the results offer some good news."

"Her vitals are the same?" Ellen questioned.

"Her vitals are normal, but her breathing is erratic. It starts off slow, then speeds up, and slows again. And still no response."

"She may be dreaming. All part of this course, I'm afraid. Okay, I'm gone. I'll let you know the outcome when I return."

"I'll be waiting with anxious breath."

*   *   *

Ellen was right on time, ten minutes to the dot, and out of breath. Charlie invited her into his office, his broom closet, as he called it. He had the papers spread on the desk when she walked in.

"Okay, Ellen, I'm going to get right down to business."

"That's why I'm here, Charlie."

"Bear with me, Ellen. I'll be going over a lot of medical jargon you already know, but I want to draw for you a complete picture and how it all leads me to a firm diagnosis. The human brain is organized in layers of interacting regions.

At the base located just behind the mouth is the brain stem, which controls the most elemental functions—breathing, blood pressure, and swallowing, appears to be normal. Above that, behind the nose and its sinuses, is the diencephalon. It controls body temperature, appetite, sleep, and wakefulness. Now, from what I understand, the medication Franki Martin is on will show slower electroencephalo organs in the brain. It appears normal meaning. I see no damage. I do need to ask one question though?"

"Shoot."

"Is this young girl a drug addict?"

"She has used crack, pot, heroin, and smurfs in the past, why?"

"I believe your girl has used heroin recently. In the past five days or so. I see tiny abnormalities on the cortex, which is a good indication of recent drug use."

"That's impossible, Charlie."

"Science doesn't lie."

Ellen sat in the chair positioned in front of his desk, waiting intently to hear the rest of Charlie's clinical mumbo jumbo.

"Circling around the central part of the brain is the limbic system and amygdala-hippocampus complex, the seat of the primitive emotions involved in sexual behavior, fear, anger, attack, and memory. Covering the entire surface of the brain and positioned just below the skull is the cerebral cortex, the thick layer of gray matter (nerve cells), are not damaged in anyway, and that is the source of conscious mental processes. The cortex is automatically separated into two regions called lobes. Vision is controlled by occipital lobes at the back of the head. Somatosensory information like touch, pain, and position space is interpreted behind and above the ears in the parietal lobes. Smell and taste are determined by the temporal lobes at the sides of the brain, near the ears. Speech and understanding of language comes from the left posterior, part of the frontal lobes that lies just in front of the ear. The left side of the body is voluntary movements, which again, are modified by deep sub cortical centers like the basal ganglia and the cerebellum. Almost all vertebrate have well-developed occipital and temporal lobes and motor control systems that are similar in humans. In other words"—he paused for dramatic affect and smile—"your kid is normal. No damage to the brain. With absentness of drug use, the kid will be just fine. Brain flow is normal."

Ellen hadn't been aware she'd been holding her breath. Now she let it out in a rush.

"Great news, Charlie, thank you!"

"Ellen, explosive, uncontrollable rage often is expressed by a person who no longer has the neurological capacity to moderate primal Libra feelings of the fight-or-flight impulse. She made a mistake and lashed out. Can't say that I blame her. You already know how I feel about Blake."

"You're not the only one. Franki hates him with a vengeance."

"So her brain is fine. If you want my opinion, watch that guy. There's just something about Blake that rubs me the wrong way. Here is my suggestion, Ellen, take it if you want."

"I'm listening." A warm sarcastic smirk washed over her lips.

"If I were you, I would quietly begin taking her down off all that crap that she's on. The kid doesn't need it, and the test results prove it." Charlie handed Ellen the paper chronicling his indisputable findings. No matter how much Blake challenged them, he wouldn't win.

"Thanks, Charlie, from the bottom of my heart! And we're still on for dinner this Saturday evening, right?"

"We'll be there with bells on. Tell that old man of yours to go and buy some decent Scotch, like Glen Flint," he ordered grinning.

"I'll put that on my priority list, Charlie."

"Good girl. Now I'm going home. It's my day off."

"Charlie, you mean you came from home on your day off to give me the results?"

"You said it was urgent." He shrugged.

"Charlie Flank, you are one of a kind! Thank you! Give my love to Ethal." She pumped his hand and walked out of Charlie's broom closet; with the results in her hand, she felt more optimistic about helping Franki than she had since the young girl darkened River Edge's doorway.

Ellen crossed the grounds, feeling a load of bricks had lifted off her shoulders. She always believed Franki Martin was not a violent girl, and now she held medical proof to back it up.

At her office, she immediately went to the photocopying machine. This very important document needed to be duplicated: one for her personal file and one for Bill Cobie.

* * *

The doctor's next stop after seeing Bill was Franki's room. She absolutely had to share the good news with Sandy. Ellen knew exactly how Sandy was going to react to learning the results of the tests, good and bad.

She opened the door. "I have good news, my dear. Franki's brain is exceedingly healthy! Perfectly normal, according to Charlie."

Sandy jumped to her feet and shook a victorious hand.

"I knew it! I just knew it, Ellen! Franki Martin is not any more violent than you or I."

"One for the good team. I believed that Franki wasn't violent, but we had to have medical proof beyond a shadow of doubt. I took a copy of the MRI results to Bill to keep on his file. There is one thing that does concern me though."

"Oh, and what's that?"

"Charlie believes Franki has used heroin in the past five days."

Sandy's bewildered expression froze. "How? I don't understand."

"That makes two of us. We'll have to ask Franki when she awakes."

"That makes no sense. Where would she get heroin?"

"It would explain the lethargy she's had."

Sandy tucked the blankets around Franki. "When she wakes up, I'm asking, that's for sure. Am I allowed to ask what happened in the meeting?"

"Dr. Blake is completely off Franki's case. She has been handed solely over to me. Blake has a suspension of five days without pay. He's lucky to only get that. Bill was not a happy camper."

"What about the other two idiots?"

"Written warnings only. They both were told that if anything like this ever happens again, they would both be fired, on the spot."

"Not good enough as far as I'm concerned. At least Blake got what was coming to him, not that he'll suffer much from his suspension." Sandy rolled her eyes.

"He wasn't too pleased, I assure you."

"I'm not too impressed with him either. Especially when I look at Franki, she should be up and bouncing down the corridor in full recovery, and look at her . . .'"

"I've ordered more blood work to be done."

"What are you hoping to find?"

"Any trace of narcotics. Don't worry, my dear. We're checking is all."

Sandy nodded. "My curiosity is now piqued. Do you believe her condition is the sole result of what that creep did to her?"

"Yes and no. Franki had been on a journey from hell before she made it here. It could be a combination of everything. Sometimes the body gives itself a rest with permission from the brain or vice versa."

"Ellen, Franki tried to tell me something that night at the beach, I wonder what."

"I'm sorry to say, her condition may last for a few more days, depending on how her subconscious is handling the fact that she was brutally traumatized again. It isn't anything you did or didn't do. You were not the one to order her upstairs. If anything, my dear, you were the one who tried to stop it. You saved Franki!"

"Ellen, she was more than traumatized. She was brutally victimized, and Blake ordered it. That's a fact!"

"I hear you, Sandy, but it won't do you or Franki any good if you're out of control with resentment. Trust me, she feels it. I'm doing everything in my power to help her. And that means staying positive. I think Blake has learned his lesson."

"I know what would make me feel better."

"What's that, or should I be afraid to ask?"

"A room, a wooden bat, and that bastard. I would show him the meaning of the word *violated*. I know, Ellen, you are doing everything you can to help Franki. I am trying to stay positive, trust me. But seeing her like this just breaks my friggin' heart."

"I understand your anger, I feel the same as you do, but he has been suspended, and that's all any of us can ask for right now."

"I think Bill should have fired his ass."

"It's not that easy."

"Why not?"

"Gloria's nose is broken, remember?"

"That's correct. I don't know how I feel about that either. I feel so confused like there is a missing piece to this puzzle."

"It will all work out, Sandy. Try to be more optimistic."

"I'm sorry, Ellen. You're right." Sandy managed a smile.

Sandy and Ellen were still discussing what was going to be best for Franki when the technologist showed up to Franki's room to take blood.

"This is our cue."

"Let's go and have a cup of coffee. But first let me show you the new schedule for Franki's care."

"I'll have a quick look. I don't really want to leave her alone with anyone else right now."

"Blake is on suspension, remember? Franki will be just fine, let's go."

Reluctantly, Sandy followed Ellen out, leaving the lab technician to do her job.

CHAPTER FORTY

Each morning for the next week, Sandy entered Franki's room, hoping to find her awake and ready for the day's challenge. It didn't happen. Franki continued to be wide-eyed and speechless. Franki looked like a statue chiseled out of stone. Sandy talked to Franki as though she were awake, keeping her voice cheery and upbeat, never letting Franki know how scared she was. She reached deep inside herself, searching for faith and hope, praying beyond conviction that Franki's condition would change for the better. All the blood work, rape exam results, and brain scans came back standard. Blood work showed a high dosage of heroin, but that was to be expected. There were no traces of curare in her bloodstream. The problem they were facing now was this: if they abruptly took Franki off all medications, she could suffer seizures. So ever so slowly, Franki's meds were reduced five milligrams at a time.

The morning began with a warm soapy sponge bath, after which Sandy applied a thick coat of lotion on Franki's skin to prevent it from drying out and cracking. Then she was changed into a pretty cotton summer dress. The nurse would lift Franki into the wheelchair, and push her over to the window so she could bask in the sunlight, while she changed the sheets.

Sandy always dressed Franki in summer dresses, knowing how much Franki despised hospital garb. Gently, Sandy took her time combing Franki's hair, making it shiny and tangle free. Placing Franki back under the covers, Sandy read the morning paper, keeping Franki abreast with world events.

An hour after breakfast, she'd take Franki for a little spin in the wheelchair. Sandy never left her side. Religiously, three days a week, she would wheel Franki to the recreational arca, parking her beside the stereo so she could be stimulated by music. It always brought back the memory of her and Franki's first drive in the BMW, music blaring from each of the six speakers as they cruised along, enjoying the fresh air and sunshine. She couldn't wait to do it again. Franki had so much living to do.

"Come back to us, baby, you can do it," Sandy would murmur, gently stroking the side of Franki's cheek, willing her to break free from her own mind.

Sandy hated to leave her at night, but exhaustion forced her to go. She continued to pray, never giving up hope that one day, Franki would return to her old vibrant self.

Dr. Smith came to visit every day as soon as her shift was over. She stayed about an hour, giving Sandy a chance to get something to eat. This also gave Nancy one hour to do other nursing duties, such as filing, medicine distribution, and meal duty. The room again went silent.

When the nurses left, Ellen pulled the leather recliner over next to the bed, enfolding Franki's frail hand in hers.

"Franki, this is Doc. I want you to listen to me. I know you can hear me. You are a survivor, Ms. Franki Martin. I know you're not a quitter. Your record speaks for itself. I know Blake has hurt you more than physically. There was a board meeting the other day, and he is no longer taking care of you. I have sole custody of you now, kiddo. But, if he has done more, I need you to come clean and tell me." Franki's hand began to spasm and then it calmed. "I promise you will not be punished nor abandoned. Right now, it's his word against yours and Gloria's. Franki, wake up and tell me why you broke her nose. I need to hear your side of the story. This is your chance to make another wrong right. If you can acknowledge what I'm saying, please squeeze my hand."

Ellen sat still, waiting for some type of response, unaware that she was holding her breath. She watched Franki's hand for some sign of movement. Nothing.

"You've been through a lot. This is why I know you will come through this too. Sandy and I miss you. And the rest of the nurses want to see you recover as well. We all have faith that you will. Now it's up to you. Franki, spread your wings of faith, peace, and happiness. I believe there isn't anything that's wrong with you that can't be fixed. Here, let me read a couple of definitions on certain disorders. You tell me if you think you have any signs of these things."

Ellen let go. "Organ mental disorder: You don't have this one because you've had no brain impairment! Did you hear me? I said you have no brain impairment! The proof of that is your MRI scan came back normal! Schizophrenia: You don't have this either. You're not suffering from delusions or hallucinations. Okay, maybe mood disorder and mild depression but nothing more. This one is called somatoform disorder: The symptoms are physical, but no organ basis can be found, and psychological factors appear to be playing a major role. If I'm wrong, tell me I'm wrong. Yell it out to me right now. Don't you dare give up! Are you listening? You have come way too far to give up now, and if you do decide to throw in the towel, then Blake will win! He will win just like all the others!"

Ellen stopped. Was it her hopeful imagination, or did she just see Franki's finger twitch?

"That's my girl." She patted Franki's hand. "You go and get real pissed off! Show them, Franki, that you're no damn quitter!" She scrutinized Franki's still face. Not an eyelid fluttered. Nothing. Ellen sighed deeply. She finally released Franki's hand and tucked it under the sheet. It was time for Ellen to go home to her husband.

*　　*　　*

The doctor made sure there was a fresh bouquet of flowers sent every few days to brighten Franki's room, as well as a few squirts of lilac fragrance to mask some of the disinfectant odor. Ellen believed it would not be long before Franki would be out in the Three-Mile Garden, picking her own flowers.

Another week passed. Franki's condition hadn't worsened, but it wasn't improving either. Ellen was baffled. By now Franki should be out of her catatonic state. She should be up and running.

Even though Blake was no longer caring for Franki, he was still seen by other nurses to be lurking around her room. Sandy and he had a verbal fight one night when she saw him as she was leaving Franki's room. He told her he could be wherever he wanted and there was nothing she could do about it. He was right; he could be on the second floor, just not in Franki's room. When Sandy reported him to Ellen, she decided to call an emergency meeting to discuss her fears. Drastic measures had to be taken. She returned to her office and made some calls.

By the time Ellen hung up the phone, the cloud of worry had lifted from her face. If James Blake were indeed doing something underhanded, she would know about it shortly.

CHAPTER FORTY-ONE

At quarter to eight the next morning, the nurses began arriving in Dr. Smith's office, including Sarah, who was able to get someone to fill in. By eight o'clock sharp, all eleven nurses were fervent to hear what Dr. Smith had to say. They filled the couch and the extra chairs she'd brought in earlier. She would have asked the janitor for help, but didn't want anyone asking questions about why she needed the extra chairs.

"Good morning, people. Thank you for coming in on your day off. I know it's very early, and I do apologize." All eleven nodded silently in agreement.

"I would not have called this meeting if I didn't believe it was of utmost importance. So drink your coffee and try to wake up." Ellen gave a playful wink. Laughter danced around the office.

"So, why are we here, Dr. Smith?" Lisa asked.

"Let me begin by saying, I believe something very wrong is happening inside the facility between Franki Martin and Dr. Blake."

"Sounds pretty serious," Mary said.

"As far as I am concerned, it is. Last month, Dr. Blake sent Franki Martin to the fourth floor. I'm sure you are all aware that Franki had a fistfight with Gloria Shelby, and yes, Franki broke Gloria's nose. This was Blake's cause for sending her up there under our no-violence policy. I told Bill Cobie, and he suspended Blake for one week without pay. He's back now, and he has been terminated from Franki's care."

"I asked Gloria what happened that day. She said a mean girl beat her up."

Dorothy commented, "I thought it was weird when she couldn't tell me her name."

"Does anyone know what started the fight?" asked Pam.

"All I know is it was over a book that apparently Franki stole from her," Ellen explained. "Two residents had a fight, and Blake sent Franki to the fourth floor and left her there overnight and confined in a straightjacket."

Loud gasps clouded the air.

"What the hell is wrong with him?" Nancy stated angrily.

"Yeah, why did he do that?" Lisa's eyes were wide in astonishment.

"So now," Ellen went on, "Franki is in a catatonic state of consciousness. I don't condone violence, but I don't believe the confrontation was just cause for the punishment she received. At this point, I only have Gloria's opinion. Blake took it upon himself to punish Franki. He ordered the two orderlies, Bruce and Gerry, to take her to the fourth floor and leave her. Franki was still wearing a straightjacket, and strapped down to the bed without food or water when we found her, approximately fifteen hours later. It wasn't a pretty sight, guys."

"He should have had his ass canned," Lisa huffed.

"I agree," Sandy seconded.

"I think you are all well aware of why Franki was sent to us. She isn't a fighter. She is very emotionally fragile. Scars around both wrists are proof of this."

"All he got was a week off?" Mary rolled her eyes. "Like that would hurt him."

"Yes, because he had an impeccable record with his patients. Franki Martin and Dr. Blake, for some reason, don't see eye to eye. It's more than mere dislike. She absolutely hates him, and no one seems to know why."

"There must be good reason. Look what he did to her. I think the kid is justified," Sarah responded.

"Franki knows something we don't," Nancy stated.

"I saw how upset she was that day. She came running to the desk demanding I get Sandy or you, Dr. Smith, and when you both couldn't be reached, she said it didn't matter. She was dead. That was the day he sent her to the fourth floor. Judy is a witness," Nurse Allan expressed.

"And we wonder why she hates the guy. Come on, guys, something isn't right here," Janice stated.

"Right now, Franki is locked inside her own mind, afraid to come out," Ellen explained.

"Can't blame her. Christ, having to go run an errand escorted to the fourth floor is scary enough, but to be sent there . . . holy hell." Lisa shivered.

"Doctor, what is it we can do to help her come out of her comatose state?" Jean asked.

"That's why we're here. Franki should have returned to normalcy by now. I have run tests on her. Everything comes back normal. It doesn't make sense." Ellen hesitated. "What I'm about to say will come as a shock. I believe Dr. Blake is trying to get rid of Franki permanently, and I need to know why. There have been complaints by other nurses that he's been lurking around on the second floor, close to Franki's room."

"I had a run-in with him last week about the same thing. I wanted to reach out and wipe that smirk right off his face when he so arrogantly said, 'I have the privilege to be on the second floor.' It's not what he said. It was how the prick said it." Nurse Allan scowled.

"And a week ago, Lander told me, she told Blake not to go into Franki's room, and he ignored her. She ran across the hall to see what he was up to, but when she opened the door, he was walking out," Pam said.

"I knew that jerk was up to no good," Sandy retorted, almost coming out of her chair. "We need a bodyguard outside Franki's door, is what we need."

"I need you people to watch Blake's every move. If he goes into that room, I want you to follow him and then I want to know immediately. Call me at home, if you have to. If he's doing what I suspect he's doing, he'll need to be caught in the act. Some poisons can't be traced in the bloodstream. Dr. Blake would know this."

"You honestly believe he's trying to kill her?" Pam asked, horror resonating in her eyes.

"Yes, I do. I want this meeting to go no further. It's imperative that this information remains inside this room for Franki Martin's safety. If Blake suspects we're on to him, there will be nothing to hold him back. He stands to lose a lot. And this is the most important part: I am going to start administering L-DOPA in hopes that will bring Franki back to consciousness."

"What are you saying, Doctor?" Nancy asked.

"I suspect Dr. Blake is responsible for Franki's condition. Why? I don't yet have the answer. I need proof before I can go to the board. And Franki, being catatonic, can't help answer the question. I need your help in finding that proof, which means, see who his patients are, what is their condition before and after visits, especially females. Most importantly, what floor are they coming from? It will take this team to put this jigsaw puzzle together."

"Do you believe he's sexually abusing his female patients?" Mary asked.

"I need proof."

"We can't do rape examinations on all of our female patients, Dr. Smith. He has a shit load . . . no offense," Jean piped up. "It's hard enough getting them to the doctor for a simple pap smear."

"No, use your own discretion. If you feel something is wrong with a patient that was fine before her visit with Blake, then that's when you make the judgment. If you feel uncomfortable, please call Sandy or myself to assist. Everything should be documented. Just to be clear about this: You don't have to participate. You can turn around right now and walk out the door, no questions asked. I can't follow him 24-7. If I could, we would not be having this meeting."

"You want us to spy on him, like detectives?" Nancy grinned.

"Double O Seven, move aside, River Edge has a team of the best investigators on the planet!" Lisa bellowed.

The office room filled with excited energy.

"Why is it that living on the edge is far more interesting than being a straight arrow?" Pam chuckled; the other nurses joined in.

"Okay, back to business. Franki is in danger, and I can't stress that enough. Unless we find something on him soon, he'll be free to come and go as he pleases, and that scares the hell out of me. Right now, he's under the watchful eye of Bill Cobie and myself, but like I said, we're not here 24-7."

"So, what is it you want us to do?" Nurse Allan asked.

"Once a week, blood work is ordered to check the enzymes in Franki's liver. If he's feeding her toxins, it should show up. That is, if blood work is done regularly. She is almost finished with the mood stabilizer and antidepressants, but I have to leave her at the dosage she's at now. I'm afraid if I don't, she'll have a seizure, which will only complicate her condition further. L-DOPA is experimental, but I am optimistic and confident it will work. I did a lot of research last night at home. I will administer the drug, and you professionals will document the progress. How's that for a plan?"

"So the outstanding doctor is a rape hound. Who would have thunked that? But I must admit, he even looks creepy. Like the kind of guy I wouldn't want to bump into in a dark alley." Sarah shuddered.

"He doesn't scare me. He reminds me too much of a weasel," Lisa said.

"Enough about his looks. The toxins can't extract from their organs because Franki is immobile. She isn't producing sweat. This is going to be a long process, and what I am asking is, are all of you up to the task of rescuing Franki Martin? Your help and the L-DOPA, I speculate, Franki will be back with us in no time."

"Great! But how do you want us to do this?" Mary inquired. "Do you want us to follow the guy, what?"

"Yes, but do it unobtrusively. We don't want Blake to think for one second he's being watched."

"Do you really think she'll come around?" Lisa questioned, serious.

"She is in pretty bad shape right now. There's no response." Sandy's face was grim.

"I can't say with absolute surety that she will, but I am hopeful." Ellen hated to admit this to the nurses, let alone herself. "My second fear is if she does come around, Blake may sanction to have her meds increased, claiming she's a high-risk patient. He'll use the fight to keep her controlled. The longer she stays in her sedated state, the farther Franki has to fight to come back!"

"I'm in," Pam answered.

"Yeah. Whatever it is you want me to do," replied Nurse Allan.

"I am going to be Blake's shadow. I'll do whatever it takes. If he's doing something he shouldn't be, then I feel sorry for his lily-white ass because it's just about to be kicked all over kingdom come." Conviction ran in Lisa's voice.

"You can count on me, Dr. Smith," Donna added, who'd been sitting quietly the entire time.

"It's risky, but what the hell." Mary shrugged.

"Me too," Sarah agreed. "Even if he does creep me out."

"God help him because I have a feeling that man is going down hard," Judy proclaimed.

"I sure hope he isn't doing anything evil, for Franki's sake." Nancy shook her head thoroughly disgusted.

"I already know your answer." Ellen pointed her index finger at Sandy.

"Yeah, it's payback time for that evil man." And she meant it.

"You, my friend, should go home. That's an order."

"Yeah, you heard the doctor. God, Sandy, you're here day and night. You're going to burn out if you're not careful . . . and besides, Franki's in good hands." Lisa looked at Sandy and winked.

"I know she is." She tried to smile, dabbing her green eyes with a Kleenex.

"Now listen up, people. I will be placing a book in the drawer of Franki's nightstand. Every day, I want you to log anything and everything in it—from how much she drools to if she blinks her eyes or moves her pinky finger. And please talk to her like she's awake. She is listening. If you see Blake going in the left direction when you think he should be going in the right, let me know. Write it down please. If you feel there is abuse going on inside the walls of his office, go and check. He'll no doubt slam the door in your face, but at least, it will be written down. I have a key here to lock and unlock the drawer. If for some reason a colleague should ask you what you're doing, tell him or her that I have requested this. If they want to explore the question further, please send them to me. If you leave Franki's room for any reason, please make sure the drawer is locked at all times and keep the key on you. Since she is comatose, her medication is being administered intravenously."

"Thank you all very much, and I know Franki will thank you personally when she comes around. Now, Sarah, you can go back to caring for Franki. The rest of you, get out of here and enjoy the day, especially you!" Sandy knew exactly to whom the comment was directed.

"I'm going, but I'll be back tonight." Sandy yelled as the nurses hustled out the door.

"Let's stop at Smitty's for a bite to eat," Lisa suggested.

"Sounds good," Sandy agreed, along with the chorus.

*　　*　　*

No one was aware that while the meeting was taking place in Ellen's office, Dr. Blake managed to slip past the busy nurses at the station and into Franki's room. He took the syringe from his jacket pocket, flicked the bubbles of air, and injected the poison into the bleed line, promptly emptying the barrel of the syringe. Franki's whole body stiffened as the poison dripped in to her vein. Dr. Blake slipped out before being seen.

CHAPTER FORTY-TWO

Monday morning at seven twenty-two, the sun rose with a vengeance, spreading a heat almost unbearable. The humidity hung heavy in the air. It was going to be a scorcher. On her way to work, Sandy listened to the weatherman calling for rain showers throughout the day. Glancing up into the cloudless sky, she shrugged; didn't look like it, but the meteorologist could be right, she thought. As a precaution, she left the top up on her BMW. The last thing she needed was to come out after work and find the interior soaked. She'd experienced blue skies change to torrential rains in a matter of seconds. Sandy was hoping for rain. It had been so hot the last few days. The lawns looked like straw, and the wilting flowers begged for water.

Sandy strolled into work in a fairly rested mood. As she rounded the corner, heading to the staff room to put away her belongings, she and Dr. Blake collided. She stooped to pick up her purse from the floor, then glaring into the monster's eyes without hesitation.

"Beautiful day, wouldn't you say?" Dr. Blake oozed sweetly.

"It's going to rain." She fired back.

"Oh, Sandy, how is Franki doing these days?"

"She is the same, no thanks to you."

"Ah, that's too bad." He smirked; his eyebrows rose high above the rim of his glasses.

"Yeah, I guess it is." Sandy would have loved to wipe that grin from his smug, ugly face.

"Well, I should be going. Have a nice day." The doctor strutted down the hall and out of sight. *What an asshole,* she thought. Her high spirits sank down to her ankles.

Dr. Blake was feeling particularly friendly this morning. Once again, he'd succeeded with keeping Franki Martin out of commission. *No one can touch me,* he thought, heading for his office. *No one!*

Dr. Smith, on the other hand, was not feeling so great. She'd had an awful sleep, waking up every hour on the hour. Nightmares poured into her mind like a heavy rain. She dreamt about patients who looked like zombies with gray skin and hollow eyes and mouths sewn shut with thick rope.

Last night, she and Tom went for a walk along the beautiful trails, where the scent of nature came alive. When they returned home, they sat out on the patio overlooking the splendid garden and had their tea. By eleven o'clock, Ellen felt exhausted and retired to bed for a restful night's sleep, which she didn't get. Five minutes in her office, she heard her first interruption at the door. "This better be real important," she grumbled.

"Come in!" she bellowed. The door opened, and in stepped Dr. Blake, a huge smile stretching his face.

"Good morning, Ellen, and how are you this morning?"

"Morning." She continued taking her files out of her briefcase.

"Is there something wrong?" he inquired politely.

"Yes, there is, as a matter of fact. I had a crappy sleep last night, and right now, I'm in dire need of coffee." She snapped. "So what brings you to my office, James? This is unusual for you."

"I'm not allowed to stop by and say hello?"

"Hello, and now what do you want?"

"Wow, someone sure woke up on the wrong side of the bed this morning."

"I have a lot on my mind."

"Like the upcoming hearing?" He smiled confidently.

"Still going through with it, I see. James, what you did to Franki Martin is despicable and highly unprofessional, and I am going to make sure that the appropriate disciplinary action is taken against you. I hope you realize you are putting your entire career on the line if you go through with this ridiculous hearing stunt."

"You're entitled to your opinion, Ellen. I feel I was unjustly persecuted. A week's suspension is fine. I can afford that. But what I can't afford is the black mark on my perfect record. I want that expunged." His features tightened. "In my defense, I did not in any way deliberately set out to abuse anyone. I was following policy."

"What did you say?"

"I said, I did not deliberately set out to abuse anyone. I acted in accordance with the no-violence policy."

"Your story." Her lip furled in disgust.

"I wrote an affidavit explaining my decision and why I ordered Franki Martin to be sent to the fourth floor. Now it's up to the board to decide my fate."

"You don't seem to be unnerved about the outcome."

"I'm not. I made a decision based on what I witnessed that day."

Ellen could feel her temper beginning to boil as she recalled the shocking image of Franki Martin tied down to that bed. His lack of conscience almost made her lose control and throw him out of her office.

"James, I don't want to discuss this with you. You will get the opportunity to justify your inexcusable actions in front of the board. Not here, not today."

"I respect that, Ellen."

"I don't mean to be doubly rude, but I must get my work done, so I can leave this afternoon."

"I have bad news for you then."

"What now?" she snapped.

"Did you forget about our scheduled board meeting?"

"Shit, is that today?"

"I'm afraid so. This facility can't run without financial executives." He grinned, almost laughing at his colleague's frustration.

"I should have known better than to think I could have the afternoon off."

"How many years before you can retire?"

"Too damn many," she barked.

Dr. Blake made himself comfortable on the couch, his hands folded arrogantly behind his head.

"Comfortable?" Ellen asked, glaring over the top of her specks.

"Yes, thank you."

Ellen wished he would leave. But she needed to stay close to him until she figured out what he was up to. She didn't want to blow the chance of finding out exactly what prompted this good mood of his. Stay close to your enemy, would be the best way to find out what was going on.

"Coffee?"

She held up a mug, hoping he would decline.

"Sure." The answer she didn't want to hear. She turned, making a sour face. "Is there something you want to talk about?"

"Nothing of real importance."

The aroma of coffee sifted through out her office. She would have preferred her coffee without company. Carrying a cup in each hand, Ellen walked over to where James was seated.

"Now out with it, James. What is on your mind?"

"Nothing. How is Franki making out?"

"Her condition is the same. Why do you ask?"

"Ellen, I want to apologize to you for behaving the way I did that day. It wasn't called for."

"Thanks."

"I know how badly you wanted her to get well."

"She will. I haven't lost hope," Ellen snapped.

"I hadn't expected that you would. That's not what I'm trying to imply."

"Good. I think we should change the subject. You have your side to present to the board and I have mine."

"Why, are you taping our conversation?"

"Don't flatter yourself, James, you're not that important." Ellen flapped a hand in the air like she was swatting a fly. "I won't discuss Franki Martin with you. We both have our differences and let's leave it at that, shall we?"

He slurped his coffee. "Fine by me."

"What order of business is on our agenda for the board meeting today?"

"I believe it's more about the funding we need. We still have to find financial support to get that wing up and running again."

"Oh great. More talk about revenue we're supposed to pull out of our ass."

James laughed. "You seem to be in an exceptionally good mood this morning."

"Nothing special or no one special. The sun is shining, and the birds are singing. The weather is warm. I make really good money, and I love my job. What is there not to love about my life?" *And every day, I slowly poison that little bitch with the big mouth,* he thought. *And I have all the fringe benefits a man could want, and no one is the wiser.*

"I am sorry to have to rush you out, James, but I have a therapy session in ten minutes, and I still have to prepare."

"Not a problem. I have to go make my rounds as well. Thanks for the coffee and the chitchat."

"See you at the board meeting."

*   *   *

Sandy performed physical therapy on Franki's frail little body. She stretched her arms and legs, encouraging the circulation to flow, keeping her body warm.

After exercise, Sandy gave Franki a real bath, holding her like an infant while she soaped her down. Sandy was an ace at maneuvering the wires and plugs that were hooked up to the intravenous bags.

"It's a gorgeous day today, kiddo. The sun is shining, yet the weatherman insists that we are going to have rain. At lunchtime, I think I'll take you outside to look at the pretty flowers. Would you like that, Franki? If it's not raining, that is."

After her bath, Sandy dressed her little buddy in a mint-colored cotton sundress. She placed a white button-up sweater around her shoulders for warmth and pulled on a pair of white ankle socks, covering her pretty painted toenails. She placed her into the wheelchair and pushed her over to the window so she could see how sunny it was outside.

Sandy was pulling the sheets off the bed when she suddenly stopped. She swung around, listening attentively. Nothing. She thought she was hearing things. She went back to finishing the bed when she heard it again. It was her name.

"Sandy," Franki whispered. "I'm right here, baby." Sandy rushed to her side.

"Help me," Franki whispered again.

Sandy was overwhelmed with joy. She wanted to run to the hallway and scream at the top of her lungs, "Franki spoke!" But she restrained herself.

"Franki, how can I help you? What do you want me to do?" The room fell silent. "If you can hear me, Franki, I want you to blink or squeeze my hand. Come on, I know you can do it." Sandy knelt in front of Franki's wheelchair, her eyes and ears straining to see or hear any further signs of communication. Franki remained immobile, silent, and unreachable.

Chapter Forty-Three

Back in his office, James sat in his comfortable desk chair, reminiscing about his childhood. At first the meager memories were pleasant. Then to his mind's eye came the vivid image of his mother beside him on the bed, wearing only a see-through slip. The ugly scene lurked in the darkness of his thoughts, festering, like a yellow puss leaking from the cortex of his brain and seeping down into his heart. This all started two weeks after his father was murdered and buried in the shallow grave in the backyard.

That horrible day began so innocuously. As usual, his mother called up to James at seven twelve. The clock radio on his dresser confirmed the time. The smell of yummy pancakes and bacon wafted throughout the air, making his stomach gnaw with hunger, yet his belly lurched at the thought of food. Before that horror happened, James had a healthy appetite for a nine-year-old. He threw back the covers and hurried to the bathroom for his ritual morning pee and quickly ran his hands under the water, then rushed down the stairs. Mustn't keep Mother waiting; she didn't like waiting. He plunked himself onto his chair and waited for his mother to pile the hotcakes onto his plate. That morning, he forced himself to eat six pancakes, four slices of bacon, and two slices of toast, slathered in his mother's homemade jam and finished his breakfast with a glass of orange juice. While James ate his breakfast, his mother slipped upstairs into his room. When James cleared away his dishes and put them in the sink, he returned to his room. He was surprised to find his bed made and clothes laid out. *These aren't mine,* he thought, picking up the jeans. He spotted a new Spider-Man T-shirt. Looking closer, his jeans had Spider-Man embroidered down the front right leg. At the foot of the bed on the floor was a brand-new pair of high-cut sneakers, which he'd wanted for months. He wasn't too thrilled with his new underwear and socks, but what nine-year-old kid gets excited about that stuff? He ran to the top of the stairs and yelled to his mom.

To his surprise, she came out of her bedroom, up the hall from his, partially naked. James was so excited; he didn't notice his forty-seven-year-old mother had on next to nothing. His mind was only filled with whether all those new clothes were his.

"Are they mine, Mom?" He jumped up and down, eager for her answer.

"Yes. Do you like them?"

"Mommy, they are the best! Spider-Man is my hero."

"I thought I was your hero?" she asked coolly.

"You're not Spider-Man, Mommy. But I love you almost as much as I love my hero."

"I guess that will have to do. I want you to dress in your new clothes. Today is a special day. We're going on an adventure!"

"Where, Mommy? Where are we going?"

"It's a surprise, son."

"Another surprise, Mommy? Wow!" James's voice shrilled with enthusiasm and curiosity.

After dressing in his new outfit, James bounced down the stairs like Tigger in the animated movie *Winnie the Pooh*, impatiently waiting for Alma to dress. He sat on the Japanese throw rug in the living room, reading *DISCOVER*, science magazine. It felt like hours to a nine-year-old little boy waiting for another surprise.

Finally, he yelled upstairs, "Mommy, are you almost ready yet?" He stood at the foot of the stairs.

"Almost, James."

True to her word, in only moments, he glanced up at the shadow blocking the sunlight from the top of the stairs.

"Wow, Mommy, you look pretty!" His eyes grew large with awe.

She smiled elegantly, making her way down each of the twelve steps. As she reached the bottom stair, James sprang to his feet, fully geared for . . . an adventure. Where, he had no idea, but he was ready.

"You look like a cool dude yourself," she countered.

"Mommy, do you think I'm cool?"

"Cool as a cucumber." She smiled.

"Cucumbers aren't cool. Oh, Mommy, you're so silly." He broke out laughing.

Alma wore powder-blue slacks with a matching blazer and a pink-and-blue hat that coordinated with her suit. On her feet, she wore a pair of baby pink pumps with a smaller heel. She slung a beige purse over her shoulder. Hand in hand, the two walked proudly out the door, locking it first, before heading to the old Honda Accord.

*   *   *

James's eyes sprang wide open when they drove into the parking lot of the amusement park of Adventure Land. His mother shut off the engine, taking the keys out of the ignition and put them in her purse. James just stared out the window, dumbfounded.

"Are you ready, son?"

James was speechless. As strict as Alma was, even James could tell these rare outings to the amusement park gave her great pleasure.

"James, are you going to sit there all day, or are you going to get out of the car? Let's go have some fun." She reached across the seat and nudged him with her elbow. James threw his arms around his mother.

"Oh, Mommy! Thank you!" His eyes sparkled with exhilaration.

"It's only me and you now, James. You understand that, don't you?"

"Yes. I think so, Mommy." He didn't want to think of his dead father rotting away in the backyard. Today, just for a while, he wanted to escape the pain and guilt. He didn't want to cry today. Pushing aside the sadness, he smiled up at his mother.

"If you don't understand right now," she said, tousling his dirty blond hair, "you will in time. Everything I do now is for you, James. You understand me right, son?"

"Yes, Mommy."

His mother seemed so different today. Two weeks ago, he had witnessed something so horrible, that he would never forget it. A rage, he didn't know could exist in human beings had burst from his mother. She hissed and growled and swore words he'd never heard before, but he knew they were bad. Alma stabbed and stabbed at his fallen father while he stood immobilized in wide-eyed terror, unable to take his eyes off the ghastly, unbelievable scene unfolding before him. He still felt as though that bloodstained knife had been plunged into his own heart. Now, he had no love for that mommy. Only fear. But this mommy did not seem like the same mommy who was taking him to Adventure Land and being so nice to him. James shook his head. It was all so confusing.

Alma got out of the car, walked around to the passenger side, and opened the door. The door wouldn't open from the inside. Alma made a mental note to get it fixed next week. She grabbed her son's hand and practically dragged him out of the car and across the parking lot. Then the two were standing at the ticket booth, with the thrill pouring into his veins, he had forgotten what had made him so unhappy.

"Two tickets please." His mother searched in her wallet for money.

"And how old are you?" the clerk asked James.

"I'm nine, sir." James's smile was as bright as the midmorning sun.

"Nine, eh. You have a very well-mannered boy, ma'am."

"Thank you." She looked down at James and smiled. "Did you hear that, honey? This gentleman here says you are a polite young boy. I told you learning your manners would pay off."

"Thank you, sir," James replied prudishly.

"I see politeness is taking a second seat to getting into the park," his mother said frowning down at James.

"Ah, he's just excited that's all," said the ticket man.

"I guess, you're right." She rolled her eyes. "Thank you." She placed the change back in her wallet, and the clerk handed her two tickets to enter the park.

"Enjoy your day."

"We will, won't we, Mommy?"

"Of course, we will."

As they entered the gate, they heard loud shouts of laughter and mind-bending screams from the people riding roller coasters and the Drop of Doom. James started laughing.

"What would you like to do first, son?"

"I don't know. I'm too happy to pick."

"How about we go and get a booklet of tickets for the rides first."

"Sure." He held her hand as they walked across the lumpy grass, carpeted with blue tarps, protecting the wires that surged electricity to the rides.

"A booklet of tickets please."

"Adult or child?"

"Is there a difference?"

"The book with half adult and half child is five dollars less."

"That's the one we want. Right, James?"

"Are you going to come on the rides with me, Mommy?"

"I sure am."

"Oh, that is so cool! But you'll have to hold on to your hat because it will blow away."

"Good advice, James. Am I almost as cool as Spider-Man?"

James giggled. "Almost, Mommy." She tousled his hair.

"What ride would you like to go on first?"

"Zipper."

"The Zipper. Are you sure?"

"Yep." He nodded confidently.

"You won't get sick now, will you?"

"Nope." He pulled her in the direction of the loud screams coming from the Zipper. Together, they waited in line, James jumping up and down, hardly able to contain himself. When the ride finally stopped, people staggered toward the exit gate on the opposite side.

James and Alma rode on every ride. James felt great. His mother on the other hand was noticeably pale.

"Are you okay, Mommy?"

"Yes. But my stomach says it's glad we're out of tickets."

James snickered. "Now what, Mommy?"

"How about you try your hand at a couple of games. Maybe you can win a stuffed animal for me."

"Okay, but I don't think I'm very good."

"How do you know that, James? You haven't tried."

"I don't know. Kids at school tell me all the time."

"What, James? What do the other children tell you?"

"They call me a nerd. A bookworm. Seth always calls me a freak and pushes me down."

"I won't put up with that, James. First thing Monday morning, I will report that boy to the principal's office."

"Mommy, no!" He cried out.

"James, what do you mean no?"

"If you do that, Mommy, he will beat me up even more."

"No, he won't. I'll see to it that he doesn't."

"He will. I know he will!" James jumped up and down in protest.

"Okay, James, let's not worry about it right now."

"Promise me, Mommy, that you won't tell?" he begged.

"James." She placed her hand on her hip.

"Promise me, please, Mommy!" His voice panicked.

"Calm down, James. I'll let you handle it."

James released the air out of his lungs.

"Enough about that Seth character. Come on, aren't we supposed to be having a fun day?"

"Okay. I'm going to win the biggest stuffed animal that they have in the park just for you!"

"You are, are you?"

"I am because my name is James Blake, and I'm cool."

"You're cool, son, and don't let anyone tell you differently."

They walked across the grounds to where the games were, opposite to the rides. There he chose a game of rings to be thrown around Coke bottles. The grand prize was a huge giraffe with a red ribbon tied around its long neck. Two customers ahead of him lost. James closed his eyes and concentrated. Then he threw it with all his might. He did it! With a heart bunting with pride, he handed the giraffe to his mother.

By four in the afternoon, they decided they'd had their fill of rides, games, and of course, cotton candy, popcorn, and pop. James's skin was turning red from the sun. Once inside the vehicle, Alma applied a thick layer of lotion on his hot face and gangly arms.

"Are you hungry?" she asked.

"I'm a little hungry." He wasn't.

"Let's stop off at Burger King and pick up dinner for tonight and then the video store. You can choose the movie." She smiled.

"You mean a Spider-Man movie?"

"Exactly."

"Can we go there first, just in case they're all gone?"

"Well, I guess so."

"You are as great as Spider-Man, Mommy."

"I'll take that as a compliment."

"A what?"

"Never mind." She tweaked his earlobe.

James felt blessed that day. Everything he'd wanted had come true. He couldn't imagine what he had done to deserve such a wonderful day.

He had no idea he was being groomed.

*   *   *

Back at home, James sat on the couch beside the giraffe he'd won, inhaling deeply the aroma of burgers and fries his mother placed on the coffee table. He was stunned at this kind gesture; his mother never let him eat in the living room while he watched television.

James went to bed that night exhausted and happy. He didn't know how long he'd been asleep. The last time she stood in his doorway, he'd been in for another one of her raise-the-rod-less-spoil-the-child beatings. His heart began pounding with heavy doom. His room suddenly filled with light when she flicked the switch.

"James, wake up. It's Mommy."

"Mommy . . . what is it?" He covered his eyes from the glaring light.

She walked over to his bed and sat down, nipples exposed through the sheer slip.

"James, I'm scared, and I don't know what to do."

"Why are you scared, Mommy?" He sat up in one sudden motion.

"Oh, James, I just am."

"You don't have to be afraid, Mommy. Me and Spider-Man will protect you."

"Will you make me feel better?"

"How?"

She walked over to the doorway and shut out the light and then came back to his bed, sliding in beside him. She stroked his hair and ran her hand along his arm and across his chest and down his leg. James began feeling uncomfortable sensations. Then, without warning, she placed her hot mouth over his. He struggled to breath. She moved away long enough to remove her slip. Then gently but firmly, she pulled him to her.

CHAPTER FORTY-FOUR

That afternoon, Sandy tried to reach Ellen with the good news of Franki's awakening. The drug L-DOPA was working. She was very disappointed to find the doctor had gone for the day. Before leaving, Sandy pushed an envelope under Dr. Smith's door. She wasn't going to bother her at home. Ellen needed a night off from this place.

A few minutes later, she was exiting the front doors of River Edge, heading across the parking lot to her car. The weatherman's prediction was correct; it had rained hard all afternoon. The muggy air created a waxen, floating haze.

The long days and nights were finally catching up to Sandy. She was beat, but before going home, she had to stop at the grocery store for some necessary items. She drove into the parking lot of Sam's Grocery Store on Bloom Street, a block from where she lived. She'd forgotten her list on the fridge but knew her stomach would decide what she needed.

That evening, Sandy lay on her couch, eating chips and chocolate and watching television. It was a relief not to be so concerned about Franki's potential; recovery was just around the corner. Ellen was right. Franki would be fine. At eleven, she called it quits and went to bed.

*   *   *

The next morning, when Dr. Smith entered her office, she picked up the envelope bearing the institute's insignia and threw it on her desk, assuming the letter was the minutes of yesterday's financial strategies.

*   *   *

Before leaving for work, Sandy caught the tail end of the weather. It was already mideighties and climbing well into the nineties by mid-afternoon. There was a warning for the elderly to stay indoors and keep cool.

Sandy had her day with Franki planned. First up was getting her ready for the day. Second, she decided on a stroll through the Three-Mile Garden and then locate a nice shady spot under a maple tree. Sandy loved reading poetry from Franki's own personal collection. Franki loved to write, and Sandy needed to make her aware of what she was missing.

After tending to all of Franki's needs, the thought had occurred that it was odd she hadn't heard from Ellen. But then it was time to take Franki for a ride in the wheelchair. It was still necessary to occasionally wipe the drool from her lips. Such an indignity for her, Sandy knew. It would be wonderful when she was completely recovered. Sandy parked the wheelchair under the big maple as she planned. She scanned Franki's book for a new poem to read. She came across the one titled "Guidance."

GUIDANCE

I close my eyes and pray to the Lord
Asking and pleading to unlock the door
Please help me to set myself free
To follow every road to every dream
I heard the Lord reply,
My dearest, dearest child,
You must have patience for your many roads and many miles
So again, I asked the good Lord above,
How many more trials will I have to overcome?
My child, he said, there is many surprises to endure in life
Stay strong and I will guide you out of darkness into the light
I guess what you're saying, Lord, is I need to trust?
So I'll find the strength to never give up
My child, he said, be honest in everything you do
Always know I am standing beside you
Thank you, I said, for the guidance, to do my ultimate best.
I then closed my eyes a heart filled with peaceful rest.

Franki Martin

"Franki, are you listening, kiddo? This is your stuff remember? You know, you will be famous one day." Sandy waited anxiously, looking for a response. "I just know it."

Franki was still pretty closed off from the rest of the world. Even with the eleven nurses standing united and the L-DOPA going up in dosage day by day, her little buddy remained cocooned from the world.

"Now it's my turn, Franki. I wrote this one last night. It's called, 'Come Back.'"

COME BACK

Little one, it's time to wake
To be a part of this wondrous day
There are things to be done
To enjoy all around you—an abundance of love
Please, find the strength to come awake
For this the Lord, I pray
I will teach you skills to live
With everything in me, I will give
Franki, I know we could be a great team
I promise I won't hurt you—or ever leave
Together experiencing all of life's fun
Memories to cherish of many setting suns
Franki, when I look at you, a version of me
Unleash the chains, child, and be free
To see and hear the birds sing
To feel a rose petal caress your skin
Franki, wake, there is too much to do
Dreams to fulfill and make come true
All the gentleness flows out of you

Sandy Miller

"Now, no more sleeping, kiddo. We both have so much to see, hear, touch, taste and smell."

Sandy squeezed Franki's hand. The only sounds were the birds chirruping in the trees. Franki hadn't uttered a word since yesterday.

CHAPTER FORTY-FIVE

Ellen was sitting at her desk, reading all the reports pouring in from the eleven nurses playing James Bond. She was disappointed to find nothing concrete. By now, the drug L-DOPA should have induced positive results for Franki.

Dr. Smith tucked the pages back inside the file folder; it was time to go and check on her little friend.

* * *

Sandy watched as Gloria crossed the Three-Mile manicured lawn. The redhead stopped in front of Franki's wheelchair.

"What's wrong with her?" Gloria asked shyly, putting her fingers into her mouth and sucked.

"Franki isn't feeling good today," Sandy replied, stroking Franki's hair, trying to remain neutral.

"Her name Franki?"

"Yes, it is."

"Can I give her this?" She held up a daisy she'd picked from the Three-Mile Garden.

"Franki would like that." Sandy smiled.

When Franki didn't reach out to take the flower, Gloria tried to force it into her limp hand.

"Why won't she take it? She mad at me stealing her book?"

"Here, let me help you, Gloria." Gently, Sandy lifted Frank's hand so Gloria could slip the stem between her fingers.

"Oh, did you steal Franki's book?" Sandy asked casually.

"Yeah. I lie."

Sandy pointed to Dr. Smith who was striding toward the maple tree. Today, Ellen seemed to have a spring in her step that Sandy hadn't seen in a while since all this crisis started with Franki.

"Did that man hurt?" Gloria asked, patting Franki on the shoulder.

"What did you lie to Dr. Smith about, Gloria?" Sandy probed.

"Her." She pointed at Franki. "She didn't steal book." She shook her head from side to side.

"What book, honey?" Sandy asked calmly while her heart raced inside her chest.

"The book," Gloria stuttered. "You . . . know . . . book." Gloria was getting agitated.

"Maybe you should tell Dr. Smith. She'll know what book you are talking about, won't she?"

Gloria shook Franki roughly. "Come on, wake up."

"Not so rough, Gloria. Be gentle."

"She won't talk."

"I think you're just in time, Doctor," Sandy announced to Ellen.

"Hello, Gloria. How are you today?" Dr. Smith asked.

"You're that doctor in office?"

"Yes, I am. You remembered. I see your nose is better." Dr. Smith commented.

She shook her head up and down. "Better."

"Gloria, why don't you tell this nice doctor what you told me? You know, about the book." Sandy smiled reassuringly and then looked up at Ellen. "I think you are going to want to hear what Gloria has to say, Dr. Smith. Oh, and before I forget, did you get my letter?"

"That was from you?" Ellen sat down beside Sandy on the bench.

"Yes. You haven't read it yet?"

"No. I thought it was the minutes of yesterday's board meeting. Why, what's up?"

"The L-DOPA is working. Franki spoke yesterday."

"What did she say?"

"Sandy, help me."

"That's a good start because that's exactly what we're going to do. Franki, can you hear me?"

"There's been nothing since."

"That's pretty normal. I knew she'd come around. Sometimes the medication takes a while to get into the system. Before I leave tonight, I'll inject her again with 20 cc's." Ellen looked at the deep bruising in the crook of her arm. "Change the needle to the other arm today. That contusion is pretty sable."

"Why would she ask me to help her?"

"It's probably the last memory she had while being confined to the bed on the fourth floor. Secondly, take it as a compliment. It's you she trusts the most."

"Great news." She exhaled a deep breath. "And Gloria was just telling me something that I think might be interesting, right, Gloria?" The woman with the young girl's mentality nodded.

"Gloria, would you like to come to my office and talk with me?" Ellen offered.

"No! I want to stay. My friend, she sick. She sick, you know, won't talk."

"Gloria, honey, tell Dr. Smith about the book."

"No one is going to hurt you if you tell me the truth about the book. It's okay, Gloria, you won't get in trouble, I promise." Ellen's smile was trusting.

"I stole the book, not Fra— . . . her," Gloria whispered, patting Franki's shoulder.

The doctor and nurse exchanged grim glances. Just as they'd suspected, the truth had finally come to light about Dr. Blake. The man everyone respected and admired. Beneath that perfect mask was a twisted monster. Franki was hiding something out of sheer terror.

"Gloria," Dr. Smith spoke warmly, "why don't you and I go for a walk, and you can visit with your friend a little later, okay? We can go to the garden and pick some nice flowers for your new friend. Franki will like that."

"Okay, bye." Gloria bent over and gave Franki a kiss on the cheek, then took Dr. Smith's extended hand as they walked away.

Dr. Smith wasn't shocked to hear the truth. He was a deceitful bastard. Dr. Blake had convinced Gloria to lie. By her now telling the truth about what really happened, Gloria is put in jeopardy. They all needed to protect these two from that devil. And they needed more proof. Speculation wouldn't nail him.

* * *

Before leaving for the day, Sandy stopped by Ellen's office. Ellen had just returned from Bill Cobie's office, and Sandy opened the door to find the good doctor in a far from jovial mood, not because of the meeting with Bill, but by Blake's deception. *Slam!* Down went the files she had in her hand. *Slam!* Down went the stapler, then her briefcase.

"I can see that you're busy, Ellen. I'll come back another time."

The doctor looked hard at Sandy, and then roared with laughter. "Come in and sit down. I promise I won't throw anything at you. I just need to vent. I need to talk to someone before I go up to Blake's office and strangle him with my own hands. That bastard—how dare he!"

"I'm seated. Fire away."

"I don't even know where to start, Sandy."

"The beginning works for me." She shrugged.

"It's getting really scary around here. I mean, Blake convinces Gloria to lie about the fight, and then, he ordered Franki to the fourth floor. What in hell is going on?"

"We know something isn't right. That's why we had the meeting, remember?"

"I am so angry at Blake right now I could just spit. Dr. Blake has betrayed my trust and tried to make me look like a fool for defending Franki, and I don't take that lightly."

"So Gloria was able to tell you the truth?"

"Yes. Franki didn't steal Gloria's book. She was trying to take her book back. When in Blake's office that day, I asked Gloria what kind of book it was and she couldn't answer me. Today, she took me to Franki's room and showed it to me. It was one of Franki's scribblers that she had written her poetry in." She held the book in the air. "I thought it was odd that when I asked, Blake quickly cut me off with 'Isn't-a-broken-nose-enough-for-you?' bullshit. I didn't like it, but I still trusted he wasn't a devil."

"Ellen, this isn't your fault. Franki is the way she is because of Blake's breach of sanity, not yours."

"I know that, but it doesn't help the situation."

"Ellen, when I came to you . . . how long ago? I didn't want to believe that a trusted colleague of yours would be capable of abusing one of our patients. But when you said that he had told you that Franki had made a pass at him. I knew in my gut he was a liar. Franki wouldn't go near him for any reason."

"And I still gave that son-of-a-bitch the benefit of the doubt. Not anymore."

"Was Gloria threatened if she told the truth?"

"Yeah. She wouldn't be 'his special girl' for starters, whatever the hell that means, and that she would be punished. She wouldn't elaborate on 'his special girl,' and I couldn't push it. It's one hell of an accusation, wouldn't you say?"

"Absolutely. The day I told you about our beach outing, you went to Blake about it, and that's when he told you she'd made a pass at him but not to worry."

"Yes. He told me to leave it alone, that Franki had had enough to deal with. I believed him, and now look at her!"

"Then, she mysteriously disappears to the fourth floor shortly after that because she had a fight with Gloria. Franki was set up!" Sandy smacked her hands together.

"I played right into Blake's hands, Sandy. He created the scenario so he could have her put up and shut up."

Both women felt an eerie shiver run up their spines. They looked at each other, reality and terror reflected in their eyes. At that exact moment, they knew they had to find out what kind of abuse he was bestowing on Franki and Gloria, and who knew how many other women he'd threatened inside this facility that was supposed to help patients get better. It was beyond belief!

"Franki is safe as long as she's not talking. As for Gloria, we'll have to up our game and make sure she's safe at all times. And monitor how many visits per week she sees Blake."

"Damn it, Ellen, can't we call the police?"

"And say what, the women had a fight? There is no concrete proof of any abuse going on. We need some goddamn proof." Ellen slammed her hand down hard on the desk. Papers quivered off her desk.

"For Christ's sakes, please don't go and ask him," Sandy blurted. "He's sexually assaulting these women, and we know it. I will prove it, by golly. I'm not going to rest until he's behind bars."

"Trust me, I have no intentions of doing that again. One major mistake almost cost Franki her life. I'll be damned if I'm going to let him have any more ammunition against any of our patients."

"Good to hear. How many years have you worked alongside that man?"

"Too fucking long, excuse my language."

For a long moment, they remained silent. Then, "And . . . what do you think we should do?" Sandy asked the dreaded question.

Ellen sighed. "I'm not sure. I am not going to put Gloria Shelby in any kind of danger by calling the police and having them question her. I believe she's been through enough. If he suspects she told on him, who knows what he will do to her. Physicians who are so inclined have access to drugs that are impossible to trace."

"According to the examinations we have performed, there's no indication he's raped either of the women."

"I'm not so sure that's great news. We need to stay on alert though and continue doing what we're doing."

"I pray, he never finds out about your conversation with Gloria." Sandy rubbed her bare arms. The mere thought turned her cold.

"If I go back to Bill again with our suspicions, when I have nothing concrete, he's going to think I'm out on a witch hunt. I need something of real substance, not a bunch of accusations or feelings."

"How close is Bill Cobie to Blake?"

"They're not." Ellen smiled, and it wasn't warmth shining in her eyes." Bill is fair, doing everything by the book, but he's no fool. Although he doesn't like Blake, he wouldn't sabotage the man's career on a presumption."

"Sounds like he's an honorable guy. Didn't fire Blake, did he?"

"No, he didn't." Ellen took a sip of her now cold coffee.

"And you think Franki's better off not saying anything for a little bit longer?"

"Unfortunately, yes."

"I don't think we should wait," Sandy countered.

"We have no goddamn evidence, Sandy!" Ellen yelled, rising out of her chair. "I will not put these women through anymore than they've already been through. This is as upsetting to me as it is to you, trust me. I have interviewed evil. I know how their minds operate. These people are devoid of any feeling."

"When Franki comes to, will she even remember?"

"Maybe not. At least, she'll be safe if she doesn't." Ellen sat back down in her chair. The room went silent. "I'm sorry. I'm not mad at you."

"I understand. You're just frustrated."

"This goes way beyond frustration, Sandy." Ellen scowled.

"Oh shoot, what time is it?"

"Time for both of us to get out of here. Want to go for a drink at Teasers?"

"I'm sorry, I'll have to take a rain check. I almost forgot I'm having a guest over for dinner tonight."

"Anyone special?"

"No, just a friend. I like it that way. No complications, if you know what I mean?"

"Complications my ass. Sandy, you're just a big chicken."

"I'm clucking my way out of here now."

"I hope you have a nice dinner. You sure deserve someone special in your life. And don't you dare sell yourself to the lowest bidder. You hear me?" Ellen waggled a finger.

"Loud and clear, boss," she said, saluting.

"Do any of the other nurses know that Franki called out to you?"

"I logged it in the book."

"Thank you, Sandy, for listening to me."

"Hey, you're human like the rest of us."

"Have a good night, chicken."

"See you tomorrow. Cluck-cluck."

Sandy closed the door, leaving Ellen alone with her thoughts. Ellen took in a deep breath. She knew what she needed to do first before visiting Franki.

CHAPTER FORTY-SIX

Dr. Blake had no idea that his mistress patient had ratted him out. Ellen told Gloria that whatever she did, she was not to tell Dr. Blake that they had talked. It was to be their special secret. Gloria didn't understand why, but she thought Ellen was her friend and agreed.

Gloria kind of liked Dr. Blake too but in a different way. He kissed her and held her and liked to put his thing inside her. She liked to make him happy. He told her that she was his "special girl," that this was their important secret. But sometimes he hurt her. Afterward, he always said he was sorry and gave her chocolates. But Dr. Smith made her smile and played games with her, and they had a different kind of fun. Dr. Smith never ever hurt her.

*   *   *

Dr. Smith hoped she'd made Gloria understand the importance of secrecy without scaring the daylights out of her or putting her in harm's way. How she wanted to storm into Blake's office and confront the son of a bitch. Ellen would demand to know why Franki Martin hated him and why she was so terrified of him. But she knew it wouldn't get her anywhere. He'd refute the whole allegation against him. The gratification would have to wait until he was behind bars. As it stood, his sending a patient to the fourth floor was ethically questionable, but not a criminal offense.

Teeth grinding and stomach tense, she knew exactly who she needed to give her a good dose of feeling better. She picked up the phone and dialed.

"Hi, darling."

"Hello, my love. How are you?"

"Not as good as I want to be," she grumped.

"Oh? And why is that, my love? Are you missing the man of your dreams?"

"You could say that."

"You could say that or are you saying that?" Tom teased.

"I love you, honey."

"That's better. What's bothering you?"

"I just wanted to hear your comforting voice."

"You called me just to hear my voice? Ellen, how long have we been married?"

"A while now." She laughed.

"A while now and you just decided to call so you could hear my voice?"

"Something like that."

"My dear, dear beautiful wife of thirty-plus years, if you don't mind me saying this, you're full of it! You have never called me before to listen to my voice unless something was wrong."

"Do you have to know me so well?"

"It comes with the territory, my darling. Happy wife, happy life."

"I have the smartest husband on this planet."

"Thank you, and I have the best woman a guy could ever hope for. So am I going to have to drag it out of you?"

"I . . . you know what, can you come and get me? We'll go out for a bite to eat. Does that sound good to you, Tom?"

"Sure, but it also sounds like after we have a meal together, you have plans to go back to work. Is that statement correct?"

"I'm afraid so," she sighed.

"You work too hard."

"No rest for the wicked." She forced a laugh, hiding her fear.

"I'll come and get you, and if you look as exhausted as you sound, you're not going back to work. Deal?"

"You drive a hard bargain, sir."

"I know that's one of the thousand reasons why you fell in love with me."

"Is that so?" She smiled on the other end of the phone. Tom could always be counted on to make her feel so much better.

"You know it, babe." Tom was also grinning on his end.

"You haven't already eaten, have you?"

"No. I was puttering around in the garden, waiting for my adoring wife to come walking through the front door, telling me how much she missed me."

"I'm sorry."

"Don't be sorry, Ellen. You can make it up to me in about fifteen minutes. I have to get cleaned up first."

"Fifteen minutes is perfect."

"Don't tell me, checking in on the little one?"

"How did you know?"

"I am your husband in case you've forgotten."

Ellen laughed. "I'll be in the parking lot, my love." She hung up feeling better, then hurried to the second-floor nurse's station. It was time for Franki's L-DOPA.

CHAPTER FORTY-SEVEN

Sandy pulled into her driveway, feeling grimy and unbalanced from the rush of the day. A cool shower would revive her to feeling clean and centered. She dropped her soiled nurse's uniform and underclothes into the laundry basket and then headed to the bathroom. The steaks she intended to cook were submerged in a teriyaki marinating sauce. The only chore left was to make a garden salad. Sandy never thought much about a romantic relationship with Peter Frost. Not because she didn't want one. She learned early on not to set herself up for a fall. The prospect of having a romantic interlude with Peter did intrigue her.

"This is your fault, Ellen!" she said aloud, laughing. Living alone, she found the best way to stay sane was to sometimes talk to herself. She wasn't nuts. Some of her solitary pals did too. "I was fine until you went ahead and called me chicken. It isn't like I'm not attracted to Peter, but we're just friends." She vigorously shampooed her hair. Then, "Stop it, Sandy! You know better than to get your head wrapped around some lame fantasy that ends up dropping on its head. The inner battle was on. One side telling her that she wanted romance with Peter, the other telling she wasn't his type. The scar on her face ran a lot deeper than she let on.

Sandy stepped out of the tub, drying herself off, sprinkling powder on the spaces and places that mattered. She dropped the towel on to the tiled floor and strode naked into her bedroom. She rummaged through her closet for something cool to wear. The temperature outside was still in the mid-thirties, with the humidity hanging intense in the air. She decided on a sundress, one way she could get away with not having to wear a bra and panties. She giggled, feeling naughty. This little secret excited Sandy in a way that she'd never experienced. It was as if she were exploring her own sexuality for the first time. She stood looking into the full-length mirror on the back of her bedroom door, swaying playfully before spinning around on one foot. "Yahoo!"

She stood at the kitchen counter preparing the "Martha Stewart" salad, which Peter loved so much. She opened a can of mandarin oranges, pouring the juice down the drain. The lettuce and vegetables were already washed and dried and waiting in the wooden salad bowl. From the pantry, she took out a jar filled with yummy trail mix. She sprinkled a fair amount over the salad, placed the mandarin oranges on top, and set the bowl on a shelf in the fridge. Then she poured herself a glass of Chardonnay to take outside. Peter wasn't due for another twenty minutes. This would give her time to calm her perverted thoughts before he arrived.

She stretched out in the lawn chaise, under the umbrella, her muscles sighing with relief. Nursing was tough on the legs.

Lost in sweet thoughts about Peter, she didn't hear the doorbell, but he heard music coming from the back. *She'll never hear me,* he thought, grinning mischievously. She jumped when he touched her shoulder, spilling wine all down the front of her dress.

"Jesus, you scared the hell out of me!" She placed her hand on her chest.

"Sorry." He laughed.

"Didn't you ring the bell?"

"Yes, I did, but obviously, you didn't hear me. With the smile I saw, fantasy must've been pretty good, eh?"

"Yeah, right." She flushed.

"So tell me, was it that sexually delicious?"

"Shut up, you pervert!" She smacked him across the shoulder.

"You're calling *moi* a pervert after that dirty little smirk you just had pasted on your face?"

"You have a one-track mind."

"I don't believe I'm the only one with a dirty mind." He smirked.

"You're sick."

"Oh, talk dirty to me please."

"You're incorrigible."

"Come on, baby, share."

"Whatever, Peter. Glass of wine or cold beer?" Sandy swung her legs over the chair when Peter's hand pressed down on her shoulder.

"Hey, don't get up. I know my way around. Would you like a refill?"

"Please." She handed him her wineglass and glanced down at her stained, wet dress. She should change but felt just too comfy to move.

Sandy was glad fantasies were hidden in the dark corners of the mind. Especially the hot and sweaty fantasy she'd just had about Peter.

He returned with a fresh glass of wine and a Labatts' Blue for himself.

"You should be happy that I'm not some sick killer, or you would have been dead. Seriously, what were you thinking about earlier?"

"Oh, it was nothing."

"You appeared pretty pleased with yourself, whatever it was."

"It's for me to know."

"I'm changing the subject since you won't tell me who you were daydreaming about."

"Thank you."

"How did work go today?" he asked, settling into the patio chair.

"It was busy."

"I don't know how you can work in a place like that."

"Like what?"

"You know, with a bunch of nuts."

"Those people are not any nuttier than some of the people outside the place. You can trust me on that one."

"Don't you get depressed always being around men and women with mental problems?"

"No. I don't look at my job that way, Peter."

"I don't know how you do it, Sandy. I personally know that I couldn't do it."

"How do you know if you have never tried?"

"Just assuming."

"You know what *assuming* means?"

"Yes, yes, it makes an *ass* out of *you* and *me*, funny, very funny. So what's new in your life? And don't lie to me. I know something's going on because I haven't been able to get a hold of you in weeks. Is there someone special in your life that you won't tell me about?"

"No!"

"No. What do you mean no?"

"I mean there is no one special in my life."

"So, where in the hell have you been? I know you haven't taken a trip. Out with it." Peter took a pull on his beer.

"I've been working."

"Bull."

"Honest."

"Then you must have made a million. Like I said, I've been trying to get a hold of you for weeks now."

"I've been spending a lot of time with Franki."

"Is she the young girl with all the talent you told me about?"

"She is the one."

"How is she?"

"Not good. She's catatonic right now. I can't go into details about her circumstances, though."

"What?"

"I just can't."

"Why? Sounds pretty creepy to me."

"It would to you."

"Come on, what's the big secret? Has she gone AWOL or something?"

"How can she go AWOL if she's catatonic, stupid? No, she's in bed with her eyes open, staring up at the ceiling, completely disassociated from the rest of the world. Don't ask me to go into more detail because I can't."

"Is she going to get better? Can you answer that?"

"We hope so, but right now, her progress is a lot slower than what we anticipated."

"She's a fighter, right?"

"Yes, she is. But for how much longer, we don't know."

"This sounds really serious?"

"It is, Peter, and that's why I've been with her almost 24-7."

"Hey, girl, you're such a great person!" He saluted her with his bottle of beer.

"Thank you, Peter. That's really nice of you to say. I needed to hear that right now. So, how are you?"

"I'm good, working hard at the construction site, nothing major."

"How's your girlfriend?"

"Oh, that nutcase. With great relief, I can say we are no longer seeing each other."

"What did you do this time?"

"Can't blame this one on me. More like she belongs in the place where you work."

"Why, what did she do?"

"More like, what didn't the freak do?"

"Okay, you have my attention. Spill it."

"I like Erika and all. It was just that she was a complete cling on. You know, the fatal attraction type." Peter gave his body a shake as though getting rid of invisible body lice."

"When I'd go out with boys for some drinks, she had to know why and what time I was going to be home. I mean, really! It's not like we were living together." Peter's eyes widened with disbelief. "She was good in bed, that I'll miss." He started laughing.

"See, you are a perv. I also told you not to be picking up women in bars."

"She seemed pretty normal to me. She's a secretary at a lawyer's firm, a killer body. The bonus, so I thought, was that she was smart."

"She was bright all right. She knew how to get to you, didn't she?"

"She got to me all right, and now she is gone, thank Christ."

"Until next week."

"Sandy, my love, if I didn't know any better, I'd say you think I'm a sleazeball."

"Aren't you?"

"That's cold. In fact that was so cold I'm going to get myself another beer. And since I'm such a sleazeball, can I top up your wine?"

"Yes, please, tramp." Sandy cracked up. She pulled a face. "I'm joking with you, Peter."

"Could have fooled me."

"Ah, I didn't mean anything by it. I just wish you would stop picking up women in nightclubs. I'm not saying the relationships that come out of bars don't ever work, but from what you've told me, the rates, my dear, haven't been that great for you. True?"

"And what's that supposed to mean?"

"I just mean—"

"Hold that thought. I'll be back in a minute, Ms. Pure as the Driven Snow."

"I'm not judging," she yelled after him.

"Could have fooled me," Peter countered.

Sandy shook her head. She didn't mean to make Peter think she was better than him. It was her insecurity talking: how can a guy like Peter be interested in someone like me?

Peter returned moments later with their refills. He plunked his almost perfect frame into the lawn chair but not before moving it closer to hers.

"So, Ms. Expert on Relationships, when was the last time you had a date?"

"It's not me we're talking about."

"Oh, yes it is. You made it that way by calling me a sleazeball. Short memory, Sandy."

"I told you, I didn't mean to hurt your feelings."

"Maybe not, so enlighten me. When was the last time you had a date with someone, other than work-related?"

"You know as well as I do that I don't date."

"What do you mean, you don't date? That sounds like a poor excuse to me."

"I'm not trying to come up with any excuses, Peter. That's just the way it is. If I was going to date any man, the prerequisite is that he would have to be blind."

"And why is that?" He folded his arms across his now bare chest.

"Are you losing your sight?" She pointed to the disfigurement on the right side of her face.

"You know, Sandy, one of these days, you're going to have to stop hiding behind that so-called imperfection. It's not a big deal. So what you have a purplish mark on the side of your face. Anyone who looks at you doesn't see the so-called ugliness you do. Within five minutes of talking with you, honest, you don't see the scar. What I see is how amazing you are. The light in your eyes, the pure heart you have, and let's not forget that drop-dead body hiding under that tent, you call a dress."

Now, it was her turn to protect her shield of armor. She folded her arms across her chest. The moments ticked by slowly as he stared into her meadow-green eyes filled with fear and insecurity.

"You can be a real jerk sometimes."

He gave her one of his famous boyish grins to soften his words. "Tell me something I don't already know." Before she could move away, Peter leaned down and kissed the blemished side of her face. Then he took off into the house. "It's time to barbecue those tenderloin steaks," he yelled over his shoulder. Sandy sat stunned. She was not expecting this kind of affection, or was it pity? Was he being truthful, or was he really looking beyond the ugly scar?

Sandy whispered when he closed the patio door, "Oh, Peter, you have no idea how I feel about you . . ."

While Peter was inside retrieving the steaks, Sandy turned on the barbecue. She had no idea that Peter was working up the courage to ask her out on a real date. But he knew she was as skittish as a doe. Tonight, he would not give up. His last remark put a chink in her armor. When he returned, the barbecue was fired up. The steaks sizzled with juice as the smoke rose from the sides of the black barbecue lid. There was an uncomfortable silence between the two of them, so Sandy went inside to return a few minutes later with plates, forks, knives, bowls, napkins, and of course, Peter's favorite salad. The table was set, and the steaks were ready. The two sat down to eat, and then Peter got up again, looked up at the dwindling blue sky, ran a hand through his mane of black thick curls, and cleared his throat.

Sandy shot him a bewildered look.

"Something wrong with the food?"

"No, food is fine." He exhaled.

"Are you okay?"

"I'm okay, yes." He nodded, almost laughing.

"Why are you so . . . I don't know." She shrugged. "I've never seen you like this."

"Like what?"

"I can't articulate it in one sentence."

"Well, is it bad?"

"I wouldn't call it bad . . . odd perhaps." She pointed a finger. "Is it my cooking? What is it?"

"Nothing like that. It's delicious."

"How would you know, you've barely touched your plate. Is this about my comment earlier when I called you a sleazeball? I was only kidding. You didn't take me seriously, did you?"

"Yes and no. Oh hell. I'm just going to come out and ask. The worst case scenario, you'll say no."

"Say no to what, Peter?"

"Sandy, I've known you for a long time. Will you go out with me on a real date? I mean, I like you . . . a lot. More than just friends, a lot."

"This isn't funny."

"I'm not laughing."

"Me!" Flabbergasted, her jaw fell open.

"Yes, Sandy—" He took a deep breath and let it go. "You're . . . a beautiful woman, and I love being around you. You make me feel alive inside like no other woman has. I mean there is nothing, I dislike about you. We get along great. And that body of yours." He gave a shudder.

Sandy wanted to smack him. "Is this some kind of pity trip because I haven't had a date in forever?"

"Absolutely not. For a very long time, I've wanted to get to know you on a deeper level. But I was afraid—"

"Are you drunk?" she interrupted.

"Pardon?"

"I think you heard me."

"No, I'm not drunk, damn it. So what's it going to be?" He sat back down in his chair next to her. "Will you go out on a date with me?"

"What about our friendship?"

"Will you for once take a risk? Who knows, you might even like me."

"I don't take risks."

"Take one with me."

"A real date, huh?"

"The whole nine yards, Sandy." He leaned forward and took her hand in his.

"I would love to go on a real date with you, P—"

Before she finished the sentence, he lifted her out of her chair and pulled her into his arms, gently kissing her mouth. Sandy melted at the feel of his soft lips on hers.

That night, they made love, at first tentatively, tenderly, and then with mounting uninhibited passion. Where it would go after these wonderful moments Sandy didn't care. Tonight, she was risking love to the fullest.

CHAPTER FORTY-EIGHT

Dr. Blake sat at his desk, reading the medical report just delivered to him by special courier. An evil sneer moved slowly across his face as his eyes zoomed on the word he had longed to see. Positive stood out from all other words on the page. His experiment with the deadly mixture he'd injected into his craving vein was an unprecedented success. He was going to be someone special the world would not soon forget. Had anyone been watching, Blake's smile could have been right out of the movie *How the Grinch Stole Christmas*, right before Jim Carrey slides down the snowy mountain and into Whoville to steal the Whoville presents.

He checked his watch and picked up the phone, calling the third-floor nurse's station for his late appointment. He didn't make a habit of seeing patients this late at night unless it was an emergency. This time was an exception to the rule; he felt like celebrating.

Nora Elmer was his dessert of the day. He would indulge in his guilty pleasure. Nora Elmer arrived in almost the same fashion as Franki Martin, escorted by two nurses. Only this time, Nora was wheeled in. This one would be a piece of cake; she was already too high from the Tylox and Vicodin to comprehend what was really going to happen to her. His practiced eyes looked her over like a vulture on a piece of roadkill. Not bad. A little plump for his taste, but young enough for her skin to be soft and supple. He plunged into her arm one more injection of Tylox and raped her. By the time he'd finished with Nora Elmer, she wouldn't know fiction from fantasy. She was just another whore in his collection of disposable souls.

Lust exhausted, he used a douche to remove evidence of semen. He then washed and redressed her back into the hospital gown and panties and sat her in the chair. He stared down at her, distaste curling his lips. She would soon be eliminated and all others like her. He would single-handedly rid this world of its filth. He felt he was untouchable.

Chapter Forty-Nine

Tom surprised Ellen with a nice romantic picnic basket filled with her favorite foods. Instead of going to a noisy restaurant, he wanted closeness and privacy. He picked Jimane Park on Mist Street, a few blocks from their home. Ellen was not surprised by his loving gesture. This was one out of the many things that made her love him. She smiled as she watched him unroll the black-and-red-checkered blanket over the grass. Then, he helped her down onto the blanket. Tom poured apple juice into their plastic wineglasses while the birds serenaded them with sweet melodies in the branches above where they sat.

"Oh, Tom, you amaze me."

"Please, Ellen, my ego is big enough, thank you. I just thought it would be a nice distraction to get out and away from people."

"I don't know how you know what's good for me but keep doing it, okay?"

"It's my job to make my wife happy." He kissed her hand. "Hope you're hungry?"

"Starved."

"What did you eat today?" he asked.

"A tuna sandwich from the cafeteria. I've been so busy it's been unreal."

"You look beat." He observed the dark circles beneath her weary eyes.

"I can't lie, I am." She rubbed her eyes, trying not to rub off what was left of her makeup.

"I meant what I said earlier. I think you should come home after this."

"Once I sink my teeth into this delicious food you've packed, my energy level will soar again."

"I'll be the judge of that."

"So, what's in the basket?"

"We have leftover chicken, my famous potato salad, carrots, celery, fresh baby tomatoes and cucumber from the garden, and of course, fresh strawberries, your favorite. What would you like to start with?"

"Chicken sounds wonderful."

"How about I make a plate with everything."

"Tom, you truly are the best. Will you marry me?" They both laughed.

Tom didn't ask Ellen what was going on; he knew her well enough that if she wanted to talk about what was troubling her, she would.

"I was thinking, honey, for next weekend, why don't we invite a few of our friends over for a barbecue?" Ellen asked.

"Sounds like a good plan. This is a bit of a change for you."

"I'm beginning to realize I need a variety of people in my life. You know, to see how the other half lives."

Tom chuckled. "Ah, I see, tired of the old retired guy here."

"Oh, honey, don't be silly. I could never get tired of you. I thought it would be nice to entertain. It feels like years since we've had our friends over or been out with friends."

"Sounds good to me. You know how I love to cook and show off my garden. That's it, we'll have a garden party."

"And a very good cook indeed."

They both dug into their well-stacked plates.

"So, what's the verdict here, Doc?" Tom asked when they were finished, knowing what the answer would be.

"I really do have something very important I have to do, Tom."

"And it can't wait?"

"No, Tom. This is pretty serious."

"Want to talk about it?"

"Let's just say that James Blake is up to no good. I don't know exactly what it is yet, but I know he's rotten to the core. I'm certain he's intentionally hurting our female patients. But I need proof." Tom looked like he just got hit in the head with a two-by-four. "I'm certain he's victimized Franki, and he's afraid she'll talk. That's why he sent Franki Martin to the fourth floor. I got the true story on what happened between Gloria Shelby and Franki. It didn't happen the way Blake told me. Sandy said Franki tried to tell her something about James the night they went to the beach. I have to be very careful when dealing with this guy. This facility can't afford any more women getting hurt or worse dead. Blake is not to be trusted. I have to contact Bill when I get back to the office."

"This sounds dangerous, Ellen. I think you should call the proper authorities and stop playing detective. If this Blake character is as deranged as you think, you could be in a whole heap of trouble yourself."

"First, it's too risky to call the police. Besides, what do we have: two women had a fight, and Blake sent my patient to the fourth floor because he believed she was a danger to the rest of the residents. I'm only going on a feeling. I need something more substantial so I can nail his ass to the wall when the time comes."

"I don't like this, Ellen. It sounds too dangerous."

"It won't be if I go about it the right way."

"And calling the police won't help?"

"There's no evidence that he's violating any of these residents. The police won't interrogate him for being dishonest about two women having a fight. The only one who knows the truth is Franki. Now, you know why it's imperative that I return to River Edge."

"I don't like you playing Nancy Drew in this."

"Oh, Tom, please don't worry about me."

"It's a little late for that."

"Really, I'm fine. Honey, really." She leaned across the blanket and kissed her worried husband. "We suspect that Blake is doing unspeakable acts on Franki and others, and that's why he tried to subdue Franki Martin from telling either Sandy or me the truth. I think, he's been sexually abusing her. She was going to tell, and that's when his evil plan came into play. He had to set up the fight between Gloria and Franki. He needed an excuse to send her to the fourth floor and leave her, hoping we'd believe she ran away. The rooms are off-limits to the cleaning staff unless accompanied by medics. He could have murdered her in a number of ways—through injections, let her starve to death . . ."

"Ellen, that's a hell of an accusation! But I know you wouldn't say something this damaging if it weren't true." He sighed noisily. "Do whatever you need to do. I'm standing behind you 100 percent. I could always go and take a round out of Blake myself."

"Thank you, darling. Once this is over, I promise, I will spend a lot more time at home."

"Better. I miss you." He kissed his wife on her forehead. "Well, I better get you back to work."

*   *   *

Dr. Smith walked down the hall toward her office, her mind racing. She flopped down in her chair and took a deep breath and released it. As much as she hated to get anyone else involved, it had to be done.

Ellen lifted the receiver from its cradle and dialed 555-6226. No one answered. She hung up, reached for her Rolodex, and flipped through the card selection until she found Bill Cobie's home number. She redialed. After the second ring, he answered.

"Hello."

"Hi, Bill, it's Ellen. I'm sorry to have to bother you at home. Got a minute to talk?"

"Sure. Anything for you, doll."

"What I'm about to tell you is going to sound completely crazy, but please trust me."

"What's this about?"

"Blake."

"You know he's gone ahead and demanded another hearing. Is that the reason you're calling?"

"No, it's far more sinister, I'm afraid."

Ellen went on to tell Bill the story of what she suspected. When she had given the details of all her fears, they both agreed it was best not to get the police involved at this time. That could only put the patients in more peril. Bill advised Ellen to be careful, that he never did trust Blake from the get-go. There was something about him that had always rubbed him the wrong way in spite of his excellent track record.

Ellen thanked Bill and said good-bye. Enough of playing Nancy Drew; time to play psychiatrist. There was a male patient on the fourth floor she needed to see; apparently his request for more medication was not being met.

CHAPTER FIFTY

Dr. Blake was pleasantly pleased with the outcome of Franki Martin's condition. He was giving her just enough lethal lily poison to keep her frozen in time, but not to be detected or to kill her. To do so at this moment would look too suspicious. Anyway, she deserved to suffer because she wouldn't obey his wishes. All she had to do was go along with his little sex games and all would have been fine. If word got out that he was a sexual predator, his career would be destroyed. That was unacceptable. Those women hid behind desires that only he could bring to the surface. He gave them what they secretly begged for.

He hung his doctor's jacket on the back of his chair and strolled out to the Three-Mile Garden to take in some fresh air. Air-conditioning made his lungs feel as if they were going to freeze up. He sat on the bench across from the patch of lilies and studied them. An evil sneer washed over his face. How could something so white and pure-looking be so lethal? Injecting their toxins into Franki's body gave him a sense of sovereignty and control, like a God. Something he'd yearned for, for most of his life. Each time he thought he'd overcome a hurdle, one more would crop up, bigger and worse than the last one. He was powerless as a kid. He could never get close to women. Alma sucked every ounce of love he had until there was nothing left. It was he and his mother against the big bad world. Blake never knew if she liked the power and control or didn't trust that he was capable. He couldn't win no matter what he did.

Like the time, he refused to take a bath . . .

"No, Mommy. I don't want to take a bath."

"What did you say?" When she got mad at him, her voice reminded him of a dog's growl.

"I don't want a bath."

Without hesitation, his mother's hand struck the side of his face, knocking him backward against the wall.

"You will do as I say!"

He stood his ground, defying her power. He wanted to prove to himself that he could stand up to the woman he feared. "No! I am not having a bath." He yelled at her, stomping his feet. She backhanded him in the mouth, splitting his bottom lip wide open. Blood dribbled down his chin. He stood strong against her wrath.

"You're having a bath and that's final!"

James made a run for it, but he was too slow. She caught him by the arm, dragging him back into the bathroom, and sat on the toilet. He struggled, trying to get away from the vicelike grip hold. She pulled him over her knee and slapped his butt, until he could no longer feel the burning sting of her thick hand. His spirit was broken. He took a bath. The one-inch welts on his backside stung the instant his skin touched the hot, soapy water. She took a facecloth from the closet and scrubbed him, ensuring he was good and clean. She had plans for them both later on.

"You know I don't like dirty little boys, James."

"Yes, Mommy."

His face, torso and limbs scrubbed clean, he stood up in the tub. Utterly humiliated, he let her wash his private parts. Anger clawed at his body's betrayal, at his erected penis. She had stolen his power over his own body. That power, he vowed, he would take back one day. He hated her. He loved her. He was terrified of her. He could never forget watching what she did to his father that fatal day.

Many nights, Alma came to James for comfort. He didn't understand how he knew it was wrong, but sensed pleasure as commanding as the betrayal. In a tiny moment of clarity, he knew she would never stop touching him and decided to run away. He would find a place where she could never hurt him again.

The next morning, the sun was just breaking the charcoal dawn when he awoke. James quickly tossed some clothes, toys, books, and a couple of apples into his packsack. He was torn between what would happen if she caught him and what would happen if he stayed. He quietly closed the front door; his short legs practically flew down the sidewalk. Past the silent houses, one block, two blocks, until he could run no further. Across the street was freedom. He stopped momentarily, chest heaving in and out, like a piston. With enough air to go on, he walked across the street to Missle Park.

Alma found him five hours later, tired, hungry, and huddling behind a cluster of honeysuckle. Semi-dozing, he jumped at the sound of the bushes rustling. He looked up, horror dawning in his eyes. There stood his mother towering over him like an evil demon about to devour its victim. In one quick motion, she grabbed James by the back of his shirt, yanking him out of the bush. James's feet barely touched the ground as she rushed back to the car and threw him into the backseat. He did not go willingly. He could see the rage in her eyes; he knew his punishment would be extra severe this time. She dragged him into the house and up the stairs. She threw him into the bedroom, ordering him to remove all his clothes. She returned with the leather strap, commanding him to lie flat on the bed. Then she whipped the soles of his feet until they blistered. If he wanted to run away, he'd have to crawl. This was a lesson he'd never forget. His feet still pained at the recollection. He didn't dare disobey her again.

CHAPTER FIFTY-ONE

Blake won his appeal in front of the board. The black mark was expunged from his record. He did admit he was wrong to send Franki Martin to the fourth floor but claimed he never anticipated the orderlies would not remove the straightjacket. It was the word of a prominent physician against two orderlies. Bill and Ellen were absolutely disappointed with the board's decision. Reluctantly, Bill Cobie shook his hand. He couldn't let Blake know he was on to him; he had to keep the peace. He didn't like it, but if he were going to save Franki Martin and Gloria Shelby and who knew how many others, he'd have kissed his own ass if he had to. Blake strutted arrogantly out of the conference room, leaving Bill wanting to beat the arrogant prick within an inch of his life.

Another week passed, and still Franki lay in a comatose state, unable to tell anyone what Dr. Blake was doing, how he injected clear solution into her bleed line when no one was watching. Dr. Smith reassured Sandy that Franki soon enough would come awake, pissed off and yelling at the nurses, just like before.

The eleven nurses were still playing the role of detective and giving physical examinations to every female patient with the doctor's expertise of course. Nothing. As more time passed, doubt began to set in. They wondered if this situation were being blown out of proportion. Was Blake really the serial rapist Ellen and Sandy believed? Or was this a secret vendetta against the doctor? The nurses all wondered, if Franki should be taken to Morial Hospital. It didn't take Ellen long to convince all eleven why she should stay: Franki not only was getting the best care possible. If she were sent to Morial, Dr. Blake would have an easier time getting access. There would be no way of protecting her from Blake's coming and goings. Sandy still had concerns. She could see a hint of reservation in the nurse's eyes.

* * *

Sandy gave Franki her physical therapy each morning before her bath. Her hair was shoulder-length and sparkled with a healthy shine. A good sign. Sandy remembered the poor state Franki's hair was in when she first arrived, awful. Filled with knots the size of rope and lacked luster. Her appearance was hard and tough like someone who had survived brutal emotional storms in life. She swore like a bunch of sailors out on the sea. Now, she was transformed: beautiful, clean, and soft. She was maturing into a blossoming young adolescent, full of talent and great promise to succeed in life. Each layer beneath the surface was a treasure of discovery. Sandy vowed Franki's every dream would come true. Including a loving family, if she had to adopt the child herself.

It had been rainy and windy all morning. A veil of low stratus clouds hung over the institution. The trees were bending in the force of the wind. The rain was pelting against the window as though clamoring to come inside. The dreariness seeped into everyone's mood. Too wet to take Franki outside, Sandy wheeled her into the recreational area. There, she could listen to the music coming out of the ghetto blaster. It was strange how adversity could become an asset; Franki had a new best friend, Gloria Shelby. The instant Sandy wheeled Franki out of her room, Gloria was right there, shadowing her every move. This was a friendship Blake could not control. Gloria had become Franki's trusted friend. Gloria stopped going to the doctor's office when summoned. She was a lot smarter than he gave her credit for, Sandy noted. She had a million excuses why she couldn't see him, and he actually believed every one. So who was mentally challenged?

The music was blasting U2's song "It's a Beautiful Day." Gloria danced for Franki, telling her that she would teach her how to dance when she was feeling better. Gloria couldn't talk well, but she sure could belt out the lyrics to any song. She had an amazing voice, and Sandy told her so. "Wish mine were as nice," she said and meant it.

By midafternoon, the summer storm finally eased up, and the sun was drying the pathways and benches. It was time to take Franki for a stroll outside. Gloria tagged along, sitting beside her new best friend. Her hands folded on her lap, Gloria listened attentively to Sandy read them stories. From time to time, Gloria read to Franki, doing the best she could. Sandy didn't discourage her, mistakes or no mistakes. Sandy never interrupted to correct. She saw the hard work being put into making stories up. She gave Gloria the praise for trying.

Ten minutes to five, Nancy entered Franki's room to check her vitals.

"Why are you still here?" she scolded the nurse. "Sandy, go home and get a life! Find a date or something. Franki is fine."

"Nice try, girl. What's the matter, the gossip running low?" Sandy chuckled.

"You know what they say?"

"What's that?"

"All work and no play makes Sandy very dull and boring."

"Thanks for the compliment. For your information, I'm just fine, and my life is anything but dull and boring."

"Why, because you never leave River Edge? If you're not careful, the nurses are going to mistake you for a patient and have you committed."

"Bullshit," Sandy whispered. But she had to admit to herself; the last couple of months were catching up to her. Exhaustion was slowing her pace. Even being with Peter was draining. He'd want to go out and do fun things while she wanted to curl up on the couch and watch movies. Their compatibility was beginning to slide. She couldn't bear not to be watching over Franki. Peter wanted more and more of her time. She loved him. She was afraid of losing him. And both scared the hell out of her.

Sandy rose out of the leather recliner.

"I'm going to the cafeteria for a bite to eat, and then I'll be back to say good-bye."

"Enjoy your meal." Nancy smiled. "Bet it would taste better in the company of a man."

"Thank you, Nancy, but some of us are able to enjoy our own company, you know."

"Too much obviously," Nancy countered.

Sandy waved a hand and made for the elevator.

*   *   *

At quarter to six, Sandy was straightening the already tidy pile of magazines. She yawned; Nancy was right. It was time for her to get lost. She pulled on her sweater, took four steps toward the door, and suddenly stopped dead in her tracks. Was it her imagination or did she really hear what she thought she heard? She whirled around and rushed back to the bed. She took Franki's hand in hers and held her breath, watching for movement. Then it came.

"Sandy . . ." Franki's voice dry and muffled sounded as old as dry leaves.

"I'm right here, sweetheart."

"Sandy . . ." Franki's eyelids fluttered.

"What, honey? I'm right here."

"I'm afraid." Her body began to shiver like she was cold. The sensation of her body coming back to life was heightened. She had lain in bed for weeks moving, only when the nurses exercised her limbs.

"You don't have to be afraid. I'm here, kiddo."

Sandy gently lifted Franki forward and propped her higher against the pillows. She held her close like a mother comforting a frightened child. Sweet adrenaline shot through her every cell, knowing Franki was on her way back to life.

"Welcome back, baby." Tears of joy streaming down Sandy's cheeks, dripping off her chin and plunked into Franki's hair. She rocked Franki's frail frame in her arms, crooning to her, as would a mother to her near-lost child.

"I won't let anything bad ever happen to you again. This I promise."

Franki said nothing but held on tightly to Sandy like a scared, injured child embracing the comfort.

Then Nancy walked in and gasped at the scene with excitement. Sandy brought her index finger to her lips, warning Nancy not to startle Franki.

"Franki, sweetheart," she spoke softly, "Nancy is here now to also take care of you."

"No." Franki whispered. "Don't leave me." For all her weakness, Franki's grip tightened.

"Of course I won't leave you, honey." Sandy looked up at Nancy. "Would you hurry and get Dr. Smith? She'll want to examine Franki."

Nancy was so elated she ran down the flight of stairs to Dr. Smith's office. She knocked so hard it resonated along the corridor like a series of explosions. *Boom! Boom! Boom!* Ellen lifted halfway out of her seat.

"Who the hell could this be?" She grumbled, looking at her watch, and then proceeded across the room to the door.

"Doctor, Doctor!" Nancy tried to catch her breath. "You have to come and see this. It's Franki! She's awake, and Sandy is holding her. Hurry!" Nancy bounced up and down like an excited child on Christmas morning, rushing into the bedroom to wake her parents.

Ellen didn't hesitate. She and Nancy dashed down the hallway and then the stairs to the second floor, down the hall to the patient's ward. In all the excitement, neither noticed James Blake lurking around the corner, listening to every word the nurse had just told the doctor.

When they approached Franki's room, the two forced themselves to slow down. Any sudden noises could send Franki back into a deep shock. In small doses, she would have to get used to all the noises around her.

"Franki. Hi, sweetheart, it's me, Doc."

Weakly, Franki lifted her head off Sandy's shoulder and looked at her. "Doc." A slow smile washed over her frail features.

Ellen wanted to snatch Franki from Sandy's arms and hug the stuffing right out of her. "Welcome back, Franki." Dr. Smith beamed.

The doctor's hand gently stroked her hair while Franki continued to cling onto Sandy and would not let go.

"Water . . . please?" Franki asked.

Nancy poured a half glass and handed it to Sandy who held the straw to Franki's lips.

"Do you remember Nancy?" Doc asked.

Franki nodded her head, happy to see familiar faces.

"I guess that means yes." Nancy grinned, elated. "Hi, Franki," she said, "we've all been anxiously awaiting your return."

"I'm back."

Ellen did her quick examination; everything appeared to be normal and suggested they not stay too long. It wasn't wise to drain Franki. Of course, Franki disagreed adamantly, shaking her head from side to side. Sandy wanted to stay the night with Franki. Under any other circumstances, the answer would have been no, but with the current situation, Dr. Smith thought it to be a great idea.

*   *   *

There was a cot they could bring in for Sandy to sleep on. She'd be close if Franki needed her, and Nancy would check in from time to time, just to make sure all was quiet and safe on the home front.

Sandy pulled the curtain to give Franki privacy. The nurse removed the catheter and the intravenous line, then placed a Band-Aid over the tiny wound, preventing any infection. It was obvious Franki had a weakened immune system; it showed in the last test results. Then it was time for Franki to have something real to eat. They started her on apple juice and cherry Jell-O.

Immediately after, Franki was fighting to keep her eyes open. The only way Sandy was going to get her to relax was to pull the cot closer to the bed. Side by side, Franki felt safe. Now she could close her eyes and drift into sleep. Sandy thought the ploy had worked. Franki hadn't stirred for a while. Then, "I have something I need to tell you," Franki whispered.

"What is it, my little love?"

"Sandy, that doctor, you know which one?"

"You mean Blake?"

"Yeah him." Franki tried to rise up on her elbow.

"What about him?" Sandy sat up.

"He's been raping me since I got here." Franki started to cry, and Sandy felt the sting of her own tears. She rose and sat next to Franki on her bed, wiping away her tears. *That rotten bastard,* Sandy thought.

"I wanted to tell you, but I got scared. He said he would turn my life into a real nightmare. He said, he could lock me away and no one would ever find me."

Sandy kept her voice calm. "Do you want to make a statement right now? I know you're too weak to write it down, but you could tell me what to say and just sign it."

"No. Can I do it tomorrow? You guys were right, I'm starting to fade."

"That's fine, but for sure tomorrow."

"I want that pervert to pay for what he's done to me."

"My exact sentiment. Don't worry. He's going to get everything that's coming to him, that I promise you, Franki."

"Don't leave me, okay?"

"I'll stay with you all night, or however long it takes you to feel strong and brave again."

"Thank you."

"I'm so sorry, Franki."

"Sandy . . ."

"What, sweetheart?"

"Thanks for caring about me. I love you." Franki's voice quivered.

"My pleasure. I love you too, Franki." Sandy's eyes spilled over with tears.

In seconds, Franki had fallen asleep. During the night, Franki jolted awake a couple of times, shaking and sweating from the fear that raged inside her chest. Sandy retrieved a dry nightgown, reassuring her she was safe from harm until exhaustion forced her back to sleep.

Judy, the nurse on the midnight shift, came in often throughout the night just to ensure all was safe and quiet.

*   *   *

Twilight was blanketing the sky when Ellen drove home. Tom was watering the front garden beds when Ellen pulled into their double-car driveway. He noticed his wife looked very bright-eyed and eager. *How could that be?* he wondered. *She'd worked almost sixteen hours.* He shook his head, not knowing how she did it. She had amazing stamina, but he still worried about her. It had been a horrible burden on Ellen the last couple of months, with Franki being in a coma state and Blake being such a vicious predator. Yet there wasn't a moment she'd given up in her search for the truth. That's what attracted Tom to her thirty-five years ago and still did today.

Ellen reached across to the passenger seat for her briefcase and suddenly stopped.

"Nope, not tonight," she said to the attractive leather valise stuffed with papers. "Tonight, I am going to enjoy an uninterrupted evening with my darling husband. You can wait until tomorrow!" She got out of the car and trotted over to where her husband was standing, his face wearing a happy expression. Seeing good news coming, he quickly released the hose nozzle and dropped it on the grass.

"Tom, she's awake!" She threw herself into his waiting arms.

"Thank you, Jesus, yes! Franki made it!" He yelled so loudly Ellen thought, *the whole neighborhood must have heard him.* He picked up Ellen and twirled her around in the air, both rejoicing for Franki Martin's recovery.

"This is cause for a celebration, wouldn't you agree?"

"It sure is, darling. It sure is!"

Tom rushed over to turn off the tap. Ellen met him at the front door with a smile that he hadn't seen in what seemed like forever. He picked her up and carried her across the threshold like two giggling like teenagers.

CHAPTER FIFTY-TWO

The next morning, Franki arose, inhaling the delicious aroma. Breakfast had arrived. The second Franki stirred, Sandy immediately jolted awake and sprang up on her cot. She hoped her expression showed Franki how happy she was to see her awake again. She wanted Franki to know how much she was missed and loved unconditionally.

"Oh, look, breakfast is here." Rolling her tongue around the inside of her mouth, searching for saliva, Sandy slid off the cot.

"You must be hungry?"

"A little."

"Starved, more like it."

"Starved." Franki laughed.

Sandy lifted the lid on the breakfast tray. "You, my dear, have toast with strawberry jam, juice, and a half cup of Cheerios."

"Is that all?" Franki wrinkled her nose. "But I'm really hungry."

"Try this and see how you do."

"Can I have my juice first? I'm so thirsty."

"I know how you feel. A large coffee sure would wet my whistle right about now." She handed Franki a glass of cold fresh orange juice.

"Why don't you grab a coffee from the resident's eating area? But only if you hurry back!"

"You sure?"

"Go!" Franki pointed to the door.

"I'll be right back." Sandy hurried out of the room and returned before Franki finished her juice. Sandy folded up the cot and sat on the edge of the bed, keeping the subject of conversation light. They chatted about writing, which Franki couldn't wait to get back into. The topics of finishing her schooling and outings in the BMW put a light touch on the horrible situation that she'd just endured. All seemed right with the world again like evil had no place in their lives.

*　　*　　*

Dr. Blake was beside himself, pacing back and forth in his office like a gorilla that had just been caged. He muttered and cursed. His face was flared and eyes bulging in their sockets with barbarous rage. He kept smacking one fist into the palm of the other.

"How is this possible? She isn't supposed to be coherent. Did I not give her the right amount of poison? This is impossible. The dosage was to keep that little bitch silent for at least another month, maybe two. How could I have failed?" Sweat trickled down his temples. He now feared the worst.

"My experiment should not have failed. I measured it precisely."

He sank into his chair, veins in his neck pulsating with his gathering heartbeat. He must calm himself. He placed a hand to his chest. His heartbeat strong and rapid, 160 pulses per minute. He rocked in his chair, thinking, thinking. He had to come up with a plan and fast. He didn't know what Franki had already told them. His thoughts tumbled upon themselves. He didn't want to go to jail for humiliating those whores. He'd never survive. He had to kill her. She'd left him no choice. Dead people can't testify in court.

*　　*　　*

At nine o'clock sharp, Dr. Smith showed up to see her favorite patient. Ellen looked like she'd had a restful sleep, unlike Sandy. A happy peacefulness seemed to be floating along the corridors, especially the second floor and room 210, Franki Martin's room.

Ellen had enjoyed a wonderful, relaxing evening with her husband. She and Tom sat on the patio until dusk turned dark, admiring their garden and drinking Pinot Noir in celebration of Franki's awakening. Around eleven o'clock, they went to bed and made love, afterward holding each other in delight of what great, unexpected gifts the universe offered. Tom was happy just to hold Ellen in his arms, not to be worrying about her getting out of bed to burn the midnight oil. When it came to her patients, his wife nurtured them along with the same care and attentiveness as he devoted to his splendid garden. He understood the passion rooted in her commitment.

To Ellen's astonishment, Franki was sitting up eating a bowl of oatmeal when she strolled in.

"Good morning and how is my star patient feeling?"

"I'm better, Doc."

Ellen peered into her bowl. "Oatmeal! It's a tad early for that. You don't want to upset your stomach."

"She kept at me until I got her some." Sandy smiled.

"Sandy, I have decided to give you the day off with pay."

"Ellen, please, you don't have to do that."

"I know. I have the authority though, right, Franki?" She gave Franki a wink.

"Big bucks. Right, Doc?" The room lit up with laughter. "Hey, you remembered."

"I'm not completely gone yet, Doc. I could hear what everyone was saying around me. I couldn't talk to let you know I could hear you. My mind felt frozen, along with my fuckin' limbs."

"That must have been scary?"

"You think." Franki raised a brow.

"I think you'll be just fine." Ellen laughed.

"Oh yeah, here's more. That jerk-off doctor came into my room and filled my intravenous line with something from his needle. Like I said, I could hear you guys talking, and correct me if I'm wrong, but he wasn't supposed to be in here, was he?"

"Pardon?" Dr. Smith's face paled.

"Didn't you know?"

"No, I didn't." Ellen stared at Sandy.

"Yeah, he was in here like every second day, I think. I'm still a little fuzzy on the time thing."

"Franki, I'm going to have the hospital tech do another tox screen. Hopefully, we'll see the results sometime today. I have a sneaky suspicion Blake was up to no good. These results could answer the mystery of why it took you so long to come back to us."

"Like what are you thinking, Ellen?" Wide-eyed shock registered in Sandy's eyes.

"Poison. It's only a speculation remember? We'll know for certain once I have the outcome in my hand."

"Was that fucker trying to kill me because I decided to tell on him?"

"That's a loaded question. I don't know if he was or wasn't trying to get rid of you, but the second half of the question makes me curious as to what did you want to tell on him about? Franki, there are many questions I have that only you can answer."

"I told Sandy last night how he's been raping me since I got here. I mean brutal." She tossed her spoon back into the bowl, too disgusted to finish. "The day, I was going to tell on him was the day I had the fight in the hallway with Gloria. He set me up. I know he did. He's been gunning to shut me up from the very first time I threatened to rat him out. Shit, this time, he almost succeeded. I'm telling you that creep is crazier than a shit house rat. *He* belongs on the fourth floor."

Silence fell upon the room like a big black cloud, smothering the rainbow energy that was just there. Every second ticking by felt like an eternity. At last, the questions had been answered as to why Franki hated him, and rightly so. Blake was the monster they suspected him to be. Finally, Doc went to Franki and wrapped her arms around her. Ellen glanced across the bed at Sandy; she was dabbing away tears from her eyes. Now they knew the ugly truth about their trusted colleague.

"Oh, child, I am so sorry. Damn, I am so sorry, Franki." Ellen held Franki in her arms for a long moment, choking back her own tears. Rage and sorrow engulfed her very soul.

"It's okay, Doc." Franki patted Ellen's shoulder. "You have to promise to keep me safe. He'll kill me for sure if he knows that I told you guys that he's a rape hound."

"Consider it already done, Franki. He's not allowed near you, that is an order from the higher up, Bill Cobie. I know this is a lot to ask at this point in your recovery. Are you willing to file criminal charges against Dr. Blake?"

"He scares the hell out of me, but yes, I'll do it."

"Good." Doc gave the brave young girl a high five. "I'll have something drawn up for you to sign. I think that's how it works. Hell, I'm not even sure. I'll have to make some calls. This is pretty intense shit."

"Try being the one living it."

"A little stressed, Ellen?" Sandy asked.

"You could say that." She sighed heavily.

"So you guys believe me, right?"

"Of course we do! I know you can get angry at times, but you're not a malicious troublemaker. Franki, do you know if he's sexually assaulted any other female patients?"

"I wouldn't put it past him."

"Franki, I promise this will be taken care of."

"Thanks, Doc. No one has ever taken the time to try and help me. They've just told me I was a troublemaker or attention seeker. Some bullshit like that."

"You are more than a patient. You are like a daughter to Sandy and a granddaughter to me."

"Really?"

Sandy broke in. "Really. So now you have the two of us to count on, and I promise we will not let you down. There will be times when you won't like what we have to say, but it'll always be out of love."

"Wow! Now I know I'm going to be okay for sure. The dream team is on my side. Yahoo!" Franki yelled.

Doc wagged a finger. "No more overdoing it, young lady. I know you feel pretty good, but the energy won't last long if you don't rest. You"—she pointed at Sandy—"I'm sending you home to take a shower and change your clothes. She smells a little funky, won't you agree with me?" Doc whispered in Franki's ear, making her chuckle out loud.

"Franki, I called Nancy in for a couple of hours. She's right across the hall. Buzz if you need her. I have some important telephone calls to make, but I'll be back to check in on you a little later. Is that cool with you? Sandy, when you return, take Franki to the lab at Morial for her blood work. I'll call over and have everything arranged."

"What are you looking for, Doc?"

"Any alien toxins in your system that shouldn't be there."

"If there is any, the blood work will find it?"

"We hope so, Franki."

"Okay, Doc. I hope you know I hate needles."

Sandy saw right through the brave mask. She was still apprehensive and full of fear. Who could blame her? Sandy wanted to take Franki to her house, but Franki wasn't strong enough; a hospital visit would be enough for one day.

"Come back fast, okay, Sandy?"

"I'll be back in two shakes of a lamb's tail. You get some rest while I'm gone. We'll tell the nurses to be on watch. When I return, you can take a nice long shower because I'm not the only one that smells a little ripe."

"Hurry. I don't want to be left alone too long."

"I'll hurry, I promise. Remember, there are lots of nurses around. Just push the call button. Is there anything special I can get for you before I come back?"

"Nope, just yourself."

"You are so sweet." The nurse blew Franki a kiss on her way out the door.

In moments, Nancy came in and pushed the table away from the bed, fluffed Franki's pillows and gently laid Franki back into a comfortable position. Nancy made sure her bear was next to her. Franki tensed as soon as she was alone, knowing Blake was somewhere on the premises. At the same time, she was so relieved she had finally told on the psychopath. He had caused her so much pain and shame. The mere thought of Blake going to jail so he could never hurt her again felt like chains breaking away from her soul.

"The truth will set you free, Franki," she murmured and closed her eyes.

*   *   *

A few minutes later, Franki's room seemed so empty and quiet. So quiet in fact that she peeked out from underneath her blankets, making sure all was safe. No one was lurking in the corners of the room. She closed her eyes again.

Then, she heard it, the sound of footsteps tiptoeing into her room. She held her breath and kept her eyes shut tight until she heard that person tiptoeing away. She opened her eyes in time to see a redheaded woman leaving her room.

Franki smiled. It was Gloria, her new best friend. With that pleasant thought, she drifted off to sleep.

CHAPTER FIFTY-THREE

Dr. Smith plunked down in the chair behind her desk. She took a sip of her steaming hot brew, then picked up the receiver and dialed 555-6226.

"Hello, Bill. It's Ellen here."

"Hi, Ellen, how are you this beautiful sunny morning?"

"I'm better now that our star patient is making an excellent recovery. She is awake and semi-functioning."

"Best news so far today."

"I'm so happy, Bill."

"Has she said anything?"

"She has and it's not good. This is the reason I'm ringing you up this early."

"I take it your suspicions are correct?"

"Yes."

"Say the words, Ellen, please."

"Dr. James Blake has been raping Franki since her arrival."

"Do you believe her, Ellen? I mean as much as I dislike the guy, we have to be positive on this."

"I do believe her without a doubt. He sent her to the fourth floor to shut her up."

"Now, it all makes sense."

"He would have succeeded with his diabolical plan if it weren't for Sandy Miller. Franki also told us that Blake has been coming into her room and putting something from a syringe into her intravenous line, but of course, she doesn't know what it was. This was after you ordered him to stay away."

"What do you think it was?"

"I've ordered a complete hemoglobin analyses. If there are poisonous toxins in her system, they'll be detected. Now, the allegation of rape is my priority. What steps would you like me to take?"

"The goal is to get him the hell out of this facility. I'm going to call my buddy at the precinct. I would like to keep this low-key for as long as needed. I'm not sure, Ellen, but I think Dr. Blake will be taken in for questioning today. Where is he? Do you know?"

"No."

"Find out where he is and watch him until you hear back from me. Trust me, I want that man brought to justice. This is my facility, and I'll be damned if I'll sit idly by and watch him destroy innocent victims that can't protect themselves."

"Good, that's exactly how I see it."

"Ellen, is Franki up to writing a statement?"

"She will be, once she wakes up. She's taking a little nap right now."

"Get her to write a statement of all Dr. Blake has done to her, leaving out no details. That will carry a lot of weight. Ellen, pardon my medical ignorance, but how is our Franki Martin doing?"

"Physically, she'll be back to her energetic self in no time. She is confused, scared, and completely emotionally drained, which will take a lot longer to heal than the physical. She has been through hell, Bill."

"Well, it's not the best, but at least, she's alive. And we're going to do everything in our power to help her progress along. I know it won't be easy, but she has you and Sandy Miller. Oh, any word on Blake's parents?"

"Nothing of real importance. His father left his mother for another woman. It's odd, however, that neither parent can be verified. My lawyer friend is double-checking the archives. If there is anything dubious, it will show up. We know he was born to someone."

"Strange. Parents don't just vanish unless he had something to do with their disappearance or worse, death."

"Who knows what he's capable of?"

"Nothing would surprise me at this point."

"Ellen, thank you."

"Don't thank me yet. He's still not in a cage."

"Ellen, your only job is to keep that little girl safe until Blake is rounded up and taken out of our facility."

"The arrangements have already been made. Nancy came in early to take care of Franki until Sandy gets back. She stayed with Franki last night. I told her to go home for a shower and get fresh clothes. Her mission is not to let Franki out of her sight. I told Nancy that she would be paid for a double shift."

"Fine by me. Ellen, I'm going to let you go, and I promise you'll be hearing from me soon."

"Thanks, Bill."

Ellen replaced the receiver into its cradle and then put the palms of her hands together. "Please, Lord, I know you're listening. Let the punishment fit the crime. If James is guilty, nail him because you and I both know Franki deserves a little payback here. She's been through too many emotional storms to walk away unscarred. Amen." She looked down at her watch. Her first patient was expected in a few seconds. She stood up and walked slowly to the door. "Seven, six, five, four, three, two, one!" She opened the door, and there he was: Jackson Muller, right on time. This guy hated being late for anything.

* * *

Nancy was leaning over the file cabinet pulling out a patient's chart when she heard her name being paged to come to room 246.

"Was that for me?" Confused, she glanced up from the cabinet. "Who could be paging me?"

"If your name is Nancy, you better go and see what is going on in 246," Lander said, strolling by with a cart of goodies.

"I'll hurry." Nancy rushed to room 246, around the corner from the station.

Mere seconds was all it took. Dr. Blake slipped into Franki's room. He stood quietly staring down at her. Good, she was asleep. Quickly, he pressed his hand over her mouth to prevent her from screaming. Franki's eyes went wild with horror when she stared into his black orbs of rage. With all the strength she could muster, she tried fighting him off, but she was far too weak.

"Don't scream or I'll kill you right here." He showed her the four-inch stainless steel knife hidden inside his doctor's coat. "You and I are going for a little ride."

In one rapid motion, he lifted her out of bed and plunked her down into the wheelchair and rushed out of the room to the closest elevator, in the opposite direction of the nurse's station. He knew those sluts were all against him. He could smell their resentment like a strong perfume. Their phony smiles and nods turned his stomach.

* * *

The doctor was unaware he was being watched the entire time. "Franki, my friend," she whispered into her hand. She followed the doctor to the basement, using the stairs after counting the numbers on the elevator drop to the bottom level.

*   *   *

Franki was being pushed along a dark passageway. She wanted to scream but discovered she had no voice. Panic tightened her vocal cords; only a tiny croak escaped her lips. They stopped in front of an old windowless metal door.

Franki's horror spilled out of her eyes in tears. Terror filled her every cell as she watched Blake undo one dead bolt after another, until all four were unlocked. This room hadn't been opened in a long time. Blake kicked open the entrance, sending dirt and dust flying into the air. Franki coughed and gagged as the dust flew up into her nostrils and into her airway. Terror hammered her heart against her ribcage, threatening to break the bones.

Blake yanked her out of the wheelchair and threw her onto the dirty metal table. She eyed a machine with plastic-coated wires like an octopus's tentacles. The dials and yellow buttons spoke volumes as to the torture she was about to undergo. Blake began: he strapped her down with two-inch leather restraints. He thought about giving her atropine, but that would stop the pleasure of knowing Franki could have a heart attack. He needed to see her suffer a slow and painful death. He gelled four pads before sticking two on her forehead and two on her temples, left and right. Franki tried to struggle, but she just didn't have the strength to fight the monster. Blake walked to the foot of the bed and stared down at her, smirking. This was it, Franki thought. He had won. She was going to die a horrible, painful death at the hands of this sick and twisted maniac. Her one pleasant thought he could not take away from her was that she was going to be reunited with her parents.

Blake climbed up on the table, his pants pulled down to his knees. He enjoyed raping Franki Martin one last time. When he finished, he laughed and shoved the plastic mouthpiece inside her mouth.

Franki's body stiffened and lifted off the bed as the electricity coursed through her anatomy. He gave it a count of fifteen seconds. There came a brief respite. Sweat rolled off her neck. Her hands clenched against the restraints. He zapped her again. Pleasure beamed from his eyes, watching Franki convulse. She was barely conscious but enough to think dimly.

Blake is going to electrocute me, thought Franki, horrified. *Oh my god—*

He placed his hand on the dial to zap her one last time when he got the surprise of his life. The door flew open, and Gloria barged into the room.

"Hurt my friend!" She flung herself at Blake, knocking him off balance. Gloria tried to scratch out his eyes, but Blake overpowered her. He punched at her until she fell onto the dirty floor. Not satisfied, then he punched and kicked at her head and body until she lay motionless. Grabbing a fistful of red hair, he dragged her unconscious body out of the room to where no one would find her. By the time they did, there would be nothing left but bones.

His time at River Edge was up. Blake slipped away without anyone seeing him.

Chapter Fifty-Four

Sandy returned to River Edge, skipping down the corridor, carrying an armload of gifts for Franki. She held balloons, chocolates, and goodies from the bakery on the corner where she lived. Wrapped in pretty boxes were new clothes. And she couldn't forget a matching teddy bear for the one she'd bought earlier. Sandy couldn't wait to spoil her with all these presents.

Hardly able to contain her excitement, she opened the door, yelling, "Surprise!" Oddly Franki was not in her bed. "Hey, where are you?" Silence. The door to her bathroom was ajar and the light turned off. Immediately, ice clawed at her heart. Her eyes swept the room again, darting from corner to corner. Her wheelchair was missing. The room's atmosphere felt cold, an unexplainable, bone-chilling kind of cold. She just knew something terrible had happened to Franki. Sandy dropped the gifts on the bed and bolted out the door and across the hall. Bobby-Jo was sitting at the nurse's station.

"Where's Franki?"

"She's in her bed, is she not?"

"No. Did anyone see her leave?" The nurse who'd been filling in temporarily had no idea what Sandy was talking about. She had the same bewildered expression as Sandy.

"Where is she?"

"The young girl left in the wheelchair with Dr. Blake a while ago. Why? Wasn't he supposed to take her?" Kelly asked.

"No!" Sandy screamed, slamming her hands on the desk. "Do you know where they went? Where is Nancy?"

"N-n-no," Kelly stammered. "He didn't say. I didn't ask."

Just then, Nancy came around the corner. Seeing the pained expression on Sandy's face, she rushed to her side.

"What's going on, Sandy?"

"She's gone. Franki's gone and Blake took her."

"No." Her rosy cheeks paled.

"Give me the phone," Sandy demanded.

Nancy rushed into the nurse's station. Pushing Kelly and Bobby-Jo out of the way. She fumbled nervously for the cordless phone and handed it over.

Ellen picked up the telephone on the second ring. "Dr. Smith speaking."

"Ellen, Franki is gone!" Sandy yelled into the receiver. "Dr. Blake took her!"

"Where are you?"

"At the nurse's station beside her room."

"Stay put, I'll be right there. I'm calling the police immediately. And page Blake to the nurse's station." Ellen hung up and dialed 911 and reported a dangerous kidnapping situation. Next, she raced up the stairs and down the hall to the nurse's station to learn Blake had not responded to Sandy's page. His phone was on voice mail. Sandy left a message that it was urgent he called the desk.

Sandy felt she was going to jump right out of her skin; she was shaking so badly. She felt sick to her stomach. Then Ellen came running toward her.

"The police are on their way. Nancy, what happened?"

"I received a page, so I went to room 246."

"Nancy, Bobby-Jo, I want this entire second floor searched top to bottom. Broom closets, under the beds, anywhere you think someone could be hiding. Franki just might be doing that. And once you've done that checking, thoroughly check again. Nancy, you should have never left Franki unattended."

"I'm sorry." Nancy wrung her hands. "I was paged to room 246."

"We'll find her, Sandy." Ellen placed her hand on the nurse's shoulder. "Any clues left behind?" the doctor questioned.

"Her wheelchair is gone."

"How did this happen? Everyone was supposed to be on the lookout for Blake, not running around on some bloody errand. Do you have any idea who paged Nancy?"

"I wasn't here."

"Well I do, she was set up, and by you know who."

"Jesus Christ." Sandy shook her head.

"Anyone check the fourth floor?" Ellen said.

"No."

"I will be right back. He hid Franki there once before, I don't doubt he'd do it again," she yelled, disappearing into the elevator.

Sandy went behind the station desk to check whether Franki's chart was still there. Blake might have stolen it if he knew his actions were being documented as evidence to use against him in the future. Franki's chart was still up on the peg.

Ellen's return was quicker than she anticipated. Sandy saw the disappointed look on Ellen's face when she rounded the corner.

"She's not in any of the rooms. Sandy has anyone seen Gloria in the last couple of hours?" Ellen knew Gloria shadowed Franki as much as she could.

"Is it possible she took Franki for a walk?"

"No. Kelly saw Blake taking her." Ellen stared at Sandy. "Oh my god, Ellen. Where is Gloria?"

"I'll go check her room. Sandy, you stay here and page her to come to the nurse's station. While you're at it, page all orderlies to the second-floor station and tell them to organize a search of the facility and the outside grounds."

As instructed, Sandy paged the men to come to the second floor, pronto. In less than five minutes, the orderlies gathered at the station. Sandy gave the instruction and watched the orderlies disperse in all direction in search of finding Franki Martin and Gloria Shelby.

Sandy paced nervously back and forth, waiting for Ellen to return with news of Gloria. Sandy saw the same disappointed expression on Ellen's face as she came toward her.

"Gloria is not in her room and obviously hasn't answered the page."

"Where in the hell could she be?"

"Sandy, calm down. We'll find both of them. I promise."

"Where could he have taken them?"

"Sandy, Franki knows we're doing everything in our power to find her. You have to believe that."

"Before time runs out. Where are the police? They should have been here by now," Sandy snapped.

Ellen drummed her fingernails on the countertop and was about to phone again when she glanced down the hall to see two men in plain clothing, walking down the corridor toward them.

"Here they are." Ellen pointed down the passageway.

"I'm Detective David Sorrel, and this is my partner, Guy Thompson." They presented their badges.

"Thank you for coming. I'm Dr. Ellen Smith, the one who placed the call. This is Sandy Miller, the missing girl's caretaker."

They all politely shook hands. "According to the report, we have one fifteen-year-old, female, Franki Martin, missing?" Sorrel began. "And a Dr. James Blake. Is that correct?"

"And you can now add another patient, Gloria Shelby."

"Is it possible that either woman could have run away?" Thompson queried.

"No, the fences are too high. Franki Martin has just come out of a coma state and is still too weak to even walk. Dr. Blake was the last person seen with

Franki Martin. Gloria has been with us for many years," Sandy stressed. "Her mind is that of about a four-year-old. She loves it here. This is the only home she's known."

"Have you checked all floors?" Sorrel asked.

"We're doing that as we speak." Ellen answered.

"So you don't know for certain if these two women are really missing?" Thompson raised his eyebrows.

"Dr. Blake was seen taking Franki from her room."

"And . . . that is that out of character for a doctor to be taking a patient?" Sorrel looked at both women like they might need mental help.

"Yes, when the doctor's been pulled off her care. Franki Martin has accused Dr. Blake of rape." Thompson began thumbing through his notepad for the allegation report made against the doctor.

"Sorry, ladies. There's nothing here about any rape charge." A little dumbfounded, Sorrel stared at both women. "I have to make a call." He pulled out his metallic cell phone.

"Gentlemen, why don't we go to my office, and I'll explain the current situation." She left Sandy in charge in case Franki or Gloria happened to show up.

Once inside her office, Ellen explained everything while Thompson talked quietly into his cell phone. Sorrel sat taking notes. He didn't want to miss a detail because he knew how hard it was to make a rape case stick in the court of law. Especially when the accuser, a young girl with a past, was accusing an outstanding member of society, such as Dr. Blake.

Thompson closed his phone.

"The call came in a little while ago. It seems that even if you hadn't called us, we were coming for this suspect, Dr. Blake, taking him in for questioning. The report came in from a Bill Cobie."

"The president of the board." Ellen nodded.

It was Sorrel who suggested that they pay a visit to the doctor's office first. Maybe they would find a clue to the disappearance of Franki Martin and Gloria Shelby or, better yet, find him waiting. It was pretty farfetched. They took directions to Blake's office and strolled away while Ellen answered her phone that was ringing off the hook.

"Dr. Smith speaking."

"Ellen, it's Bill here."

"What impeccable timing you have."

"I phoned to let you know that I filed a report, and they are sending two officers over."

"It's too late, Bill."

"What do you mean, it's too late?"

"Blake is gone and so are Franki Martin and Gloria Shelby."

"Did he find out we were on to him?"

"I'm not sure, Bill. Two detectives are here right now. They've gone to Blake's office, hoping to find a clue to his whereabouts."

"Pardon? The son-of-a-bitch couldn't have just vanished with two women. He isn't a bloody magician!"

"They're calling a search team now. Thanks for all your help, Bill, but I should go and join the detectives."

"Keep me posted, Ellen."

"I will."

"Ellen, maybe I should come over there?"

"If we don't find them by mid-afternoon, I'll be calling you for assistance."

"Deal. And Ellen, good luck."

"Thanks again, Bill."

"They are in my prayers, Ellen."

"I have a feeling those women are going to need all the help they can get."

* * *

After a few more hard bangs against the door, the two detectives glanced down the hall to see Ellen heading toward them, keys in hand.

"No answer?"

They shook their heads and stepped back so Ellen could unlock the door.

The doctor's office was bare. All his personal belongings and files were cleaned out. Not so much as a paper clip was left behind. He'd made sure there was no trail of evidence to implicate him of any crime. It was as if he'd vanished into the air like he never existed at River Edge. His office was a dead end. They reported to the station that they needed an APB on James Blake and an AMBER Alert on Franki Martin and Gloria Shelby.

Within a half an hour, River Edge was swarming with men and women in uniforms. They searched the entire premises of River Edge, or so they thought. Nothing. Sandy watched the sunlight disappear from the sky; it was hard to hold on to hope. The acidic taste of bile rose in her empty stomach. Guilt came on like waves crashing against the eroding rocks. She'd promised to keep Franki safe and had failed. She was angry at Nancy for leaving Franki unattended and at herself for being gone so long. She'd promised Franki her safety, and now this evil predator had kidnapped her. And maybe Gloria too . . .

It was one thirty in the morning and still no sign of them. The detectives had sent officers over to Blake's house, not surprised to find his clothes and personal belongings gone. Everything else was left behind in precise order.

Bill Cobie had been at River Edge for hours, helping search for the two missing women. Coffee from the vending machine flowed like hot lava. Every time Ellen looked around, someone was sipping a cup of mud.

The detectives had the uniforms check every square inch of the grounds. When they still came up empty-handed, they brought in the cadaver dogs to search the premises. Another hour went by and still nothing. Desperation, like a storm pressed down on all of them. Sandy was beside herself with worry. The traffic of blue uniforms was unending. The press was out behind the gate, scavenging for any tidbit of information they could get. Tragedy sold papers.

Ellen, Tom, Sandy, Bill Cobie, and the two detectives in charge were in Ellen's office going over the building's blueprints for missing places and spaces that perhaps they'd overlooked. They were searching for any clues that could help the dogs, orderlies, and police find these missing women.

Detective Sorrel asked Ellen if there were other sections of the institution that, for any reason, they could have missed. The detectives were mystified. They appeared to have searched everywhere possible and found zilch. At first Ellen's reply was no, she wasn't aware of anything.

"Are you absolutely certain, Doctor?" Thompson asked, massaging the back of his neck.

Bill suddenly jumped in. "Wait." He rubbed his forehead. "I have an idea. Please follow me."

Bill in the lead; he took them into a part of the institution that was no longer being used. It would be up and functioning one day, but right now, it was off-limits due to the safety of the structure.

Next, Thompson shone his flashlight. They could see small pools of blood in the dust on the steps. Hope and dread pounded in Sandy's chest. Ellen didn't hesitate. She bolted up the stairs, realizing she didn't have the right key for the lock.

"Damn it, we need bolt cutters!" Ellen yelled.

"Who needs bolt cutters when I have good strong manpower," Thompson said firmly.

"I've kicked in a few doors in my time." Sorrel nodded, moving Ellen out of the way.

"Okay, on the count of three. One, two, three!" The two men crashed through the door, splintering the frame. The stench of death exploded out of the room and into their faces. Sorrel threw his hand over his nose, shining his flashlight around the room. Ellen located the switch. The grisly discovery almost made even the detectives vomit.

A half-decomposed body, clad in a purple dress, lay on an old metal bed. Ellen quickly scanned the room. Gloria was on the floor in the far corner, her knees drawn up to her chest, rocking back and forth, crying uncontrollably.

Ellen and Sandy rushed to her to see whether she was physically injured. She had a one-inch gash above her right eyebrow. Her lips were cut and massively swollen. She had severe contusions on her face and body.

"My friend die. My friend, she die," Gloria cried, wiping snot and blood on her shirtsleeve. Sandy felt her heart shatter into a million pieces. But she couldn't lose it, not now.

"Bad man hurt me." Gloria pointed to her eye.

Sorrel ran to the sink and grabbed a roll of paper towels, running them under cold water. *Who left these here?* he wondered. He placed the cold wad against the mouth of the woman rocking back and forth, scared out of her mind and in shock. Meanwhile, Detective Thompson stood at the bed, closely viewing the body. The victim had been dead for possibly a month, month and a half; maggots and blowflies were devouring the flesh on the corpse. The loud buzzing shocked Tom, standing just far enough away.

Ellen took the cold compress from the detective and wiped away the blood from Gloria's eyes and mouth. "Gloria, honey, where is Franki? Can you show me where the bad man took your best friend?"

"Let's get her out of here." Sorrel pointed to the corpse. "I'd say she's been through enough."

It surprised everyone standing in that abandoned room as Gloria threw down the bloodied compress and bolted out the door, rushing down the steps and up the dark corridor, like a bat out of hell.

"My friend die, my friend die," she sobbed over and over. Gloria led the pack. The only three who could keep up were the two detectives and Sandy. The others weren't far behind. Gloria took them to the basement and ran to a door at the very end of the long hallway and stopped.

Detective Thompson opened the door. Sandy couldn't contain herself and screamed when she saw Franki strapped down, wrists and ankles to the bed. Ellen took one look and told Detective Sorrel to radio for an ambulance. His hand was already speed-dialing to summon it.

Dr. Smith checked quickly to see if Franki was still alive while Sandy tore frantically at the buckles until Franki was freed. Ellen gently removed the electric shock pads from the young girl's temples. Young Franki lay on the bed, staring unblinking at the ceiling. Suddenly, her body began convulsing. Ellen threw herself on the thrashing girl so she wouldn't spasm off the bed. A few long moments past, and Franki settled into a motionlessness state. Ellen checked her heartbeat; it was weak. Sandy leaned down to lift Franki into her arms when Detective Thompson touched Sandy on the shoulder.

"Please, ma'am, allow me." Sandy turned Franki over to the detective.

By the time Thompson carried Franki up the flight of stairs, the ambulance was parked at the front entrance waiting to take Franki and Gloria next door to the hospital's emergency room. Gloria couldn't believe her eyes when she saw Franki being carried past.

"My friend, Franki, alive! She alive!" She tried to smile through her tears and swollen lips.

"Gloria, thanks to you, Franki is going to be okay. You are a hero."

The paramedics took Franki out of the detective's arms and placed her on the stretcher. Ellen gave them the quick medical data needed to transport Franki. Then she helped Gloria climb into the back of the ambulance. She was having nothing to do with the stretcher.

Sandy received permission to ride along next to Gloria. This time, she wasn't leaving either of them for a minute. Blake was still out there. Franki and Gloria needed to see and be with someone whom they trusted.

"Will I see you later, Ellen?" Sandy called out from the back.

"I'll be there just as soon as I can. I have some unfinished business to do right now."

The paramedic closed the back of the van, and they were off. No sirens or lights were necessary. The media would know soon enough what took place inside the trusted institution of River Edge.

Ellen turned to the two detectives. "Find that bastard."

"We will," Detective Sorrel assured her.

The two detectives left her office an hour later, after they noted every detail about the so-called monster, James Blake. They didn't have much to go on. Bill and Ellen realized they knew very little about Blake outside the facility. Bill knew one thing: he hadn't liked the man since he was first hired.

Tom decided it was time for him to go home; there wasn't anything more to be accomplished. He invited Bill over for a good stiff drink of Jack Daniel's. He didn't want to leave Ellen, but he knew there were other pressing issues that needed to be attended to, like calling the coroner's office to come and retrieve the corpse found earlier in the abandoned wing. But first, there was something she needed to do, and it couldn't wait. Ellen said good-bye to everyone and walked back down to the deserted basement.

*　　*　　*

Ellen entered the last room at the end of the passageway. With each step, she could feel the storm of emotion mounting inside her. She unleashed some of her fury by flipping the bed over on to its side as if it had the weight of a feather. She tore the plastic wires from the electric convulsive apparatus and threw them to the floor, then kicked them at the wall. The tiny yellow button broke off and flew across to the other side of the room. Then with all her might, she flung the metal stand, which cradled the small deadly weapon of electricity. The loud bang echoed within the almost empty room. Moments later, she stood in the doorway, evaluating what she had done. Satisfied, she swiped the wisps of hair from her eyes and rubbed her hands together to get rid of some of the dirt. *This room will never be used again as a torture chamber,* she vowed. Calmly, she closed the door behind her, locked all four dead bolts and walked away. Now, she needed to call the coroner's office.

*   *   *

By late afternoon, the next day, the detectives had the name of the elderly woman found in the abandoned room. The autopsy confirmed it was Alma Blake.

CHAPTER FIFTY-FIVE

The next morning, Franki opened her eyes; she almost couldn't believe she was alive, no longer confined to the metal bed. Her body felt as if it had been run over by a steamroller. Every muscle ached from the received current of the shock treatment. It hurt even to move her tongue. It had been held down so she wouldn't bite it in half and swallow it. *Thank God for small favors,* she thought. But was she alone? She started to panic, eyes darting around the hospital room. Finally, she saw Sandy, asleep in a vinyl-covered recliner next to the bed. Groaning in pain, Franki rolled to the edge of her bed and gave Sandy a little shake. The nurse leaped immediately to her feet. For an instant, she'd forgotten where she was, then regained her mental composure. She had big black circles under her eyes. Slumber had not come easy, knowing Blake was still out there lurking around somewhere.

Without thinking, she swept Franki into her arms and gave her a hug she wouldn't soon forget. Franki let out a yelp of pain.

"Oh, sorry, honey." She loosened her grip and softly rocked her in her arms. Tears of happiness streamed down her face. "I'm so sorry I didn't protect you like I promised."

"It's not your fault," Franki whispered, relief streaming from her eyes. They clung to each other, both grateful that Franki was alive.

"I've got a surprise for you." Sandy pulled back the curtain separating the beds. Gloria sprang from her bed and leaped onto Franki's.

"My friend, Franki!" she shouted, patting Franki on the shoulder.

"My best friend, Gloria," Franki giggled, giving Gloria a big hug. "Oh, Gloria, your mouth looks so sore. And how did you get all those bruises?"

"She talk now," she said, happy as a clam.

"Yes, I can talk."

"I make her not sick."

"You sure did."

The room was filled with an array of emotion by the time Ellen returned for the second time. Immediately, she wrapped her arms around and kissed both of them.

"Let me have a look at you two," she said, drawing back. "Well, at the moment, you won't win any beauty prizes, but at least, you're both still alive. You'll be better in no time." Everyone laughed.

Ellen was so proud of these two incredible, strong girls, surviving their horrible ordeal. What the human spirit could endure in order to stay alive always astounded the doctor. She had seen many cases where one assumed the worst but received the gift of opposite.

"Gloria, I have a gift for you. It's out in the hall. Let me go and get it. Stay here."

The doctor came back with a teddy bear, her own children's storybooks, and a red balloon, her favorite color. Hidden behind her back was a huge silver Medal of Bravery with a pretty red ribbon to hang on her wall. That, of course, was Tom's idea. Gloria, he said, was the real hero in all of this.

"This is for you being as brave as you were yesterday."

Gloria's proud smile would have outshone a lighthouse. "My . . . my friend, Franki, she talk now."

"Yes, she does, and Gloria it's all thanks to your bravery. You are the best friend a girl could ever want."

"I need a pee." She jumped off the bed and raced to the bathroom.

"Franki, I don't mean to rain on the party, but I need to ask you some important questions. Okay?" Ellen pulled a chair over and sat beside the bed.

The happy expression on Franki's face dropped. "I know, Doc. I'm ready to answer any questions you have."

Sandy took Franki's hand and squeezed.

"When was the first time Dr. Blake raped you?"

"The first day I got here."

"The police are going to ask you the same questions. You do understand this?"

"I get it."

"Franki, why didn't you tell anyone earlier?"

"He told me no one would believe me. Talk about your turn of events, hey? I came here because I wanted to die, and weeks later I'm fighting for my life. I realized my life had meaning, what it is yet, I don't know, but I know I want to hang around long enough to find out. I mean, Doc, he tried to kill me."

"Franki, he didn't succeed."

Gloria had returned. She sat on the opposite side of Sandy, holding Franki's other hand.

"I know, I should have told you earlier. But when he demonstrated his real power, I got scared. I'm a tough street kid, but even I can't handle that brutality. Then the fight with Gloria and being sent to the fucking fourth floor didn't help matters. It all spun way out of control." She fought back her anger.

"I know this can't be easy, Franki, but I need to know exactly how he demonstrated his power."

Franki looked away, her eyes roaming everywhere but into Ellen's. Sandy felt the nervous sweat making both their hands slick. Finally, her eyes settled again on the doctor's. She took a deep breath.

"He sodomized me, Doc."

"What a despicable bastard!" Ellen could feel her blood boil.

"Bastard, bastard, bastard!" Gloria second.

Ellen raised a finger to hush her and then stopped midair. She looked keenly at the child-woman. A cold chill clawed up her spine. *Special girl.*

"Oh, Jesus!" Ellen gasped.

"What?" But Sandy already knew what Ellen was thinking.

Gently the doctor took Gloria's hand in hers and searched her eyes. "Gloria, why did you call Dr. Blake a bastard?"

"He mean."

"Was he mean to you?"

"He punch me. Kick me. He loves me, special girl." Gloria suckled her fingers.

"How did he *love* you, honey?"

"Shhh, don't tell." She lightly pressed her index finger against her swollen lips.

Ellen looked over at Sandy; they now both knew how "special" Gloria was to Blake.

"Franki, you weren't the only victim in Blake's reign of terror." She nodded at Gloria, nestling next to Franki on the bed. Franki spoke with clenched teeth. "If only I could get my hands around his neck—"

Bored with the conversation, Gloria got out of bed and played with her red balloon.

"I wonder how many others," Sandy questioned. She kept her voice low. They shouldn't frighten Gloria; she'd been through enough horror already.

"I don't know. I promise you this much: I will find out." Ellen's voice was hard as flint.

"I'll help in every way I can. You know that," said Sandy.

"Doc, what's going to happen to him?"

"Sweetheart, they have to find him first."

"What? What do you mean?" Sheer terror twisted Franki's face.

"Franki, he must have known his day would come. He had a plan because his office is as bare as Mother Hubbard's cupboard. He packed everything up. There wasn't even a paper clip left in his drawer. His home is empty."

"Jesus Christ, he's still out there?"

"Yes."

"That means that . . . oh, shit shit shit . . ." She put her head down, defeated.

"That means nothing."

"Doc, he got me once before. You can't tell me that he won't or can't do it again," she cried out.

"I can't argue with that, but if Sandy and I have to sit in this room day after day or week after week to make sure nothing happens to either of you, then that is exactly what we're prepared to do!"

Franki tried to get out of bed but quickly realized her body was far too weak and hurt. She fell back against the pillows, pounding the mattress with her fists.

"Franki, believe me, he won't get within fifty yards of you. Either Sandy or myself or both of us will be in your room at all times."

"I want to trust you guys, I really do, but you don't know him the way I do. He is dangerous and a sadistic, fucking, crazy man that gets his jollies inflicting pain. If he wants something, he makes sure nothing stands in his way."

"I hear you, Franki. But the last thing Blake wants is to get caught."

"Doc, you don't know that for sure. He probably thinks you haven't found us yet."

"Okay, if it will make you feel safer, I'll request an officer be posted at the door. Will that make you feel a bit safer?"

"Yes, providing he has permission to shoot the prick and ask questions later. I can't ever go through that torture he put me through again."

"We are going to make sure this never ever happens to you again. There is one more question I need you to answer, if you can?"

"What's that, Doc?"

"Can you tell me how he managed to grab you yesterday?"

"I was sleeping in my room when he crept in, covered my mouth with his hand, and showed me a big knife. He told me if I screamed, he'd kill me right there. I didn't scream. He shoved me into the wheelchair and whizzed me out to the elevator. He took me to the basement. I think it was the basement?"

"The basement is where you were found."

"Okay. He unlocked the locks and rolled me in. I wanted to fight, but I had no energy. I couldn't scream because my voice was gone. He threw me onto the table and strapped me down. I couldn't move a muscle. He climbed on top of me and raped me again. He hooked me up to those pads and clicked on the machine. All I remember is the burning pain going through my body. Jesus, it hurt. Don't ask me how many times he zapped me because I don't remember. Thank God for Gloria. I wouldn't be here telling you the story if it weren't for her. Just when I thought it was lights out, the door flew open. Gloria charged at Blake like a fearless bull. I saw her struggling, but there was nothing I could do to help her. He kept punching and kicking her until she wasn't moving. I will never forget those awful, horrible sounds when his fist and shoes connected to her face and body. Jesus Christ, I thought she was dead." Franki took a shuddering breath. "That's when he dragged her out of the room by her hair."

"The bad man, drag me. Crash into something hard. Make me cry hard," Gloria cut in.

"He did drag you by your hair. And he hurt you really bad."

"Hurt." She pointed to her face. "I cry and cry."

"Blake would have killed her, given enough time," Ellen said quietly. "He beat her up pretty badly. No broken bones, thank goodness."

"Bad man kick here." She again pointed to a number of bruises from her face and down her torso.

"Yes, he is a bad man, horrible man. And you were very brave," Franki praised.

"Bastard, bastard, bastard," Gloria sang out in a surprisingly pretty voice. She got back on the bed and snuggled against Franki. It was evident Gloria was angry. She just didn't know how to articulate her feelings. Art therapy would now become part of Gloria's care for the next couple of months. Ellen didn't want this horror to be suppressed. This would be a good way for Gloria to express her emotional pain.

"Gloria, is there anything you need?" asked Ellen.

"My best friend, Franki. We hang out." She smiled.

"Don't worry. I won't leave you. Promise." Franki looked down at Gloria, kissing the top of her head. She smiled shyly, trying to hide her painful mouth with her hand.

"Okay, ladies, I have to get back to River Edge," Ellen announced. "I have a meeting with Bill Cobie. And you"—she pointed a finger at Sandy—"are not booked. So your time is your own to do with it what you will."

"Thank you. I'll be right here, guarding these two lovely ladies. And when are you going to take off a couple of days?"

"Not today." She smiled.

"Big bucks, right, Doc?"

"That's right, Franki." Ellen laughed. "I have one more thing to do before I leave."

Ellen left the room to use the phone and returned five minutes later, a big smile spilling across her precious face.

"Good news! Detective Sorrel has informed me that your request is on prompt order."

"What in the hell does that mean, Doc?"

"An officer will be posted at the door to ensure that you both will be safe. He couldn't guarantee the shoot and ask questions later though." Ellen smiled, shaking her head.

Franki grinned, shaking her head. When Doc said something was going to get done, she made it happen.

"The detectives will be stopping by within the next half hour to ask the both of you questions. More questions to you, Franki than Gloria." With a wave of her hand, Ellen disappeared out the door.

Right on time, Sorrel and Thompson came walking into the ward with another officer in tow.

"You must be Franki Martin?" Thompson asked.

"In the hurting flesh." She gave him a half a smirk. She still didn't like cops very much.

"Happy to be alive, I assume."

"Depends on what you guys have planned for me?"

"We just want to ask you some questions, that's all. Are you up to it?"

"No, but I will answer."

"Franki, before we get started, I want to be totally honest with you."

"Here we go." Franki rolled her eyes. "Who's that?" She pointed to the man wearing the blue uniform with a gun holstered on his left side, leaning against the far wall."

"That guy is your knight in shining armor. His name is Constable John Bean. He's going to be your shadow for the next few days or however long it takes to find Blake."

"Hey, know how to shoot that thing?"

"Highly trained, ma'am."

"Then you can stay. And what about Gloria?"

"The doctor tells me that you two are pretty much inseparable. Is that correct?"

Franki grinned at Gloria. "Yep, she's my buddy, that's for sure."

"Okay. Now that we have that squared away . . . Franki, you do understand that you will have to testify in court?"

"I'll do it, but I don't have to like it."

"Since his alleged attack, Dr. Blake will be charged and tried with statutory rape, kidnapping, and attempted murder."

"That sums it up. I need to see that son-of-a-bitch rot in jail for the rest of his life."

"Son-of-a-bitch," Gloria echoed.

"Young lady, I think it's time you cleaned up your language. It sounds horrible coming from such a pretty young girl. It, in no way, enhances your beauty." Thompson waggled a finger.

"I didn't realize I was trying to impress you."

"Franki, be nice. These detectives are here to help you." Sandy shook her head.

"Sorry," Franki apologized.

"Yeah, sorry," Gloria followed suit, smiling at the two detectives who grinned back at her.

Franki gave a detailed play-by-play of her ordeal, answering politely all of the detective's questions. It wasn't easy. A couple of times, she had to stop to regain her composure. Franki had truly been tortured. Gloria had been severely punished for her disloyalty. It was incredible they'd survived. Finally, the detectives were finished, satisfied with the victims statements. They knew more would be revealed through Gloria's art therapy. Sorrel and Thompson shook the girl's hands before saying good-bye, assuring Franki and Gloria that they would be in touch.

"Catch him please before he hurts anyone else," Franki pleaded.

"You can bet on it, kid," Sorrel pledged. "He will go to jail for a long time for what he's done."

"Thank you."

"Get some rest now."

"We will."

"If you need anything, just yell for Constable John. He'll come running."

"Not with that belly, he won't."

"Okay, a slow jog then." Thompson laughed.

CHAPTER FIFTY-SIX

After one week of almost driving Constable John Bean nuts, Franki and Gloria were discharged from the hospital and returned to River Edge. Gloria had three stitches above her right eye. One of her eyeteeth had been knocked out from the brutal punches to her face. The swelling in her lips was slowly decreasing and replaced by light bruising. Franki's wrists and ankles suffered severe bruising from the leather restraints. The inside of her thighs had faded from black to yellow caused by the brutal sexual assault. This time, forensic had the DNA that tied Blake to the rape of Franki Martin. Neither Gloria nor Franki wanted to talk anymore about what the predator had done to them. Franki made her statement accusing Blake of rape, kidnapping, and attempted murder. Dr. Smith videotaped Gloria during her sessions with art therapy. The prosecutor, Shallow Brooks, felt she had enough evidence to stick Blake with one count of assault causing bodily harm for Gloria.

On sunny days, Gloria and Franki were found together, sitting under their favorite maple tree. Franki read aloud poems she'd written. Gloria read from her children's books. It was soul filling to watch the way they cared so much for one another. Life had almost returned to normal.

* * *

Days later, Sandy was getting Nora Elmer ready for her morning shower when Nora unexpectedly asked Sandy how she felt about that doctor that gave her the creeps. She couldn't remember his name, just the smell of his strong aftershave.

"Sandy, you know that weird-looking doctor?"

"Nora, there are many doctors here. Can you be more specific?"

"I think it starts with a *B*, something . . ."

"You mean, Dr. Blake?"

"That's him."

"He's gone."

"Why is that?"

"He's been accused of doing some very vile things. Nora, why are you asking me about Dr. Blake?"

"I think, he did a bad thing to me."

Sandy left the bed and walked over to the window, taking Nora's hand. "Do you want to report this to your doctor?"

"I'm not sure there is anything to report."

"Why don't you tell me?"

"I think it was the first day I arrived. Two nurses took me to the doctor's office. He stuck me in the arm with a needle, then the room began to swim, but . . . I think he forced himself on me. I know it sounds pretty stupid, doesn't it?"

"No. Nora, I think you should talk to Dr. Smith."

"I will, but I'm not sure if I was hallucinating or not. I don't want to appear to be crazier than I am you know what I mean? But when I think about it, I get a cold chill. It was probably a nightmare. Maybe I should just forget it."

Sandy knew differently. Here was another victim. Dr. Blake had committed the same atrocity on to Franki Martin when she arrived. How many others were there?

Sandy would promptly report this to Ellen. Meanwhile, she told Nora she would make an appointment for her to see Dr. Smith, and she could talk about what she had just told Sandy. Nora agreed. If Blake had raped Nora Elmer, she wanted his ass doubly nailed to the wall. The damage Blake caused was incomprehensible.

*　*　*

Three weeks from the date of finding Franki Martin in the basement and Gloria in the abandoned room, Detectives Sorrel and Thompson located Dr. James Blake. He was living in India, in a small village called Shotapur. He was still practicing medicine. The proper documents were filed, and he was being extradited back to Canada. There, he was to stand trial for the kidnapping, rape, and attempted murder of Franki Martin and assault causing bodily harm on Gloria Shelby. The prosecutor had enough evidence to put him away for a long, long time.

*　*　*

The media was in its full glory about this sensational story. Franki and Gloria held hands as they watched the news. They watched Blake being led in shackles and chains from the van into the jailhouse. Franki thought, she would be cheering the moment the police caught him; oddly, she wasn't. She was bombarded with a hoard of emotions ranging from rage to fear. Her stomach clenched in tight knots, and her hands trembled at the mere sight of him. She felt she was going to heave her cookies. Then, he stared directly into the camera and smirked. The hairs on the back of her neck stood straight up in shock at his arrogant expression. Franki felt as though he was looking into her soul. Fear ran through her like a sickness; she couldn't slow her rapid heartbeat. How could she even face him in the courtroom if even the mere sight of him on television shook her to the core?

*   *   *

Blake never did stand trial. Two days after his capture, Blake was found in the shower stall, hanging by his neck. He'd knotted together strips of bed sheets. Rudimentary. It worked. The same morning, Detectives Thompson and Sorrel knocked on Dr. Smith's door at eight o'clock. They didn't want her finding out through the media. They owed her that much. The previous day, the two men had shown up at her office, explaining the procedure of how Blake's trial was going to perform and what was expected of Franki Martin. This morning, they were there to inform her that James Blake committed suicide.

As soon as the detectives departed, Dr. Smith immediately went to see Franki and Gloria. As long as she lived, she would never forget the looks of utter betrayal on their faces. Blake's suicide meant he would never be publicly humiliated in court. He would never endure time in a cage or suffer sexual sadism at the hands of the other inmates. For Franki Martin, justice would never be served. As far as she was concerned, he'd taken the easy way out. Ellen too had been deprived the pleasure of seeing Blake sentenced and locked up, unable to commit any more carnage. Sandy was stunned by the news. Certainly, she wanted to see him pay for the heinous crimes he'd committed.

The following morning, Ellen felt completely exhausted. She'd been dealing with accusation from the media, dealing with the families of the patients in River Edge, questioning patients about their relationship with the late Dr. Blake. Her days were endless. This Blake business seeped into the marrow of her bones. She was now trying to occupy her mind on the task of reviewing a patient's chart and sipping her morning coffee, when she heard a knock. She glanced at her watch; it was too early for her patient to arrive. Ellen yelled,

"Come in," assuming it was Sandy. The door opened, and in marched the two detectives wearing pained expressions.

"Morning, gentlemen. This is a surprise."

They sat down with a nod, no smile.

"Why the long faces? Blake is dead. Surely, he can't harm anyone from the grave."

"Don't be too sure about that, Dr. Smith," Sorrel spoke seriously.

"Don't be too sure of what?"

The detective leaned forward, sliding an envelope across her desk, addressed to her. Her eyes filled with trepidation as she recognized the penmanship. She tore open the envelope and began reading:

> Dear Ellen:
>
> I know you believe I'm guilty, in which I am. All these years working side by side and you didn't even know me. Yes, I am dead now, and in a small corner of your heart, I believe you're happy. I know you think I'm evil, disturbed, blah, blah, blah, and if you could, my name would never be uttered from your sweet lips again. Unfortunately, you don't have the power to make that little dream come true. The fact is that you will never be rid of my presence because I am a genius. In my professional opinion, I have sacrificed everything in the name of greatness. Month's back, I injected a deadly virus into my bloodstream, for which there is no cure. I was the one chosen to do this. It was my destiny. Mine all mine to cleanse the world of filthy whores like Franki Martin. You see, Ellen, I did something you could not. I helped society. I did not fail it like you. Every time I raped those filthy pieces of trash, I, Ellen, made the world a better place. My body will turn to ashes, but I will never die. My legacy is immortalized. I will live forever. Not as a monster some will claim but as a hero."

As if the letter burnt her hand, Ellen dropped it onto her desk. She stared up at the two detectives, tears of anguish streaming down her cheeks.

Quietly, they turned away and left. The letter said it all.

THE END

Thank you to everyone that supported me over the years.
You know who you are.
A special thank-you to my wonderful sister,
Colleen Harley, who never stopped believing in me.
My editor, Joan Rickard, for polishing my
magnum opus, thank you.
Thank you to Cory Giroux for drawing an accurate depiction on
the face of *Breach of Sanity*.

Edwards Brothers, Inc.
Thorofare, NI USA
February 10, 2012